In *Mogollon: A Tale of Mysticism & Mayhem*, Sandy Nathan reveals her characters early on like well-drawn chessmen on a board, and from the beginning we're waiting and nervous about the clashes that will come. As intriguing as the characters are, it's the stakes that are the real grabber because she has taken the higher feelings of compassion and goodness and flung them against ruthlessness and evil. We see the news every day and all its battlegrounds—and in Mogollon we see this same battle made human and spiritual, and *we hang on and hope.*

Gerald DiPego
Screenwriter of Phenomenon, Instinct, The Forgotten

Mogollon: A Tale of Mysticism & Mayhem is one of those books that transports you into a mystical world where the supernatural is eminently believable. Mogollon is about nothing less than the battle between the forces of light and dark — in the real world and in worlds that feel incredibly real though they stretch the imagination way beyond its normal boundaries. With unexpected story twists and characters that I want to know better and better, *Mogollon is sheer enjoyment, page after page after page.*

Laren Bright
Award-winning television writer
Co-author of Golden Voyages, a spiritual children's book

A really talented storyteller captures your mind and heart with the story's first words. In *Mogollon: A Tale of Mysticism & Mayhem*, Sandy Nathan once again demonstrates her amazing story-telling talent. Her writing stimulates our subconscious minds, helping us to explore and deal with the incredible pressures and changes of our times, *weaving a tale that is slated to become a literary classic.*

Ilene Dillon, MSW
Radio Host, Mentor, Coach & Speaker
Author: The Exchange Student Model for Parenting

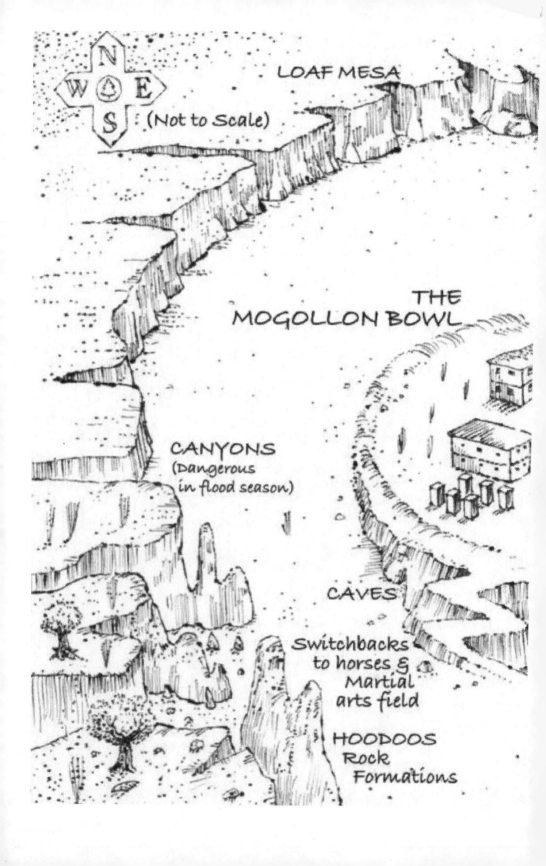

To the Main Road

PARK HERE

BADLANDS: DANGER!

Camping Area
Grab a spot.
First come, first served

NUMENON CAMP
(Proposed)

THE PIT
Amphitheater

Grandfather's
Lean to

The
Wedding Tepee

CAVES

DO
NOT
ENTER

The Mogollon Bowl is a fictitious place.

ALSO BY SANDY NATHAN

Stepping Off the Edge: Learning & Living Spiritual Practice

Numenon: A Tale of Mysticism & Money
(Bloodsong 1)

Tecolote: The Little Horse That Could

The Angel & the Brown-Eyed Boy
(Earth's End 1)

Lady Grace & the War for a New World
(Earth's End 2)

The Headman & the Assassin
(Earth's End 3)

The Earth's End Trilogy
(Earth's End 1 to 3 in a single eBook)

MOGOLLON

A TALE OF MYSTICISM & MAYHEM

MOGOLLON

THE BLOODSONG SERIES 2

SANDY NATHAN

VILASA
PRESS

SANTA YNEZ, CA

First Edition

First Printing: 2014

Library of Congress Control Number: 2013952297

Editor: Melanie Rigney
Cover & Interior Design of Print & eBook Editions: Damonza.com
Cover Model: Rick Mora
Cover photograph of Rick Mora: Rick Mora

Publisher's Cataloging-in-Publication Data

Nathan, Sandy.
Mogollon: a tale of mysticism & mayhem / Sandy Nathan.
pages cm. – (Bloodsong, bk 2)
ISBN: 978-1-937927-07-3 (pbk.)
ISBN: 978-1-937927-08-0 (e-book)
1. Indians of North America—Fiction.   2. Shamans—Fiction.   3. Good and evil—Fiction.   4. New Mexico—Fiction.   I. Title. II. Series: Bloodsong.
PS3614.A865 M64 2014
813—dc23
          2013952297

To the great souls like Grandfather who have sustained this planet

and shown us what human beings can be.

Is it real, this life I'm living? Is it real?

Pawnee Warrior Song

AUTHOR'S NOTE

What's a Mogollon? The Mogollon are an extinct Native American people who lived in Southern New Mexico and Arizona roughly between 150 AD and 1450 AD. The name Mogollon came from the Mogollon Mountains, which were named after Juan Ignacio Flores Mogollon, the Spanish governor of New Mexico from 1712 to 1715. So there's a Native American and a Spanish influence. The New Mexican pronounciation of Mogollon is Muggy-own; the Spanish pronunciation is Mow-go-yone. I pronounce it Mow-go-lawn. Use whichever you like as you read.

Mogollon: A Tale of Mysticism & Mayhem is the second book in the Bloodsong Series. *Numenon: A Tale of Mysticism & Money* was the first. Both books contain supernatural and spiritual elements that feature mystical experience, in addition to many more down-to-earth subjects. Both Bloodsong books contain mature content and would be rated R if they were movies. They are not kids' books.

This book is complete fantasy. FANTASY. FANTASY. Even the ground on which the story takes place is fictitious. The desert terrain I describe in the book is flat, like Arizona's Painted Desert. The actual area of New Mexico where the book takes place is a mountain range.

The character *Grandfather* is fictional. He does not represent or portray any living or historical Native American shaman or holy man. What he says and teaches, his People and their practices, what happens at the Meeting, and the Meeting itself—they all are made up.

I'm saying this for a reason: American Indians have had their religion stolen from them, their spiritual beliefs and experiences misinterpreted, and their spiritual leaders killed and discredited by European-based society from the minute we came in contact with them.

To avoid perpetuating this barbarism, I set a few boundaries for myself. I don't write about American Indian ceremonies unless they're something that *everyone* has heard of, like the sweat lodge. With the exceptions of a quote from Black Elk at the end of this book and the quote from the Pawnee warrior song above, I don't use the actual names of the Sovereign Nations to which my Native American characters belong. This immediately marks my work as fiction, since the People always refer to themselves by their Nation or Band. I believe omitting tribal names is necessary when non-Natives write fiction about Native American life.

I am not a spiritual tourist who Googled "spirituality" and "shamans" to get material for this book. Visionary experiences have been with me for most of my life. I began having spiritual experiences in my early teens, while riding my horse through the redwood forests of the coastal range of the San Francisco Peninsula. Since then, I've had explosive, life changing spiritual experiences and subtler, daily guidance.

After reading *Numenon,* the first book in the Bloodsong Series, someone who had studied with a Native American shaman told me, "You really *nailed* the shaman. That's what he was like, and that's exactly how I felt around him."

How did I do that? In addition to my own spontaneous experiences, I spent close to thirty years studying with two East Indian meditation masters. As a result, I know what an elevated soul like Grandfather is like. I thank the monks and those associated with them for their teaching and inspiration.

While this story emerged from my heart and brain and I claim responsibility for it, I hope my readers will also feel the unseen power that imparted it to me.

I'd like to thank a few people for their contributions to this book. My husband, Barry Nathan, provides excellent feedback and support. He's my first fan and best friend.

My developmental editor, Melanie Rigney, used her golden machete to cut *Mogollon* from a monstrous 240,000 words to a svelte 127,000. As a result, the print version no longer resembles a telephone book and reads better, too.

Thanks to Kate McGuinness, J.D. for legal advice. Kate was partner in a top corporate law firm for ten years. She retired as the general counsel of a Fortune 300 company. Kate gave me a clear perspective on how the law really works, which resulted in me changing key passages of this and coming books.

Finally, I'd like to thank Rick Mora for allowing me to use his image on the cover. Rick is a Native American (Apache/Yaqui) model, actor, and philanthropist. He is a dead ringer for the image of Wesley Silverhorse that I carry in my brain. When I was looking for cover material, I was immediately drawn to Rick. What a delight to have his photo on the cover. Thanks!

I hope you enjoy *Mogollon: A Tale of Mysticism & Mayhem!*

INTRODUCTION:
GRANDFATHER'S INVOCATION

He stood in the deepest place. He stood in a place that was closest to the core. He stood in the sacred place and held the eagle feather. He raised the feather to the sky people, to the guardians of the world above.

"I pray to you, people of the sky, be with us this week. Stay with us and keep us safe." The shaman spoke in the old language, his voice rising and falling. It was neither querulous nor weak. No one hearing it would guess his age.

Hundreds of warriors watched silently, sitting in the deepest place. Grandfather turned to the four directions, one by one.

"I pray to you, guardians of the North, for the strength to overcome the cold time, to get us through the hard time. Let the People come to this last Meeting. Let them come with clear eyes to see what is here. Let them see the Great One, behind and beyond and through all places and directions."

Let them give up their strife and fault finding, the old man prayed silently. *Let them stop picking each word I say apart. Let them see you, O Great One, and stop fighting me. I am your tool and your soldier, nothing more.*

Grandfather swayed on his feet, feeling the Presence of the One. *O Great One! You who fills all the earth, and the stars; the things that we can see, and the things that we cannot see. I love you! I praise you! I worship you!*

"Let the People feel the river of love this week. Let each of them learn what he came here to learn. Let each learn what she came to learn. Take away the darkness, O Lord, and bring us your light."

He turned to the East. "I praise you, guardians of the East. Give us your power, the power of new life, the power of spring over winter, of awakening. Watch over us and give us victory."

Give us victory over the intruders from the outside, and over the intruders from the inside, he prayed within his heart. *Free us from our poisonous thoughts and feelings, from the desire to see only small things and differences. Let us see that we are the same. As you are the One, so we are one.*

Bud Creeman stood next to Grandfather, circulating the smoke with his feather fan. He let out a piercing cry. "I see you, Great One! I see you!" He raised his hands high.

The old man turned and held the eagle feather over his head. "I praise you, great Southern warriors. I praise you with great love. Thank you for your peace, your serenity. Your plenty, the plenty of summer and the good harvest. Be with us this week, show us your bounty."

Let us accept your bounty with graciousness and love, he prayed. *Let us recognize a great gift when it may appear small, or not what we wanted, or not a gift at all.*

Then Grandfather turned to the Western gate, the passage between this world and the other side. "Watcher of the Gate, let us die and die again, the little deaths that mean growth and change. Let the parts of us that need to die go, and the parts that need to live stay. May we pass through your doorway in glory when the last dying comes!"

And may our visitors from the great corporation get what they need this week. May they have the love and courage they need; may they have the will to die and be reborn.

He sang in the old language, his voice rising over the Bowl. He stood in the deepest part—in the amphitheater they called the Pit—where the meteor struck long before the dawn of days. Grandfather knew that the meteor did not give the Power. The Power was there before anything. The Power made everything.

"I love you, I worship you, I praise your name and glory. Be with me all of my days. Protect us, O Great One, from our enemies inside and outside."

He sat cross-legged on the earth. The warriors were around. Rapture overcame him, followed by tears of joy as they rose from the bliss inside. Like a sun, came the Great One; like the sun of suns, splitting his heart in two, tearing him in pieces until the bliss was so great that the universe broke open and he dropped, a shining pearl, a brilliant diamond, dropped into the nothing that exists beneath all that is.

He heard no more until the sun was high.

1

WILL DUANE STARED out of the motor home's tinted window, scowling. The *Ashley*, his luxurious RV and the hallmark of the Numenon caravan, jolted across the desert in fine form. Will wasn't doing quite as well.

He turned away from his view, not wanting to face the light. That damned New Mexico sunlight had done something to him. That and all the space. The desert had too much space; it made him feel weird.

He felt as if the core of himself, the hard center that was him, had cracked. He blamed it on the damn light. All day, they'd passed through that bright emptiness. Who he was began to melt away. His control, his purpose, all of him was being undermined.

The terrain did the same thing. All day long dirt, rocks, and cacti surrounded them. Plus those stupid round trees that dotted the landscape like lice. They weren't even eight feet high. Will hated New Mexico more than he thought possible. *They can't even grow a proper tree.*

Will rubbed his chin, feeling a screamer coming on. He would not give in to it. He would stay in control.

"Mark, how much longer?" he shouted.

"It's right up ahead, Mr. Duane. Over that rise. See the cars." The driver pointed at a ridge a short distance away. For the last few miles, phalanxes of junker cars from the 1970s had dogged them. Those were their fellow retreat attendees. It was 1997. What kind of people drove cars that old?

Will could see laden vehicles disappearing over the crest. Other cars returned, obviously having dumped their loads. They turned left and entered an enormous parking lot just outside the Mogollon Bowl. Light reflected off the vehicles and hit him like bullets. The parking lot was a junk yard of wrecks with alligatored vinyl tops and mottled paint. He clenched his jaw.

Will sat in his command seat, directly behind the driver, with his back against the cabin's rear wall.

Looking to his left, Will observed the anxious faces of Betty and Gil. They sat on the banquette that ran along the *Ashley's* wall, twisting to see through the big picture window behind them. The opposite wall was covered floor to ceiling with cabinets stuffed with electronic gear, the super computer being the most important. The super computer was the most advanced in existence. Numenon's technology had been ahead of the pack since the late 1950s when Will founded the corporation.

Will furrowed his brow. Why were Betty, Gil, their driver, and he the only ones in the cabin? When they started, the cabin was almost full. Now there were just four people. Where were the others? He felt so fuzzy; he couldn't remember what happened five minutes ago.

Sunlight reflected off the chrome of one of the vehicles outside. It struck Will's eye and he rocked back in his seat. His eyes rolled back and quivered.

Red rock walls rose high above them. He was running, breathing convulsively, sobbing. Thrashing on the ground, fighting. Something crushed him into the rock.

Will blinked, coming back to himself. Something had happened in the desert. He could recall it dimly, like someone else's dream. Their drive wasn't just across the desert floor. There had been a canyon, and red cliffs.

He put his hand on his chest. The day before, his doctor told him the tight sensations he felt were nothing. His heart was good. He was okay.

Will rubbed his chin again and tried to remember.

Something came out of the buzzing, disintegrating void inside of him. The old shaman had appeared in the desert in front of them in a golf cart. Will had walked out to him and the light surrounded them. Light had come off the old man, even more than from the sun it seemed. Will had broken down for some reason; he had fallen at the holy man's feet, sobbing.

Why, why? His disintegration had accelerated since then.

"We're here," Mark called. The *Ashley* pulled over the bank. Will jumped up and grabbed the back of the driver's chair.

"What is it, Will?" Betty asked. She and Gil moved forward, straining for a look at the sacred place where they would spend the next week.

"Oh, my God," she said.

The others were speechless.

Betty peered through the windshield. The Mogollon Bowl spread out before them; as far as she could see, a writhing mass of people were interspersed with camping equipment. Well, some of it was camping equipment. Shabby tents and tarps on poles. Shade canopies on aluminum legs. People unloaded cars and headed back to the parking lot outside the Bowl. Other cars inched around, searching for a place to camp. The Bowl crawled with movement.

That's all it had; no trees, no lawn, and no structures existed except two derelict buildings in the distance. The Indians' hallowed sacred ground looked like the desert they'd crossed, but less interesting. It was rocks and dirt and chaos.

This was the legendary Mogollon Bowl where anyone could become psychic and all of your problems disappeared? Betty thought of all the

work she'd done to prepare her brief on Grandfather, the famous shaman who led the retreat, and on those closest to him. On Indian history.
On the Bowl itself. For *this?*

She looked at Will, knowing what his reaction would be. Will only
stayed at five-star hotels. Living in the luxurious *Ashley* was his idea
of camping. Her boss's face grayed with horror. He turned to her, his
mouth gaping.

Before Will could speak, Doug Saunders charged out of the bedroom. "Will, I will not stay in this *dump!* If we have to stay here for a
week, I *quit.*"

Betty glanced at Gil Canao, who looked out the window in glum
silence. She opened her mouth to echo Doug's sentiment, when Will
grabbed Doug and hugged him like a grieving father.

"I thought we'd lost you," Will cried.

With that, the memory descended upon her—what had happened
on the drive in. Will lying in that canyon, covered with blood, bones
bent at impossible angles, squashed. Really, squashed *flat.* Doug lay next
to him, foam coming out of his mouth, his body bent backward in a
crescent arc. Blue and bloodless, both of them.

Her sobs took her by surprise. Her hands went to her face and she
doubled over. Will, Gil, and Doug jumped toward her. Will caught her
in his arms, and the other two men joined the hug. The minute they
touched her, her backbone stiffened. She pulled herself erect, trapped in
the circle of solicitous males.

Tears streaked her face. "Oh, I'm sorry. I can't …" Will handed her
his handkerchief. She snatched it gratefully.

"It's okay, Betty," they said at once.

But it wasn't okay. They almost died, all of them. A flash flood
would have killed them in that narrow ribbon canyon. Floods happened
right now, in early spring. It had been a horrible, horrible trip. But Bud
Creeman had saved them.

"We have to find Bud and thank him again." She looked up at Will. "He was so good to us. Let's find him, and then let's leave. Okay, Will?"

Will's brow lowered and his jaw tightened. "I'll get you out of here tomorrow, I promise. I'm going to stay." They stared at him. "I have to stay here—I have business to complete."

Betty pulled out of her despair enough to stammer, "But, Will, you told us that the mine deal was dead."

"It is, Betty. I promise you." He glanced out the windshield. The Indians were beginning to cluster around the *Ashley*. "I have personal business with Grandfather."

She had heard so many of Will's empty promises that she didn't know what to think. "I want to go home to John." The tears came again. She wiped her face, conscious that she'd shed more tears in public in the previous five minutes than she had in twenty-eight years of being the head of Will's secretarial staff. *Private* tears didn't count.

"I'll make arrangements for all of you to leave. You don't have to deal with this …" Will's arm swept the crowd outside.

Betty looked out the window. Indians wearing hats and jeans and shirts of every color surrounded the RV. Faces. Braids. Bodies, short and tall; fat and thin. Some were very dark, almost like African Americans. Others were as light as Gil Canao. Their eyes grabbed hers. Black to hazel, those eyes bored into the *Ashley,* trying to see past the tinted windows. Trying to see *them*. But they couldn't, of course.

Not one face was friendly, not one mouth smiled. They stared, a half circle of intense eyes, brown skin, dark hair. The first ring was followed by another, and another. Some began to point at the *Ashley* and laugh. Two Indians dashed out and stood in front of the vehicle, posing. Others took their picture. They ran back to their friends, laughing uproariously. Another pair came forward for a souvenir photograph, and then another. The crowd roared.

They were *laughing* at them! The representatives of the largest corporation on the earth. Not representatives—the *founder* of the largest corporation in history and the richest man in the world, and his top staff.

Betty would have been more offended, but she knew why the Indians were so hostile. Grandfather was retiring from public life in a week, and this was his People's last chance to spend time with their shaman. And here *they* were, Will Duane and his fancy Numenon crew, crashing it.

If they dislike us so, what must they think of Grandfather for inviting us?

More Natives gathered, forming a circle around all five vehicles in the caravan. Betty couldn't see where the crowd ended.

Will looked out the window. "Drive over them, Mark."

"I can't, sir."

"Why?"

"There's someone at the door."

2

ENZO DONATORE SAT on one of the finely carved marble benches ringing the wide patio behind the palace. He was contemplating a little problem that had been worrying him more than was seemly. Ruining his afternoon, truth be told. Despite his gloom, light flooded the area where he sat. It shimmered on Enzo's silver-flecked blond hair and closely trimmed beard; it shone on his strong teeth and jaw. His body was perfectly formed. His tailored jacket could not hide the breadth of his chest or his muscular physique, yet he carried his massive form with grace and ease.

His brother emerged from the castle's nearest door with a very attractive young lady. He beckoned for his brother to bring the girl over. He was so distraught by the difficulty gnawing at him that he neglected to rise to greet her.

"Lorenzo, this is Andrea Beckman, the young woman I told you about," Diego said. "We had a lovely time at the Alhambra yesterday. I invited Miss Beckman to the party this evening, and to stay as long as she wanted." Diego smiled at her. "I'll let you two get acquainted. I have work to do in the office."

She looked at him with huge, trusting eyes. "Señor Donatore—"

"No, my dear, call me Enzo. Everyone who knows me does."

"You're a very long way from home, my dear," said Enzo. "You've travelled all the way from California to my little abode." He waved his hand to indicate the vast terrace around them, the lower courtyards cascading down the mountain, the vast blue skies, and the expansive fields and orchards of his domain. "You traveled all this way by yourself. You're quite the adventuress."

Enzo's face radiated bonhomie, obscuring the sharpness of his gaze. Andrea stood next to him on the stone balcony, a slim young woman in a traveler's cheap, wrinkle-proof dress. The dress couldn't disguise the bounty of her breasts. She had dark hair and a fine, straight nose. Magnificent gray eyes.

He could tell she was awed by her surroundings, but managed to appear poised. From what Diego told him, this trip must have been the greatest adventure of her life. Most probably, it would be the last. His lips curved into a smile.

"I ran into Diego—Señor Donatore—at the Alhambra, as he said," she replied. "He invited me to stay here. I hope you don't mind. I don't usually just meet people and then show up at their *castle*. But he was so kind and he said that you have company all the time, and parties … It didn't matter that we'd just met."

Her voice had the ingenuous inflection of the American West. He loved it. As she blinked her wide eyes, Andrea's flaws were perfectly apparent to him: greed, ambition, and a willingness to believe anything that seemed to serve her purpose. Enzo smiled broadly. She was far better than Diego had indicated.

"I'm delighted to have you, my dear. What Diego said was true. Sometimes it does seem that we have a continuous party." He chuckled. "My brother has impeccable judgment about whom to include in our social circle, and, as you can see," he indicated the massive stone palace behind them, "we have plenty of room. Please stay as long as you like."

ℵ A delicate flush rose from her neck. "Thank you. I can only stay a week. I have a new job waiting for me at home. I just finished my master's degree in computer science at Berkeley. This trip is a graduation present from my parents."

"Tell me about your job. I'm interested in jobs. I provide many. You've heard of Donatore Indústrial?"

"Of course. The Donatore name is famous all over the world." Her tongue darted around her lips before she answered, a defensive gesture. It told him who her employer was before she said the name. Of course, he already knew from what Diego told him. Everyone knew of the feud between him and Will Duane. He tensed in anticipation of the word. "Well, my new job is at Numenon, in their Palo Alto headquarters."

A hiss escaped him. She pulled away.

"Don't mind me," Enzo said, recovering. "Will Duane is an old rival." He waved his hand. "His refusal to leave Europe and take his products with him has caused me much grief."

A band struck up from the terrace's lower level. "Ah, the party has begun. Would you like to meet your fellow guests?" He rose and indicated she should join him by the balustrade.

Andrea stood so close that he could have nestled his palm into the soft valley joining her waist and hip. He glanced at her face. A thin film of moisture glistened on her upper lip. A wisp of dark hair had loosened from her chignon and whipped in the wind. She reached up and secured it, neat as an adder.

She reacted to him the way everyone did when they saw him stand for the first time. She stood stiffly. Her eyes traveled up to his chest, and up again until her neck was craned back. When her head stopped moving, he knew she saw the underside of his nose and jaw. Her mouth opened; her face registered dismay and then, pity.

"I've a bit of gigantism, my dear," he said. "Runs in the family. My father was much taller than I am. You must get used to me, and then you will think of me as your uncle Enzo."

⅄ Enzo closed his eyes, inhaling sharply. He put his fingers to his forehead and winced.

"Are you all right, Señor Donatore?" Andrea asked.

He grimaced. "My dear," he said, and then lifted her hand and brushed her knuckles against his lips. "I must attend to a bit of business. I'll find you some company."

They stood on the castle's highest terrace. Buff-colored stone patios spread out behind them, and cypress-flanked stairways descended from each side. The staircases dropped and dropped again, until they reached the distant walls that surrounded the castle's lands.

Enzo moved to the stone balustrade and looked down. The terrace below was crowded with people sipping drinks and dancing to black-clad musicians. A tall, auburn-haired woman looked up. He caught her eye and beckoned. She immediately headed for the stairs, moving toward them with surprising speed. The silk of her dark green gown pressed against her body as she walked, revealing its outlines.

"Andrea, this is Penelope. I'm going to leave you in her care." Andrea looked flustered when she saw the other woman's silk gown and jewel-draped arms and neck. Her hair was lacquered and wrapped as though she was a model in *Vogue*.

"Don't feel embarrassed, my dear. We are formal here at the castle. Our guests are often taken by surprise. Penelope, get Andrea something to wear." He kissed Andrea's hand. "I'll meet you for dinner. I'd like to continue our conversation, if that suits you."

"Oh, yes!"

Enzo spun and charged into the castle. Tall bronze doors opened inward as he approached. The castle was made of the same buff-colored stone as the patios. The stonework continued inside, lovely soft beige columns and arches, all beautifully carved and complemented by ancient ironwork. Massive pillars held up the ceiling's beams. Medieval banners hung from the joists and polished suits of armor stood at attention along the hallway.

Enzo ran down a set of stairs, and then the next. The gloom grew deeper at each landing, but he paid no attention to the darkness. Finally, he reached the castle's lowest level.

Ancient wooden doors, metal-bound and six inches thick, guarded his secret quarters. Enzo's chest heaved as he approached the entry. He had to get to his stronghold. He needed to see. Something was happening in the desert. His quarry was slipping out of his grasp. He held his palm to a sensor by the door.

The massive portals opened and he entered his domain. His movement caused a few lights to go on, but Enzo's lair remained shadowed. Outlines of stone columns, leather, and wrought iron furniture were barely visible, hinting at the masculine opulence of the room. The room had one window, sunk into the wall and glazed with rock crystal. Sitting before the window was a polished stone table.

He planted his palms on the table's surface. The slab was six feet across, its unadorned surface polished ultra smooth. A clear, pyramidal gem two feet in diameter rose from the center. The see-stone.

"Show me," he commanded. The stone lit up, light spiraling from its core and rising above the table. The spiral coalesced into a wide beam, which showed him his target. The wretched caravan of motor homes bounced across the desert. They were approaching the Mogollon Bowl.

He should have dealt with Duane and his friends before they got this far, but something had intervened. Enzo looked at his hand, which was carefully bandaged.

The old Indian shaman had come *here*—to his stronghold—and thrown a lance through his hand. While the Numenon caravan was stuck in the ribbon canyon where he'd planned on killing them, the shaman had invaded Enzo's most secret place and stopped him. The old man had more magic in him than Enzo knew.

Will Duane and his patsy, Doug Saunders, were alive because of the old man. And that other Indian, Bud Creeman. The see-stone had shown the fat slob healing them. Rage erupted inside Enzo. He'd show them what an invasion was. No place would be safe to any of them this week—or ever.

"Show me more," he hissed at the table. The crystal revealed a glimpse inside the first vehicle. He saw a tall, white-haired man. Duane. The see-stone's focus shifted. He could see the Numenon caravan approaching something vast and obscure. And then nothing. Something blocked the stone's vision. Enzo knew what had happened: The caravan entered the Mogollon Bowl.

"Fix it!" he shouted. Darkness filled the area over the table. The blackness became absolute as the spiral of light disappeared into the stone. He cursed. The see-stone couldn't reach them. What could stop a *see-stone?*

What could he do? Nothing. Until that afternoon, he'd had an operative in Will Duane's office, a spy under deep cover. Sandy Sydney was Betty Fogarty's right hand and most trusted assistant. She was so valuable to Betty that she'd been included in the Numenon group going to the retreat. *She* should have been his eyes in the Mogollon Bowl.

But she had finished her transformation early and, not knowing what to do with her new powers, attacked the members of the Numenon party. Then she had run into the desert and abandoned her responsibility to him. Enzo could feel her hiding on the edges of the Mogollon Bowl where he couldn't touch her.

That was the issue that had been shredding his guts all afternoon. He had no one in the Bowl to inform him. He couldn't *see;* he had no source of information. Anything could happen and he wouldn't know about it.

Enzo threw himself into one of the huge chairs and bunched his hands into fists. Pain from his pierced palm shot up his arm. He cursed again. He couldn't sit on the sidelines; there was too much was at stake.

If that old fake shaman converted Will Duane and his people, they would be powerful enough to use Numenon to change how corporations operated worldwide. If that happened, everything could change. People would devote themselves to sentimentality and foolishness, love and good deeds, instead of healthy self-interest.

Enzo paced around his lair. *He* was supposed to be the ruler of the universe. *His* kind and their lore was to triumph, not the myths that fools like the shaman worshipped. *His* kingdom was supposed to rule the earth, forever and for all time.

This was the week. Duane would come to him, or be lost forever.

A chime caused him to raise his head. "Yes?"

"Enzo, it's late." Diego's voice came from a speaker.

"Tell them to serve supper."

"They already have."

"Tell them to dance."

"They are."

"Don't bother me, Diego. I'm thinking."

"Enzo, the new girl is upset. She's talking about leaving."

"What new girl?"

"Andrea."

"Who?"

"The new girl."

Enzo's eyes widened. "Keep her where she is. I'll be right there."

3

WHEN MARK OPENED the *Ashley*'s door, a tall gray-haired Indian leaped into the cabin. Everyone pulled away as though a cougar had burst through the entry. Will knew who the guy was: Dr. Tyler Brand, Professor of Religious Studies at UC Santa Barbara. The brief Betty had presented gave them the facts about Grandfather's main people, including photos—and Dr. Brand was one of them.

Brand was the author of eleven critically acclaimed books, and a world authority on Native American religions and Eastern philosophical systems. He was believed to have been Grandfather's student for more than twenty years and a founder of the Meeting. Betty's brief could not indicate the guy's personal impact. The air around him vibrated.

"I'm Tyler Brand," a deep voice announced as he shook Will's hand. "Grandfather wanted me to meet you and lead you to your camping spot. I'll be your liaison for the week." The professor's face said he didn't like them or being their contact. "The Bowl is filling up fast. Let's get to your campsite. We'll do introductions when we get there." Tyler pointed the way, standing next to Mark with one hand on the back of the driver's seat.

Brand was an academic. Will didn't like academics, but this one was sharp and tough and a big success. He could excuse his unfortunate gaffe in job selection. Whatever he was, he was better than Paul Running Bird.

As they moved deeper into the Bowl, Will realized that it looked better from a distance. Up close, he could hear the crowd's racket, even behind the *Ashley's* closed windows and the engine noise. Dust swirled around the vehicle. The crowd seemed to press at the RV's sides.

"Stop," Tyler Brand said, as he pointed to someone outside.

Mark stopped the vehicle and opened the door. A paunchy Indian, his khaki shirt pulled taut across a bulging abdomen, climbed in. Below the belly, his waist nipped in over improbably slim hips. He took off a high-crowned hat and wiped his wet forehead with the back of his wrist. A few strands of hair were plastered across the front of his head. The rest fell in skimpy braids.

Dr. Brand's voice was sonorous as he introduced the visitor. "This is Tribal Police Chief Elmo Gregg."

Elmo looked around warily. "I want to welcome you all on behalf of the tribe. The rest of the Tribal Council will meet you at an official ceremony, when Grandfather says they can have it."

He wiped his forehead again. Will noticed a wet half moon under his arm. The police chief chuckled. "It's hot out there. You all will be glad for your air conditioning." He looked around the *Ashley*, appearing perplexed and a bit slow. But Will knew that for what it was. Elmo's eyes didn't miss a thing; he covered them and the *Ashley's* interior like he was making copies of everything he saw.

"I want you to know that you have the full protection of the Tribal Police and our justice system, if you need it. However, the Meeting is strictly Grandfather's show, so he and his warriors will be doing the actual protecting. But we'll jump in if they need help." The Police Chief grimaced and shifted uncomfortably. "Grandfather don't want the Tribal Council here on an official basis because they might try to ... uh,...

well hit you up for the new casino." Elmo rubbed his forehead again and looked acutely embarrassed. "The Tribal Finance Chief is hot about gettin' it goin' …" He looked directly at Will, then ducked his head and glanced out the window.

"Is there a problem, Chief Gregg?" Will asked. His tension was ratcheting up with each of Elmo's nervous gestures.

"Oh, nah. Nothin' we can't handle. I thought I saw Lena back there. She's the Tribal Chairman's daughter. Went to college and run wild."

"What did she study?" Betty asked. Will could see that Elmo's anxiety made Betty nervous, too.

"*Art.*" The chief looked even sadder, bending over to speak to the driver. "You got alarms on these things?"

"Yes," Mark answered.

"Motion sensors?"

"Yes."

"Well, you might want to use them at night. In the day, too. I'll be leavin' you now. Any trouble, call me, but call the spirit warriors first." He nodded at Tyler Brand. "That's the way it's done at the Meeting." Elmo put his hat on and trotted down the stairs.

"What was *that* all about?" Will turned to Tyler.

"The relations between Grandfather and the tribe can be … *are*—"

"About as tricky as relations between me and my Board of Directors," Will finished for Dr. Brand.

"The Bowl is on reservation land, and so it is in the jurisdiction of the Tribal Council and Police. But Grandfather …" Tyler shrugged. "He doesn't follow anyone's rules but the ones the Great One gives him. And *all* the warriors are here. The ones who aren't still in jail."

"Jail!"

"Yes, Grandfather works extensively in the prisons. Many inmates are among his followers. Some of them are here—those who have been released."

"There are *ex-convicts* here?" Betty's voice rose.

"Men and women who have paid their debts to society." Tyler looked pained. "Grandfather decides who comes here and who stays. If he says you come, you come. If he says you go, you're gone.

"Now, you need to claim your space. I'll show you where to park."

Their designated camping spot was a large open space next to the head-quarters—that's what the Indians called the funky, two-story buildings visible since they cleared the Rim. The structures' crumbling cement-block construction and missing windows seemed ominous up close. Will and the others got out of the *Ashley* and looked around.

Showers formed by tarps and poles fanned out behind one of the buildings. The tarps billowed in the wind, allowing glimpses of the bath-ers. Beyond the headquarters an ancient water tank tottered on stilts.

The other cement-block building looked empty, and between them, Will saw a decrepit generator.

That was the camp headquarters.

The Numenon team moved into the open space. Banks of portable toilets flanked their campsite. They had been obscured by the buildings earlier. Will did a quick count: *Hundreds* of porta-potties were available, enough to serve thousands of people. The potties stood in turquoise rows. Flies had already discovered them, and the Meeting hadn't even started.

The symbolism implied by their location was obvious. The Indians had put them next to the crappers. They were implying that he and his people were crap.

Their neighbors noticed their arrival. They stared at them stone-faced like the Indians they'd met when they entered the Bowl. Beyond them, multitudes of campers chatted and laughed with friends, catching up on a year's worth of news. The racket of thousands of people talking surrounded them. It would go on all night; there would be no peace in this place.

"*Paul Running Bird* did this! That son of a bitch got us lost, and then he put us *here!*" Will spit out the words like bullets, heedless of the professor standing next to him. His face grew white, then red.

He noticed his employees were regarding him nervously, so Will pulled himself in. He knew that his anger was legendary. If he blew, he'd turn the whole crowd against them, more than they already were. He had to stay in control.

Betty put a hand on Will's forearm. "I don't think they're trying to be insulting. There's got to be a good explanation for this. Let's go find out what it is."

4

"BUT SHE'S NOT one of us," Diego sputtered.

"Of *course* she's not one of us," Enzo replied. "If she were one of us, she couldn't set foot in the Mogollon Bowl, and she couldn't get near Will Duane."

"But can you trust her?"

Enzo chuckled. "Making her trustworthy is my problem. This is what I want you to do …"

Andrea sat in the lushly appointed salon. Brocade sofas were grouped around the room; a stone table laden with fruit and cheese sat in the middle. Tapestries and Renaissance paintings covered the pale rock walls. She knew the paintings were famous from her art appreciation course. Andrea clutched the hankie Diego had given her, and wished to God that Enzo would come so that she could say goodbye and leave.

What started out as a dream, had ended as a nightmare. When Enzo left, Penelope had taken her to the castle wardrobe, which would have put a Hollywood star's dressing room to shame. Just being around Penelope was magical—she looked like a supermodel and moved like a dancer. She went into a closet and brought out a silvery silk designer sheath, the type of dress Andrea had only seen in magazines. "It brings out your gray eyes," Penelope said. "And now for the rest." A hairdresser and makeup artist materialized.

While they worked, Penelope told her about the wardrobe and life in the castle. Apparently, actresses and rich women, even nobility, left clothes there so that they could be "dressed" at a moment's notice. Sometimes, they never wore the gowns, and just left them hanging. The glitterati usually brought their own personal attendants, but when he was having a party, Enzo hired a hairdresser and beautician for his guests.

Andrea gasped when saw herself in the mirror. She looked beautiful and sophisticated; nothing like the self-conscious dope she had felt like her whole life. This was the way she was meant to be, except for the front of the dress. When Penelope wasn't looking, she tried to pull it up a little, but there wasn't enough fabric. Maybe no one would notice.

Penelope led her to the dining hall. The distances in the castle were so vast that Andrea almost wished she had roller skates. Walking in the stiletto heels they'd found for her was hard work. As she walked, Andrea scanned the corners of the hallway, looking for bugs and spiders. She couldn't help it, even though she'd taken her medication.

When they reached the dining hall, Andrea ducked her head, intimidated by the room full of new people. Penelope sat her to the right of Enzo's empty chair, an immense wooden and leather thing that commanded the head of the table. The room glittered with jewels and brightly colored gowns. Every face turned to her. Andrea picked up her napkin and smoothed it across her lap, and looked down.

The table was covered with fine linen and dotted with candelabras. It seemed to extend forever. Every seat was filled. The little guy sitting next to her was the Prime Minister of some Asian country. She had seen his picture on the cover of *Forbes*. The lead singer of GothPhantoms was three seats down from her. Enzo's chair remained vacant, which seemed to peeve the aging actress across the table.

"Ah. A *young* lovely. How long have you been here, my dear?"

"I got here today—" Andrea began, aware that the actress had narrowed her eyes at her.

"Here we have *today*. And who will sit there *tomorrow?*" She spoke gaily, waving to the rest of the table, drawing them into her joke. With her bright red lipstick, bleached teeth, and one too many facelifts, the woman looked like a witch.

Andrea flushed and would have shot something back, but she suddenly realized that they were talking about her sexual availability—and dispensability. Just as fast, she realized that Diego had picked her up at the Alhambra and brought her to the castle for his brother's pleasure. He was nothing but a pimp. But why would Enzo want *her?* Did she look easy? The thought made her choke.

"What do you do, young lady?" said the Asian head of state next to her.

"Well, I just got a master's degree in computer sciences. I'm going to work at Numenon—"

"Numenon?" he cried with horror. Everyone laughed. The word Numenon careened around the hall, hilarity increasing with every repetition.

"What's the matter with Numenon? It's the best corporation in the world!" Andrea cried.

"Don't tell Enzo that!" the actress chortled.

When the food came, Andrea couldn't eat. The others kept eyeing her and making comments she didn't understand.

The courses kept coming, part of a feast that was as sumptuous as her dress was elegant and sexy. The snickers and malicious jibes vaulted across the table like devilish condiments. Many were directed at her.

"How many little girls came to stay last week?" said the actress.

"I don't know. If Enzo wanted to keep track of a year, he'd have to use a computer," the Prime Minister giggled.

"At least they were smart enough not to mention Numenon." That brought a guffaw from the whole table.

Andrea ran from the hall. She couldn't stop the tears and didn't have a hankie or a tissue. Her nose always ran when she cried. Andrea dashed through the corridors, searching for a ladies' lounge. Anywhere to hide. Penelope found her and called Diego.

"Oh, my poor dear." Diego was the soul of remorse.

"It was because Enzo wasn't there," Penelope said. "They were jealous because she was seated next to him. You know how they are."

"I am so sorry. Please, let my brother talk to you. He will wish to apologize."

She sat in the pretty room waiting. Never again would she let a handsome stranger turn her head. She shouldn't have spoken to Diego at the Alhambra and she shouldn't have come to the castle. She wanted to go home and start her job with Numenon. That was all she'd wanted to do for years, since she heard Will Duane speak at the NumoFair in San Francisco.

5

TYLER WAS EMBARRASSED. He knew the Numenon campsite was a hellhole. He and his wife were set up on the other side of the open space, next to the hospital tent. They stayed there every year, wanting to show the People that success hadn't changed them. They were right next to Elizabeth Bright Eagle, who camped there for the same reason, he presumed.

He looked across the field and saw Bert Creeman standing by a tent, cradling her belly with both hands and looking pained. Why Bud would bring such an enormously pregnant woman to the Meeting, Tyler didn't know. If she made it through the week, he'd be surprised. At least she was close to the doctors.

Tyler pulled his attention back to the Numenon camp. Despite its proximity to physicians, the site *was* hell. The noise never stopped. People moved around all night despite the curfew. Add in the porta potties and bathhouse, and Dante could have used the place as inspiration for a lower level of hades when he wrote *The Inferno*.

"We're sorry about this location. We were attempting to accommodate your needs, Mr. Duane. The electricity and phone for the camp are right there." He pointed to a four plug electric outlet on the outside of the headquarters. "Sometimes the generator works. There's a cell phone for emergencies inside. We don't have phone lines."

"We have generators in the motor homes," Will spoke rapidly. "We can use our cell phones. They're satellite-based. But we need phone lines for faxes. We can't be without faxes for a week. Or the Internet." Will ran his hands through his hair. "Doug, how long would it take to get phone lines out here? A week?"

"Actually, Mr. Duane, none of your equipment is likely to work, even if you had phone and electrical lines. This Bowl is a holy site for many reasons. One is that an anomaly in the earth's electromagnetic field exists here. There are only a few spots on the planet like this—and this is the strongest by far. Scientists used to come out here to study the place. They built those," Tyler said as he pointed at the headquarter buildings, "but they never figured out why the Bowl is this way.

"Grandfather says the Bowl is alive. After staying here for years, I agree. It has a will and values. The Bowl controls what happens here and what works and what doesn't. It sounds crazy, but if it doesn't want you to use," he waved his hand at the phone on Will's belt, "your cell phone for a particular purpose, it won't work. But if you want to use it for another purpose, that the Bowl deems fit, it *will* work." He shrugged apologetically. "The phone in the headquarter's main building will work for emergencies, even though there's no signal here."

"That's impossible," Will barked. "It's against the laws of physics."

"They don't apply here. Didn't Paul Running Bird brief you? He was supposed to tell you about the Bowl."

"All he did was give us a map that almost got us killed," Will snapped.

Tyler's breath caught as he realized what had happened. That's why Grandfather had given him this miserable duty at the last minute. Almost killing their guest of honor definitely would get Grandfather's ire up. He hadn't seen Paul, either. That was strange; he usually glad-handed every important arrival.

"Paul said it was like the Santa Cruz Mystery Spot," Betty added. "Strange, but harmless."

Tyler coughed into his hand to cover a laugh. "Not *quite*. Grandfather is a great healer and holy man, but he doesn't do it by himself. In the end, the Bowl calls the shots. Don't mess with Mother Nature." Tyler raised his brows in an attempt at light-heartedness, and failed.

"Are my people in danger?" Will scowled.

"Not really. If I get the sense that something I'm going to do or say is wrong, I don't do it. And that's *in addition* to following the Rules. Paul did give you copies of those, didn't he?"

All but the middle-aged woman looked blank.

"They were in the briefing I gave you. Doesn't anyone remember? I went over them at length." Betty looked peeved. "The binders are in the *Ashley*. You can look at them later."

"We didn't get a briefing," said one of the other RV drivers, the only African American in the group. He had an unforgetable deep voice with a Southern inflection.

The ripple that went through the drivers told Tyler volumes about how Numenon worked. The drivers didn't get complete information; they weren't full members of the team.

"I'll summarize the Rules and make sure you get copies," Tyler said, primarily addressing the drivers. He couldn't ignore that social-class based omission. "The Rules are *no nuthin'*: no drugs, alcohol, sex, violence, or gambling. Nothing that will distract you from experiencing the Spirit is allowed at the Meeting. If you break the Rules, Grandfather will throw you out." He looked at Will and then the others. "Even you, Mr. Duane. He will know. You're warned."

"The Bowl's power and ethical principles are in addition to the Rules. If the Bowl doesn't want you to use your technology, you won't be able to use it. That's probably why the scientists always abandoned their studies. Anything electronic may be affected. Look at your watches and calculators."

They did—digital watches moved randomly forward and backward in time. Will pulled out his pocket calculator. It made a fizzing noise and black guck oozed from the display panel.

"I wouldn't even think about turning on your computers."

Melissa Weir's eyes shot open. Numenon's star female MBA sat up and looked around. Will Duane had an affection for the nation's top graduate schools of business. He loved the products of their master's of business administration programs. All the executives on the trip were MBAs, including Will. Melissa was a prodigy; she earned her master's degree before she was twenty, at Harvard, no less. She moved on to conquer Numenon.

She was fully clothed, wearing jeans, a shirt, and running shoes. She distinctly remembered dressing in a business suit when she left that morning. She didn't remember changing. Worse, she was in Will's bed in the *Ashley*. Holy shit—rumors would fly. She had a vague recollection that Doug had been sleeping there, too. That was even worse, given their vendetta.

The RV wasn't moving, and the bed didn't have any sheets on it; she was lying on a bare mattress with Will's raw silk bedspread draped over her. They had been going somewhere—but where? She couldn't remember. She remembered clawing her way across the floor screaming, and then a brown-skinned man helping her. Melissa crept to the window and peered out.

A crumbling cement building was next to the *Ashley*. A hose with a showerhead on the end was slung over a tarpaulin, creating a shower on the other side. A wet brown shoulder became visible between the sheets of plastic. Melissa ran from the bedroom toward the main cabin.

Finding it empty, she made for the entrance door and squatted as low as she could to avoid being seen.

Looking through the windshield, she saw the whole Numenon group—Will, Betty, Gil, and Doug, Jon, and then Mark and the rest of the drivers—standing in a ring around a distinguished looking Indian. Dr. Tyler Brand. It was coming back.

The *Ashley's* door was open; she could hear Dr. Brand trying to put a pretty face on a shameful deceit.

"In past years, people have turned on their laptops," he said. "Sometimes they work; sometimes they go up in smoke. We had a real fire once." He laughed.

Melissa couldn't believe what she heard. *They burned laptops!* She bounded out of the *Ashley* and threw herself in front of the professor. She knew who he was from Betty's brief. Melissa leaped at him without a thought. "What did you say?"

"The Bowl is a geo—"

"A geomagnetic anomaly. The rules of physics don't work right here. I know all about that. *But why didn't you tell us that we couldn't bring our laptops?* For Christ's sake, your Rules cover everything else, why didn't you tell us about something so serious. We came all the way out here to your retreat. What are we supposed to do when we're not listening to lectures? Twiddle our thumbs? What kind of retreat is this?"

"Sometimes everything works fine," Brand said. "During the lightning storms—"

"Lightning storms?" Melissa interrupted.

"Yes, we get lightning storms that you wouldn't believe out here. But don't worry—the storms have never killed anyone."

"You didn't tell us about lightning storms, either!" A fleck of saliva shot from Melissa's mouth.

Tyler Brand stepped back and crossed his arms over his chest.

"What other *little surprises* do you have for us?" Melissa snapped.

Tyler clenched his jaw and raised his head, refusing to speak.

6

WILL OPENED HIS mouth to order his staff back into the motor homes. They were going home. Before he could say anything, a vision stopped him. She walked toward them from the gigantic tent across the empty field. She was with another woman. Will recognized them from their photos in the briefing, but only one caused him to catch his breath.

Elizabeth Bright Eagle moved like an Indian goddess. She was a large woman with perfect posture. She held herself upright, her erect torso accenting her magnificent, very large, *huge*—

Will stopped himself. He couldn't believe what he was thinking about Dr. Bright Eagle. She was an internationally known physician and philanthropist. She'd been on *Oprah* and the cover of a dozen magazines. She was *People's* Woman of the Year, for heaven's sake.

After a while, he noticed the woman with Elizabeth. She was as tall as the doctor and much thinner, moving with a dancer's ease.

Tyler Brand smiled and stretched out his arm. "I'd like you to meet my wife, Leona Brand, and Dr. Elizabeth Bright Eagle."

Leona and Elizabeth shook hands with all of the professionals, starting with Will.

When he touched Elizabeth's skin, Will's hand and forearm seemed to ignite. Pleasure filled him, emanating from the few square inches where his skin touched hers. His mind went blank, but his soul understood.

Will had had spiritual raptures for most of his life. They came over him unexpectedly. He felt bliss and saw lights and amazing creatures, which seemed perfectly real. He got insights and solved business problems in those magical states. All his life, he'd hidden his visions, knowing everyone would think he was crazy—even *he* felt crazy for having them.

Elizabeth's handshake felt like the touch of one of the wondrous creatures from his visionary world. Will looked into her eyes in awe.

She yanked her hand away. Horror flickered over her face, replaced almost instantly by unflappable dignity. She smiled stiffly and shook Doug's hand, moving quickly down the line. Will looked after her, wanting to say, "Did you feel that? What was *that?*"

"We are so pleased to have you here," Leona Brand said. "Sharing our culture and lives with you means so much to us. Welcome to our Meeting and to our hearts. If you don't need the utilities, you're welcome to take that spot over there." She pointed to an empty space on the ridge across the Bowl and next to a primitive lean-to. "That's Grandfather's lean-to. That's the best spot in the Bowl."

"Certainly, Mrs. Brand, we'll take it. When do I get to see Grandfather?" Will sort of danced on his toes, like a fighter. Despite his efforts, he knew that he couldn't be polite much longer. He was about to pull a famous Will Duane screamer.

"He can see you privately, Mr. Duane, on Thursday from four to six p.m.—or a.m., whichever you prefer. He will do a purification ceremony with you at that time. He can also see you for a few minutes on Saturday morning before everyone leaves. And you are welcome to attend the public meetings, of course." She smiled brightly.

"*Do you know how much it's costing me to be here?*" Will seemed to sink a few inches before exploding. He screamed, his face reddening, his mouth snarling. He always seemed about three times his normal size when he blew up. "I drag my staff out to the middle of nowhere—and give up my business for a week—to stay in this dump and see an old man for a couple of hours on Thursday? Thursday! *Are you out of your minds?*"

7

GRANDFATHER STOOD A short distance from the Numenon group, watching and listening. These people would be lucky not to get struck by lightning. He didn't know how they found the Bowl, even with the Ancestors and Supernaturals guiding them. His shoulders shook and he couldn't stop himself.

His laughter burst out, rolling from him, covering the Bowl and the wretched headquarters and all his cranky People who wished these tattered scraps of humanity ill. He laughed and laughed, pulling out his handkerchief and wiping his eyes.

The Numenon group stared at him. There they were: the tall, handsome Will Duane, the richest man in the world. He had white hair like Grandfather's, except he didn't wear his in braids. The old man guffawed; maybe Will Duane would grow braids by the time this was over! There was pretty Betty Fogarty, long suffering and faithful. The brilliant, explosive Melissa Weir. Loyal Gil Canao. And Doug Saunders, Will's enforcer and the corporate bad boy. There were also the drivers and a chef, each with a story and a reason for being there.

Still, he laughed. They had a *brief* about him and his People—but he had all the knowledge of the Great One about *them*. Oh, he had been *briefed.* His laughter continued. Tears ran down his cheeks. He blew his nose.

The warriors behind him started to titter, and then the by-standers. Even Tyler Brand, the biggest prune of all, began shaking with mirth. They thought he was laughing at his guests. He wasn't; he was simply laughing because he couldn't contain his joy at the glorious play Creator had put in motion. At last, the Numenon crew started giggling, and then chuckling. Finally, they cracked up, as the younger people like to say. Grandfather knew a thing or two about the way people spoke these days.

When the mirth had run its course, he raised his hands.

"Oh, my dear friends, I'm so glad you're here." He walked toward them, holding out his hands. Their faces softened, all of them, and some seemed as though they might weep. "Yes, this is a place where feelings arise. Sometimes laughter, and sometimes tears. Whatever comes, remember that the will of the Great One is behind it. The Great One loves us and will see that we succeed this week." He reached Will Duane.

"Welcome, Will Duane," Grandfather said softly. "I welcome you with all the love in my heart and all the love of my Ancestors." When he took Will's hands, his guest began to tremble. "It's good to see you again. I came to see you in the desert when you were on the way here. Do you remember that?" Will shook his head.

"That is fine. This is a place where what should be remembered is, and what should be forgotten is buried in darkness. You may forget many things, and remember others that happened long ago. If you cannot think the way you usually do, it is the Mogollon Bowl, and it is the presence of Spirit. The Creator plays music here, and we are the instruments."

Will looked down at Grandfather, and began to breathe hard through his dry lips.

"You are a brave warrior, my son. The memory of what happened on the trip will return when it should. You are safe here." He reached up and brushed Will's cheek, gently caressing it. "Such a good boy. Good boy."

Will swayed with the words. Grandfather looked into his eyes and saw his spirit. He could see all of Will Duane's past, and some of his future. This week would decide the fate of his soul. He looked into those blue eyes, knowing everything about the mine Duane wished to perpetrate on their Holy Lands.

"We will be neighbors, Will Duane. Your camp will be next to mine. You will see so much of me, you will grow tired of this old face." He beamed and patted Will's hand. "You do want to stay this week, don't you? If you want to leave, that is fine. Just turn around and go home." He read the hunger in Will's eyes, the pain.

"No, no. I want to stay. I want to … learn what you have to teach me. I want …"

Will suddenly clasped his hands tighter. Gazing intently into the shaman's eyes, the billionaire said, "I'm so sorry about the BIA."

Grandfather blinked. "What about—"

"The Bureau of Indian Affairs. Betty told us about it. I'm so sorry about what they did to you, investment-wise. Losing all of your money. And for the Indian schools. I'm really sorry. If you ever want any consultants or lawyers, please, call me. I've got the best."

Grandfather nodded. No one had ever said that to him before, yet the offer was sincere—Will's energy surged through the shaman's hands and he read all of it. Will Duane had great potential, if he could be healed.

"Will Duane, I have many duties this week," Grandfather said. "We will have our sweat on Thursday, as we planned on the phone, remember?" Will seemed bewildered, clinging to the old man's hand. "I will say hello to your friends. Then I must leave. Go set up your camp, have a nap. At four o'clock, there will be a special treat for you: Wesley Silverhorse will give you a horsemanship and martial arts demonstration."

The old man moved on to Betty and Gil, taking their hands and gazing into their eyes. When Grandfather got to Melissa, something unforeseen happened. Her moods were swinging wild and fast. He had seen her dressing down Tyler Brand and knew that she treated others the same way. He looked into her eyes and the Power took him. He could see inside her mind as though he had lived her life.

He could see images of a red-haired man screaming through her memories. Her moods ricocheted between rage, terror, loneliness, and despair. She was in desperate need of healing. Her soul was whole and good. And he discovered something—something shocking.

He kept holding Melissa's hand, hoping he was wrong. *This nasty woman is my Wesley's partner? This hostile creature is my Wesley's soul mate?*

Wesley Silverhorse was his most advanced warrior and would probably succeed him. He knew Wesley's spirit as well as he knew his own.

He kept holding her hand, searching for an explanation, when something inside Melissa shifted, allowing him to see her extreme loneliness. He realized how she suffered. Poor thing!

If Melissa could be cured, she would be perfect for Wesley. Grandfather sighed. She'd eat him alive if she wasn't healed. He pulled her to him and hugged her to his heart.

She almost collapsed. He allowed his energy to pass into her. She relaxed, not fighting him. A good sign. *You're a good girl*, his soul said to hers. *You'll be fine, little one. Follow your heart this week.* Grandfather whispered, "If you need me, I'll come to you. Just call."

He let go of her, and Melissa wobbled on her feet. She looked peaceful and unafraid. "You do want to stay this week, don't you?" He had to ask. She nodded vigorously.

He was about to leave when he remembered. "The other woman. Where is she? The blond."

Will jumped forward and said loudly, "Sandy Sydney is an industrial spy. She's more than that; I don't know what she is. She attacked us on the way here. She's out in the desert somewhere. She's very dangerous."

Grandfather nodded. He felt Sandy Sydney become a demon the instant it had happened while they were traveling in the *Ashley*. He was also glad that the hundreds of people gathered around them had heard Will Duane. Hopefully they'd remember when events played out.

"We have the best trackers in the world, Will Duane. We'll find her before she does any damage," Grandfather replied. "Carl, we will go to the Bowl now." He turned to a huge man waiting in a decrepit golf cart. The shaman climbed in and they drove away, followed by the crowds.

He didn't know all of what Sandy Sydney would do, just enough to turn to Carl and say, "Send many warriors out. If you find her, kill her. Use all of your power and show no mercy."

He knew they would find nothing, but he was honor bound to try to avert what was coming.

8

"MY DEAR, I am so sorry." Enzo looked into Andrea's eyes as they sat in the elegant salon at the castle. "They are jealous of you because you are fresh and lovely. They want your youth and beauty. I am so sorry that I left you alone, but something very important came up. Will you forgive me?"

She looked down, knowing that weeping had given her a red, dripping nose, splotchy face, and swollen eyes. Despite that, Andrea sat up as straight as she could, trying to accommodate herself to the formality of Enzo's manner and the overwhelming effect he had on her.

He *was* sincere. She could tell that. The sincerity of his apology flattened her hurt and anger—that and the fact that she knew she looked terrible, a rag-muffin to his prince. Her voice was a squeak. "All right. I forgive you."

"You want to leave the castle, I understand," Enzo said. "Please know that I will reprimand my guests; they will not go unpunished."

"*Punished?*"

"Gently, my dear. We are gentle here." He looked around the room, eyes lighting on the table in the center. "Are you hungry? I am ravenous. I haven't eaten since this morning."

Andrea nodded. She'd hardly touched a thing at dinner.

"Good! You will share a bit of food while my jet is readied."

Her mouth slackened. "Your jet?"

"I have many jets, my dear. The fleet of Donatore Indústrial is at my disposal. And I have my personal jets." He laughed. "When you work for Will Duane, you will notice that my world is far more luxurious than his. Even if he is alleged to have more money." His chuckle died, but he kept smiling.

"Ah, our meal is here." Liveried servants carried trays into the room, quickly setting the table and laying out the food, then silently disappearing. "We will eat, and then my pilot will deliver you back to the Alhambra where Diego met you, or home to California. Wherever you would like to go."

Sitting quietly with Enzo, she wasn't so sure she wanted to leave. He was charming and sweet. His size was a little scary when she first met him, but once she was used to him …

Something deep within her body trembled. She felt a familiar slippery sensation. *Oh, God, don't let me fall for him.*

"It's rather nice, isn't it?" he said, filing her glass again. She nodded. She'd had so much of his wine that she should have been snockered, but she wasn't. "It's a special vintage from this estate. I keep it for occasions such as this."

Diego walked into the room and placed a manila folder and a laptop next to Enzo, then withdrew. Enzo pulled the folder in front of him and laid his forearms onto it.

"Are you feeling better, my dear?"

"Yes, much better, thank you."

"I hope you will forgive me, but I have something I'd like to discuss with you. A bit of business." He looked at her for permission to go on. She nodded.

"Diego did not bring you here by chance. Donatore Indústrial needs good people. Diego did a bit of research on you before he approached you at the Alhambra." He flipped open the file Diego brought him. Her transcript from UC Berkeley was on the top. Enzo rifled through the file. She saw her resume and the letter from the Numenon personnel department. More material she'd posted on the Net, and one of her graduate school papers.

"How did you get all of that?" She pushed her chair back and rose to her feet, making a lunge for the folder. Enzo pulled it away. "You researched me and sent Diego to—"

"He is a, what do you call it? A headhunter. We were interested in employing you when he found the paper you wrote on Internet security." He patted her hand. "I know this seems surprising, my dear, but you need to know how corporations work. I assure you that Will Duane has a file on you twice as thick as this. Diego noticed your resume on the Internet, that's why you put it there, yes? For people to see? Diego was going to discuss it with you when he met you at the Alhambra, but you told him you had signed with Numenon. He invited you here anyway."

She could see that Enzo was telling the truth. The file wasn't so sneaky; she had put her resume on the Web so that it could be seen— and it was. How Diego got all the rest, she didn't know. Another sip of wine.

He ran a hand through his short hair, leaning toward her and lowering his voice. "Will Duane is such a problem. A matter related to him kept me from joining you at dinner." Enzo heaved a huge sigh and leaned closer.

"How can I tell you what I need to if you do not know the real Will Duane? He is not the man in the magazine articles." He looked at her, distress in his eyes. "Duane is a monster. In business, there is nothing he will not do. You do not believe me? Let me tell you about him.

"Have you ever heard of 'bricks'? These are boxes printed to look like they hold computers. They really hold ordinary bricks used for building. Will Duane ordered thousands of them to be made, filling warehouses. Before a new stock release came out, he represented the contents of the warehouses to SEC representatives as finished products available for sale." She looked puzzled. "He inflated the value of his inventory and gave Numenon the look of being better able to fulfill orders than it was. He *lied* to the SEC. That is a very illegal deception. Who knows what else he's done?

"His personal life is the worst." Enzo shook his head, and dropped his voice to a hoarse whisper. The atmosphere in the room grew darker. "The man is a fiend. Everything you've heard of him—the worst rumor—is true."

Andrea had heard that Will Duane was a womanizer in his younger days. She'd also heard that Numenon once had a sexual double standard, but that Will Duane had cleaned the place up. She'd heard Melissa Weir speak at a Women in Business seminar. She praised Numenon's treatment of women. Was she lying?

"What they say about him using prostitutes understates the truth. He devours them and tosses them away," Enzo said, gazing at her. Her eyes widened. *That* she didn't know about. "Ask any of the Madames on the Peninsula; they will tell you. What they *won't* tell you is how he assaulted a young girl. She vanished from the hospital. All the evidence against him disappeared with her. No body. No evidence. No crime. Very neat.

"The man is dangerous. At the very least, let me protect you when you're in Numenon. I told you that I have friends everywhere. I do, inside Numenon as well. You can become part of my network. If he makes advances toward you, my friends will spirit you away, or protect you with their lives."

"Part of your *network?*"

"Yes. I have a network of people devoted to protecting me and what I stand for." His eyes bored into hers.

"What do you stand for?"

"Excellence in everything, even more than Will Duane. The highest quality products. And freedom. I want people to be free to experience whatever they want—*everything*. I don't want artificial rules to separate people. Most of all, I want my people to have the lives of their dreams. What are your dreams, Andrea? What do you really want?"

Her breath stopped. She'd never thought of that. "Hmm. I'd like to look like I did when I first put on this dress, for the rest of my life. I'd like to be really good at what I do, be the 'best of the best,' as they say at Numenon." She noticed how saying Numenon made him wince. And then it came to her.

"I want *anything* but the life I've lived. I grew up in a tract house in the Oakland hills. My dad is an engineer. He's worked for the same company for thirty-eight years. My mom took care of my brother and I until we grew up. Now she raises purebred Pomeranians that she calls 'Oodles.' My mom and dad argue about what kind of fertilizer to buy. They're so boring I can't stand it."

She leaned forward, her voice becoming almost frantic. "I want *anything* but that. But that's what I'm turning into. I've got a four hundred-square foot studio apartment in a basement in Berkeley. When I'm at Numenon, I won't be able to afford much better. I think about insurance policies and retirement funds. I'm turning out just like my parents! Except that I don't have a husband. Or anyone."

He patted her hand, the soul of kindness. "Would you join me if I could give you what you desire? A lovely apartment. Sufficient money for you to live however you want? A job with real purpose? Freedom to act in ways you never imagined?" His smile had a hint of something in it. Was he coming on to her?

"Well, yeah. I'd go for that. I don't want to do anything illegal, but I'd do pretty much anything else." She gulped the wine.

"Well, Andrea, the difference between legal and illegal is often a fine distinction. Did Will Duane commit murder if there was no evidence or body?" He filled her glass and she sipped.

"I don't know. I'm confused."

✗ "Think of it this way. I'm offering you escape from the sentence your parents imposed upon you: a life of boredom and mediocrity. Does what I described sound good? Would you carry out the assignments I give you?" His gaze seemed to penetrate all the way to her brain.

Her brow furrowed. "I wouldn't have to kill anyone, would I?"

"Of course not." He laughed heartily.

"Well, yeah. I'd do *anything* not to be like my parents." Her chest heaved unexpectedly and she grabbed the hanky again.

Enzo smiled at her. "I understand, my dear. You want a chance at a life like this." He indicated their sumptuous surroundings. "With a man like me." His smile was matter of fact, as though she could actually have a relationship with him.

"Are you making me a job offer?"

"Not yet. We need to talk more. You have to know everything before you can decide. And I have to know if you're the one for the job I have in mind." Enzo stopped speaking and appraised her, as though searching for some hidden quality. He must have found it, because he continued.

"Will Duane hates me. He knows that I know all about him; he knows that I watch him, waiting for him to make a fatal mistake. We compete in business, but more than that, there is ... what you say, a blood feud between us." Enzo hung his head, looking charming. "I took a woman from Will Duane once, years ago. She came willingly; she wanted me rather than him. He's never forgiven me. I am safe here, and a few other places, but I must stay out of his reach. He knows many of my people, too; they are not safe."

Andrea could see the fear in Enzo's eyes, the raw kind that couldn't be faked.

"This week, Duane has gone to a Native American retreat in New Mexico to convince the old shaman leading it to let Numenon mine their sacred burial grounds."

"*Really?* That's awful. Isn't that illegal?" Her eyes flashed. "Will Duane wants to mine their burial grounds? How can he do it?"

"He can do it because he has influence in Washington and can convince the Indians to let him do it. The shaman is a weak old man." He scrubbed his face with his hands and spoke slowly.

"I feel horror at what Will Duane proposes to do. And yet, I cannot stop it. I cannot go there and warn the poor, simple shaman about what he is facing. I cannot send my people to stop him—the Indians think Will Duane is a friend!"

Enzo's mouth contorted in despair. Andrea quickly filled his wine glass, then her own.

"Can I help?" she said.

"Oh, if you would," he gulped the claret-colored liquid. "I have thought of something that only you could do. You're a Numenon hire; they've checked you carefully. You could go to the retreat and keep an eye on him."

"*Spy* on Will Duane?"

"Think of if more like being a member of the resistance. I will have a team of my best people waiting outside the Mogollon Bowl—that is the place where the retreat is held. We'll create an identity for you. You can say you are tracing the lineage of your great-grandmother, who was a full-blooded Indian taken from her family when she married."

"Would anyone believe that?"

He smiled sadly. "It happened all the time. Native Americans were taken from their families and lost all touch with their Indian heritage. That story will convince anyone.

"You must know that the retreat will be very large. About four thousand people are expected—"

"Four *thousand?*"

"Yes. The shaman has declared this is the last retreat, so all of his followers are coming, and many curious newcomers, too. Duane's a cheeky bastard, I must say. His party has ten people. The Indians number almost four thousand. I hope they don't find out about his mining plan." Enzo chuckled.

"How can I find *ten* people in a crowd that large?"

"Very easily, my dear. They're traveling in a convoy of five motor homes, including Duane's magnificent moving palace, the *Ashley III.* My sources have told me that they will be the only vehicles allowed to park inside the Bowl. You'll be able to spot them anywhere. The Bowl is almost flat. Look for the motor homes, and you're almost there."

"Will Duane is the most secretive person on earth. He's probably got guards all over. Why would he trust me?"

"Duane brought three MBAs, his secretary, some drivers, and a cook—become friends with them. Get them to trust you. You're a new hire at Numenon, you saw the camp and thought you'd stop by and say hello. How are you, what a surprise to see you here. You can start a conversation, yes?"

"Yeah. As long as it's not too long."

"Get to know the MBAs, or the drivers. Even the drivers are well-educated. Don't try to talk to Duane until you're friends with his staff and everyone knows you in his camp. Then approach him—very carefully. Before you get that far, observe Duane through the field glasses we'll see that you have and see what he's up to. Then, once a day, or more often if there's news, go to the parking lot outside the Bowl, and report to my team."

Andrea took a healthy sip of wine. This was a real adventure, dangerous but righteous. "I still don't see why he would trust me."

"He won't trust you. Duane doesn't trust anyone but those closest to him. *They're* the people he brought. *They're* your ticket in."

"Why do *you* trust me? You don't know me, except for what's in that folder."

Enzo reached out and took her hand. She felt like her insides lurched toward him. Pleasure blossomed inside her, mostly in places she didn't like to admit she had. She gasped.

"I'm like my brother Diego, Andrea. I can always tell about people. From the moment I saw you, I knew you'd be perfect for this task and that I can trust you." He caressed her hand. Her breasts and crotch felt like they were blooming. She squirmed, not knowing what to do. Being seduced was not her area of expertise.

"Uh," she stuttered, "what about the shaman? Will he know I'm not for real?"

"He is the most adorable little man. Not even this tall." Enzo held out his hand to indicate the man's size. "Sweet and kind hearted. Beloved by his people. And a complete charlatan." He laughed. "He doesn't have any 'powers' at all, but pretends to. His people love him like a guru—you know what that is, don't you?"

She nodded. Living in the San Francisco Bay Area all her life, she'd seen a procession of gurus of all types, mostly weird.

"So he won't mind me being there?"

"He won't know. With all those people coming to the retreat, he'll be so busy 'healing,' he won't notice you."

"And Will Duane is going to talk that poor little guy into mining their holy lands?"

"Yes. Will you help me?"

"Are you making me a job offer?"

"Now I am, my darling, Here is my offer: Whatever he will pay you, I will double. Whatever benefits he gives, I will double. Vacation time, name what you want." Enzo opened the laptop and typed some numbers into it. He turned the screen around so that she could see it.

Her savings account was displayed on the computer monitor. She looked at it, speechless. How did he get into her account? The balance was $106,784. Enzo had given her $100,000. He had called her "my darling."

"That is just a token of affection, my dear," he said. "If you achieve results this week, you will see how I reward loyalty."

What he was asking her to do would be the biggest stretch of her life. Infiltrating a company she'd practically worshipped. Spying on a man she admired more than anyone. Being around all those Indians. She'd never seen an Indian up close.

A salary twice what Numenon was offering. The chance to come back to the castle. He deposited $100,000 in her savings account before she did anything. What else would come in the future? She wavered.

"I must tell you something else, to make sure you know everything. Like Will Duane, I am very careful with whom I trust, my dear. I have been hurt by women in the past." She thought he was tearing up. *Oh, my God. Someone as powerful as Enzo crying?*

"I was engaged to a beautiful woman named Sandy Sydney."

Andrea's lips curved up involuntarily at the silly name. Enzo didn't smile.

"She was as lovely as any woman I've ever seen, and seemed as innocent as an angel. She agreed to seek the information I have asked you to obtain, and traveled to the Numenon headquarters in Palo Alto to get it. But she never returned. She betrayed my trust, acting as a whore to Duane's most important executives." Andrea's eyes widened. "A harsh word, but that is what she was. I found out only days ago." He trembled slightly. Andrea had had no idea that a man could be so sensitive.

"So, I am careful. And you should be careful, too, little Andrea. Sandy Sydney ran away from the Numenon camp and hides in the desert, seeking revenge. Watch for her, my dear. She is evil. She will betray whomever she crosses. Run from her as though she was death."

Andrea put her hands on the table and narrowed her eyes at Enzo. "Wait a minute. You want me to perform industrial espionage on the most powerful man in the world—someone I've admired forever—out in the desert, surrounded by thousands of Indians, with a crazy prostitute running around who could kill me?"

"That's speaking in the most extreme words, my dear."

"Don't call me 'my dear.' You don't know me, and I don't know you. Your plan sounds crazy." She prepared to stand. "I'll take that jet."

"Let me see, Andrea, if I can make things better." He started typing on the computer again. "You are the only one who can do this. I am dependent upon you to help me." He turned the computer around showing her bank balance. Her balance was $156,784.

"You want me to put my life at risk for an additional $50,000?"

"You thought $100,000 was generous before."

"That was before I knew about Sandy Sydney. And that you have a blood feud with Will Duane. I can't do it."

They settled at $300,000 and three times what Numenon was going to pay her. She also got a new BMW.

Enzo reached out and took Andrea's hands in his. Electricity jolted up to her elbows. There, it turned into fire that rocketed throughout her body. Her eyes widened. She felt Enzo. Enzo in her pelvis, Enzo in her breasts. Enzo everywhere. She clung to his hands, wilting over the table.

"Do not worry, my darling. You will do beautifully. You are so exquisite that all barriers will fall before you." He bent over so he could look into her eyes. She wanted to throw herself on him.

"Yes, Enzo! I'll help you. I won't let you down—you can trust me."

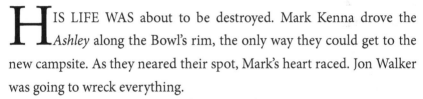

9

H IS LIFE WAS about to be destroyed. Mark Kenna drove the *Ashley* along the Bowl's rim, the only way they could get to the new campsite. As they neared their spot, Mark's heart raced. Jon Walker was going to wreck everything.

Mark and Brooke had a plan. Brooke was his lady. They weren't married, but so what? They loved each other; they'd be together forever. Their three kids were what complicated things. They needed braces and tutors and private lessons. Tuition.

They needed more money than he could make as a driver. He *could* be more than a driver if anyone could see him—the real him. He'd never been close enough to Will Duane to show the billionaire he was more than a smile that could drive. This week was his chance to get out of the drivers' pool and into the ranks of the executives. Well, if not that high, then as least he might be able to get a better job. He had to show Mr. Duane that he had more going for him than the average driver. A lot more. He had a master's degree in transpersonal psychology and had been top in his class.

He'd proven his worth on the drive in, explaining spiritual things that the MBAs were clueless about.

They heaved off the Rim at their designated camping space, a broad flat area slightly beyond Grandfather's lean-to. The Bowl dropped off at least thirty feet on its far side, with crooked fingers of rock sticking out into the plain below. Those were the Badlands. "Don't go into the Badlands. People die there," Dr. Brand had said. Mark shivered.

Turning around and looking back into the Bowl, Mark could see the Pit right behind them. That was where Grandfather spoke and they had ceremonies. All the campers and racket seemed far away. This was a great spot.

Before Mark could collect himself, someone banged on the glass top of the door. He couldn't see through the tinted window, so he opened the door. Mark's nemesis was right there, looking like an elegant woodpecker. Jon Walker was one of the best-looking men Mark had seen, and as gay and as "out" as a person could be. He'd taken to doing crazy things since his lover 'Rique died. Like dying his hair bright red.

"Let me in, Mark!" Jon demanded. "We don't have much time!" He carried a megaphone and a bunch of clipboards jammed with papers. Mark opened the door and Jon charged in, handing him one.

"These are your instructions. When you've parked, come out and help the others." He turned to Will and the professionals. "While we're setting up, I've prepared special refreshments for you. I'll bring them to you when they're ready."

Jon stepped down next to the other motor home and raised his megaphone. "People! I need your attention! I have a camp layout for each of you. If we work together, we should finish within an hour."

Will chuckled at Jon's tyrannical behavior, and then turned to the others. "That's Jon for you: over-the-top. I have a feeling we'd better do what he says." He led his team down the stairs.

Mark could hear Jon talking to Will through the open door. "Mr. Duane, the executive lounge area will be," he pointed to the Rim where the best view was, "over there. You and the executives can have refreshments while we work to set up the camp."

"You and you," Jon said, as pointed to two of the other drivers, Hector and Delroy. "Look in the third motor home. You will find umbrellas, a picnic table, and lounge chairs. Also rolls of indoor-outdoor carpeting. Set them up there." He pointed to the spot on the Rim he'd selected for the executives. "Make sure that the table doesn't wobble. The two coolers by the table contain snacks and drinks for Mr. Duane and his staff." Jon clapped his hands. "Let's go, people!"

He spoke to Will. "Mr. Duane, I hope you can serve yourselves. That way, we can finish faster."

"Of course, Jon. I'm going to go for a jog," Will said. "I can't sit still any more." He ducked back into the *Ashley*, and emerged moments later in jogging clothes.

Mark looked at the papers the chef had given him. Jon had a written plan that not only specified the camp's circular shape, but the exact location of each motor home, every stick of furniture and every other insane thing he'd brought.

"Okay, Mark," Jon bellowed on the bullhorn. "The *Ashley* goes there."

Mark had to inch the vehicle backward and forward a couple of times to get it just right, with Jon directing him from the ground. When the *Ashley* was finally parked, it had a beautiful view of the desert behind the Bowl.

He got out as Jon was positioning the other vehicles. From there, it was jump, jump, jump to Jon's megaphoned orders. The motor homes had been packed last in, first out, so that whatever they grabbed was the next thing to be installed. Jon had performed a miracle of organization, Mark had to give him that.

The kitchen motor home and its trailer overlooked the Pit and larger camp. The trailer, which Mark had thought totally unnecessary, disgorged its treasure. Jon raised his arms in triumph as they rolled a ten foot long black metal barbecue down the trailer's ramp.

As the camp shaped up, Mark felt more and more outclassed. They ran around like maniacs, Jon either screaming or using that damned bullhorn. "No! Not like that. Turn it. Like this!" Half the time Jon would run over and adjust something himself. "See? Like that."

As promised, they were done in an hour. Sweaty and open-mouthed, Mark stood by the chef next to a stainless steel serving table they'd loaded with snacks. He looked at the camp, jaw loose. The place would've looked like a men's locker room if he had set it up.

Jon looked at Mark and said, "I did this so that Will would be comfortable. Will and the rest of us."

Mark felt his emotions rising. His throat seemed like it wanted to shut down. This place … he felt so crazy.

Jon patted his shoulder solicitously. "I know," he said. "I've been feeling that way, too. Have some of my iced chai." He turned to the serving table and handed him a glass of a pale brown liquid.

Mark sniffed it. Spices and honey. He took a sip, then a gulp. It was liquid heaven. He looked at Jon, grateful and a little stunned.

10

WILL FELT TOO tired to run, but knew he'd earn his hour nap that way. He loped out of the campsite and past Grandfather's hut, then along the Bowl's rim toward the entrance of the camp. The Rim was broad and wide, an easy place to run. To his left, the Bowl ended abruptly with a steep drop off to the desert floor. He didn't have to think about what Tyler Brand had said; that cliff was dangerous.

Before he left them, Dr. Brand had shared one piece of good news. "Grandfather slipped the martial arts and horse demonstration back to five so that you can have time to rest after getting set up. Be on time. Wes is a stickler about promptness."

Will was aware of everything Dr. Brand had said as he jogged along. He slowed when he passed a tall tepee made of pale hides; it was painted and beaded and hung with pelts and objects he didn't recognize. "The Wedding Tepee," Tyler had called it. Will found it hard to believe that that anyone would want to get married in this place. He glanced over his right shoulder into the Bowl.

All four thousand or so Meeting attendees had arrived. The crawling crater revolted Will. He couldn't deal with the visual assault of all the people, or the noise. The Bowl magnified everything—sounds, feelings, his inner dialogue. He could hear squeals of delight as people greeted friends. A hum of conversation, sounds of tent poles striking each other, things being dropped. Cars moving in and moving out. A sea of life surged to his right. Will ran from it.

But he couldn't stop looking into the Bowl. A *zap!* went through his mind; he stared into the basin, then felt like he was looking down on its floor like a map. He saw it instantly: the human structure in the Bowl.

Will could walk into a meeting anywhere on the planet and see the pattern. He knew immediately who had the power, who voted with whom, where the coalitions lay, and most importantly, who was a friend and who was an enemy, even among strangers.

His eyes shot open—these people were arranged by *tribe!*

He couldn't conceive of being in a group of people who were related by blood or held together by bonds of kinship. Will couldn't imagine being with his family voluntarily. He had two sisters and hadn't seen them for years.

His family's gothic stone mansion on Lake Michigan filled his mind. Feelings of hate and fear seeped from it. Marina Selene had loosened up the memories so that they came out anywhere and everywhere. Marina used to hold him until they stopped, but there had been no protection since she kicked him out.

Will shuddered as he stood on the Rim, and recalled what had happened for the thousandth time. His father's nicotine-stained fingers pointed at him and his words struck him like a cane. "You're *nothing.* You'll never be anything."

He had vowed that he would never be like his father. No screaming fits, vindictiveness, vendettas, or rage. No fancy women and nights of smoke and booze. He would never be like that. He swore he would succed and be *happy.* He'd be *faithful.*

Will ran along the Rim. His father had won. Will Duane was just a fancier, tougher, bolder, smarter, more up-scale version of his dad.

Stumbling, Will flailed blindly. A golf cart pulled up next to him. A huge dark man dressed in a black shirt and jeans climbed out. Will had seen him with Grandfather. He'd been in the cart when the old man met him in the desert. He had tattoos all over.

The giant said, "I'll give you a ride." He didn't ask, "Are you okay?" Will wasn't, anyone could see that. They rode back to the Numenon camp silently. When Will asked to be let off, the man stopped the cart.

In a deep voice he said, "The Meeting is hard, but if you face it, you will win."

Will felt himself deflate. This stranger had captured exactly what he felt.

11

WHILE THE DRIVERS and Jon set up the camp, the MBAs looked around. Melissa could see that their new location was the best in the house. She turned her back on the Bowl, looking past the cliff and maze of canyons and out into the desert. She discovered something amazing on the desert floor.

"Oh, wow, look at that!" she exclaimed, pointing to the foot of the rock formations. The other MBAs ran to her. "It's a ropes course! A big one."

"Wow!" Gil and Doug exclaimed at the same time.

They were saved. They were experts at these types of courses, designed to physically and psychologically challenge those training on them. On ropes courses, Melissa and Numenon's top executives had learned a fundamental truth: work like a team or fall off a cliff.

Lengths of telephone poles about three feet apart stuck out of the ground. They protruded at heights varying from one to four feet.

"Look," said Gil, indicating the poles. "Didn't we do that one in Death Valley?"

Doug looked. "I think it was in Baja."

"No. It was Colorado," Melissa said. "We all stood on poles and had to arrange ourselves in alphabetical order by our mother's maiden names."

"Yeah. Without speaking." Doug added.

"Was that the one where you could swear but not talk?" asked Gil.

"No, that one was building bridges over the canyon," Doug said.

"The one where Billy broke his arm?" Melissa crinkled her forehead. "I can't remember."

"That was Palm Springs. In the atrium of the St. Regis Hotel," Doug said.

"Well, someone broke something on the cliff in Colorado." Melissa remained puzzled.

"May Sun Lin broke her collar bone." Gil looked at the poles suspiciously.

"Oh, yeah. I remember!" Melissa smiled. "I can hardly wait to tell Will. We'll beat the Indians cold."

Betty sat at the table in the "executive lounge area" behind the *Ashley*, sipping iced chai tea. She had called home again, chancing damage to her cell phone. The phone worked but she didn't succeed. John had left no message on her cell and didn't answer at home or at his office.

She blew her nose and searched in her purse for her lipstick as the MBAs looked around the desert. Betty found her lipstick wrapped in a sheet of paper.

She unwrapped the paper and read it, drawing her eyebrows together. *What on earth is this?* Will needed to see it right away.

Moments later, he appeared on the Rim, stepping out the way he always did, the picture of confidence. She jumped to her feet and tucked the paper into her pocket. "Will …"

Before she could get his attention, Will disappeared between the motor homes into the camp's central area. He looked around, eyes wide. Betty followed him into the courtyard.

Betty's eyes darted from one spot to another. Light purple carpet covered the entire area between the motor homes. Heavy wooden furniture with pale canvas upholstery was arranged in seating groups. Big comfy chairs, tables with canvas umbrellas, chaise lounges, everything. It looked like a resort.

She could see a food prep area peeking from behind the kitchen motor home, which was the one closest to the Bowl. Inside the patio, Jon arranged a buffet-style serving area and busing station in front of the kitchen RV. The professional people and the staff had separate eating areas.

Stylish kerosene lamps on posts dotted the camp. Strings of tiny white electric lights were hung in a grid over the courtyard, strung on the ribs of the umbrellas, wrapped around the palms, and draped between the motor homes. At the corner of each vehicle, long banners whipped in the wind; they were each white and burgundy with gold braid, all with the Numenon logo appliquéd in gold.

"It's perfect, Jon," said Will. "You'd never know we'd left home."

"That was the idea."

As everyone departed, Betty felt her sadness threaten to overwhelm her. "Will, can we talk for a moment?"

"Sure, Betty. What's the matter?" He piloted her to the sitting area behind the *Ashley*.

Tears formed despite her resolve to be strong. "I can't get through to John. I guess it's over … And look at this."

She showed her boss the note she'd found in her purse. Sandy Sydney's loopy handwriting filled the page. Betty had been surprised the first time she saw it. Sandy's handwriting was the affected scrawl of the most popular girl in high school.

The letter read:

"*Dear Betty, I don't want to die without telling you this. I'm sorry. I never wanted to hurt anyone.*" The handwriting faltered.

"I love you, Betty. You were the only person who believed in me."

There was a space, then printing that looked like it had been done by someone in agony.

"Be careful. I'm changing. They're coming."

Will read it and shook his head.

"It sounds like Sandy was dying, but she was very alive when she attacked us and escaped." He read the last part again. *"Be careful. I'm changing. They're coming."*

"I don't know what that means. We should tell someone. I'll give this to Grandfather. Give me that bad map Paul Running Bird faxed you, and I'll show him that, too," Will said.

Having delivered Sandy's message, Betty realized how exhausted she was. She looked at her watch; it was four fifteen in the afternoon— assuming the watch worked. They had forty-five minutes to rest before the martial arts and horse demonstration.

She climbed into her motor home. The vehicle was boiling inside. She flipped on the air conditioner.

12

A S EVERYONE ELSE got settled, Bud Creeman was still out in the desert, walking an insane mare back to the camp. Ol' Squirrel Brains didn't have enough brainpower to find a carrot in a carrot bin, but she had given her all in the race to save the Numenon crew. She'd hurt her legs and couldn't be ridden.

Even though Bud knew he was doing the right thing walking the mare in, he wished he could be doing anything else. Once the Numenon caravan pulled out of sight, he was a little speck of horse and man, walking through the huge desert.

He felt as though he was being watched by something. It wasn't Sandy Sydney; something *huge* lurked out there, stalking *him*. He felt like something very, very bad followed his every move. He heard a disgusting noise, too, like rocks rubbing together. He wished he could hurry up, but he couldn't with the injured horse.

Like an angel from heaven, Lisa Cheewa rode up with a fresh horse for him. Unfortunately, the news she had wasn't as good. Lisa was almost in tears when she said, "Paul Running Bird almost rode that dun-colored stallion to death. You've got to save that horse, Bud."

He took off right away, forgetting to tell Lisa about the stalker and Sandy Sydney, the runaway secretary from hell. Bud was so mad at Paul Running Bird, he would have forgotten his mother's birthday.

When he got to the stable area, a knot of men stood around something on the ground. Bud swung off of his horse and went straight to the group. They parted. Bud recoiled at the sight before him. The stallion was on the ground, struggling to get up, but couldn't.

His long winter coat was separated into stiff ringlets formed by dried sweat. A dried lather like old shaving cream covered his neck and chest, reaching almost up to his mane, running across his belly and flanks, and up between his hind legs.

"Who did this?" Bud shouted. But he already knew. Out in the desert when he had found the Numenon caravan and saved Mr. Duane and one of his people, Paul Running Bird had run away like a fiend was on his tail. Everyone knew that he was the one who gave the Numenon people the map that got them lost. Paul ran the stud all the way in, accounting for his present condition.

Bud put his hands on the horse, a healing trance taking him in an instant. Something covered him like a mantle. He couldn't see it, but he could feel it moving through him. He laid his hands on the horse's legs and just let whatever happened happen. He heard a voice in his mind saying, *Put your hand here. There. Rub here.* He could feel the horse's legs as if he was inside of them. Tattered flexor tendons, micro-tears in the suspensory ligaments. Paul had destroyed this horse, and Bud was healing him.

When he was done, he put one hand on each side of the stallion's face. He stayed there for a while, eyes closed, feeling his connection to the animal. He stepped back and let the horse get up. He said, "Does anyone have a carrot?" Someone got him a couple.

"Well, I think this horse will be all right. If one of you would like to take him out to the springs and give him a bath, I think he'd appreciate it." Everyone jumped for the chance.

"When you're done, just turn him loose out in the desert. I told him that would never happen to him again, but if he wanted to leave, I understood."

Bud looked up and saw Grandfather sitting in a golf cart watching him. The shaman drove over to them and climbed out of the cart. When he patted Bud's arm, his shoulders started to heave, as his feelings let loose. Next thing he knew, he was wiping his eyes with his handkerchief.

"See," Grandfather said to the group watching. "Bud's heart is right here." He touched Bud's chest. "So close. A man with that much feeling in his heart can't do evil. It will hurt him. Only a man who doesn't feel his own heart can hurt others."

The shaman hugged Bud. "Very good work, my son. You are a warrior of warriors. Your time has come." Then Grandfather was silent, appraising his student. "Is there something you need to do now?"

Bud stiffened. The energy came over him again, but it felt different this time. Hotter. His breathing deepened, his hands clenched. Bud nodded. His mouth took on a grim set. "Where is he?"

Grandfather replied, "You tell me."

Bud went inside himself and turned eastward. "He's at the springs," Bud said softly.

"Yes. Go, my son. Do what you need to do." Bud nodded and started to jog toward the hot springs. "Wait," Grandfather called. "I'll drop you off."

13

GRANDFATHER DROPPED BUD off at the canyon that formed the entrance to the hot springs. The canyon hid one of the area's mysteries. It looked just like any blind canyon in the Badlands: fifty feet from side to side, with red rock walls thirty feet high. You couldn't see a hundred yards into it—the ravine twisted and blocked your view. Just past the bend, the gully elevated slightly and then spilled out into a fantasy of rock and water. Acres of waterfalls, ponds, and slides hid just out of sight.

Hot and cold baths, hidden grottos with private ponds. Everywhere, the sound of water, running, trickling, falling, and dripping. Just being at the springs was healing. The camp got all of its water from this wonderland; the crew delivered fresh water to the camp every day in the decrepit, but functional, water truck.

The springs flowed together just after the bend and made a good-sized creek that emptied into a pond that drained underground. Its water was always fresh, even though they washed the horses in it all the time. The private bathing ponds were farther into the springs, hidden in clefts off the main canyon.

Bud could feel Paul Running Bird's presence and walked up one of the side canyons to a hot spring in a sandstone grotto.

Sure enough, Paul was there. He stood by the side of the steaming pool, fully dressed and buttoning his shirt. A pile of dirty clothes lay at his feet.

"Ah, Bud!" Paul saw him and smiled. "Time to wash off the trail dust? I came here the minute I got back. That was a long ride. I'm sure you got the Numenon crew back safely."

Bud stood quietly, watching him. The Power settled on him again; he felt his breath deepening. He clenched his hands, but held back; he'd give Paul a chance to apologize and explain. Paul didn't.

"Well, it's all yours. Time to get back to work." Paul started to walk away.

"Aren't you going to say anything?" Bud's voice was low and steady.

Paul looked alarmed. "Oh, sorry to run off on you like that, I remembered something back here that I had to do right away. You were handling everything fine."

"What did you have to do that was so important?"

Paul's eyes widened.

Bud could hear Paul's thoughts. *This fat slob is questioning me?*

"Well,... I had to decide the final location of the campsite for the Numenon party. That had to be done before they got here. I had to ... uh ... make preparations for the day's schedule. That sort of thing."

"Two sites have been set aside for them—everyone in camp knows that. I want to know what was so important that you almost killed that horse."

Paul jerked and pulled away, but his words were as smooth as ever. "That horse was fine when I left. He was a little hot, but I had someone walk him. If something happened to him, I didn't do it."

The energy became a dull throbbing deep inside Bud. Blackness spread in a spiral from his feet. He heard himself say, "You *ran* him all the way in, Paul. You scared him almost to death."

Paul ducked his head a little and looked away. "Well, yeah. I did run him, heading back to the stable. What do you expect? He wanted to go and I let him." He looked at Bud cautiously. "Okay, Bud, I might have gotten carried away. It was fun."

A rumble came out of Bud's chest. "The horse collapsed. Blood was running out of his nose; his legs were ruined, his wind, his mind—all ruined. Is that how you *have fun?*"

Paul scooted around Bud. "Look, Bud," he said. "It's a lousy wild horse. The Bureau of Land Management sells them for a hundred bucks. If I hurt him, I'll pay you that back at the camp—" He didn't complete his sentence. Something whirled him around to face Bud.

A terrible voice came from Bud. "*Grandfather's People do not hurt horses. Do you understand?*"

Paul looked at Bud with horror on his face.

Bud's mouth wasn't moving, but that *voice* came from him. "*Grandfather brought me here. He left me with you. He told me to do what I had to do. This is it.*"

Paul jerked three feet off the ground and remained there, suspended. His body convulsed as though a giant was shaking it, his hands clawing at the air in front of him. When blood spurted from both nostrils, he fell in a heap. Paul rubbed his wrists and ankles, sobbing. "Oh—What did you do?"

The horrible voice replied, "*I let you feel what that horse felt. Feel it, Paul. Maybe you'll learn something.*"

14

ANDREA RAN HER hand over the jet's seat. The leather was smooth, soft, and reeked of money. The Donatore Indústrial logo—two bold, contemporary Ds back to back—was embroidered on the backs of the seats. The cabin's walls were printed with a subtle form of the design. The logo was etched on her wine glass and woven into the carpet.

"Would you like another glass of wine, Ms. Beckman?" the crisply uniformed steward asked.

"No. Well, okay." She'd never flown in a private jet before. It was heady and exhilarating and terrifying. She was the only passenger until Atlanta, where they'd land. She'd go through U.S. Customs and board again, to be joined by two Donatore executives going to Los Angeles. They'd drop her off in Las Cruces, New Mexico. She'd never heard of it.

"Oh, thank you," she said as the attendant brought her a fresh glass of merlot.

"Shall I leave the bottle?"

"No, thank you." She picked up the folio lying on the seat next to her. It was her homework, the magic carpet to an existence better than her dreams.

Despite the wine, her mouth felt dry. She was almost panting. In fear, she realized. *It will be okay. Will Duane isn't the person I thought he was. This isn't wrong. You're protecting the Indians.* The memory of $300,000 sparkling on the computer's screen blotted out her misgivings. Triple salary, quadruple when you added in her Numenon salary. Ditto on the benefits. Vacations. He said he rewarded loyalty. If she got some good results, how much more would he pay her?

Enzo's people got her ready to go so fast that she felt dizzy. Less than an hour passed from the time she and Enzo reached an agreement until she was sitting in the jet. Someone had taken her bags from her room at the castle and put her things in brand new Louis Vuitton luggage—a matching set.

She didn't like someone going through her things. She hoped they'd included her medication. That really mattered. She'd start being afraid of dust bunnies in the corners in a day or two. Fortunately, Penelope, the beautiful woman who'd gotten her dressed, was the one who moved her clothes. She had assured Andrea that she included everything.

What Enzo wanted wasn't so bad, once he spelled it all out. He wanted lots of financial and strategic information, stuff you would expect. But he also wanted something so secret he whispered it in her ear and didn't write it down.

"If you discover his secret, don't tell anyone, my dear," he'd said. "Only me."

Why he'd want to know that so much didn't make sense, but he was the one paying her. When she thought about him, the way she felt when he touched her came flooding back. She didn't know how she could bear sitting in the plane for hours and hours, feeling her body's tingling and throbbing.

The steward approached again. "May I get you anything?"

"I'll take the rest of that bottle of wine."

Everything Enzo wanted her to do was illegal. What had she gotten herself into?

A trill of terror started to rise inside her, but the image of Enzo's face covered it immediately. All she could see was his kind face. His wise eyes. His smile. The way his touch felt. Her body responded as though he was touching her there, in the plane. Over and over he stroked her. She felt her hips rising—No!

Andrea grabbed the leather folio from the seat next to her and got to work. A thick report with the title *Grandfather & Company* sat on top of a collection of documents and photos. She had to memorize all of this and leave it with her contacts in New Mexico.

The plane would land in Las Cruces. A group of Enzo's associates— the "outside team"—would pick her up there. They would drive to the retreat site and camp far enough away from the Mogollon Bowl so that the Indians wouldn't notice them. They would remain there to receive her reports and help her if she needed it.

Enzo had been apologetic. "I can't let them go inside the Bowl, my dear. Will Duane knows my people. He'd spot them immediately. But you won't be alone—any trouble and they'll be there for you."

That reassured her. All she had to do was learn the stuff in the folio and follow Enzo's directions. He'd also assured her that he didn't care if she wasn't able to get everything he wanted; she should feel no pressure. No pressure! She knew she'd blow her chance if she failed. All the future years of benefits and bonuses. The huge salary.

Back to work. *Grandfather & Company* was a report put together by Will Duane's secretary, Betty Fogarty. It covered the retreat and pretty much everything associated with it, including bios of the major Native players.

A dossier for someone named Paul Running Bird was the longest, several single-spaced pages with an 8"x10" color, glossy photo. A note clipped to his file said that he'd given the Numenon party a bad map that had gotten them lost. He sounded like bad news, but Enzo had told her to seek him out and befriend him. Why?

Leafing through *Grandfather & Company*, Andrea's eyes widened. This was a "for participants' eyes only document—that meant Will Duane and his top executives—dated *the day before*. The note about the map was only *hours* old. Enzo said he had secret friends inside Numenon. This showed her how secret and how far inside.

Get to work. Additional material focused on the Numenon team and Will Duane. His bio outlined what she already knew: he was an innovator, brilliant financier, and visionary. She'd been infatuated with him for most of her adult life.

Instantly, Enzo's image filled the screen of her mind. Smiling, holding her hand. Giving her those incredible amounts of money. Repeating what he had said about Will Duane. The truth.

15

WESLEY SILVERHORSE LAY on Grandfather's bed in the shaman's lean-to. Half asleep, he moved his arms and flexed his legs. No pain anywhere. Grandfather had put him back together as good as new. Wes floated in a cloud of good feelings and robust health.

A horse he'd taken in to train had almost killed him a few days ago. Usually, he got busted up by bulls. Wes rodeoed for the money, little as it was. The Silverhorse family had to keep their ranch. They were the only Indian ranch owners near Smallbone, Wyoming.

Days before, a rogue mare he'd taken in to train had thrown herself down and rolled on him when she couldn't buck him off. She'd done the same with other riders, he later found out; but no one had told Wes when it would have done him any good.

Before dawn, Grandfather had healed him of injuries inflicted by the mare and from the rest of his life: the residue of his father's death and years of caring for siblings who paid him back by running from the ranch the moment they could. Wesley had finally broken down and given the shaman control of his life.

Grandfather's voice was sharp. Wes would stay with him after the Meeting and not go back to the ranch. He would never again rodeo or bull clown. "You may only ride horses I approve."

That meant his family would lose their ranch. Wesley had wept and Grandfather had held him gently.

"Now, my son, you will live your own life, instead of trying to finish your father's." And then the shaman had told him something wonderful. "I had a vision about you this morning, Wesley. You will be married at this Meeting."

Wesley's recovery took a giant leap forward. "Do you know who she is?"

"No, my son. The Great One never tells me."

Because of his devotion and the Power it conferred, Wesley was a warrior with miraculous abilities. Everyone knew that Grandfather was likely to name Wesley his successor, over Leroy Watches, his grandson.

He'd fallen asleep in Grandfather's bed early that morning, healed and ecstatic. He was getting married this Meeting! Wesley drifted into a deep sleep, dreaming of his bride. For hours, he had tossed in golden flames, enjoying the bliss of the world of the Ancestors.

When the Numenon people arrived and set up their camp, their noise knocked him out of that bliss. He dropped into ordinary dreaming, still partly immersed in the golden flames. He was looking for his bride. She was just out of his sight, hidden in streaming amber fog.

He reached for her through the mist. It evaporated so that he could see her face.

A monster's bulging eyes glared back at him. Flames shot from her mouth. Her teeth and claws ripped his flesh.

Wes's eyes sprang open. Someone was in the lean-to. He lay still.

16

MELISSA WAS TOO agitated to nap. Something seemed to be uncoiling inside of her. The bravado she'd shown confronting Dr. Brand had crumbled.

She and Betty were in the motor home reserved for them and Sandy Sydney. Sandy's departure made dividing up the sleeping space easier. Melissa grabbed the bedroom; she wanted a locked door between her and everyone else.

Betty seemed relieved to give Melissa the room. "I'll be fine here," she said, pulling down the cabin's wall bed.

She thinks I'm gay. Doug had spread rumors that she was a lesbian all over the corporation after their … *incident*. It wasn't true, but people believed Doug's lies.

Melissa's mind ran wild. She lived with a feeling of pending disaster every day, but it was sharper than usual. And things bugged her. She couldn't figure out why she'd been sleeping on Will's bed when they'd arrived. There had to be a reason.

It came back to her all at once. She felt like she was back in the *Ashley's* cabin. Something had attacked them; the men were screaming and holding themselves between the legs. The motor home veered since the driver had also been hurt. She wasn't injured, but she felt fingers or something *inside* of her. She shrieked, out of control and terrified, clawing her way across the cabin floor. And then Bud had picked her up. She didn't remember anything else.

Her cheeks flushed. She could see herself, jammed up against the door, screaming. Melissa shuddered with embarrassment.

Why hadn't she been able to remember what happened until now?

Grandfather told Will that the Mogollon Bowl caused memory lapses. People remembered things when the time was right. The time must have been right. Would she remember more awful things? Was that why she felt so spooked?

Unable to stand being in the small bedroom any longer, Melissa threw on jogging shorts and her new running shoes, and slipped past the slumbering Betty and out the door.

She took off, darting toward the Rim. Like everyone else who wanted to rise at

Numenon, Melissa was an exercise nut. Will was as compulsive about exercise as he was everything else, and anyone who wanted to make it with him followed his example.

Melissa Weir was running now for an additional reason: She'd been having panic attacks since the incident with Doug. Six months ago, she'd been in a conference room, composing herself after a rough presentation. Doug went to the reception in the foyer and got drunk. He came back into the room and grabbed her.

She reacted without thinking, throwing her arms up and shoving him. He flew across the room, his body moving like someone was kicking him. He ended up in the hospital with all sorts of broken bones; she was taken to jail for assault. Except it turned out that Doug was at fault because he grabbed her breasts first. That made it sexual assault. The cops released her. Doug stayed in the hospital.

He would have been charged for the assault and fired, except that she and Doug were Will's favorites. Plus, no one could figure out what really happened, including Doug and her. Will fixed it with the law, but he'd been distant since. Melissa wondered why he'd invited the two of them on the trip.

The last six months had been rough. In addition to keeping up with her work load at Numenon, she had to contend with gibes from everyone. Doug slandered her the moment he could. "She's a bull dyke. She beat the crap out of me when I suggested a quicky," he told the whole Headquarters.

She had visited her doctor and gotten medication for the attacks only when running failed to curb her anxiety. Heading out of their encampment, her agitation practically shouted.

Her attention jumped to a primitive lean-to next to the trail in front of her. Examining the lean-to was better than giving in to her craziness. This must be Grandfather's hut.

The shelter looked like something her anthropologist mother would love. It was made from unpeeled wooden poles bound with natural fibers. The panels were lashed to uprights made of small tree trunks. Rawhide cords tied animal hides to the framework, providing wind-protection and waterproofing. She looked inside and saw no one. She stepped in, intrigued.

The interior was even more interesting. Rough wood shelves held various objects: herbs, crystals, a book or two, a few items of clothing; more sat on a low table by the bed. The bed was primitive and modern: a mattress with a messy heap of hides on it. No pillow. The bed wasn't made—Grandfather wasn't a housekeeper. Other objects captured her eye: a medicine bag, a beaded pipe bag, tools, primitive weapons, and carved stone bowls. She picked up some of the things on a small table by the bed, not touching the medicine pipe bag. She knew from her mother that it was considered sacred.

Melissa picked up what appeared to be a Tibetan singing bowl, and examined the writing on the rim with wonder. She placed the bowl in the palm of her left hand. She took its wooden striker, made a wish that her dream lover would appear, and struck the bowl's side. A clear, bright sound filled the lean-to.

Wesley awoke from his nightmare totally alert. He didn't move.

The person in Grandfather's hut had to be one of those people from Numenon; no one else would intrude. He heard someone moving around the room, handling Grandfather's things. Wes was outraged. Only two things kept him under the hide, one being that he was naked. But when he heard the bowl sing, he couldn't restrain himself.

In one quick motion, he reached under the bed and grabbed the hunting knife Grandfather kept there, threw off the hides, and leapt to his feet to face the intruder.

He looked straight into the eyes of a beautiful white woman. She froze, turning whiter than he knew a person could.

In an instant, she was ten feet outside the lean-to. Wes didn't know how she got out there—she was just there. She put the bowl and wooden striker down, and said in a tight voice, "Please forgive me. I didn't mean to intrude."

She dashed away. She was down the Rim of the Bowl in seconds.

He could hear her mind as she ran. At home, he and his mother read each other's thoughts; sometimes they didn't actually talk for days. At the Mogollon Bowl, his powers multiplied. Grandfather and he were like parts of the same person, they were so connected. He felt almost as close to the other spirit warriors and could read their minds. By the end of the Meeting, he would be able to read the mind of anyone there.

But this was more than that. The woman was a stranger, yet he could hear her thoughts and feel her emotions as though she was a warrior he'd known for years.

One part of her mind spoke to the rest. *Breathe. Stay in control. Keep going, you're okay; you're not hurt. You didn't belong there. He thought you were stealing. It's all right. Keep going. Relax.*

Under her grown up thoughts, Wesley could hear a child's voice screaming, *Help me. Please help me!* Then the inner voice changed back to an adult's. *Calm down. You're over-reacting. Calm down.* Switching again, Wes heard the child's voice begging, *Please don't hurt me!* This was followed by screams.

Wes had no idea he could scare anyone so much. He looked down. His erection was gone. He was so embarrassed. He'd been dreaming about his intended. He would have stayed hidden in bed, but for her striking Grandfather's bowl.

Shit! Wesley threw on his clothes for the horse exhibit. She was the first woman who had seen him like that. Would his *bride* start screaming?

17

LISA CHEEWA STOOD in the court formed by the Numenon motor homes. The skin on the inside of her legs vibrated with pleasure. Her breasts ached and hummed and throbbed at the same time. She could still feel Sandy Sydney's fingers inside her. Lisa blushed.

She was waiting for one of the Numenon people to get out of the shower so that she could guide her down the switchbacks to the horse exhibit. She'd already taken most of them down, but this woman had been out running and needed to clean up first. She could hear the water running. How long was she going to take? Lisa waited. Her body's sensations were almost unbearable.

The trip back to the Bowl after she gave the fresh horse to Bud that afternoon was a little different than what she had imagined. She was riding along, leading the lame mare and daydreaming, when a beautiful blond woman stepped out from behind some rocks.

"Hi! I'm Sandy Sydney," she said, beaming. "I'm with Numenon. I like to hike so they dropped me off so that I could walk in."

They laughed, having fun. The attraction between them was incredible. Lisa got off her horse and led the two animals.

Sandy Sydney knew that Lisa was a lesbian right away. It was nice to meet someone like herself. Pretty soon, Sandy was holding Lisa's hand. Like all the warriors, Lisa was bound by Grandfather's rules. They were supposed to be celibate until they met their soul mates and married. Touching Sandy's hand, Lisa was sure that's how a soul mate's touch would feel.

They'd held hands for a while, and then wanted to do more. She hobbled the horses and walked to a rock shelf and sat down. Sandy stood in front of Lisa and smiled. Lisa unbuttoned her blouse and let Sandy touch her breasts and kiss them. Sandy did other things to her; lots of things. Things Lisa had never done with anyone.

Lisa found herself screaming, moaning, and doing whatever Sandy wanted without question. Sandy could stand back, not even touching her, and Lisa could feel her inside. She couldn't refuse Sandy. Or stop her. She felt excited and a bit guilty, as they'd jumped the gun, but she was sure Sandy was her soul mate. Grandfather would approve—everything would be okay.

They would still be there on that rock ledge, except that Lisa had to go help with Wesley's demonstration. "They're waiting for me," she said. Sandy didn't want to let her go, but when Lisa said, "They'll send people for me if I don't get back," Sandy gave in.

As she rode off, her lips swollen and red, Lisa heard Sandy's voice inside her mind, *Would you like to meet tonight?*

Lisa thought, *Yes!*

Where shall we meet?

Lisa thought. *By the line shack down by the horses. After dark.* She felt Sandy's smile fill her soul. And pleasure flooded her pelvis as she heard Sandy's voice say, *We'll play all night, if you like.*

Sandy also issued a warning, *Don't tell them you saw me.*

Melissa stood in the shower, trying to wash away what was erupting inside her. The face of that man in the lean-to kept reappearing in

Melissa's mind. Actually, she couldn't remember it well. All she could remember was the knife and his penis. The rest disappeared.

The images wouldn't stay fixed. The brown face of the man in the lean-to faded into another man's, one ringed with curly red hair. Blue eyes. A rough voice rang in her head. "Is that how you like it, Jew-bitch?"

Melissa began washing herself, scrubbing her body. She scrubbed so hard that the skin between her legs felt raw. She was wiping herself furiously with the towel when she remembered an Indian woman was waiting for her, to take her to the horse exhibition. She hurriedly dressed and went outside.

Melissa smiled at Lisa. "Sorry I took so long. I lost track of time."

As Lisa walked to Wesley's exhibition with this other white woman, she felt conflicted. She was wildly, wildly in love with Sandy Sydney. But when she got back to the Bowl, little nagging doubts came up. Grandfather always told people when he'd had a vision that they'd meet their soul mates. Maybe what happened with Sandy wasn't what she thought.

Lisa decided to meet Sandy that evening, and tell her they couldn't do anything more until Grandfather married them. That would be easy.

Lisa could feel her hands on her skin. Oh, yes, she would see Sandy Sydney again.

18

WHAT AN IDIOT she was for letting that little bitch get away. Sandy Sydney wiped her mouth with her forearm. She'd barely gotten started and hadn't gotten much of any thing for herself. That's how she was: always pleasing others even if she got shafted.

Well, that's how her previous life had been, but not this one. Sandy stretched out her arm, which was covered by its pink-checked blouse. She rolled up the sleeve and made a fist, admiring the size and definition of her muscles. Something had happened out in that canyon, that was for sure.

She'd transformed into her true identity. Powerful. In command. Capable. Much stronger than a human. And still, very beautiful.

Was she human? Seemed like it. What she could see of herself seemed the same: pale complexion, blond hair. She didn't have a mirror to really look at herself, but she touched her face with her fingers. Felt the same.

Sandy looked around the desert, feeling exposed. She shouldn't be out in the open. Enzo would be able to track her with the see-stone. He would *not* be pleased that the first thing she'd done with her new powers was wreck his plan to co-opt Will Duane.

But how was she to know? Enzo didn't tell her what was happening to her. She didn't know every little bit of herself was being transformed. If he'd told her, she would have known when she began to feel that she was dying that she was really turning into something wonderful. Her new body couldn't be destroyed. Well, maybe if a missile hit her.

She'd studied the brief Betty wrote about the retreat as much as anyone. The Mogollon Bowl was a special place that protected its occupants from evil. Enzo would be classified as evil, though how anyone who was such a good lover could be evil was a mystery. But she knew what he'd do if cheated or enraged. He could kill her.

Sandy began jogging toward the cliffs that ran along the southeast edge of the Bowl. Jogging was so easy. She covered ground effortlessly. She began to run, stretching out like an athelete. She *was* an athlete. Pouring on the steam, Sandy laughed. Nothing could catch her. Not a car, not a jet even.

She pulled up when she reached the edge of the cliff, not even winded. She felt *wonderful!* Glancing down at the back of her hand, Sandy gasped. Something dark was under her skin. What was it? She pulled up both sleeves. Both arms had a blackish tinge like something under her skin was emerging. What was happening to her? Enzo didn't tell her about *this*, either.

Making her way along the base of the cliff, Sandy dodged the Indians at the stable area. They didn't see her, but the horses sure noticed. She loved their panicked cries and terror. She'd have to remember that.

Running came naturally. She traveled to the far side of the cliffs before she found what she was looking for: a group of hidden blind canyons. The Indians would never go there and Enzo couldn't find her with the see-stone. When she stopped running, she looked ar her hands again. Pebbly black skin began to protrude through her flesh. She pulled off her clothes.

The black skin kept coming, until her arms were clothed with shining black scales. She looked at her body. All of her was covered with sparkling plates. She stared at her limbs and gasped. What was she? She felt her face. It had small bumps over it. Scales.

What had happened? How could she use her power around humans if she looked like this? How could she meet Lisa? She wanted their little get together that evening.

Sandy ran her finger along a boulder. The stone sizzled and smoked. Its surface was marked everywhere she touched it, as though etched by acid. She was an acid-skinned monster.

Her condition made her want to cry. "Why did this happen? This isn't fair. I want to look like I did."

As soon as the words cleared her mouth, her fair skin began to emerge and cover the black plated coat. She examined her hand and forearm. Soft peach flesh. What she could see of herself looked like the Sandy Sydney of old.

"Oh!" She put her hand to her cheek. "This is swell. I can change whenever I want to." A baby-doll smile came to her lips. Nothing could stop her.

The rest of the afternoon, Sandy practiced transforming herself. What she could do was thrilling!

"Now I can keep my date with Lisa!"

19

W ES PACED. ABOUT thirty people dressed in black waited near the stable. This was a closed show—warriors only. Wes told everyone to wear their uniforms—black jeans and shirts. He noticed that Bud was the only one who wasn't in black. Back too late to change, he assumed.

Other warriors patrolled the perimeter of the area, keeping everyone but the Numenon people away. All the people in the Bowl would resent this, Wes knew, but it was important that the Numenon people, and only the Numenon people, knew what Grandfather's warriors could do. The atmosphere was tense, and Wes was twice as tense as the rest. It was his show.

Wes looked at his watch, which was working. The presentation must be very important. Five o'clock. Grandfather had said the show was supposed to start at four. There wouldn't be enough light to show what he wanted to; he would have to change his plan. Wes hated changing anything. He hated performing for people he didn't know, and he hated corporate people.

And though Grandfather had lectured him on this shortcoming, he had a tendency to hate white people. Especially this week, when that mare had tried to kill him. She belonged to one of the richest ranchers in Wyoming, who happened to be white.

He kept looking at the path from the Bowl, expecting to see the Numenon people coming, to see dust, or something.

At five thirty-five, Will Duane and his entourage straggled into the stable yard. He dragged his feet, paying little attention to his surroundings. Wesley leaped toward him, planning on chewing him out. Lisa Cheewa intercepted him before he got to Will and took him aside.

The damage was already done. When Will and the Numenon team met Grandfather, the shaman had looked past normal reality and glimpsed their souls; they had done the same with him. A profound experience followed. When Wesley Silverhorse met Will Duane, they splattered against each other's surfaces, reaping reflections of their own imperfections.

Wesley was dressed for the show—black shirt, jeans, and boots. He had buttoned his shirt all the way up and wore a stylized silver pin at his throat in lieu of a tie. His long, shiny hair was pulled back in a ponytail tied with a leather thong.

He regarded the Numenon crew. They wore spotless, ironed jeans, brand new white athletic shoes, and maroon baseball caps with the Numenon logo embroidered in gold. Even an hour and a half late, they acted like they owned the place.

He knew who Will Duane was right away and who was his second in command. Doug and Will reminded him of coyotes. Not the roguish teachers of his People's lore, or even the fuzzy bits of Americana cherished by animal lovers, but the coyotes he knew. Those rotten sons of bitches that would steal every lamb on your place and wipe out your chickens. One of those yellow thieves that would make your cow dog so mad that he charged after the varmint, only to be gutted by the pack.

Lisa Cheewa tugged on his sleeve and whispered, "Wes, they're late because the Chinese guy passed out on the way over here. He fell and hit his head on a rock."

"What?" Wes hadn't realized anyone was missing.

"He keeled over on the way down the switchbacks. We called for Elizabeth and she came out in one of the golf carts. The guy came to, but he wasn't making much sense—he kept talking about his wife and baby at home. Elizabeth stopped the bleeding and took him to the hospital tent. They didn't want to come," Lisa whispered, indicating the people from Numenon, "but Elizabeth ordered them down here. You'd better get their attention right now. They're talking about going home tomorrow."

Wes made a snap change of plans—easily, for once. He walked up to the Numenon group, his demeanor changed.

"I'm Wes Silverhorse. I'm very sorry about your friend. Elizabeth will take good care of him. She's patched me up enough times. I'm going to change the show so that you can get close to the horses right away. A lot of people find horses are good to be around when you're feeling bad. Before we get started, tell me about yourselves, especially what you know about horses."

The introductions started with Will. "I'm Will Duane. I don't ride, but my former wife and daughter did. We had horses once."

Doug and Betty spoke about their experience with horses: they had none.

The drivers and cook hung back, acting as though they didn't expect to be included.

Wes pulled them forward and talked to each one. Hector Carrillo was the only one in the group who knew anything about horses.

"My family raised *los caballos Peruanos de paso* on our hacienda in Peru." The intensity of Hector's Spanish-accented voice told Wes there was a lot more to his story. He didn't know a thing about Peru or its horses, so he moved on.

Wesley introduced himself last, his voice soft and unassuming. "I train horses, just like my father and grandfather. We have a ranch in Wyoming. I'll be in the martial arts demonstration, too.

Bud watched Wes face off with the corporate visitors. Eight black-clad men and women stood behind him. More were scattered around the field. The Numenon people looked edgy in their presence. Bud felt their energy; it was so powerful that the Numenon people *had* to feel it. The warriors gained power by the minute—that's what happened when they gathered anywhere. Here in the Bowl, the effect was magnified.

Bud watched their guests looking around nervously. It was kind of a thrill, scaring the richest man in the world and his *compadres*.

He pulled himself up short. That wasn't nice. He had felt just as ill at ease at his first Meeting, ten years ago. He'd arrived his first year in his second *day* of sobriety. He had puked all the way from Texas, but he'd been sober since.

The Numenon people were fish flopping on the bank, wondering why their gills didn't work. Bud tuned into them with his mind. He was surprised by what he could perceive. His psychic powers were much greater this year.

Will and Doug disliked the warriors more than the rest; they could feel their power and didn't like being "one-down." Their eyes swept the Indians, looking for a way to restore their advantage. There wasn't any, so they waited.

Then Bud heard Will Duane think, *How can we get out of here?* He looked at Doug.

Shit if I know, was the unspoken response.

They were becoming psychic, too?

20

WILL FOLLOWED AS Wesley led the group toward the mustangs in the desert pasture. A large herd of horses stood a few hundred yards out, watching them. Will had no idea how many there were, hundreds, probably. Wes whistled and a bunch of them headed toward them.

"The horses coming toward us are different from the rest," Wes said. "They are descendants of the horses the Spanish brought to the Americas. Grandfather's lineage of holy men has been caring for them for hundreds of years. We're showing them to you because they need help. Their grazing lands are threatened, and so are their lives. The horses coming over aren't for sale. They're special—you'll see why."

The approaching horses quickened their pace. The sound of hoof beats intensified and dust overwhelmed them. Will stood still while his staff huddled behind him. He was surprised when Hector Carrillo broke away and walked *toward* the horses. He cupped his hands behind his ears and dropped on to one knee.

"*Es paso llano! Eso es paso llano!*" he exclaimed. He stopped, transfixed, as the mustangs stampeded toward him.

The animals stopped a polite distance from Hector. One came up to him. Hector extended the back of his hand and the horse sniffed it. He rubbed the animal's head along the bridge of the nose and between the eyes; the horse relaxed as Hector talked to it softly.

Will knew a good horseman when he saw one. He'd bet that the herd stallion had never been touched before. Hector did it perfectly. The driver walked back to the group, with the stallion and the rest of the horses following him.

"That eez a very good horse," he said to Wesley, his voice thick with emotion. "Ze …" Then he was off in Spanish. He and Wes walked over to the horse, Hector gesturing and speaking a mixture of Spanish and English.

Will took a closer look and said, "That horse looks like my former wife's Andalusians, but smaller and rougher." Will smiled for the first time in days. "Like they've been on their own for a few hundred years."

A messenger galloped up on a brown horse splashed with white. It had a flashy way of moving, picking up its feet very high. The rider slowed and then stopped next to Wes, handing him a piece of paper. Wes took the message and read it quickly, and then stuffed it into his pocket.

When the new horse approached, Hector threw up his hands and exclaimed, "Look at ze *thread!* Gallop. *Sobreandando! Paso llano!* Only," he said a few words that might be horse names in Spanish, "could do that. My father would *cry* if he see thees horse!"

Will and the others stared at Hector. He was a different person than the man they knew at Numenon. The elegant Peruvian usually wore a look of bored sophistication as he performed his duties. Now he stood next to the horses, babbling in Spanish.

Indicating the pinto that had just arrived, Wesley asked, "Would you like to ride this horse?"

Hector nodded. "Si. Very much." The rider dismounted and Hector expertly checked the horse's girth and adjusted the stirrups, then mounted.

Hector walked the horse, getting used to him, and then shortened the reins a tad. The horse arched its neck and raised its back. The cues were so subtle that Will barely saw them. Hector rode around looking like a connoisseur sampling a fine wine.

Wesley explained the horse's gait. "When the Spanish came to the Americas, they had riding horses like this. Instead of trotting—that one-two, one-two gait that bounces you up and down—these horses' legs move first on one side, then the other." He showed how they moved with his arms and legs. "We call it a two-step or an amble. Hector called it a *paso llano*. You can travel for hours with this gait and not get tired."

The horse was moving faster, while Hector barely moved in the saddle. Hector was riding very fast now, and they could hear the rhythm of the horse's hooves, an even one-two-three-four.

Will was beginning to want what he saw. Wesley had said the mustangs needed a safe place. They'd fit on his ranch in Montana without anybody noticing them.

Hector made a series of serpentines down the arena. He rode the horse in figure eights, then put it into a gallop and stopped it fast. The horse slid when it stopped, kicking up dust.

When Hector brought him in, the horse was dripping with sweat. His ribs heaved with exertion. Before Wes could get mad at him about the animal's condition, Hector said, "I am sorry to ride your horse so hard. But he eez the best horse I have ever ridden. Thank you for letting me ride him. Let me walk him."

Wes softened. "We'll cool him out. Watch the rest of the show."

Hector dismounted. His co-workers clustered around him, treating him like a celebrity.

Will clapped Hector's shoulder and said, "Let's talk about your future. I've got an idea."

"Would you like to see me ride?" Wesley asked mildly.

"Yes," the Numenon group responded, and then went back to praising Hector.

"Okay. One second." While one of the black-clad warriors brought out a horse for Wes, he pulled the note the messenger had brought him out of his pocket and signaled to Will that he wanted to talk to him away from the group. Will moved a few steps away.

"The message is from Elizabeth Bright Eagle," Wesley said, handing him the paper. "She thinks that your friend collapsed from exhaustion and emotional stress. She's keeping him in the hospital tent tonight and wants to talk to you when we're done." Wes's voice was clipped and cold.

Will listened, shaken. He had coerced Gil into coming on the trip by threatening to bring his biggest rival if he didn't. "Will he be all right?"

"You'd better talk to Elizabeth." Wes pulled away from Will as though he carried an infectious disease.

One of the men led a horse over to him. Wesley took the reins and said, "This horse is farther along in its training than the horse Hector rode." The animal was shiny black, with a very long mane. His tail touched the ground. He had a long neck and brilliant black eyes. Will had never seen a more beautiful animal.

"This is a stud horse, a son of my stallion and one of the wild mares. I've messed with him a few years at the Meeting. I trained him like a ranch horse, and then I tried something called 'dressage' with him. I don't have an English saddle, so I just ride him bareback."

Wes swung up on the horse so easily it seemed as though he'd levitated.

Will stepped back when he saw Wes on the horse. On the ground, Wes was an impressive man, but on a horse he was … Will couldn't find words to describe it. The air around Wesley and the animal seemed to vibrate. He seemed bigger, and the horse looked larger. The pair glistened in the late afternoon sun.

Wesley was completely at home, totally natural, and the master of the world sitting on the horse. He picked up the reins, cueing the animal to move forward. Wes became more animated the more he rode, but he hardly moved. His excitement showed; he loved to ride.

Wes put the horse into a hard gallop, heading right at them. Will's staff clustered behind him again. When Wes almost reached them, he said, "Whoa." The horse set its hind feet under itself and slid perhaps twenty feet, stopping well away from them. The horse paused an instant, and then spun back in the direction it came. The horse turned so fast it seemed a blur. Wes did this run, stop, and spin maneuver again.

"Back," he said. The horse, its reins loosely draped, shot back as fast as it could. He let the horse settle down for a moment and then walked forward to them, stopping when he got to them.

Wes kept the demo going. The animal changed leads every stride, went diagonally all over the arena, half reared, and then jumped in the air after half rearing. Wes and the horse seemed to radiate a blue light. Will whistled and clapped with the others.

"He also does that four beat gait," Wes said, which the animal preceded to do, but with much more fire and energy than Hector's horse had shown. Wesley rode the horse one more lap around the arena in the high stepping Spanish gait. He looked displeased.

"Give it to me; I want it! Give me yourself!" Wesley shouted. He smacked the horse on the neck with the flat of his hand. The slap made a resounding sound on the wet flesh. Will jumped.

The horse leaped into the air and moved out with twice the vigor he had shown before. Wes and his fabulous steed made their way toward the group, both putting out everything they had. The horse stormed by, brilliant and animated. The rider's intensity and beauty was as blinding as the horse's.

Will knew they had seen a world-class display of horsemanship. He vowed to take Wesley and the horses home with him if he had to kidnap them.

21

WESLEY WHEELED THE stallion at the end of the field and flew toward the corporate guests. He raised his arm and smiled. As Wes rode past the visitors, he recognized Melissa, the woman he'd frightened earlier. He looked into her eyes, wanting to find a way to apologize.

Melissa stared back, delivering a look that said, *You asshole! Are you going to ride me down?* She practically leapt off the ground in rage. *Are you going to rape me? You'll have to kill me first!* Melissa stood, feet spread, just over one hundred pounds of fury.

Wesley turned the great horse again, and faced Melissa. Fully energized from the ride, he stared into her defiant eyes. He registered her full, sensuous lips, the high cheekbones, and that pale, fine-textured skin. He felt Melissa's rage and repressed sexual drive. Their eyes met and locked, and his ferocity flew back at her.

You spoiled, white bitch! You walk in here like you own the place. Who do you think you are? And surprisingly, he wanted to do exactly what she was mentally accusing him of wanting to do—rape her.

Wesley halted his horse and said, "Excuse me, folks. I need to get ready for the martial arts demonstration. Thank you for watching me ride." He waved and left the field.

He stormed back to the tack shed. He wanted to throw himself off his horse, rip off her clothes, and fuck the crap out of that nasty bitch. He could see himself tearing open her blouse, grabbing her hair and holding her head back while biting her breasts. He wanted to plow into her as violently as possible. He wanted her to fight him, so he could slap her around …

Wes was horrified. He'd never had fantasies of raping a woman, much less beating her and liking it. He locked himself in the tack shed. The images of raping her wouldn't leave. Worse—he was in the same state he was in when he scared her earlier.

While Wes tried to get a grip on himself, Bud did damage control. He sauntered over to the Numenon crew. "Hi. Good to see you guys again."

"Oh, Bud," Betty cried. "We've been wanting to thank you for what you did on the way in." They clustered around him, thanking him and shaking his hand.

Melissa stood in her tracks, growling like an unfed, untamed lioness. The expressions on the faces of the people who didn't know her well—the drivers, all the warriors, almost everyone—were cautious. Bud glanced over at Will Duane. Will, Betty, and Doug stared at her in horror. Bud figured that they knew her and there was reason to be afraid when she looked like that.

"C'mon, ma'am, you'll get a kick out of this." Melissa trudged into the pasture behind Bud, looking around and glowering. He felt like laughing.

When she saw him amble over, Melissa liked Bud as much as she hated Wes. She remembered how he picked her up off the floor of the Ashley when she was so upset and put her on Will's bed. He had put her to sleep somehow, she realized.

Bud spoke. "A lot of people like hanging around horses, even if they don't ride. I think it was Mark Twain who said, 'The outside of a horse is good for the inside of a man.'"

Melissa thought, *He's not so dumb!*

Don't ever think I'm dumb, lady.

Melissa heard the words, right in her head, but with no sound. They shocked her. She was certain they came from Bud. Had he heard what she thought about him and responded? Melissa remembered what Betty had written in her brief. *People often become psychic in the Mogollon Bowl.*

Was *she* psychic? If she heard Bud's reply, he must have heard something coming from her. Did everyone hear what she thought? She stared in horror, remembering what she'd thought about Wesley.

Bud spoke to the group. "These horses are the best in the world to hang out with. Just pick one and pet it. Move slowly and don't wave your hands around their eyes. They have a secret; see if you can figure it out."

22

WILL APPROACHED A brown horse with a black mane and tail. That color was called "bay," one of the few bits of information about horses he remembered from his ex-wife's days with her Andalusians. The animal's mane and tail were matted like dreadlocks, bearing no resemblance to the flowing locks of wild horses on film.

When he left the riding portion of the demonstration, Will was gripped by his fantasies of possessing the herd and using them for PR. The horse standing in front of him knocked that flat. The animal was big. It stood impassively as he approached, looking at him out of a shining eye that was stuck on one corner of its head.

"Nice horse," he said, keeping an eye on its horn-like, and potentially lethal, hooves. While he'd owned some of the top show horses in the world, Will had never ridden one. He may have touched one when his daughter was in pony club, holding the reins for her at a show.

He didn't want to touch the one in front of him, but he looked around. His employees were petting their respective horses. Melissa had her arms around the neck of a gray-white animal and was cooing at it and weeping. The sight made him tear up, surprisingly. Will felt like she was more his daughter than his real daughter. If Melissa could do it, then so could he.

Taking a deep breath, Will laid his palm on the bay horse's neck. It was hairy and warm. The horse didn't move. Will waited for something to happen. Maybe Bud would come by and say they could quit.

As his hand rested on the animal, Will suddenly became aware that Frank Sauvage, one of his top executives, would attempt to oust him from control of Numenon in the very near future. Will had known that Sauvage was capable of disloyalty, but not with the utter certainty he felt then. Nor did he realize the extent of Sauvage's malice or the fact that he was currently recruiting others in the corporation who felt the same way. With enough people on his side, and the cooperation of the Board, Sauvage *could* unseat Will from control of his own company. He felt the Board coalescing against him. Will's heart contracted. The chest pains that had plagued him throbbed beneath his breastbone.

He also knew with absolute certainty that the Dow would climb 300 points the next day, and fall 200 the next. He needed to do some trading. He also needed to check on Numenon's R & D department. Something was going to break there. Or was a new innovation coming his way from outside? A large technological advance was on its way. Something huge.

Will had experienced visions all of his life. This kind of insight was nothing new—except that the new batch of realizations were clearer and more powerful than any he'd ever known. He didn't question them. He looked around to see what the others were up to. They looked engrossed in their equine experiences.

The horse had something to do with the material flooding his mind. It didn't talk, but it ignited something in him that was omniscient. He put both palms on the creature's neck.

Why do you act like a jerk? a clear voice said. Will jumped. *You're not a jerk, you're a nice person. Why don't you let people see that?* He looked around. No one was there. He'd heard voices before, but voices he knew were his own mind. This one seemed to come from outside of him, as well as inside. No one else acted like they heard it. Will's jaw relaxed from surprise. He left his hands on the animal.

You're not here because of Marina or the mine. You know that. Why don't you admit it? Why don't you let everyone else know it, too? People don't have to hate you.

Why did you really come here? The sharp, direct voice cut through his defenses. *You need something that's here.*

Find it or you'll be dead in a year.

23

WESLEY SAT ON the horse, and was wrapped in a blanket. He wore a traditional and very brief breechcloth, all that he could wear for the martial arts demo. If he wore anything more, it would ignite. Wes wrapped a blanket around himself because he was too prudish to run around almost naked in front of strangers.

The exercise he thought up would tame that Melissa. He needed to get her under control so she'd stop doing whatever she was doing to him. When the Numenon group had been hanging out with the horses, Wes had seen her with Risa, his favorite horse in the world. Had she done anything to the mare?

The Numenon people wandered in from the pasture, each having had his or her experience with a horse. By the looks on their faces, all of them had discovered the horses' secret. They made the voice of Spirit louder.

"Come over here," he called. "I have something really fun to do. It's something horse masters do." They gathered round. "Who would like to analyze these two horses and tell us which is better?"

When no one stepped forward, Wes rode toward Melissa and said, "How about you?"

Though he'd merely said, "How about you," it sounded more like, "How about you, *bitch*?"

Melissa instantly rose to his bait. She replied, "If you wish." But it sounded like she was saying, "If you want to fight, buddy, watch your balls."

The horse masters brought out the two horses that Bud had healed. First was the beautiful, but weak and insane, black and white pinto mare known as Squirrel Brains. The sight of the Numenon crew set her spinning. She snorted and whirled on her lead line.

The other horse was the ugly, but truly fine, dun stallion. He had been close to death when Paul Running Bird rode him back to the stable. The stallion apparently thought better of human beings after Bud healed him, because he hadn't disappeared into the desert afterall.

Melissa walked toward the animals with *the walk*. She sauntered out, looking self assured, swaggering as if her joints and muscles were loose, her eyes soft and languid.

Her posture read, "I have an Uzi in my bra. What do you have, dip shit?" She was so insolent that Wes involuntarily rode forward, glaring at her. She reached the horses and paused.

He waved at them, saying, "What do you think ..." Wes's voice trailed off; gazing into her eyes rendered him speechless.

"Think about *what*, Mr. Silverstone?"

"Silverhorse."

"Oh, sorry. Silverhorse. What do I think about *what*? The weather? The economy? The situation in Bosnia?"

"About the horses standing in front of you."

"Ahh! The *horses*. I think that *horses* should be extinct." The crowd gasped. "Nothing needs to be that big in this day and age. They take up feed from more adaptive animals. And, they're bad for the environment. Studies have shown that."

Wesley reeled. She had invalidated his life in a couple of sentences. He was about to reply, when one of the guys shouted from the field, "Hey, Wes! There's something wrong with Risa!"

Wes jumped. What did that *woman* do to his favorite horse? He had seen her waving her hands around the mare. He galloped out to Risa, followed by everyone else. Melissa ran fastest of all. She arrived just behind Wesley.

Risa stood with her head down, front legs spread, unsteady on her feet. Her eyes rolled back and the tip of her tongue hung out of her mouth.

As Wes reached Risa and swung off his horse to help her, he lost his blanket. The reason he was wearing it became obvious: Wesley Silverhorse was almost naked. Melissa's eyes widened and she stopped, staring at him.

The rest of the crowd arrived to a dramatic tableau. The gray-white Risa was outlined against the red soil. Wes's dark figure moved like a ghost next to her, dancing in anger. In the background, the mountains' tortured outlines were black against the moonlit sky. Thunderclouds formed fantastic shapes; lightning stabbed downward, a dangerous light show.

"*What did you do to her?*" Wesley shouted.

Melissa ran forward in a panic. Lightning flashed, illuminating Wes's body. Melissa gasped. Not only was he almost naked, symbols blazed like brands flamed bright red all over his body. She leaped back, terrified of him and for Risa.

"I didn't do anything to her," she said.

The horse spoke in a voice they both could hear, *Oh, Melissa ... I love you ... Do it again.*

Melissa turned to Wes. "All I did was this ..." She positioned her hands five inches above Risa's body. She moved her left hand parallel to the horse's side with the palm and fingers flat. She held her right hand flat and poked it, fingers first, at the horse. She never touched the animal.

"See," Melissa said brightly. "That's all I did! It's what the Chinese guy taught me. I'm an expert at bodywork. I went down to L.A. and a Chinese master taught me how to do that. It's just energy. It heals. Really."

Wes glared at her, marveling that she was even more beautiful close up. He wanted to kiss her.

Risa groaned and keeled over—*whoomp!* She lay flat on her side with a dusty splash. Her legs stuck out straight. Wes turned to the mare and touched her. He could hear her mind singing,

"*Walking in a winter wonderland ...*" She sang three verses of the famous Christmas tune, followed by, "*Jingle bells, jingle bells, jingle all the way ...*"

Risa was stoned out of her mind.

Wes stood up, ready to scream at Melissa, when Risa said to him, *Wes? Wes? Is that you? Oh, Wes! Marry her! Marry her right now! Tonight! What she can do with her hands! Touch me, you'll feel it.*

Hands touching the mare, Wes had the full benefit of "The thing the Chinese guy taught Melissa" in two horse-sized jolts. His body jerked, but he did not let go of Risa. Gasping, he was finally able to say, "I see what you mean!"

When he could, Wesley addressed the crowd. "Risa's okay."

He swung up on his horse and asked Melissa to give him his blanket, which she did, being careful not to touch him. He looked at her, giving her a piercing gaze, which was made up of "Chinese guy" and Christmas carols, plus anxiety about the upcoming martial arts show.

Seeing his expression, Melissa jumped back. He heard her mind scream, *Help me! Help me.* Wesley turned back to help her.

Melissa gave him a look that said, "Come near me, you jerk, and I'll tear off your balls and feed them to you."

"Oh, yeah? See if you can, bitch!"

24

"YOU," WES SAID, pointing at Melissa. "Look at these horses. Tell me which is best, and why."

Melissa strolled toward the horses, wearing "fuck you" in her walk, her posture, her facial expression, and her incredible ass. Wesley had not really looked at all of her before. Now he did, not realizing that what he saw was the product of corporate America. Melissa had been stressed in recent months; she dealt with it by working out at the office gym. She wasn't wearing baggy jeans, either.

Melissa sauntered over to the two horses. While maintaining her casual demeanor and appearance of control, Melissa thought, *Shit.* That was all she knew about horses.

Still, she knew a test situation when she saw one. She wasn't clear why it was a test or what the prize was or even why she was in it, but a test it was. She was a Harvard MBA—a *woman* Harvard MBA with an IQ of 215—at the top of her class, and was used to beating the best. She would win now.

Calmly appraising the horses, her intellect searched for relevant data. She came up with a few tid-bits from her parents. First, from her artistic, museum-loving father, some advice from the American architect Louis Sullivan: "Form follows function."

Melissa raised her eyebrows and said in her cultured voice, "What do you intend to *do* with these horses?"

"Ride them."

"What *kind* of riding do you want to do? Are you going to make them leap over high hurdles? Harass cattle? *Race* them?" Each word was an indictment.

Wes grimaced. "Ranch work: do chores, doctor cattle, move them. Whatever needs doing."

Melissa shivered. Animal exploitation. "Well, I'll answer your question, Mr. Silversmith—"

"Silverhorse."

"Right. First, answer *my* question. Have you ever considered the *morality* of riding horses?"

"What?"

"Have you ever asked your horse how it feels about being ridden? Or do you just use the animal for your own purposes?"

Seeing that she was serious, Wes replied, "There wouldn't be any horses if they weren't ridden. That's what they're for."

"That was my original position—they should be extinct." She turned to the horses and picked up the conversation without a missed beat. "This horse is being considered for work on a ranch. Well, let's see …"

She looked at the two animals and felt like laughing. The answer was so obvious that Melissa couldn't believe it.

"The best horse is this light brown one. If he's meant to work hard, he needs to have a strong skeleton. Look at the size of his bones compared to the other horse." She went up to the dun horse and felt its legs. "The joints of this horse are large and firm. That's important—puffiness indicates inflamation and disease."

Melissa approached the crazy pinto mare, Squirrel Brains, moving her arms and hands more than an experienced horse person would. The mare looked at her suspiciously.

"This horse is very pretty, with the elegant sculptural quality of its head, flashy color, and large eyes," Melissa reached up to touch the mare's face. She snorted and half reared, almost getting away. "But she doesn't have the same thickness of bones as the other horse, nor does it have the nice joints. And look at those feet. Tiny. Also, this horse should be able to tell if I'm dangerous or not; it isn't mentally stable."

Melissa paced back and forth. She studied the primitive-looking dun horse. "Of course, of *course!* I remember where I saw that coloration. Przewalski's Horse! This horse is crossbred with the Przewalski Horse. He is *Pleistocene*—the cave paintings look like him."

Melissa was so excited that she hopped from one foot to the other. "He's a living fossil! Not only that—he's not supposed to be here! Przewalski's horse is Asiatic, and he shouldn't be on this *continent.*" She marched in front of Will and shook her finger at him.

"Listen. *Will*, you especially listen. This is a major archeological find. I know about these things; my mother is an archeologist. I would bet anything that this horse is a descendent of a Przewalski's horse. These are very primitive animals, extinct in the wild." She walked over to the dun horse.

"See the bony structure of the horse's head? Here in the front of its eyes and nose." She touched the horse's face. "This is typical of the early equus coming through the Pliocene era into the Pleistocene. I'd call the Smithsonian right away."

Everyone looked at her, amazed.

"I *knew* I would remember." She looked at the group, smiling brilliantly. "Horses originated here, in the New World. Then they all left for some reason. Scientists believe it was on a land bridge across what is now the Bering Sea.

"There were no horses here when the first European settlers arrived. The so-called wild horses here are descendants of escaped Spanish horses. They are of a different type than truly wild horses—like this horse." She indicated the dun horse.

"If he is really descended from a Przewalski's horse, his ancestors have been here, on this continent, for millions of years. If there are others like him, it would throw archeology on its head, disprove theories, and make careers." She smiled at Wes, standing near him and his horse. He looked at her, motionless, seeming to have seen her for the first time.

"I'm sorry to take up so much time. Can you still do the martial arts show?"

Wes smiled at her. He seemed to come back from a reverie. "Sure. We can do it at night." He looked into her eyes. "Where did you learn all that?"

"Deduction." She smiled warmly. "Deduction and observation. Plus my mom's a senior scientist at the Smithsonian."

Will was proud enough to burst. That was his girl! Melissa had taken the place of his daughter in Will's mind. She was the daughter who survived and won. He'd have to acquire all the horses and get the Indians' permission to study their habitat. He'd have to have that Wesley kid working for him, too. He'd shown how skilled he was earlier.

"Wesley!" Will called out.

Wes wheeled the horse. "Yes, Mr. Duane?"

"If you're interested in a job, come and see me first thing in the morning. Seven thirty. We can have breakfast and talk."

"Certainly, Mr. Duane."

25

JON WALKER BEAT the Numenon crew to the area where refreshments were served. He hoped to spiff up whatever the Indians made so that it met *his* standards. He didn't get the chance. A warrior supervised a rickety table next to the tack shed. A plastic cooler dispensed a golden liquid into paper cups. Next to the cooler was a platter of brownie-like cakes laid out on newspaper. The table's legs sat in two inches of dust.

Nice visual presentation. Jon was glad he'd organized dinner before leaving camp that afternoon; otherwise, he'd have to leave early and miss the martial arts show. The drivers were going help him cook and serve after they got back.

One of the Indians, Paul Running-something, said he'd light the barbecue so that the coals would be perfect when they returned. The guy had been hanging around the camp, so Jon pressed him into duty.

Jon looked back at the bluff they'd have to climb to get back up to the Bowl. The rock formations gave him a creepy feeling. He didn't want to walk back by himself in the dark, tonight or ever. He shuddered and sipped the drink.

"Oh ... my ... God!" he exclaimed as he tasted the drink. "What *is* this?"

He kept sipping. What was it? A fruit drink? An herb tea? Definitely not alcoholic. What was it? It was *delicious*.

Usually, Jon could analyze and duplicate any food after a single taste. Will Duane looked at him, indicating his cup with his finger and making a quizzical face. Jon shrugged. He'd figure it out. This drink was worth taking home.

He tasted the brownie, his interest up. Again, he couldn't tell what it was. He made a mental note to lift whatever was left for further study. He would figure out how to make these as soon as possible.

Then it hit him. Zowie, wowie. Their snack packed a wallop. His head buzzed and he felt like laughing. This was more fun than he'd had in a long while. Since that afternoon, actually, when they were stuck in the desert and Bud was healing Doug and Will. Whatever Bud had done gave him a contact high. He turned to the others, and saw that everyone was having his or her own reaction.

After finishing half a cup of the drink, terror swept over Melissa. She excused herself and headed for the corral fence away from everyone else. Close to tears, her stellar performance with the horses buoyed her not one bit.

She rubbed her breastbone—what did Wesley Silverhorse do to her? He had been talking to Will when he looked up directly at her. His glance hit her with something. It hurt terribly. Drinking the golden liquid made it worse. She felt dreamy, as if she were being forced to relax. Melissa didn't dare relax any more than her ancestors dared to get drunk in the land of pogroms. She looked over her shoulder at the bluffs behind her. They seemed menacing, as though they were hiding something.

The sense that something was stalking her was back. The feelings that she'd had for so long were almost overwhelming. Melissa grabbed the corral rail. She felt like a freight train was roaring down upon her, out of control.

"Ma'am? Are you all right?" a soft voice asked. She turned. It was Bud Creeman.

"No," she said. She rubbed her chest. "I'm very frightened. I'm sorry if I was awful back there. Everything seems to be hitting me hard tonight." Her face showed her distress. "I'd really like to go home." Tears welled up in her eyes.

"This is a really intense place, Miss ..." Bud Creeman had walked up to her quietly.

"Call me Melissa."

"The Bowl's energy is strong, and you've got some of the most powerful healers in the world here, led by Grandfather. There are some real healers here: Tyler Brand, Elizabeth, me. And Wes."

Her eyes widened in alarm. "I can't imagine him healing anything."

"Wes is one of our greatest healers."

"But he *hit* that horse. And he's so conceited."

Bud smiled. "He just called out the horse's spirit. The horse wasn't giving him everything he had. Wes is a very gentle, kind person. I've known him for years."

"He did something to me, Bud. Something flew off of him and hit me here." She touched her breastbone. "It really hurt. It still hurts."

Bud's brows knit. He seemed concerned. "What do you think of Wes?"

"I think he's the most arrogant, obnoxious, terrifying person I've ever met."

"Well, in this show, he's going to seem really scary. Keep in mind, it's for defense. He could *defend* you—if you needed it. Remember that. Melissa! Listen to me!" She felt herself slip far away. He reached for her.

Words barely penetrated Melissa's mind; the pain in her heart was unrelenting. The rest of her body was affected, too. Her insides felt like they were made of that golden liquid. Whatever Wesley had shot into her slowly drifted downward inside her torso, sending off bubbles. The image was beautiful: a pearl dissolving inside her as it drifted lower and lower.

How it felt was something else. She felt like she was being forced open—her pelvis was unlocking, as were her chest and abdomen. She was releasing herself to that dreadful man. She felt heavy, languid, and slow. Sensuous. Fantasies of having sex with Wesley overwhelmed her. Her legs spread involuntarily; she could barely keep them from parting.

As she opened physically, the greatest terror she had known arose within her. The stalker was right there, and she was opening to receive him. She started to cry out, when Bud touched her. She yelped.

26

"*D*AMN THAT BITCH!*" Enzo rubbed his temples. His head throbbed with the effort of maintaining contact. He had to tune in to Andrea every two minutes—literally—to keep her from ordering the pilot to land and let her out.

All the time, her mind yapped and whined about the illegality of what she was doing. It wasn't *that* illegal. Not like murder or rape or blowing things up. She was going to do a little industrial espionage. Why did she think Duane had all that security?

She was someone who could get through all of his safety nets. He had read her paper on Internet security. The stupid twat knew exactly how to break into Duane's system. She was perfect for the job. Except …

He put one hand on each side of the see-stone and watched her disembark in Atlanta. Pretty thing in the traveling suit he gave her. Pain circled his head, a crown of agony caused by holding Andrea in check. He watched her approach the customs' desk. She was thinking of turning herself in.

"Feel this, you stupid sow." He sent such a torrent of energy to her that she was lucky she didn't climax while handing her passport over. Hah! Enzo laughed as she tried to cover what she was feeling. His rush of energy brought out a new fact about her, something that would make her delicious when she returned home.

But first she had to get to New Mexico, do the job, and come back.

"Oh, Andrea, love of my heart," he said to the see-stone. "I miss you so much that my eyes fill with tears. I cannot wait until you come home to me. You will be my lady and my love. We will be together forever. All that is mine will be yours, but most importantly, my heart belongs to you." Enzo watched her though the see-stone. From the way her body jerked as she got back on the jet, he could tell that his message registered.

"I want to spread your legs and touch your ..." He gave a millimeter by millimeter description of her body and what he intended to do to it, an inventory that would make even the palace women blush. "You will feel such ecstasy ..."

He stopped when she passed out in her chair on the jet. The attendant had to belt her in.

That should hold her for a while. His head throbbed. Now maybe he could have some peace. Enzo watched her through the see-stone, her head lolling to one side, soft hair draped down her breast. Pretty even like that.

But a problem. If she doubted what she was doing as she flew across the country in his jet, which was piloted and staffed by his people, making it practically the same as being *at* the castle, what would she do when she came under the influence of the Mogollon Bowl and the shaman? They were so powerful that *he* could not see in, even with the stone.

He had to stop her senseless thinking about morals. What could he do? If he kept her so aroused she was almost climaxing, but not quite, that would get her to New Mexico and the Bowl without ruining the operation. Maybe it would work inside the Bowl. Maybe.

Enzo separated the threads of his mind, diverting the most erotic to Andrea. She'd receive a steady stream, until ... he came up with Plan B.

He needed a Plan B. Sandy Sydney had worked out badly without any morals at all. What would a computer scientist with an obsession with ethics, which were so needless, do? He needed someone already inside, well known to Grandfather, someone who would gladly betray him. Maybe even without having to be paid. Who would that be? What temptations could he offer? How could he recognize and contact this person in the Bowl, where he couldn't see him or her?

Andrea was in love. Images of Enzo would not leave her. His sculptured head and broad shoulders. His gray-flecked hair sparkled; it didn't make him look old at all. His eyes were a brilliant shade of blue she'd never seen. As she thought, more of Enzo appeared in her imagination. All of him. She gasped. He wanted *her*, too.

He wanted to marry her. The realization was blinding. She had to get the job done and get back to Enzo. The love of her life.

Burying her nose in her laptop and the brief, Andrea studied the material about Numenon as though it was the hope of her salvation. If only the throbbing of her body and racing of her mind would stop, she might be able to understand what she read. She wanted to groan.

27

TYLER BRAND, THE Master of Ceremonies for the martial arts exhibition, stood in front of the Numenon group. He had just gotten back from riding all over the desert trying to find Sandy Sydney. Not only did they not find her, he'd forgotten to tell Wesley the horse demo had been put back an hour. Wes was mad at him because he'd had a bad start with the Numenon group.

Evening shadows accented his craggy features. He was wearing black; Tyler knew he looked like a warlock and delighted in it. Poking their visitors was fun. Will Duane was everything the professor hated: a rich, WASP male—fattest of the fat cats. The rest looked like they'd walked out of a display widow of an upscale store.

"We are spirit warriors." The professor felt like he was presenting Shakespeare to baboons. These people had no clue about mystical life. "What does that mean? A warrior is involved in struggle between opposing forces.

"What about the spirit part of it? The definition of spirit is 'the vital force within living beings.' Spirit is the difference between a living person and a dead one. A spirit warrior uses his or her life force against an enemy. Evil, in our case.

"The concept of spirit as animating force is known all over the globe. The spirit warrior is a concept of our People, but also Indian and Asian cultures. In the East, they call the energy *Qi Gong* or *Kundalini—*"

Will Duane jumped in, interrupting Dr. Brand. "*Kundalini?* We're going to talk about *Kundalini?* The column of light that goes up your spine and gives you power?"

"We'll do more than talk about it." Tyler was amazed that Will Duane had heard the Sanskrit word. "You'll get your fill of *Kundalini* here. Our traditions call it something else, but that's what it is. As spirit warriors, we are on a journey to transform ourselves into people of Spirit.

"Some people have better access to this energy," Tyler continued, "and can ignite it in other people. Grandfather is one of those people.

"Hear me now, even if you've slept through everything I've said." Tyler raised his voice. "The energy I'm talking about is real and unbelievably powerful. You will see things in this show that will frighten you. Don't worry; the force is for defense, not offense.

"A warning. The content of this exhibition is confidential, even to the other people at the Meeting. Grandfather and Wesley would be most unhappy if its contents became known. People who weren't invited to the show will not be able to see or hear what happens.

"That's it! Let the show begin!" Tyler waved his arms with a flourish. He stepped back, and vanished.

Will stared at the empty field. The high that he'd gotten from the drink and brownie was gone. Except for Tyler Brand disappearing into thin air, the world seemed perfectly normal. All the black-clad people who had been hanging around were gone.

The martial arts field was next to the area that the MBAs thought was a ropes course. The tower they had assumed was used for rappelling was to the group's right, a few hundred feet away. The row of chopped telephone poles sticking out of the ground was also to the right, between them and the tower. They didn't seem like part of a training course any more; they seemed foreign and menacing.

He waited and nothing happened. The group shifted around, looking at each other. They sat on hay bales arranged on a gradual rise above a flat plain at least the size of a football field. All of them had front row seats before a very large earthen stage.

Something touched him and Will jumped up, spinning around. A chorus erupted from the others: "Oh my God!" "Will, what is it?" "Shit!" "What the hell!" All of his people were on their feet.

The warriors stood behind them. Will hadn't heard them approaching; he had no idea how they got there. There were about twenty of them. They shook hands as though they were at a cocktail party.

Then the warriors stepped back. The disgruntled Numenon crew muttered. A few of his people grinned—the drivers, primarily. They acted like it was great fun. Will turned around again, and the Indians were gone. Vanished.

Shaken, he sat on his hay bale and watched the earthen stage before them. All was silent. After a while, the silence became ominous. Lightning flickered in the mountains, illuminating the peaks. He began to feel woozy and nauseous.

"They've drugged us," Will announced. A murmur went down the line.

The red dirt stage seemed liquid, rolling with waves. The sound and movement made Will feel heavy and lethargic, but, oddly, his senses and the world around him were ultra clear. The desert's atmosphere was totally different than it had been during the day.

Lush and ripe with promise, the land was *alive*. The red dust before him quivered with vitality, smelling deep and musky. The night sky shimmered where it met the mountains, gradually darkening to luminous blackness above them. The moon, though not particularly full, drenched the scene with light.

He had the sensation that he and his crew were crossing the sea. The sound of waves receded. They had reached a new land. Forests and meadows rose from the red field, appearing and disappearing like phantoms. They crossed streams and valleys. Saw swamps, clouds of insects, alligators, rodents, deer, rabbits, elk, turkeys, birds, and flowers. Every wild thing shouted its aliveness. The Native people inhabited the land, as natural as the leaves.

New sensations battered him like gunfire. The earth spoke to him through all of his senses, showing him the coming of the Europeans. Will realized that this wasn't a show originating from the Indians at all; the *earth* was expressing its affront at what was done to *it*, at lies and broken promises made to it and its inhabitants.

"They got those enviro-Nazis from Hollywood to do this," Will fumed. "It's special effects, that's all." He signaled to Doug that they should walk out, but Doug stared at him. His eyes looked deep and dark. Clearly, he was drugged. The Indians were trying to brainwash them. He'd helicopter everyone out tomorrow and sue the bastards.

"Communists!" Will snarled.

But the inventory didn't blame the settlers. The earth showed starving Europeans shoved off of their shareholds by greedy landowners and insatiable royalty. No one came to the New World because life in the Old World was good. They fled sure death.

Will gazed at the shimmering dust before them. History marched forward. The industrial revolution transformed the world. Great fortunes arose from the labor of workers who were one step up from slaves. The modern world appeared with its stinking rivers, useless lakes, acid rain, and towns and cities whose human inhabitants killed each other in a poverty of soul.

In golden California, oak savannahs became Spanish ranchos built on Indians' bones. In Silicon Valley, new millionaires covered the hills with monstrous houses. Snobbery and greed entwined with compulsive achievement, giving birth to palaces for pseudo-royalty.

Will Duane's magnificent mansion stood above them all, crowning a hill in the Town of Woodside. A party glittered on its broad terraces. Men laughed with sleek ladies, leaving early in limousines to drink champagne in secret places.

Will blinked as the sky reflected his favorite haunts. He was in a spectacular corporate condo, the lights of San Francisco glittering through walls of glass. Caviar and champagne sat on a table. A man's naked buttocks plunged as he drove himself into a stylish woman with red lips and nails. She clawed his back, moaning and mewing as his pace increased. More interludes appeared.

That was *him! Oh, Jesus!* The images covered the sky, a documentary of Will's insatiable hunger for sex. It was real; he remembered the women and places. How did they film him? How could they broadcast it?

Will peeked at the others. They looked as embarrassed as he did, but no one pointed fingers in his direction. He guessed that the show was custom made for each person. Each saw where he or she had stepped over the line. They were looking at things no one admitted.

The sky cleared, but images quickly formed again. It looked like a view of the dust and cactus they'd passed all day. And then Will knew: this was the Indians' sacred land that he proposed mining. The others gasped, especially the drivers who didn't know what he wanted to do. They glared at him. Will realized with horror that everyone in the Bowl knew that he wanted the mine.

Radiant blue lights appeared in the desert, moving in and out of rocks and soil, blessing everything. Blessing the earth itself. The wealth of that place was in *souls,* not minerals. This was the "lifeless wasteland" that Will Duane wanted to destroy.

Will gasped as he saw the land after being mined: truly dead, devoid of light or life, stripped, raped. Will Duane's marble home was juxtaposed on the ruined earth. The mansion echoed, an empty shell occupied by a lonely, impoverished man.

His people stared at him. Had he earned his vast wealth destroying all that was good? Will shrunk into his seat, silent, like the rest of them.

He thought the show was over. They sat looking at an empty dirt field, but it wasn't. Red figures arose from the ground. They stood, bathed in moonlight. A shriek slashed the air. The figures leaped, screaming war cries. Mounted now, they rode for their lives.

Will watched open-mouthed. The horsemen became a whirling circle of flesh. Horses peeled off from the circle, leaving a single ring of galloping riders yelling ferociously and waving their lances.

In the center, a warrior stood alone. The riders veered off and the sounds of hoof beats died. Light fell on the figure's body, highlighting muscles and sinews, angles and planes. His hair was tied back, exposing his face.

It was Wesley Silverhorse, almost naked in just his breechclout. He was covered with what looked like *brands;* red symbols flamed over his skin. He stood silently, looking at the ground. Thunder stalked in the distance.

Wesley raised his head and looked at them, then raised his arms gracefully over his head. Blue lights began spinning upward from the earth around him. Fine blue and white vapors shot with silver sparkles spiraled around his body, touching it, dancing around and through it. They rose until they reached the tops of his up-stretched hands, and then continued to twist over his head. The air above him was filled with lights, spiraling as high as they could see. A column of light engulfed Wesley's lean form.

"Holy shit! What is *that?*" said Doug. Everyone turned to Will, looking to him for leadership.

Will barked, "They've given us a hallucinogen. It isn't real."

The others nodded and turned to the field before them. But what they were seeing *was* real.

Wesley was perfectly formed—a paragon of male beauty. His expression was enraptured, ecstatic. Electric blue flames danced around and through him.

Lightning ringed the Bowl, blasting volley after volley until the field was lit like daylight. Thunder deafened them. The group cowered and pulled toward Will.

Wesley spun toward the wooden tower that they assumed was for rappelling. Large rocks flew from a catapult atop the tower. Wesley swung his arm toward the stones. Blue light flew from his hand, striking and exploding the rocks. They covered their ears, trying to escape the deafening explosions. Men reloaded rocks into the catapult and released them as rapidly as they could. Wesley kept firing and exploding the targets. The blasts lit the air like fireworks, providing a gala show of destruction.

"He could kill us!" Betty gasped.

Will and Doug looked at each other. Yes, he could. Wesley Silverhorse was a valuable asset. Dangerous, but very valuable. Numenon needed him.

Melissa hid her face in Jon's shirt.

Wesley turned to face them. The energy moving around him pulled closer to his body. An eddy formed, and that became a whirlpool. An ephemeral blue and white ring rose around him, rising to the heavens, and then dropping down toward Wesley and the earth like a waterfall. It was a circular conduit of power rising hundreds of feet high. Wes stood in the middle of it, unaffected.

A white light burst from the top of his head. Cloudlike, it ascended and formed an enormous creature, a centurion of light. Its human shape was clearly visible, muscles and limbs defined by moving light. The thing stood almost three hundred feet above Wesley's head. The giant looked down on them. Immaterial, transparent, mightier than the ocean, it gazed at them with glowing blue eyes.

Will knew that it wasn't any hallucination; that thing was *real*. He cowered and it continued to look at them, as neutral as a bolt of lightning. It wasn't evil; it wasn't good. It simply *was*. The human Wesley extended an arm toward the catapult tower. The towering manifestation above him extended *its* arm, touching the tower's piers and bending them as though they were putty.

Wesley raised his arm over his head, and the giant raised its glistening arm. Lightning flew from its hand, ten, fifteen, twenty bolts. Wes aimed his hand, and lightning flew from the monster in the direction he pointed. The explosions blasted craters in the desert. The show ended as quickly as it began; Wes dropped his arms to his sides and disappeared.

Moments later, he hurtled onto the field on a huge black horse. The moonlight played on horse and rider. He galloped in a circle, then halted. He looked at the corporate strangers, his gaze hard and fierce.

His eyes sought Melissa's as his hand reached toward her. Energy pulsed from it, piercing her soul. She put her hand to her heart and staggered backward. The sensation she'd felt before was multiplied many times.

Wesley screamed, racing the horse toward the buried telephone poles. Blue flames shot from his hands and he blew up the poles: One! Two! Three! He wheeled the horse toward the tower. The horse reared as the structure flew into fragments. Wesley vanished, leaving flaming destruction behind him.

28

WILL PICKED HIS way carefully down the slope behind their camp. Pebbles and ruts made it treacherous walking. He shone a flashlight on the trail, hoping he didn't fall and break his neck. The group followed him through the darkness.

They had been ordered to attend a *party*, which was raging in the open space just below him. Will didn't want to go to a party. He wanted to sit in the *Ashley*, nurse his headache, and try to figure out what the hell happened in that martial arts exhibit.

"It's the Rules," Dr. Brand had said, crashing their morose dinner. "You must observe the Rules or you'll be asked to leave." And, he told them, they were having a party every night, which they were also required to attend.

Their destination, the amphitheater—known as the Pit—was directly behind the Numenon encampment. The Pit was the center of all the Meeting's activities. A low stage with a palm frond sunshade over it backed up to their side of a shallow crater. Grandfather sat at one end of the platform leading the thing with a hand drum and a warbling song. Native musicians rocked on the dais's other end.

Thousands of Indians danced, wearing fringed buckskins, shirts with cascading ribbons, and dresses with jingling metal bits. Some wore wild powwow outfits—*regalia,* he remembered. Betty had schooled them on the correct vocabulary. Their regalia were covered with feathers and cascades, horsehair streamers, with feathered fans on their heads, shoulders, and rumps. Will's headache ratcheted up.

At the end of the platform, a drum that had to be four feet across was set up. Men in feathers and paint sat around it, hitting it with sticks. Other people with handheld drums, flutes, shakers, and every kind of primitive instrument, including *spoons*, played next to the drum. The crashing rhythm assaulted him.

Will initially took a position near Grandfather, making sure the old man registered his presence. He slowly drifted to the side of the crowd, edging his way back to their camp. Will was partly up the hill, about six feet higher than the mob, when his drivers came careening down from the camp carrying … drums and musical instruments … strange ones that Will didn't recognize.

They approached Grandfather and spoke to him, and then stepped up on the podium near the Indian musicians. In moments, the Numenon musicians were part of the gang and the noise level exploded. Will could feel the tension between his people and the Indians dissipate and then disappear.

Betty danced in front of the stage with a group of women. She wore a beaded shawl around her shoulders. Doug was out there doing some kind of stomp that Will had never seen. He was attracting a lot of attention. Grandfather beckoned Doug to climb up on the platform. The two of them danced, looking like they'd worked out a routine.

He crept farther up the hill, aware that his white hair made him very visible; aware that he was probably the only one not having a good time. He couldn't dance—he had no rhythm.

When he saw people turning toward him and scowling, Will clawed his way out of the Pit. The tension between *him* and the others hadn't diminished at all.

Will watched the invisible wall between him and everyone else materialize. People didn't want *him*. They wanted his money, or what he had. His face. His endorsement. An invitation to his house. A job. Not *him*, Will Duane. Every time he forgot that, the wall hit him in the face.

He dashed through their campground and found himself standing in front of Grandfather's shack. He turned right, heading down the rim until he was standing by the trail heading to the horses. Will walked down it a few yards and sat on a boulder. Everything fell on his head.

He couldn't tell anyone what troubled him. A couple of weeks ago, he had received a phone call at work. The caller introduced himself as Harold Reinholder. When Will didn't recognize the name, the man elaborated.

"Harold Reinholder, the Attorney General of the United States."

That got his attention. When Marina dumped him, Will went nuts. He tried to get the authorities to shut down her restaurant in San Francisco and her clinical practices in Woodside and Palo Alto. No one had told him to get lost before. He didn't take it well.

Turned out Marina had friends in high places. Reinholder had called to tell him that because he *had bothered* Marina, the Attorney General's office was going to take a look at Numenon and him.

If he called off the dogs and repaired things for Marina, Reinholder *might* be able to stop the investigation.

After that call, he left work early for the first time in forty years. He stopped harassing Marina and made financial amends. People didn't realize that he *loved* Marina. Everyone thought she was a hooker, but she wasn't. She was a healer, the only person able to touch his pain. He wanted to marry her, but she wouldn't have him.

I can feel something moving. It's like darkening clouds. I don't know what to do.

Numenon had gone through the usual run of legal problems and spats with other companies. They had a patent infringement suit going that had reached the Supreme Court. It was a groundless claim he was sure would be decided in their favor in a few weeks.

Will didn't know that he'd done anything illegal. Numenon did what everyone in Silicon Valley was doing. But how would the Attorney General's office see it?

He would take his medicine, if he'd done something wrong. But what about Betty and Doug? Betty knew everything he'd done and Doug Saunders handled Will's "dirty work." If exposed, Doug would be ruined professionally and probably end up in jail.

Their guilt or innocence wouldn't matter once the media got a hold of the story. He could see his picture on the cover of the news magazines and papers. They'd be splattered all over the TV and Internet. Will was a good guy in the public eye. He'd never been subjected to the destruction the media could dish out.

Anguished, Will jumped up, wavering on the edge of the cliff. If he jumped, all of it would be over.

A calm voice from behind him said, "Will Duane, be still."

The fight went out of him. He turned to see Grandfather. The old man sat on the rock ledge.

"Look out over the desert, Will Duane. The Great One has a gift for you."

The desert was like the belly of a huge snake, soft and encompassing. Animals talked to each other. Stars flung themselves into oblivion.

Someone began to play a violin. It was so beautiful, the music's sadness broke his heart. Will wept. Grandfather laid a hand on his shoulder.

"Good, Will Duane. You are doing very well. Marina would be pleased."

"Marina?" Will's head shot up.

Grandfather smiled. "Yes. She said you would work hard, if you had a reason."

Will slumped. "My life is falling apart. I feel like I'm going to die. No one cares about me. I may spend the rest of my life in prison."

"Yes, Will Duane. Those are very good reasons." Grandfather stroked Will's shoulder. Will deflated. "This is the Meeting, Will Duane. The Play of the Creator, the Great One's way of getting your attention. You are doing very well, my son. You will be ready."

"For what?"

"For our sweat on Thursday. You have to be pure, Will Duane. You are taking a bath now. Not a fun bath, but a very good one. Now listen. The Great One has something to say to you."

They were silent, listening to the violin.

Will felt his chest open and his heart fly out. It flew into the blue velvet sky and danced with the stars. He couldn't see it any more, and still his heart flew higher. It came back to him with a sweet pulsation. He relaxed, peaceful, and felt the glow in his ribcage.

The violin stopped. Will looked at Grandfather, soft and quiet.

"I'll tell you a secret, Will Duane," the shaman smiled. "This world is just the start. Many worlds live beyond it. Many better worlds. Make your peace here, and aim for them."

They walked along the Rim heading back to the Numenon camp.

"Grandfather, I want to die."

The old man nodded and patted him again. "That is very good, Will Duane. You have to want to die before you can want to live. And you need to feel remorse."

They passed Grandfather's lean-to and saw Melissa standing on the Rim with her violin. The old man chuckled at something Will couldn't see.

"Come out of the shadows, Wesley. I will introduce you to your wife."

29

"OKAY, GIRLFRIEND. ALONE at last," Jon Walker sat next to Melissa in the Numenon camp. "I brought this for us."

"What is it?"

"That horse piss that they served us down below. I liberated the remains for further study."

"The drink that made us high?"

"Yes, this is a night to get very high. Can you believe that martial arts show?" He handed her a wine glass full of the stuff. They sipped.

"It's not working. I need something that works tonight, Jon."

"I know. It only makes that racket louder." The powwow was reaching a frenzied pitch. "They're going to do that every night."

"If we don't go, do you think they'll kick us out?" Melissa sounded hopeful.

"If we're lucky." He put his arm around her. "Let's make a deal. Let's not talk about how exhausted we are. Or traumatized by watching Wesley Silverhorse shoot lighting bolts and blow up things. Let's not talk about how bad our culture shock is. Or how we're afraid we won't survive the week. Are you afraid of that?" She nodded. "I don't want to talk about any of that shit. It's bad enough feeling how I feel. Okay?"

"We'll talk about strictly neutral subjects. But you have to put your arm around me if I get scared."

"As trivial and not scary as we can go. So. What shall we talk about?"

Melissa shrugged. "What about us?"

"I don't think that's so trivial. Let's talk about things people don't know about *us* and things we wouldn't tell anyone else. How many people would guess that we're best friends? The MBA prodigy and the gay chef."

"None."

"They don't know about all the dancing trophies we've won. And all the dinners at your house—"

"Mostly with you and 'Rique."

"Yes. When are we going to get it on?"

"What? You're gay."

"True, but that doesn't have to be a problem. I've lusted after you for years."

"What?" She jumped up and he grabbed her arm.

"Nope. You don't get away tonight. This is 'fess up night. We're going to share secrets. That was a big one for me. Now, I think we both agree that this was the most fucked up day of our lives. Yes?"

"Yes."

"But not all of it was bad. What was the most exciting part?"

"Wesley Silverhorse," they said at once.

"Absolutely. He's the sexiest man I've ever seen, including all of them. What do you think?"

She slumped, looking glum. "I agree with you. He's also terrifying."

"That often has to do with sexy. What's sexy about him?"

"*Jon.* Why are we talking about sex and who's sexy? We've just been traumatized."

"That's the best thing to talk about when you're traumatized. A PhD told me that."

"Who?" Her nose crinkled in scorn.

"Dr. Walt on the Afternoon Show. He was talking about fear of flying. The best thing to do is take some porn on the plane with you. Read it when you get scared."

"That's ridiculous."

"No, it's a scientific fact. You can't be sexually aroused and afraid at the same time. Physically impossible. Believe me, Melissa. Dr. Walt said it."

"Really?"

"Yes. You'll feel totally better after this conversation. Now, Silverhorse. You have to tell the truth. What's sexy about him?"

"Everything." The corners of her mouth twitched into a little smile. "I saw him naked before the horse exhibit. I walked into Grandfather's lean-to. He was asleep and jumped up. He wasn't wearing anything."

"Why didn't you tell me? That's a huge 'fess up."

"There wasn't time." She laughed out loud. "There's more."

"What?"

"He had an erection." She nodded, restraining a laugh. She explained, "Men get erections when they're sleeping."

"I *know*, Melissa. But you see Silverhorse naked with an erection and you don't tell me? That's cruel."

"I've never seen an erection before."

"Everyone's seen an erection. Why haven't you seen one?"

"I don't want to talk about this."

"Why not? Why not spend the rest of the week seducing Silverhorse? I will swoon with delight watching."

"I can't seduce anyone, Jon. I'm ugly. No one would want me."

"Melissa, I've wanted to seduce you practically since I met you." He grabbed her arm again. "Surprised? I don't just like men. Dancing with you was like holding an angel."

"Jon, don't do this."

"I have a reason for talking this way. I expect to hear that I'm HIV positive this week. Good ol' Elizabeth 'the Tank' Bright Eagle let it slip by the way she looked at me. So, as the one of us closest to the grave, tell me why you won't go after Silverhorse?"

She glared at him, shaking her head from side to side. "You're not HIV positive, Jon. I'm sure."

"You're sure? Oh, good. Just throw medical science away."

"Dr. Bright Eagle didn't say you were Positive, did she? She just looked at you funny."

"Very funny. Stop stalling. Why don't you want to jump Silverhorse?"

She frowned. "All right, I'll tell you. I'm a virgin. I'm twenty-five years old. I'm *worse* than what Doug said about me. I'm not a lesbian—I'm a virgin."

His head dropped along with his jaw. "*Really?*"

"I know I'll be terrible at it. I'll get an F in Sexual Intercourse. Or even worse, a C."

"That keeps you from attacking the beautiful Silverhorse?"

"That and the fact that we're only here for a week and it's against the Rules and I'm terrified of him and sex."

"Melissa, my dear, did it ever occur to you that he might *like* you being a virgin? They're in high demand in some cultures."

"Oh, Jon, let's not talk about this. It's been an awful day."

"Okay. But I'm not letting you dump me because I told you how I felt about you. I'm not letting you run." He grabbed her shoulders and shook her a little. "Melissa, I don't know why you haven't leapt into the vast pool of sexuality, but remember: you don't know when you're going to die."

All joking gone, he pointed to the vast, star-studded sky and blackness of the desert. "Do you know what I see when I look out there?" She shook her head. "I see my death, Melissa. Right in front of my nose." He snapped his fingers. "That close and that fast.

"I think it's time to give up the virgin princess act and get what you can from life before it's *over*. And I think you should do anything else you want and love to do, too. Starting now." He pulled her to her feet and dragged her toward her RV.

"Jon, stop it. Where are you taking me?"

He wasn't heading to her motor home. One of the chaise lounges had a sleeping bag on it. Jon climbed in. "I want you to do what you did to that horse to me."

"Really?"

"Oh, yes. After today, I want to sing Christmas carols."

She did the thing the Chinese guy taught her to him. He passed out. Melissa sat on a nearby chair, feeling like she'd been hit on the head by an axe.

Death was *that* close. What did she really want to do?

30

MELISSA DASHED INTO the motor home and pulled the plastic vial out of her purse. Entering the bathroom, she took the second vial from her makeup bag. Tense with purpose, she dumped the pills into the toilet and flushed.

She staggered against the bathroom wall, watching the orange dots swirl away. Her hands trembled. She'd been terribly anxious in recent months, going to the doctor only when she started having panic attacks. The medication he gave her took the attacks down a notch. But she'd lived for twenty-five years without taking pills; she could do it again. Whatever was chasing her, Melissa Weir had stopped running. She didn't feel brave watching the toilet refill; she was scared witless.

Turning, she dove under her bed and pulled out her real secret—the covert love that *no one* at Numenon knew about—something she hid deeper than the pills. She carefully opened its case.

Her eyes stroked the rich curved body in the velvet-lined case. She lifted the violin, held it to her chin and bowed it tentatively. Then she tuned it quickly. Melissa had loved the violin since she began to play at age twelve. She was an exceptionally talented pupil; her teacher said she would have been a prodigy if she had started younger. Melissa practiced her violin more than any student her teacher had ever had; and loved every minute of it.

When she applied to the Julliard School of Music in New York when she was fifteen, she was accepted. She recalled her admission audition: she was brilliant and they wanted her with a passion.

But Melissa was a prodigy in more ways than one. Her mind shone as brightly as her musical talent. She was barely sixteen when she went to Carleton College in Minnesota, the "Harvard of the Midwest." She graduated at eighteen and did the MBA program at Harvard in one year. Then she signed with Numenon. The rest was history. She was twenty-five and Will's top hand.

Her artsy-fartsy intellectual parents had wanted her to go to Julliard. She'd be *nothing* if she'd done that. Melissa had been at war with her folks for as long as she could remember. All they had to do was say they liked something and she'd hate it. So she shoved Julliard and what she loved away, especially the violin. She couldn't say why she hated them so, but she did.

She set the instrument aside completely when she was at the Harvard Business School; no time, she rationalized. She resumed playing a year ago. *I'm better than I've ever been.*

With the bow in one hand and the violin in the other, she walked back to the bluff. Stepping close to the edge overlooking the desert, she placed the violin beneath her chin and raised the bow.

In the Pit, the dance and party had broken up, and the drums were quiet. People were returning to their campsites, saying goodnight to friends, and thinking of sleep.

Melissa's playing swelled over the crowds, a delicious bedtime treat. But rather than a sweet taste promising repose, she played her soul in all its complexity and darkness. Her violin was the outlet of her soul's song. No one listening knew what music she was playing; no one was classically schooled. But everyone listened. The sound was irresistible.

Everyone in the Bowl felt the pain of being, the pain of existing. Each knew that a very developed, elevated spirit was playing itself. A heart that hurt more than a human being should have to bear was telling its story.

Wesley froze. He had never heard classical violin—he'd only heard country fiddles playing "Turkey in the Straw." She made these *sounds* come out of the instrument. His breathing deepened and his heart beat quicker; he was riveted by the music and the figure of the woman playing it. Melissa's slender form stood against the night sky. She was enraptured and engulfed by her music.

As she flew through those skies, she heard a *crack!* as something opened above her. She went through it. High above, the gateway was thrown wide and she soared, flowed and rejoiced in the love of the Creator on the other side; it billowed around her in ecstatic grace. She knew that she was blessed to live.

Melissa stood at the edge of the abyss. She saw Grandfather's form. He smiled at her, a brilliant sword of grace. She reached for his outstretched hand. She was disorientated, not on earth or in heaven.

Grandfather said, "Melissa, my daughter, have you met my son?"

She turned to Wesley, who stood next to the shaman, his eyes shining with tears, and his face lit by the rapture she had released. He reached out his hand, taking hers, and they both entered the bliss.

They looked at each other in wonder. She touched his face and said, "*Wesley?* Is that you?"

He reached for his soul mate and held her to him, dissolving in her.

31

WILL WALKED UP to her and said, "That was fantastic, Melissa! I didn't know you played the violin!"

Melissa raised her eyes to him, blinking. She was entwined in Wesley's arms. Grandfather had put them together and they would never be apart. But Will took her hand and pulled her away. She looked around. Wesley was gone. The others led her back into their camp, talking and laughing. Melissa turned around and couldn't see him. He wasn't there.

"Wesley?" she said. But he was gone and her own people surrounded her, laughing about the dance and her violin. They reeked of loud drums and excitement.

"'Wesley?" she said. "Where are you?"

She couldn't sleep. She could still feel him holding her, floating through space, the golden flames billowing around them, caressing them. Her body called him to her, next to her. Her soul cried, "Wesley. Wesley."

In his tent, Wesley burned. They'd snatched her from his arms. He couldn't sleep. Couldn't do anything—without her.

Time passed, and he was in her room. The door was locked, but he was there. Melissa switched on the light. No one was there. But she felt him.

Surrendering, she made him room in her bed. He lay with her, disembodied. Embracing her with his soul, stroking her and loving her. She let his spirit touch her and move and be with her and she loved him back.

Finally, Melissa slept. She dreamed bright dreams of horses and fidelity.

32

"*PLEASE* LET ME in," Andrea stood next to the beat-up truck Enzo had provided for her, begging a stone-faced Indian to let her into the Mogollon Bowl. Three more lined up on each side of him. They all wore black. "I can't go back. It's too far. It's *dark*. Please let me in."

It was the middle of the night—she had no idea what time. Her watch had stopped ages ago. She had bumped over terrifying miles of desert in the pitch black, all alone. The wind had whipped up storms of dust, obscuring her way as much as the darkness. It shrieked and battered her car like a demon bent on driving her back. All that kept her going was the thought of Enzo.

When she reached the knoll that marked the edge of the Bowl, Andrea thought she'd be safe. But the seven men materialized out of nowhere and stopped her. She could hear wild music coming from the other side of the rise in front of her. People were over there. Safety.

"You *have* to let me in!" Andrea was almost hysterical. "I thought you were supposed to welcome people. I'm trying to find out about my great-grandmother. Why don't you believe me?"

They looked at her, as dour as the presidents' faces carved into Mount Rushmore. Enzo had assured her the story about searching for her long lost great-grandmother would work with everyone at the Meeting.

The eyes of the man in front of her went blank, as though his attention was elsewhere. They snapped into focus again and he said, "Okay, you can go in. Most of the Bowl is filled, but you can camp in the back next to 'Fonzo Ramos." Something in the way he said the name told her that wasn't a good place to camp. He fished a piece of paper out of his shirt pocket. "Here are the Rules. Follow them or you'll get kicked out. Unpack your stuff and come back and park out here."

With that frosty welcome, she was permitted to drive into the Bowl. Her headlights illuminated a tangle of tents and lean-tos. The camp was pretty much filled, as the man had said. She found a vacant spot and set about putting up her tent and unloading the truck. The tent opened like an umbrella, which was a good thing. She had no idea how to pitch a tent and no one was around to help her. The pulsating drums and lights in the distance said why: everyone was at a party.

Andrea almost broke her back putting her duffle bag and coolers in the tent. Then she parked her car outside the Bowl as she had been ordered. The men had vanished. She shined her flashlight in big arcs as she stumbled back to her campsite. Cactus loomed like stalking monsters. She dove into her tent and zipped it up, cowering.

The trip had been hellish. She hadn't slept since she ran into Diego Donatore at the Alhambra two days earlier. Enzo's team met her in Las Cruces Airport as planned. There were five of them, all looking like supermodels heading out for a shoot in the desert. Three guys and two women, in two campers and the truck she was driving. They drove for hours on paved roads, then more hours off-road.

Shivering in her tent, Andrea kept thinking about the drive in. Her companions started getting sick when they got close to the Bowl. Why? Was it radioactive or something? Enzo hadn't told her about that. But she didn't get sick. Why did they? What was different about them? They were certainly weird enough.

How could they get her reports if they were miles away, rolling on the ground throwing up? She'd have to drive all the way back to their camp to let them know what she found. Like hell she'd do that.

Enzo said they would be there to protect her, no matter what. But unless they got better really fast, they wouldn't be any help at all. She was stuck in the wilderness with no backup, a spy surrounded by thousands of hostile Indians. She had to find the Numenon camp—which shouldn't be hard if theirs were the only RVs in the Bowl. But how was she supposed to infiltrate them and reach Will Duane? Given the reception the "friendly" Indians had given her when she got there, was making friends with Will Duane's people going to be as easy as Enzo had said? No.

What else had Enzo told her that wasn't the truth?

33

WES WAS EXHAUSTED. When he did a martial arts exhibit, he often slept for a full twenty-four hours afterward. The previous night, he'd slept only when he had projected his consciousness into Melissa's room. Worse, the countdown that soul mates felt after touching their beloveds had begun. If he didn't marry Melissa in the next hour, he thought he'd explode.

Wesley launched himself across the vast inner courtyard of the Numenon camp to a table where Melissa sat. With the carpet and flags and oversized furniture, Wesley had never been in a more intimidating place. He reached her table, smiled at Melissa, and nodded at Jon.

"Hi! I smelled the coffee." His voice sounded assured and confident, not like the bozo he felt he was. "May I sit down?"

Melissa responded, "Oh, sure. Join me for breakfast. I'm having Jon's cholesterol special, what would you like?"

"I'll have the same," Wes said, smiling as though he knew what cholesterol was. "And some coffee."

"Coming up," Jon said and went back to his duties.

Wesley looked around and realized that he had entered another universe. A carved wooden wall stood behind the dance floor. An outdoor kitchen was set up near their table with a serving area and everything a restaurant would have. Jon handed Wes a mug of coffee.

The mug was ivory porcelain banded in gold with the Numenon logo, also in gold, embossed on it. It told him that he didn't belong there better than a printed sign. His feeling of inferiority handled his embarrassing attraction to Melissa better than anything could. He shrank, as the reality of Numenon impressed itself on him.

"Hi." Melissa watched him sit down, looking soft and sweet. He couldn't believe their souls had spent the night together. She echoed his feelings. "I don't know what to say. This has been the most amazing time. Is it always like this at the Meeting?"

Wes smiled. "Pretty much, though I've never met anyone like you before."

A tiny smile parted her lips. This was hard going; he wanted to hold her hand so badly. Gathering his courage, he reached out and took her hand, looking at her intently.

Touching Melissa both calmed and excited him. The physical sensations flowing all over him told him that it was true—she *was* his soul mate.

When Melissa felt his touch, her mind stopped. Something came from him, into her, something delicious and comforting and wonderful. She blushed. It made her want to do things she'd never done before; made her want to lie down with him, open herself to him, let him come inside her. She wanted him to *love* her. Her breath lengthened the longer he held her hand.

Finally, she forced herself to say, "Wesley, what is it? What is *that?*"

He kept looking at her as though she was the most beautiful woman in creation.

"We're soul mates, Melissa. We can really feel it in the Bowl."

Melissa was breathing deeply, her chest rising and falling. She had to do something. "Wesley, I don't even know you. I'm a very conservative person. I'm really conservative about ..." She couldn't say "sex." She couldn't believe what she was about to say. "I've never said or done anything like this, but would you like to go into my bedroom with me?"

He pulled his hand away. "I can't do that—I'm a spirit warrior." He looked appalled. "This is a sacred thing. People are lucky if they ever find their soul mates." He looked as though he was going to get up and leave, but Jon arrived with their breakfasts.

"Is everything okay?" Jon approached the table with a platter in each hand. "I can come back."

"No, everything's fine, Jon. We're starved."

Setting the dishes down, he said, "Two cholesterol specials. Three egg omelets with bacon, cheese, avocado, and onions, with extra bacon on the side." The plates were garnished with fresh salsa and slices of papaya. "I've got more fruit if you want it. I'm bringing croissants and fresh corn bread. Okay?"

"More than okay, Jon," Melissa said.

Wes looked at the plates as though he'd never seen food before. Melissa gathered that food was in short supply at his house. He tasted his omelet as if in wonder.

"Do you eat like this every day?" he asked.

Melissa smiled. "Not me, but Will does. Jon is his private chef. Wesley, I didn't mean to suggest anything wrong. It's just that," she looked down and took a deep breath, "what I feel for you is so strong, that I almost can't resist it. It's painful when you touch me. I just want to—do something about it."

"You have to admit that our getting married would be stupid."

Wesley cringed.

She looked into his beautiful eyes. *He's so talented and gorgeous. We could work something out.* "I mean, we don't know each other. We're from different worlds." He took her hand back, stroking her arm. She shivered and pulled away.

"Please don't do that! I melt when you do that. Tell me about this soul mates stuff."

Wes ate carefully, as though he was using his best manners. Speaking slowly, and keeping his mouth as shut as much as possible while eating, he told her how the energy flow between soul mates guides them to each other, and how, once having touched, they would burn until they consummated their relationship.

"We could do what you suggested, except that I'm a spirit warrior. One of our rules is that we don't have sex until married. We get the energy to do some of the things we do because we don't have sex." Wes looked down, obviously embarrassed. "I've been with Grandfather since I was six." He smiled and shrugged. "Most everyone here knows about me. They leave me alone."

"Then you're a …" *Was it possible that Jon was right last night?* Would he like her more because she was a virgin? Like him?

"Yeah. I don't usually talk about it. It's not how twenty-two year old Indian men are supposed to be." He looked like he was asking for her forgiveness. This time she took *his* hand.

"Or twenty-five year old women from Silicon Valley," Melissa blurted out. "So what you're saying is that, this hunger for each other is going to keep growing until we have sex, and you won't have sex with me until we marry?"

Wes nodded.

"That seems coercive. I mean, I wasn't looking for anything like that when I came here."

"You weren't?"

Melissa realized she had been praying for nothing but a dream lover for most of her adult life. She just hadn't expected him to be a beautiful Native American with supernatural powers and no education.

Wesley reached into his pocket as Jon took the plates. He pulled out a beaded suede bag.

"Oh. Look at that!" said Jon, appearing behind them.

The bag was beaded with tiny black, silver, white, and blue beads. Fine fringe flowed from the bottom.

"That is beautiful, Wes!" Melissa said.

"I made it. It's for you. Look inside."

Jon hung around, waiting to see.

"Look!" Melissa said. "A silver belt buckle. It's like yours!" She stood up to put it on her belt.

"There's more. Look inside the bag." A gold and silver ring with running horses and diamonds fell into her palm. Wesley took the ring and placed on her ring finger, giving her no opportunity to put it on any other. His touch was like an electric shock. The ring continued it, pulsating.

She asked, "Did you make these things?"

"Yeah. I do silver and jewelry. So did my dad. Not as good as me."

Well, Melissa thought, not as *well* as I do.

"*Well* as I do," he corrected himself.

"Did you read my mind?"

"Yeah. It's easy in the Bowl."

"Well, let me think about it. Shall we talk tonight? You'll have a busy day. If Will wants to hire you, they'll give you the personnel packet. It's a lot of tests that everyone at Numenon has to take. That will give them a good idea of what your aptitudes are and where to place you. If you show some special ability, they'll test you more."

She touched his shoulder and left her hand there, letting them both feel the energy throbbing through them. He leaned into her. After few moments, both were breathing deeply and had half-closed eyes. Melissa broke it off.

"You'll be busy until twelve for sure. Most likely until three. Meet you then?"

"By the horses."

"Perfect."

"Melissa?"

"Yes?"

"May I kiss you?"

She sat still and he leaned over to her. His lips felt the way the soft inner parts of rose petals would if she stroked them. He smelled the same way, fresh and clean, soft. Melissa wanted to go into her room with him more than she'd ever wanted anything in her life. His hand touched her side, brushing her breast.

"Oh … Oh … my *God*," she gasped. Melissa pulled away and said, "Maybe, when you're done with the tests, you *should* talk to Grandfather about marrying us. I don't think I can stand this."

34

"SHIT! WHAT IS *that?*" Doug peered into the mirror, touching his chest with his fingers and looking at something on his skin. He went into the main cabin where there was a big mirror and turned on the lights.

They were all over him. His chest, his back. He pulled off his pants. *I slept in my clothes last night?* Must have. He didn't remember. Yeah, they were on his ass, between his legs, on his legs. Everywhere. What were they? He remembered that Silverhorse guy had them, too. Doug threw on some clean jeans and a shirt and ran out to him and Melissa.

He stormed up to them, nodding at Melissa. "Hi, Melissa. Say, Wesley, can I talk to you? In there?" He took Wes into his motor home. He pulled off his shirt and said, "Look. What is this shit?"

Wesley's eyes widened. He looked at Doug as if he was a freak.

Doug raised his arm. "Look. They're everywhere, all over me. What does it mean? You have them, too. I saw them. They look like brands."

"They're spirit marks. If the Spirits are pleased with you, they'll come to you when you're in a trance state and touch you. That's what they leave.

"They are brands. They're claiming you as their own. They're taking your soul, parts of your soul, for themselves. You will begin to do their work in the world."

Wes regarded Doug carefully, as though he was a stranger. "Did you feel it when they touched you?" Wes asked.

Doug nodded and told him what happened at the dance. "I could feel it, but didn't know what was happening. Grandfather said that I'm waking up. What does that mean? I've always felt awake."

Wes smiled. "There's awake and there's *awake*. People go around looking alive, looking awake, when in fact they are asleep or dead inside. Here, people wake up to who they really are. That's what's waking up: you."

Doug looked at himself in the mirror. "Will I always look like this?"

"No. They'll fade. Mine just come out when the Power is on me." Wes opened his shirt; his Spirit Marks were blazing. "Excitement brings them out."

Something inside Doug looked back at Wes and nodded. Doug's nostrils flared. He knew why Wesley was flushed.

"You've found her?" The voice speaking to Wes was slower and steadier than Doug's normal voice.

Wes regarded Doug carefully. "Yes."

The emerging being in Doug breathed harder, nodding slowly himself. His woman was out there, too. There was much to do, he had slept too long. He put his shirt back on and tucked it in. Looking at Wes, he said, "Good."

Wes looked at Doug carefully. "You're one of us," he said in a language that Doug had never heard. He understood it, though. Then Wes said, "Welcome home."

They left the motor home. Walking back to the table, the awakening being inside of Doug saw Melissa and said to Wes, "She's a very good woman. She'll make a good wife. You should watch out though; don't get her mad. She'll hurt you when she's mad."

As they sat down, good old Doug Saunders from Numenon popped back. He grinned at Melissa, and continued the conversation the other Doug had begun. "Yeah. I made a move on her and she broke my nose! And that was just for starters." Wes's eyes widened. "Tell him about it, Weir. He should know you're a terror. Tell him!"

Melissa blushed. "I'm sorry, Doug. I overreacted."

"No, you did the right thing. I was drunk and out of bounds. I apologize. But you pack a wallop. You should have a warning printed on you." He turned to Wes. "She knocked me across the room. Broke my jaw, front teeth. Black eyes. Concussion. Lots of time in the hospital, plastic surgery. What did you hit me with, anyway?"

"I don't know, Doug. There wasn't any blood on me or weapons in the room. The police wanted to know what hit you, too." She pulled away.

Doug ducked his head.

"You know what happened—the paramedics took you to the hospital, and your friends called the cops. I was charged with felony assault."

Doug flushed.

"But when it came out that you grabbed my breasts first, that made it sexual assault. So *you* were charged. Will handled that for you. And *then*, as soon as you could, you told everyone I was a bull dyke who decked you because you suggested a quickie." Her lips quivered. "That's made the last six months fun, Doug."

"It wouldn't make any difference to me if she was a lesbian," Jon stuck his nose in. "I've heard how you've slandered her."

Melissa got up and ran to her motor home.

Wes followed her, sickened by what he'd heard. He knocked on the door. "Melissa," he said softly. "Can I come in?"

She let him in; the cabin was dark. She looked away. "That's how it is at Numenon. Talk about sex and quickies and … what they do all the time, all of them, Will, Doug, everyone." She wiped her eyes.

Wes didn't know what to do. If it were anyone else, he would have held her. "Can we go in your room to talk, Melissa?"

She shook her head and looked up at him. "I can't do that. I can't be in a closed space with a man."

Wes smiled. "Then let's talk outside."

She and Wes walked around the back of the motor home. "I'm so tired, Wes. And I feel crazy."

He wanted to hold her and comfort her, but didn't want to make their attraction situation any worse. He kept his distance and said, "Feelings get stronger in the Bowl, Melissa, mostly so we can resolve them. I don't think Doug and Jon are bad people. I think you're going to be very surprised by Doug soon. He made a mistake. Just like you did when you asked me to go to your room. That hurt me, Melissa, and you're not a bad person."

She nodded.

Through the window, Wes saw Will Duane sitting at a table. "It's time for me to talk to Mr. Duane."

"You're on, Wes. Give it your best shot."

35

WILL TUGGED AT the top button of his shirt, trying to relieve the heaviness in his chest. He'd go running in a few minutes. Get in front of it. Will scraped his fingers through his hair again. *Come on, come on. Get over it. Think.*

The mine was the answer. If he could produce the new nanoquartz-based computer chips before his competitors and tie up the market, he could buy off the Feds no matter what they did. The world would forgive anything if enough money changed hands.

To make the chips, he needed ultra-pure quartz that could be broken into almost microscopic particles. That was found in large quantities on one place on the planet: next to this miserable Bowl on the Indians' holy lands. He had to close the mine deal with Grandfather.

But he couldn't. Every time he thought about talking to the shaman, he could see Wesley Silverhorse throwing blue lightning. *That's* why Grandfather had let them see that show. The old fox was ahead of him.

But if Wesley worked for *him* …

He had to hire Silverhorse. And he was going to right now.

*

Will expected Wesley to give them a sales spiel, talking up how hard what he did was so that he could negotiate more money—this interview was about hiring him, after all.

"I can't do what I did last night by myself." Wesley turned to Will. "The Great One does it, not me. If you wanted to hire me to do things like you saw yesterday, you can't. I wouldn't do them for money, and I couldn't do them even if I wanted to. The Power doesn't care about money or what anyone wants."

Will was dumbfounded. "You can't do *that* whenever you want to?"

"No. I can do it in the Bowl, because of what the Bowl is and because Grandfather and the other warriors are here. I couldn't do it anywhere else."

"So what good is it?"

Wesley shrugged. "I think that if a real need arose outside the Bowl—something that the Great One wanted done—I could use my Powers. But I don't know, because I haven't tried. I only do what Grandfather tells me to do."

"You wouldn't do any of what you showed us without his permission?"

"No. And if I tried to use the Power without it, I don't think it would come."

Will had planned on hiring Wesley for corporate espionage and security—he would be priceless. He also wanted to buy Grandfather's loyalty by employing his favorite.

"If someone wanted to hire me to spy or to do something the Great One didn't consider worth doing, it would be a waste of money." Wesley said, foiling Will's plans.

"I think Grandfather showed us to you so you would know who he has available for friends. If I'm going to work for you, Grandfather has to approve. I'm supposed to stay with him after the Meeting unless he tells me to do something else."

Will realized why Grandfather had given them the martial arts demo: so that Will would know the power he could command. The mine deal would never happen; he'd been outmaneuvered. It was a nice piece of negotiation without a word spoken.

Melissa broke in. "I'm going to Grandfather's lecture; it's supposed to start in a few minutes. Wesley, remember what I said about standardized tests."

He nodded. "I'll meet you by the horses when I'm done." Wesley's smile was dazzling.

He's in love with her! Melissa would break his heart; she's way over his head. But he was such a good-looking kid. When Melissa returned Wes's smile, Will was shocked. *Uh-oh. It's mutual.*

After Melissa left, Will continued interviewing Wesley. "How about training horses for me?"

"I would love to do that."

Will remembered what Melissa said about the wild horses. If verified, what she suggested about the history of the Indians' horses would be a major archeological find. It would prove out, he was certain. He wanted the Numenon mustangs.

Will continued. "You said that your wild horses are in danger. Tell me more about that."

"Mustangers have found the herds—we have two of them." Wes gave Will and Betty an expanded version of what he said previously. "If they find out what they really can do, they'll be rounded up right away. We need a safe place for them."

"How many are there?" Will asked.

"About three hundred total."

"That's no problem. My ranch in Montana is perfect. There's a big house, a barn, horse facilities, and everything. You might have seen it in *Architectural Digest* last year." He'd bought the ranch to keep Cass out of trouble. That didn't work, but maybe Cass would get interested in the mustangs. Maybe they would save her.

Wes's face said he'd never heard of *Architectural Digest*. "How big is the ranch?"

"Oh, about four hundred fifty thousand acres, give or take." Will shrugged. "I bought a couple of ranches owned by celebrities. They found out Montana was a long way from Hollywood during the first winter. Your horses should love it. They'll be completely safe."

When he heard "four hundred fifty thousand acres," Wes's face went blank. Will smiled. *Good. The kid is learning what can happen if you work for the richest man in the world.*

"Would you be interested in relocating to Montana, Wes? You could train the horses up there. You might be able to manage the ranch, eventually."

"I would do that, Mr. Duane. Is there anything for Melissa to do there?"

Betty and Will stared at him.

"What do you mean?" Betty asked.

"We're getting married today."

"You're *what?*" Will said. "You haven't known each other twenty-four hours!"

Wes nodded. "That's true …" He seemed to struggle to find the right words. "It's something that happens at the Meeting; people find their soul mates and get married right away. Melissa and I are soul mates."

Will nodded. He'd seen them come out of the motor home beaming. They were a thing already. *But they'll blow it off by the end of the week. Wes was a looker; can't blame Melissa.*

Make Melissa happy. He decided to humor Wesley and keep the romance going.

"I need you up in Montana. And, no, there's nothing for Melissa to do there. She's got a contract with me in Palo Alto. You'll have to live separately if you get married."

"Do you have anything for me in Palo Alto?"

Will hated to break up the lovebirds, but he couldn't see any use for Wes except as a horse trainer. He wouldn't hire anyone unless they filled some corporate need. He thought of Melissa's smile when she said goodbye to Wes. He'd never seen her so happy. *Oh, make her happy. She's as close to a daughter as I'll get.*

"We had horses on my estate in Woodside years ago, but none since. I might get something going again with the mustangs; we could do a show or exhibit. I'd hire you to lead that, but I don't know how fast we can get it organized." Will searched his mind. "Wes, tell me about yourself. What you can do besides horses and martial arts?"

"Well, I did really good … *well* … in school, but I dropped out after my sophomore year."

"Oh …" Will deflated in his chair. *How could Melissa marry a high school dropout? And what did he have for him to do?*

Wes hastened to say, "I didn't want to quit, but my dad got killed. My mom needed my help with my brothers and sisters and running the ranch, so I had to drop out." Wes looked down.

"That's terrible, Wesley. What happened to your father?" Betty asked.

"He was bull-clowning—you know, in rodeos? The clowns keep the bulls off the cowboys if they're thrown. A bull went after a guy who got tied up in the rigging. My dad went in to save him, but the bull got him." He added, "The cowboy was okay, though."

Wes looked down. "My brothers and sisters all got to finish high school. They're doing … *well.*"

"How many are there?" Will asked.

"Six. Three sisters and three brothers. The last one left last summer." He looked down again. "None of them wanted to stay on the ranch. I was kind of hoping one or two would stay. It's a lot to do with just Mom and me."

Betty said, "You take care of a whole *ranch* by yourself?"

"Yes, ma'am. With my mom. I hire a hand when I have money."

"How old were you when your father died?"

"Fifteen."

"How old are you now?"

"Twenty-two."

"You've worked the ranch by yourself for *seven years?*"

"The kids helped Mama and me after school. It was hard, but we got by."

"Son, if you could do anything you wanted, what would that be?" Will asked. He wanted to do something for this kid.

Wes looked like he not only hadn't been asked what he wanted to do before, he'd never asked himself. "Well, I'd like to marry Melissa, first of all. Then I'd like to go to college. I know I can do it. I'd like to study something that could help my People, and I'd like to do something with horses, too."

Will looked at Betty. If there was ever a kid who deserved a break, it was this one.

"Okay, Wesley. Take the tests. Let's see how you score and talk some more this afternoon." He remembered something. "Can we take a look at your silver jewelry, too?"

"Yes. That's the other thing I do. Silver. I made all the buckles for the Horse Masters. And the pins." He touched his throat to indicate where they wore them. "I made most of the silver jewelry that Elizabeth wears. I have some new stuff with me."

Will felt like buying the whole lot sight unseen.

Wes beat him to it. "I'd be glad to show you my work, but I need to talk to Melissa before I sell any."

Betty and Will laughed.

"She's your business manager! You got a good one! Okay, show it to me when she's here." Will excused himself, saying, "I'll let Betty do her job. I'm going to go on a run. I'll be back in an hour or so."

36

ANDREA OPENED HER eyes; her lids hurt. So did the rest of her. She lay on top of a sleeping bag in a tent, fully dressed. Her hand fell to the side and felt rubbery fabric. She jerked up, looking around in panic. The sides of the tent became a tarp that covered the floor; the bottom was sealed. Thank God! Nothing could get in. Snakes might have crawled in while she slept, or black widow spiders. Maybe other terrible things, like scorpions or ticks; ticks carried very serious diseases.

Her chest heaved as she recalled where she was and how she got there. Why was she on this crazy mission? The computer screen with her new bank balance flashed in her mind's eye. The $300,000 Enzo put in her bank account was one reason. And her new job. Then there was Enzo's smile. The way she felt when he touched her. Their future.

She rolled on to her hands and knees and examined the stuff she'd pulled into the tent the night before: four ice chests of food, a duffle bag with clothes, an airbed that she had been too exhausted to inflate, and a cot she hadn't set up.

And her laptop. Great! The fact that the supermodels were use-less wouldn't get in her way. She could e-mail her reports to Enzo. She opened it up and hit the power switch. The screen flashed, made a little *fizz*, and went dark. Sparks came out of the keyboard, and then smoke.

She recoiled, staring at the dead computer.

Andrea lunged for the tent's zipper and struggled to open it. She clawed her way out and looked around. She was on one edge of a shallow crater with a perfect view of the whole bowl. The ramshackle shelters extended all the way to the other side; it had to be miles away. *This* was the sacred Mogollon Bowl? She ducked back inside her tent and grabbed the binoculars she'd seen.

There, on a rise on the other side of the Bowl, were a bunch of motor homes in a circle. She studied them. That was the Numenon camp. Pennants sporting the Numenon logo flew between the vehicles. Palm trees filled the spaces between the RVs, shielding the Numenon team from the chaos outside.

Andrea smiled. That was Will Duane, classy all the way. And on the other side of the frigging bowl from her. She'd have to walk miles to make contact. Her mouth tightened. How could she get over there? How would she get back?

She looked away, eyes traveling to her left. Not very far away, a dark man sat by a fire in front of a ragged tent. She smelled coffee. A metal pot sat on a grill over a fire. That was enough to motivate her. She walked over to him.

"Hi, I'm Andrea Beckman." She held out her hand and smiled. She froze when she got a good look at him.

He ignored her hand, and *sneered* at her. "Y're s'posed to be at Grandfather's talk. It's the Rules." He was a very dark Indian, nose like a hatchet. Terrible scars ran down the left side of his face. He was skinny and wore torn jeans and a dirty cowboy shirt. His hair hung in greasy braids. She recoiled when his odor hit her.

He glared at her and refilled his coffee mug. He didn't offer her any. A frying pan containing bacon, eggs, and fried potatoes sat next to the coffee pot. Saliva filled her mouth. Her stomach growled. She was really hungry.

He glowered at her. "Bring anything to trade?"

"What do you mean?"

"Food." He looked at her like she was the stupidest person in the world. "Y'know. To trade for my food."

"I've got four ice chests. I don't know what's in them."

"Y'should have somethin' to trade in 'em." He narrowed his eyes. "Why don't y'know what's in yer own stuff?"

"I came at the last minute. My friends packed for me." Her stomach growled again. "I didn't see what they put in my duffle bag."

He snorted in derision, but said, "Y'have a plate?"

"I don't know." She started to go back in the tent to look for one.

"Nah. I got two." He handed her a metal plate. She tried not to think about how clean it was. "Have some coffee."

The way his hand snaked out when he grabbed the pot's handle alarmed her. He was so quick. She couldn't get away from him if she had to. He gestured at a rock and she sat on it, checking it for scorpions or snakes before taking a seat.

He was silent. She devoured the food, sneaking looks at her companion. Black eyes, brown skin, snarling face. A badass motherfucker if she'd ever seen one. Even homeless people in Berkeley weren't as down and out as him. Or as angry.

"You're not at Grandfather's talk, either," she remarked.

He grunted and went back to drinking his coffee.

She sat there, feeling stupid. "Is everyone at Grandfather's talk?"

He looked at her like she was stupid.

"When will they be back?"

He jerked his head toward the depression on the other side of the Bowl. With the binoculars, she could see tiny figures jammed inside it. "When he's done."

He made her so nervous that she kept babbling, giving him her spiel about searching for her roots, finding out about her great-grandmother, and being so glad to discover Grandfather. "Is he the real thing?" she said, trying to sound enthusiastic.

He looked her up and down. "As real as you."

She had the same feeling she did with the men trying to keep her from entering the Bowl the night before. He saw right through her. "Well, I'm real, so he must be." He didn't answer.

Andrea blushed and looked around, trying to think of something that would alleviate the embarrassment she felt around this nasty man. "What's your name?"

"'Fonzo. 'Fonzo Ramos." He took a round tin out of his pocket and put something into his mouth. "This is my territory. The back of the Bowl."

"You *own* this area?"

"I been t' 'most ev'ry Meeting. People know t'stay away unless they're my friends. An' they know to behave."

He spat a stream of dark liquid into the fire and turned his back on her. She could see his ribs through his shirt.

Andrea looked into the Bowl, thinking of how to get away. She couldn't get to Grandfather's talk in time. It was miles away.

She decided to organize her things and see what the models had packed for her. She crawled back into her tent and pawed through her stuff.

The clothes looked like designer sportswear from a top Parisian salon. It would look terrific on a runway, but stupid in real life. All of it was cut a little too tight, and too low. They'd packed the sexiest underwear she'd ever seen. Open crotches and worse. Andrea took a deep breath and let it out. She'd be the slut of the Mogollon Bowl.

Okay. She would deal with that. What did she have to eat?

She opened one of the chests and stared, aghast. Opened the next, and the next. Then the last one. They were stuffed with bags of lettuce.

Romaine, butter, mixed Italian. Lettuces she'd never heard of. Of course the models looked the way they did; this is what they ate.

Could she trade the lettuce for anything? There had to be more food. Andrea dug under the lettuce in one of the chests. The bottom half of it was full of cuts of meat wrapped in white paper. Big cuts. She opened the paper and pulled away. It didn't smell too fresh.

Great. Lettuce and rotting meat. Too tight clothes and a dead laptop. Maybe there was something she could do about the laptop. The Numenon people were here. Who knew how many were techies?

She picked the laptop up and carried it out to 'Fonzo. "Do you know how to fix laptops?"

He snorted into his coffee, laughing. "Do I *look* like I fix computers?" He regarded the smoke-streaked case and shook his head. "It's dead. You can't use anything electronic in the Bowl. Everyone knows that."

"I didn't know." She stood, helpless and close to tears, as a beat-up golf cart pulled up in a whoosh of dust. The driver jumped out. He was short and thick, dwarfish.

"Hi, 'Fonzo!" he called, beaming and waving. He had a puppy-dog earnestness that would have been cute if he wasn't so pathetic. He wore a Western shirt with fuchsia and turquoise coyotes all over it and hiked his jeans up as he walked. He was one of those guys whose crack showed when he bent down. *Stop it, Andrea. He's handicapped.* He wasn't really a dwarf, either. Short and stumpy, he waddled toward 'Fonzo. But he stopped directly in front of her.

"Hi," he said. "I'm Willy Fish. I came to get you. Grandfather wants to meet you, right now. I'm going to drive you all week. In this cart. He told me that was my job." He beamed like that was the best news in the universe.

She blinked and nodded vigorously. "I'm Andrea Beckman. I got here late last night. This was the only spot I could find."

"Oh, don't worry. 'Fonzo will let you stay. He likes pretty girls." The squat man smiled. Andrea smiled back.

The other occupant of the golf cart got out of the passenger seat and walked toward her. Tall and lanky, he wore new indigo jeans with a crease ironed down the front. His shirt was a subdued gray stripe. She recognized it from Ralph Lauren's latest collection. He removed his dove gray Stetson and nodded at her. His silver-flecked hair was cropped stylishly short. He looked like a Native American banker.

"I'm Paul Running Bird," he said, holding out his hand.

Her eyes almost bugged out. He was the one who gave the Numenon party the bad map that got them lost. But Enzo had charged her to seek him out as a possible ally. Well, she needed one now.

"Andrea Beckman." She took the proffered hand. "I got here late last night. This was the only spot I could find. I didn't know that 'Fonzo had the area tied up."

Paul smiled, courtly and polite. "Oh, I'm sure 'Fonzo won't mind if you stay here." He looked at 'Fonzo. "You don't mind, do you?"

'Fonzo shrugged and went back to spitting in the fire.

"See. All set. This is actually a very good place to camp. Out of the fray," he sniffed and waved toward the bustling campground. "The only place that's better is over there where the Numenon people are, with Grandfather, of course. He gave *them* the best spot." His voice had an edge. "Willy's got the cart for the whole Meeting, so he can ferry you around. And I'll be up here a lot." He smiled at her, taking in her figure.

Andrea smiled back. "Well, good. We'll be seeing each other."

"We gotta go now," Willy insisted. "Grandfather's waiting."

"I have to put my computer away. It's broken."

"I can fix it." Willy held out his hand.

"You can fix it?"

Paul's deep voice seconded Willy. "Willy can fix anything. He'll fix half the cars in the parking lot when the Meeting's over." He cast a doubtful eye on the computer, despite his words. The top looked lightly barbecued.

"I can fix it, but you shouldn't use it here." Willy's face was so earnest. *He's too dumb to lie. And he's really sweet.* "Come on! Grandfather's waiting. He won't start his talk without you."

"Really?"

"Yeah. He knows you're here."

37

ANDREA SLATHERED SUNSCREEN over her arms and face as they headed toward the Pit. She tied the hat to her head with a scarf. The supermodels got something right with the sunscreen and hat; she could fry in this sun. She attached a canteen of water to her belt. She was prepared for anything.

Willy Fish leaned forward, hands barely reaching the cart's steering wheel; he had to stretch to use the pedals. Andrea grabbed the rail holding up the cart's roof. The vehicle was old and its seats were torn up. It had just a roof and a cracked plastic windshield, no sides or anything. The thing *hauled*. They jolted across the Bowl, the Pit and its crowds growing closer each instant.

She didn't have time to question Willy about how Grandfather knew she was there. And why he wanted to see her so badly. When they topped the rim of the Pit, her stomach sank. She'd never seen so many people; well, yeah at Edwards Stadium for her Berkeley graduation. That held 22,000. But even jammed with happy almost-graduates, Edwards didn't seem as wild as this.

She took in the semi-circular arrangement of the seats and benches. The aluminum-legged, modern sunshades; the palm-fronded traditional ones; the tribal markers of skins and totems dilineating territories. The musty smell of thousands of bodies in the heat made her wrinkle her nose. The rest made her dizzy: brightly colored clothing. Movement. Conversation. Noise.

Willy drove along the side of the seating area straight to the front of the Pit, by-passing the audience. That was when she saw him. He was sitting cross-legged in the middle of a stage, a tiny, white-haired figure. In the surging crowd, he was the one still point. His outline was distinct, as though the air around him was super-charged. His form was more than distinct; it sang. A force radiated from him, touching her.

Not for one moment did she regard Grandfather the way Enzo had described him—as a kindly old man, a charlatan. He turned toward them and his eyes fell on her. She felt like something shot from them, something piercing. She couldn't hide anything from him. He *knew*.

"We're here," Willy announced loudly as the cart slid to a stop. "You sit here, Miss Andrea. Grandfather wants to talk to you afterward."

She sat, feeling lightheaded. Nothing made sense. Enzo and the castle. The money he gave her. Her job. This place. Him. She looked at Grandfather. He paid no attention to her, yet she knew he was acutely aware of her presence. Something moved inside her, like he'd injected something into her with that penetrating look.

They were a little late. People were passing sheets of paper back through the rows. Grandfather had been talking about something.

"The Rules matter," the shaman waved a paper over his head. "If you attain anything this week, it will be because you followed the Rules. They were given to me by Great-grandfather. They hold the power of my lineage.

"If you break the Rules, I will know." His eyes were innocent. "Don't wonder *how* I know; I will *know*. And we will have a talk, and you will stay or leave. Usually, leave."

His expression changed just the tiniest bit, and Andrea knew that he could be terrifying. She didn't want to have "a talk" with him about anything, ever. They'd given her the Rules when she'd arrived, but she had tossed them aside. Now Andrea took a sheet when it was passed to her and read it quickly.

"Everyone comes here for *one* reason," he said as he looked around. "Because they feel an emptiness inside. A hole where their hearts should be. They sense that the hole can be filled with something, and that I know what it is. They sense that I can give it to them. That is what people come to this old Indian to find."

Andrea sat motionless. That was it. Exactly what she wanted. To have the emptiness inside filled. She heard him talking, but what he said went in like a stone thrown into a deep pond. It went straight to the bottom, where it stayed. Even so, she could hear and remember what he said.

"What do I have that people want? Love. That's all. I love everyone. That's the great gift Great-grandfather and the Ancestors gave me. They cracked me like an egg and showed me where love is. And what love is. They showed me how to show it to others."

Abruptly, his posture changed and he became serious. "We are talking about love, but something else is here." He searched the crowd as though he were sniffing something out. "A *question* is here.

"New people have come with a question for me." His eyes scanned the crowd rapidly. "There—you! And you, and you, and you. Come up here." He pointed to the dirt before the stage. "That way I can see you." He chuckled. "I'm old, you know. I need people to keep me on my toes. I might be up here passing air." He made a farting sound. "Maybe that's all this old man has to give. Let's see. Come here.

"I love new people, even if they don't love me—yet. I let them come to the Meeting. Some might say that is not very smart. They might be enemies ...," He shrugged.

From the center of the crowd and toward the rear, seven young men made their way to the front. They were dressed in leggings with colorful shirts belted with leather. They all wore knives. Andrea noted that the

Rules did not prohibit traditional weapons. She saw knives and hatchets on the belts of people around her.

The men moved together, their eyes narrowed and filled with … hatred. They huddled together. As they approached the stage, a mutter arose. Who were these strangers?

Andrea felt the anxiety. Why did Grandfather let them come so close? They were young and vigorous; Grandfather was so old. When they arrived at the stage, Tyler Brand, whom she recognized from the briefing she'd read, and a huge tattooed man jumped up and stood in front of Grandfather.

"Sit down, my friends," Grandfather said to his protectors. "These nice boys do not want to hurt me."

Smiling, he waved his warriors away and said to the leader of the young men, "You have come to ask me a question. You are studying with an indigenous Teacher who is *the real thing*. He told you to expose me as a fake. What is the question he gave you?" The shaman stood with surprising grace and walked along the edge of the platform, searching their eyes.

Andrea was afraid. This wasn't part of the proceedings. Violence rippled through the soft haze Grandfather had created.

"What is it you wish to ask me?" He stood before the leader.

"How can you say you're an *Indian?*" the man spat. He said more in a language Andrea didn't understand. Some people in the crowed gasped. The spirit warriors jumped up.

"No, my friends. He's just showing us his manners." He explained to the crowd, "He said some very bad things about my mother." Grandfather narrowed his eyes, but his smile remained.

The young man flew into the air, arms overhead, legs spread. He fell hard on his back. He pulled at his neck as though trying to dislodge something that was choking him. The crowd shot to its feet, cries filling the air.

"Great-grandfather insisted on good manners." Grandfather said mildly, making no effort to help the choking visitor. "He taught me to be kind and speak highly of the Ancestors." The guy on the ground was turning blue. "He taught me that Power isn't the same as strength. He taught me what a warrior is.

X   "So, my fine warriors," he addressed the newcomers standing before him, "what did you come to ask me? The real question."

The third one from the end said, "You're *killing* him." The gasps were horrifying.

"He won't die. Not yet. What was your real question?"

"How can you say you're an Indian and love our Gods and say you're a Christian and love Jesus?" The stranger turned to the fellow on the ground. He'd stopped moving. "Please! He's my brother!"

"Wake up!" Grandfather cried. "You need to hear." The fallen man sat up and looked around, bewildered. "You need to say something, and then I'll answer your question."

Wide-eyed, the man got to his feet and said, "I apologize for how I acted. I apologize for what I said about his mother," he nodded at Grandfather, and spoke to the crowd. "His mother said she would do that to anyone who disrespects her, or her son."

The young man stumbled back, his friends holding him up.

Andrea gawked like everyone else. The ghost of Grandfather's mother did that?

The shaman waved his hands. "Magic? Am I magic? No. But I have the good will of the Ancestors." He chuckled. "You should see my mother when she's *really* mad!"

Laughter played around the crowd, laughter edged with fear.

"Now I will answer the real question. I am an Ordained Minister and a Holy Man of my People." His smile broadened. "Some people hear that and go crazy. They come to the Meeting wanting to scalp me. I *can't* be both, because *their* religion says I can't." He laughed, that exuberant laugh that was the soul of mirth.

"Those of you who have been here for years—do I make you follow *my* beliefs? Do I tell you you'll go to hell if you don't do as I say?" He waived his arm to indicate everyone in the Pit. "Have I ever said anything like that?"

"No, never!" arose from the crowd.

"That's right. Do I tell you Secret Indian Ways? How to make Big Magic? No. You are beginners. You can't understand 'the Big Picture.'" Grandfather whooped. "I love the new people—they bring such great new words. I pick them up like this." He moved his hand like he was picking things out of the air. "Bits and bytes and cyber this." He leaned toward the Numenon group and laughed.

"I am *not* a Christian." He repeated it a few times. "And I love Jesus with all of my heart. Jesus came to me when I was stolen from my family and protected me from the missionaries and what could have happened to me at Indian schools.

"He came to me and *stayed*. He has been with me since the first night I was stolen and has been with me every day and every night. He is here *now*. He talks to me, He protects me. I love Him like my family and like God. He *is God*.

"But I am not a *Christian*, full of rules and judgment and hatred of those who don't believe the way I say. Not all Christians are like that, but many are. Do you know who killed Jesus? Christians. They kill Him by killing others in His name. They kill Him by not seeing Him as He is: a holy man and not a magic toy. He told me that.

"Has Jesus ever spoken to you?" He pointed to the leader of the young men, who shook his head and pulled away.

"If He talks to you, you will never forget it. He isn't like what *they* say: The King of the Birdbath. He doesn't look like a plastic statue to put on your car's dashboard." He held his arms at his sides, palms facing up, a mawkish look on his face.

"He is not something you pray to so your team wins!" Grandfather paced along the edge of the stage, feelings flying from him like missiles.

They struck people, who burst into tears or laughter. Some rolled on the ground, crying out in languages Andrea didn't know.

"Have you ever heard Jesus weep? HAVE YOU?" Andrea trembled in her seat. She had no idea why anyone should care about what Grandfather was discussing, but she was still terrified.

Grandfather raised his hands over his head and pulled his hair. A cry of grief escaped him. It flew from him like a tidal wave, knocking people over. When they righted themselves, they saw Grandfather on the stage, his tears splattering the wooden floor, streaking his cheeks and braids. "Have you heard Him cry?"

The crowd moaned, "*No.*"

"I have. He came to me, weeping. The sight was so horrible that it branded me forever. What made Jesus cry?

"Was it because there are still Hindus? Because there are Buddhists and Muslims? Was it because his Holy Army hasn't converted everyone in the world to *believe* only in Him?

"No. Only a fool thinks that. Jesus cried *because of what had been done in His name.* Because of what Christians have done because they thought they were doing *His* will."

He looked at the crowd. "So, you see I am not a Christian. I don't believe that this Christian sect is better than that one. Or that Christianity is better than any other religion. I don't think that only those who believe the *right* way can go to heaven.

"Do you think God is so stupid? God runs the whole universe. Why should God care about such things?"

He looked down at the young men groveling before him. "You can see that I am not a Christian. You're safe, all you *traditional* people.

"It's just that Jesus is right *here*," he said, as he touched his chest. "He won't leave me. And I would die if He left."

He shrugged. "Others say I'm not a Native American Holy Man because I know Jesus. According to them, I can't be a Holy Man and know Christ. They say it's impossible.

"Sorry. I'm much worse than that. Not only do I know Jesus, I know Moses, and saints from all over the world and many traditions. Foreign deities. They're real to me. Real as you. As real as Her ..." He looked up to the sky.

Andrea ducked as she looked up. She'd heard thunder breaking around the Bowl when Grandfather spoke and had seen flashes of lighting in the corners of her eyes. Now it seemed to strike all at once, in a circle just outside the Pit.

"As real as Her and as real as Them." Thunder beat the ground, shaking the Bowl. Shaking all of the improvised sunshades that kept people from frying in the Pit, jangling the wooden benches and plastic chairs. When the thunder struck, the sunshades rattled like a cosmic dog had them in its teeth. Andrea thought she could see giant forms standing around them, huge forms beating drums. She was about to try to roll under the golf cart, when something shot across the sky.

Curved wings spanned the heavens. Sparks shot from the edge of the bird's wings where she touched the air. Andrea knew the bird was female without asking. The creature opened her mouth and shrieked. Andrea would remember the sound as long as she lived. Primal. Ecstatic. Ferocious.

Andrea looked at Grandfather, who sat unconcerned. When the eagle passed, the clouds disappeared, the mighty drummers faded and sunny skies returned.

"Yes, those were the Thunderbeings, our People's Gods. And my totem, the eagle. Nothing cute or nice about them. They are *powerful*.

"Other 'Holy Men' will tell you, as they did these boys," he indcated the young men in front of him, "'Only the *pure* can see our Gods. It's dangerous if you don't believe *only* in them and do fifty ceremonies with *me*. No other way of worshipping exists.'

"I can't say that, because *there they are,* for everyone to see. You don't have to do anything or believe anything.

"So, you see, I'm not a Holy Man, because I'm not like *the others* say I should be. But my Teacher, Great-grandfather, gave me his Power when he died. It lives in me and is me and is my life.

"Did you know that I am dangerous because of the way I am? An old man who does what God tells him to do is so dangerous that the FBI and the CIA chase me?

"The rumors are true—they say I'm a *revolutionary!* Maybe they'll show up here and visit." He laughed long and hard. "How would you like that?

"All of you who have been indoctrinated by religion—the religion of white people or brown people or yellow or black, it doesn't matter—you will hear what I say and hate me.

"God made me as *me.*" He struck his chest. "Don't ask me how I can be a Christian and Holy Man at the same time. Ask *Them.*"

The sky was roiling with them: kachinas, saints, the brilliant eagle. Thunder shook the desert. And Andrea felt a whisper in her heart. A fine mist of opalescent pearl. She felt the presence of a man who came to earth to save it, a man who was God. She shivered. Had Grandfather brought Jesus to her?

"That's all you can handle for now," he addressed the young men before him. They looked half conscious. "We will sit quietly."

As she fell into some kind of swoon, Andrea heard someone say, "Grandfather wants to talk to you."

38

ANDREA FELT DIZZY. Grandfather had done something to her. Hearing him talk—she almost felt as if Jesus was real, and all of those other deities. How could she doubt it? They were flying all over the place.

"Over here, miss." A dark man guided her toward the stage.

Every feeling she could possibly have reared up inside as she approached the shaman. Something came off of him; it made her cough. A force. She fought it. She had to fight it. He was so foreign to her. Everything he'd done was so unreal. A war raged inside her.

The old man was speaking to the crowd. "Every year, Great-grandfather and the Ancestors come to me before the Meeting and tell me what to do. This year," he paused, shaking his head in mirth and amazement, "they told me we will have a management seminar!" Angry murmurs played around the Bowl.

"Oh, yes, my friends, our visitors from the great corporation need something they can 'relate to.' So, we will give them a seminar. I even know who will speak." He pointed at someone sitting across the Pit in the front row, a dark-haired athletic-looking man wearing a Numenon cap. "You, psychologist. You will speak. You will explain psychology."

"All of it?"

"Just the parts that matter." He looked up at the sun, which was directly overhead.

"When will I talk?"

The old man shrugged. "I don't know. When we have time. Today, tomorrow ..."

Abruptly, Grandfather smiled at Andrea, holding out his hand. "Don't worry, my daughter, you have nothing to fear from this dried up old man." Everyone laughed. Almost no one left the Pit after his talk. "I hear that you came here very late last night, driving across the desert." He closed his eyes and began nodding back and forth, singing something.

Her eyes focused on him as he sat cross-legged in bliss. He was the real thing, all right. This was another thing that Enzo had told her that wasn't true. Did Enzo do it because he didn't know Grandfather, or to deceive her?

The shaman knew what she really wanted. He'd named it in his speech. She wanted the ache inside to stop and to fill the emptiness. She wanted to feel truly happy. She wanted her life to mean something. She wanted peace and love. She wanted a husband and a family.

She wanted to tell him, *I'm a spy. Someone I really don't know sent me here to spy on Will Duane. He wants me to get secrets from him.* The words drifted up to her throat, and then lingered on her tongue. They were almost strong enough to emerge.

He opened his eyes abruptly and stared into hers. She gasped. His eyes had no bottom; you could fall into them and drop forever. He saw everything. He knew everything. He was love itself. He was knowledge itself. She couldn't get away, his eyes held her captive. She didn't know how long she was transfixed.

When he finally let her go, she rocked backward. He knew everything about her. Or did he? Had she been able to hide her mission?

"What do you want, my daughter? Choose."

The war inside ratcheted up. Someone spat near her. Another coughed noisily. She looked at the crowd. They wore Indian costumes and rags. They worshiped an old man while standing in dirt. The dirt and mess spread out all around her. That's what he offered her. Dirt. The words in her throat drifted back inside. She was made for better things than this.

"My name is Andrea Beckman. I came here because my great-grandmother was an Indian but I didn't know it until …" she heard herself repeat the words Enzo had given her. She felt as if she was moving farther and farther away from the shaman, drifting from shore.

Grandfather reached out and held her hand. She could feel herself moving back toward him. Something was calling to her silently, *Stay with him. He's real and good.* A battle was going on; tides pulled her, drawing her forward and back.

Andrea saw a dusty tiered skirt out of the corner of her eye. Worn moccasins. No one here had any style.

What could the old man give her? He didn't own a pot to pee in. All he had was a big smile and dizziness.

Her laptop appeared in her mind. The screen showed her bank balance. Enzo gave her $300,000 and she didn't even do anything for him. She could see the stone terraces and the castle. Designer dresses. Fine food. He had everything, and he would give it to her.

The old man peered into her eyes. "How are you, my daughter?"

"I'm fine. A little dizzy. I guess it's the altitude." She pushed her hat back on her head.

He kept smiling and holding her hand, as though waiting for something.

Someone cleared his throat. "There's a lot of people who need healing, Grandfather."

He dropped her hand and sat back, keeping those all-knowing eyes on her. "Good luck with your search, my daughter. Have a good Meeting."

Willy Fish drew her away, taking her to the golf cart. "Did you like him?" he said.

"Uh, yeah. He's something." Her heart felt like it might leap out of her chest and drag her back to the old man. The urge to go tell him everything was almost overwhelming. Andrea wanted to go to the Numenon camp and warn Will Duane. She wanted Grandfather to forgive her. And all those gods to absolve her.

She had turned her back on something wonderful.

But she sat silently as Willy zoomed away. A smile touched Andrea's lips. She'd fooled him. He didn't know why she was there.

39

MELISSA LOOKED AROUND at the desert. "It's so beautiful here!" It wasn't as hot as the day before or as windy; the air was like crystal. The distant mountains looked like they were a block away. The decrepit tack shack and ramshackle fences of the horse facilities looked picturesque, rather than shabby.

Maybe it's from being in love.

Bud was down by the horses where Wes said he would be, and he looked absolutely adorable to Melissa, especially the duct tape on his boot. *He* was authentic!

"Hi! Wes wants me to take good care of you."

Melissa laughed. "Does everyone know about Wes and me?"

He nodded. "The whole camp. Congratulations, Melissa!"

"They know psychically?"

"Yeah. This year everybody's blazing. We're about where we were at the end of the last Meeting."

"What do people think?"

Bud hesitated. "Uh … They think Wes has sold out his People to marry a rich white woman."

Her eyes widened. "But they don't know me."

"If they knew you, they'd know you're perfect for Wes, like I do."

"But Bud, I've never felt anything for anyone in my life like I feel for Wes. It's like a miracle."

Bud smiled. "That's how I feel about my wife. We got married last year. We're soul mates, Bert and I, just like you and Wes. We'll be together 'til we die." He glanced at the place where the trail from the Bowl zigzagged up the cliff. It was the third time he'd done that.

"Is there something wrong, Bud?"

"Well, maybe yes and maybe no. My wife, Bert, is expecting a baby in a couple of weeks. I didn't think she should come to this Meeting, but she's stubborner than me. She's *here.* Up in our tent, which is next to the hospital tent. If she wasn't there and her sister wasn't with her, no way I'd be down here working."

"Is her sister a doctor?"

"Student nurse. Roxy knows a lot, mostly when to find a doctor. Grandather told her to stay with her sister all week. Bert will be fine. I hope."

"Maybe you should go see her."

"I will when we get this place buttoned down for the night. If I didn't do my job, Bert and me would be the first divorce in Grandfather's people. That woman is fierce."

"Really? No divorces?"

"There's never been a divorce between people married by Grandfather. Not one, out of hundreds of couples. Some people have problems, but they don't split up."

"I wish that everyone could see how happy Wes and I are to have found each other."

"That's just how it is. We got screwed by whites so bad that there's a lot of bitterness about it."

She thought of a dozen responses. Her family was Jewish. Her father's family had fled Russia and the pogroms a hundred years before. *They* didn't hate white people.

"That's how it is everywhere, Bud," she continued. "It's not just about race. People who look exactly like each other are massacring each other right now."

Her shoulders slumped as she realized the magnitude of what was against them. Wes's people weren't happy about their marriage. That was all it took; exhaustion settled upon her. She hadn't slept well for days. She couldn't fight everyone. Melissa swayed on her feet.

Bud grabbed her shoulders. "Are you okay, Melissa?"

"I'm exhausted." Tears filled her eyes. She couldn't help it; the tough girl had met her match. She sighed, an enormous ragged breath. "I just want to go somewhere and sleep forever."

She looked into Bud's eyes. The kindness she saw there made her unravel further. Bud was so nice.

"I can do something about that," he said. "But just know that whatever happens,

you'll be safe. Wes would wipe out everyone at the Meeting if they tried to hurt you.

"Come over here. We've got a place where you can take a nap." He led her to a series of large rock formations that poked up out of the desert floor. Tucked behind one was a weathered, wooden shack.

"People riding through stay here. We fixed it up for the Meeting. You can sleep in there as long as you like. I'll keep people away. But let me know if you go anywhere. I've got to watch you or Wes will kill me."

"When he gets done taking all the tests Betty's giving him, he won't be able to kill anyone. You're safe."

Melissa entered the line shack. Inside was a cozy bunkhouse. It had a built-in wooden table and an ancient wood-burning stove. New patchwork blankets covered each bed; matching curtains graced the windows.

"It's so cute!" Melissa exclaimed. She laid down on one of the beds. That was the last she remembered, sleep came so fast.

40

SWEAT RAN DOWN Will's face as he walked slowly, cooling off from his second run of the day. He was down by the horses, checking the area out as a place to jog. He noticed unusual activity on the switchbacks going back up to the Bowl. Spirit warriors were keeping people away from the horses and the entire lower area of the mesa and shooing the ones already down there back up.

More warriors were clustered in front of one of the canyons a short distance away. His intuition was working at full blast. Something had happened and Sandy Sydney did it. Will considered her his personal responsibility. He brought her to the Meeting. He jogged over to the group of warriors in front of the canyon.

"What happened?" They looked at him with undisguised hostility. "Is Grandfather in there? I need to speak to him."

They wouldn't let him in.

"Look, I'm not going away. I want to know what's going on." They looked at him with expressionless black eyes and didn't move. He couldn't force them; he knew their Powers. "Look here, I'm Will Duane. I want in!" he half-shouted.

Grandfather came out. "Let him in, my warriors. He needs to know." The old man led him back into the canyon. It didn't go very far before dead-ending into the mouth of a cave. The warriors stayed away.

"Elizabeth, can you come out?" the shaman called into the cave. Dr. Bright Eagle emerged wearing a lab coat stained with grisly, bloody areas marked with black charring. Her face was grave. "Tell him what happened, Elizabeth."

She turned to Will. "One of our spirit warriors was attacked last night, by your Sandy Sydney. She was sexually assaulted and tortured."

Will staggered back. "She was raped?"

"Worse than that. She looks as though someone threw acid on her and also used electricity. Her external genitals are burned off, as are most of her breasts and face. I've never seen such an attack. She was also branded with some symbol; we don't know what it is." She glanced at the shaman. "It may be satanic or demonic. She may have internal injuries. She's lost a great deal of blood." Elizabeth crossed her arms over her chest. "She told Grandfather and me, and one of your people and Kit Jay, that the perpetrator was Sandy Sydney."

Will was staggered. He'd seen pictures of middle eastern and east Indian women who'd been drenched with acid because their father-in-laws thought they made breakfast too slowly or something similar. As horrific as those pictures were, this was worse? He shuddered.

"Lisa is a lesbian," Elizabeth went on. "Sandy lured her to the badlands and seduced her. Then she began hurting her, reveling in Lisa's pain. Lisa told us that psychically. Too much of her tongue is burned off to say all that." Elizabeth glared at Will. "She tortured Lisa, thinking of ways to hurt her more. It looks like Sidney stopped because she thought Lisa was dead. She's alive now, and will probably survive if she gets to a hospital soon. She'll be a cripple emotionally. Without very good plastic surgery, she'll be a physical cripple, too."

"How could Sandy do that? Where would she get acid? She didn't have any weapons."

"She didn't need weapons." Grandfather's voice and expression were kinder than Elizabeth's. "She used her body."

"What are you saying?"

"Sandy Sydney is no longer human. She is an alien life form—a demon. Her flesh is poison to us. She can do what she did to Lisa to anyone she touches, if she wants."

"What?!"

"She is a servant of the Dark Lord. She completed her transformation—into what she is now—on your journey here. She is a mature demon, almost impossible to kill. She will spawn by killing her victims. A person killed by a demon becomes a demon. And she has other ways to reproduce. She will use all of them."

Elizabeth broke in, "Lisa's sedated and Grandfather has used his healing energy on her, so she's quiet now. I don't know how long that will last."

Grandfather agreed. "I have done my best to heal Lisa, but her spirit is too wounded. I kept her alive and eased her pain, but she needs a hospital and care for many months."

Grandfather frowned. "What happened gets worse and worse as I think about it. She has chemical *and* electrical burns. That means that the energy you saw Wesley use—which is electrical—can be used to hurt and maim. I thought it could only be used for good. Part of me suspected this would happen one day." He shrugged helplessly. "But who is prepared when 'one day' comes?"

"We can talk about the implications later, Grandfather. We need to get Lisa to a hospital," Elizabeth said.

"Can Lisa travel?"

"She has to, if she's going to live," Elizabeth said. "And yes, with medics on board, she can travel. We have plenty of doctors here who can accompany her, as well."

"Elizabeth, get a medi-vac helicopter out here. Let's get Lisa to Stanford Hospital. Someone needs to figure the logistics out." Will was having trouble thinking. "I'll pay for it all. Whatever she needs—the best."

Elizabeth smiled. "We'll handle it, Will."

"I need to talk to you," he said to the doctor. "After we get Lisa off?"

"Absolutely, Will. First thing."

At this point, Wesley arrived at the healing cave. He had fallen asleep in his tent after hours of testing. When he awoke, he headed for Bud and the stable area, looking for Melissa. He heard about Lisa and came running. "Is she okay?" he asked.

Elizabeth shook her head. "No. She's not. Will is sending her to the hospital; he's paying for her treatment."

Wes scowled. "Who did it?"

"Sandy Sydney, the secretary who disappeared."

"*He* brought her here." Wes pointed at Will. "He *should* pay for what she did."

Grandfather rebuked him sharply. "Wesley! Where are your manners? Did the men who sent you the bad horse offer to pay for a doctor?" Wes shook his head. "And they knew the horse was bad. Will Duane did not know this woman was a killer. Did you?"

Will shook his head. "I thought she was an industrial spy. I told everyone that I thought she was dangerous the minute we got here."

Grandfather turned to Wesley and said, "This is true. We can be angry with *ourselves* for not protecting Lisa."

As Wesley simmered down, Grandfather considered his reaction, then said to Will, "Many at the Meeting are not as reasonable as Wesley. If all that happened to Lisa were known, you could be in danger." Grandfather thought a moment. "I will not lie to my People about what happened."

He looked at Will. "I may have to ask you to leave the Meeting, my friend. Not out of blame, but because I cannot guarantee your safety."

Will opened his mouth to protest. "If you go, we will continue our work together somehow. Do not despair." He patted Will's shoulder.

The old man was grave as he continued. "There is one more thing I must tell you. Lisa 'transmitted' it to Elizabeth and me. Sandy Sydney said it while she was torturing her: the woman she wanted was not Lisa. It was *Melissa*. She is in love with Melissa. She fell in love with her working at Numenon."

Silence followed his announcement. Will broke it. "She wants to do what she did to Lisa to *Melissa?*"

Grandfather shook his head. "No. Much worse. She wants to take her home for the sport of her friends and herself. She wants Melissa for her slave."

Wes reeled. "No!"

Grandfather asked, "Where is Melissa?"

"She's with Bud down by the horses," replied Wes.

Will contradicted this. "I saw Bud in front of the cave when I got here. He's not with Melissa."

Wes left the cave at a run, heading for the horse corrals.

"Where is she?" Wes asked Bud, who was on duty at the corrals.

"She's sleeping in the line shack. I left for a while when I heard about Lisa. But Sammy was watching."

They burst into the line shack. It was empty.

Melissa was nowhere in sight.

41

"MISS ANDREA?" WILLY Fish piped up. She'd forgotten about him as they bounced across the Bowl and headed back to her camp.

"Yes, Willy." *You cretin*, she wanted to snap.

"I can fix your laptop." He beamed. "I studied it. I can fix it."

"Really?"

"Uh-huh. I'll finish it tomorrow. I'll bring it to you." His grin was infuriating. But he could fix her computer. She could go out in the parking lot and send messages to Enzo directly.

"How can you do it? It was melted."

"I don't know. I can fix it like I fix everything. Cars an' things. Boats. TVs. Computers. Everything." He nodded happily. "My boss—he owns Mike the Mechanic's Garage. His name is *Mike*."

Andrea nodded, her bad temper now focused on Willy.

"Mike says I'm a ..." Willy crinkled his nose. "I can't remember. Id'jit is the first word. The other one isn't in American. I'll tell you if I remember."

"You do that, Willy." Why did Grandfather assign Willy Fish to drive her? Why not one of the handsome Indian braves all over the place? She couldn't help but notice them as she jolted back to her camping site.

"Miss Andrea?" He looked at her timidly, about to ask a favor, she could tell.

She sucked in her breath. "Yes, Willy?"

"Have you been to college?"

"Yes, Willy." How long was she going to have to talk to this cretin?

"Did they teach you about 'quations in college?"

"'Quations? No, I've never heard of them." When would he shut up?

"Oh. That's just my name for them. They're really *e*-quations. They're where there's a little mark in the middle, two little lines on top of each other. And then what's on one side of the mark is the same amount as what's on the other side. That's called an equals mark and the whole thing is a 'quation. Do you know about them?" He flashed her a beaming smile full of hope. "Because I can fix things, an' I can do more. I can do 'quations. I can do 'quations to make all sorts of things. 'Ventions. TVs that are really flat, an' cell phones that are small. Lots of things. I write them in my notebook. Do you know 'quations?"

Did she know about equations? In addition to fifty-six units of quantitative methods—statistics, linear programming, econometrics and the like—she'd taken the full math series. Three quarters of calculus, then differential equations, followed with linear equations. She knew more about math than anyone but Einstein. "No, I don't know anything about 'quations, Willy. Why do you ask?"

He sighed and his shoulders slumped. "Well, lotsa times when I'm not working, 'quations come to me. I write 'em down and draw plans for my 'ventions in my notebook, but I don't have anyone to talk to about 'em. I thought you could maybe talk to me about 'em. You've been to college and all."

"I've been to graduate school, Willy. That's more than college. I'm sorry, I'd love to help you, but I don't know anything about 'quations.

I'll tell you what ..." A smile darted across her face. Why not have some fun? "Why don't you take your notebook and all your drawings and ask Will Duane to look at them. He knows *everything*." She would love to see Willy bugging Will Duane with his stupid notebook.

"Gee, Miss Andrea. That's a great idea. But do you think he'd talk to me?" Willy looked down at his purple and green striped shirt.

"You're right, Willy. I think he'd like the magenta and turquoise one with the coyotes better." She had to turn away to hide her smirk.

"Well, we're here, Miss Andrea." They pulled up into the shabby camp. Her tent was the only decent thing in it: new and super hi-tech. She could see that 'Fonzo Ramos had his jeans and shirt spread over the top of his tent, drying. A clean 'Fonzo would probably be just as disgusting as a dirty one. He was nowhere in sight.

Andrea got out of the cart and walked toward her tent. The ragged shelters and depressed people at the back of the Bowl hadn't improved during her absence.

Willy called to her, "I remember what Mike the Mechanic called me: a *savant!* I'm a id'jit *savant.*"

Andrea waved her hand. "That's nice, Willy. I'm sure you are."

She looked around a moment before entering her tent. It was zipped all the way up, the way she'd left it. She didn't have a lock for it, unfortunately. The people around here probably would steal anything that wasn't tied down. But her camp seemed untouched. She pulled the zipper down and stepped inside, glad for the privacy. Andrea lifted one arm. A wet crescent greeted her. She sniffed. Yech. She'd have to take a shower today. And change her clothes.

The clothes Enzo had given her poured out of the bag. Slut clothes. She'd never dress like that. Low necks and lace cut-outs that would show her boobs and everything else. Pants that would look painted on and barely cover her ass. She'd have to wear them while her clothes dried, but that's all. What was Enzo thinking giving her a wardrobe like that? Just another mistake? Or was he setting her up for something? She'd do what 'Fonzo had done, wash what she was wearing in the shower and dry it on the tent. Shouldn't take long for jeans to dry here. She would look like a whore, but just for a little while.

The four white ice chests marched across the side of the tent. She was supposed to share the lettuce with everyone. 'Fonzo would handle parceling out the meat. She lifted the bag that had held her clothes and froze in horror.

It lay on the tent floor looking up at her. Bright black eyes like small beads were almost hidden in the rest of the beading pocking its bulging body. Its black skin looked pox-ridden; its hide was knobby and splattered with orange and white. It looked at her, monstrous. A fat tail stuck out behind. Four hideous legs protruded.

Her eyes widened and her mouth opened. The edges of her vision faded. Terror took her; she was locked in the tent with a monster. The thing raised its head and sniffed, then waddled toward her, opening its triangular mouth. It had a huge beak with tiny teeth like she'd seen on Moray eels at the Steinhart Aquarium in San Francisco. Deadly tiny teeth. Something dripped off the fangs. Venom.

She stepped away, not turning her back on the thing, feeling for the tent's zippered opening. When her butt touched the tent wall, she panicked. Turning, she grappled with the zipper while looking over her shoulder. The beast waddled after her, body undulating like a chunky snake, its fat tail dragging. When it was right behind her, the beak raised and opened, dripping. The creature hissed.

Andrea yanked the zipper and tripped when she went through the opening. She rolled on the ground, clawing away from the tent and screaming. People came out. She didn't see them. All she could see was that mouth with its venom-dribbling fangs moving toward her. Her ribs pumped and lungs filled convulsively. Her screams and scrambling terror didn't stop. The Indians gathered around, but no one helped her. She could hear their laughter.

Rolling up on all fours, Andrea tried to get her feet under her to run. But she couldn't. She dropped back, fell on her side and sobbed. Whimpers escaped her and snot ran down her upper lip and into her mouth. The high-volume cries petered out, but her broken moaning didn't. She shook as though she had been immersed in ice water. 'Fonzo ran up and grabbed her shoulders. "What is it? What happened?"

"It's in there. It tried to get me." She pointed and went back to shaking and crying. 'Fonzo entered the tent. She heard him swearing as loudly as she was sobbing. He wasn't speaking English, but she knew he was cursing.

He leaped through the tent door. He held the thing behind its front legs with his right hand. It fought lazily, whipping slowly from side to side, unable to bite him. It wasn't so big now that she could see all of it. Two feet long, maybe. Cursing viciously in his language, he ran down the row of tents. Some of the Indians had been looking over at her, laughing and joking. 'Fonzo stood in front of them, waving the monster and bellowing. It was a lizard, she could see; nothing that should unhinge an honors graduate from UC Berkeley. She began to cry again, this time about how stupid she was. Her cheeks flamed with embarrassment.

'Fonzo swore, Indian words rising and falling. From the looks on the faces around him, she guessed what he was saying was really bad. She also guessed that they were more than a little afraid of him. He tossed the lizard at one of the men and waved his arms at him and his tent.

"One more thing, Chu, and you're out of the meeting. You and them." He waved at the group, and then went back to yelling in his language. He yelled at the on-lookers who hadn't helped her. They cringed.

Finally 'Fonzo stopped, pointed at her and said in English, "If anyone does anything to her—anything *at all*—he will answer to ME." He struck his chest with his hand and walked back to her where she sprawled on the ground.

"You all right?" 'Fonzo bent over her.

She couldn't stop hiccupping and sniffling. Her nose ran all over. She wiped it with her sleeve. He sat down next to her and put his arm around her. It felt so good. He wasn't dirty and smelly now. He'd taken a shower. His braids were shiny. She wanted to grab him and hold on forever. Something about touching him …

"Thank you," she said, and then went back to shuddering. "I know I acted crazy. I have a problem." Words began to fail her, but she forced herself. She had to explain. "I'm afraid," she finally got out, stammering. "I'm afraid of everything. Bugs. Spiders. Snakes. Lizards. I'm afraid of dogs. Big ones *and* little ones." She glanced at him. "I'm not afraid of cats, though they carry diseases. I'm afraid of diseases. I'm afraid of dirt and getting sick and germs. I'm afraid of traveling. I see a therapist and take medication." The tears came back and 'Fonzo held her and listened. "I've never been so scared of *anything* as that *thing*." Tears came again.

'Fonzo kept his arm around her. It felt wonderful. She didn't know someone touching her could feel so good. She wanted to bury into him and stay there forever.

"I'll make sure no one else plays a joke on you." He stroked her hair. It felt good. He also spoke better English than she remembered. "That was a Gila monster. A big one. They live out here. Anybody'd be scared of it. That was poison dripping from its mouth." He removed his arm from around her. It felt like a great loss. "It's Chu's pet. He was just having fun.

"Nobody's gonna bother you any more, Andrea." She blinked, liking how her name sounded coming from her lips. She realized what his protection meant. He didn't seem horrible and scary the way he did when she first met him.

He went inside her tent and searched it. She followed him. Enzo's people hadn't put her medication in the duffle bag. He set up the cot and put her sleeping bag and pillow on it. She had a blouse and some jeans out to put on after her shower. And some underwear that only a fancy prostitute would wear. He looked at the clothes, but didn't seem surprised.

"Those aren't mine. Some people packed for me. I don't dress like that." She hid the garments under the pillow.

"Your friends set y' up real good. I'm not sure for what, though."

"I was going to take a shower and wash these clothes." Her snot-smeared blouse and filthy chinos. "This is how I usually dress." Except the top was tight.

"Want me to come over an' make sure no one plays any jokes while you're in the shower?"

Her eyes widened. "Would they do that?"

"If they didn't hear me yellin' at Chu and the rest. People know you're not one of us."

He turned to the white ice chests. "We need t' do somethin' with the meat an' th' lettuce," he shook his head at that. "*Lettuce.* You sure got *some* friends."

The lettuce had rotted and the meat was worse than that. It wasn't just rotten, either. It stank horribly. 'Fonzo held it to his nose and slammed the chests shut. "This is bad. I thought it was elk; aged elk will smell like this. But this smells like the white man's devil got it." His laser black eyes lit on her.

"What's your friend up to, Andrea? What's he doing to you?" 'Fonzo appeared to be suspicious and troubled.

"I didn't think anything. I just thought ..." You couldn't lie to 'Fonzo. He moved closer so that no one could hear him.

"You in trouble, Andrea?" He glanced at the pillow that hid the panties with their open crotch. The bra had holes around the nipples. "Does he want you to fuck someone to get something?"

She gasped. Enzo did. That's what the clothes were about. And the way her body felt. She felt like she was bursting out of her skin. Everything throbbed and ached. Even 'Fonzo touching her made her feel all … like fucking. Not making love. Fucking. That's what Enzo set her up for. She didn't know him. But she did. Part of her wanted to put those clothes on and go to town. Enzo Donatore had wound her up and set her loose to go after Will Duane.

Her knees buckled and she sat down on her cot.

"You in trouble, Andrea?" 'Fonzo dropped to one knee and whispered in her ear.

All she could do was nod. Her mouth wouldn't move.

Carl Redstone, the tattooed giant she'd seen in the Bowl, drove up with three other huge guys in a couple of golf carts. He looked at her as she sat outside her tent, but spoke to 'Fonzo in their language. They went inside her tent. She heard the ice chest open. A stench flowed out, hitting her like a slap. She heard exclamations and curses. They came out with the containers, scowls on their faces. They loaded the trunks on the cart, then took down her tent and threw it on another cart. The duffle bag and clothes were tossed on top.

"I don't have anything to wear," Andrea squeaked.

"Get off all what you're wearing, too. Anything they touched," Carl growled.

"I'll get a blanket." 'Fonzo got one from his tent and wrapped it around her as Carl waited for her to strip. Carl said something to 'Fonzo and the caravan drove straight into the desert with all of her stuff.

She stood naked under the blanket and watched the cart take off with everything she had.

'Fonzo tapped her shoulder and looked at her with that crooked grin. "Well, it's you and me, babe."

"What do you mean?"

"Grandfather assigned me to watch you this week." He looked at her as though that couldn't be something she wanted. "We're gonna be tight."

"Are you a spirit warrior, 'Fonzo?"

"I'm sorry ma'am, that is classified information." His mocking smile said he wasn't worth taking seriously. Was he a warrior? Or a broken down bum? "Come into my tent. I'll give you some spare clothes. I'll get the ladies to put together more stuff for you."

They looked up when a helicopter flew over, heading for the other side of the Bowl and the horse facilities. A pall followed it. Outside the Bowl, a column of stinking black smoke rose out in the desert where Carl and the others had gone. They were burning the food Enzo had left her and the all the rest of her stuff. The drifting fumes made her nauseous. It was all poison.

'Fonzo looked at her, his black eyes guarded. "You're going to have to fight for your life this week, Andrea. Are you up to that? You're going to have to fight or you'll die." He wrapped his arms around her, burying his face in her hair. He was too thin, and covered with scrawny ropes of muscles. Being in his arms felt like heaven. No one had ever felt like that. She grabbed him back.

Sandy Sydney had done something to someone. That's what the helicopter was about.

Enzo had set her on Sandy Sydney's course. But she wouldn't end up like Sandy because of 'Fonzo. He would protect her.

What if someone had been there to save Sandy Sydney?

42

MELISSA AWAKENED AROUND three or four in the afternoon. Or did she awaken? Her eyes opened. She saw light and shapes and colors; she heard sounds. Recognized the line shack. She moved, raising herself on one elbow; the light was dimming, it was late afternoon.

Wesley! Wesley would be coming soon. Sensation flooded her body, causing her to gasp and fall back on the bed. He was coming. Her pelvis felt liquid, heavy, throbbing; her breasts ached. The nipples hardened.

That was all the thought she could muster. *Wesley was coming …* Her body seemed too weighty to move, filled with luscious, delicious sensations. She could feel Wesley inside her. He'd reconsidered, she realized, and they would have sex before they married. Oh, they'd marry, but they'd fulfill … answer … she felt they were already doing it. Melissa rocked on the bunk, moaning.

Something came to her: Wes wanted her to leave the shack and meet him … at a secret place. He was communicating with her psychically; his mind knew her every thought, knew every crevice of her body, and he'd soon know them physically, as well. Very soon. She stood, weaving, unsteady. She was supposed to meet him in a safe place. They would lie together, flow together, and release this unbearable heaviness. Another thought came: He wanted her to make sure that no one saw her leave. He was a spirit warrior, no one must see what he was doing. She smiled softly. Of course.

Peeking out the curtained window, she waited until no one watched. There was some sort of commotion, and Bud drove off toward the cliffs in a golf cart. Perfect! She crept out of the line shack silently, bent on her rendezvous. Wesley … Wesley … She could feel his hands, his lips. She saw him as she had that first naked instant: erect, powerful, huge.

Not once did she marvel that Wesley would throw aside principles he'd held his entire life, nor did she notice that her body's sensations were darker than her earlier bright passion. She wasn't thinking properly, or, indeed, thinking much at all. Certainly not questioning. Was she awake?

Images appeared in her mind as she darted from the shack: a stone outcropping, like a bench, over in the Badlands. She was supposed to meet Wesley there. She could find it, easily. Her feet flew as if they knew where they were going; like an arrow, she homed to the bench. It was quite far; how long it took her to get to it, she had no idea whatsoever. It was up a small canyon, very private and secluded, a good place to meet.

She sat on the ledge, waiting for Wesley. The late afternoon sun felt warm beating down on her; and the sensual feelings she'd had in the line shack intensified. Everything felt so wonderful: fear didn't exist. She stretched out her feet in front of her; her body felt open, vital, throbbing. She couldn't hold her legs together; they wanted to part, so she let them. She relaxed, lying back on the rocks behind the bench; it felt as if Wesley was stroking the insides of her legs, feeling inside her body. She couldn't see anyone or anything. She remembered the spirit warriors' psychic abilities. This must be what was happening. Wesley was making her ready. Simple and uncritical, like a young child with a woman's lust, she would do whatever he directed.

He wanted something else. Without a moment's hesitation, Melissa sat up and took off her shirt; she removed her bra and threw it down, putting her shirt back on. She left it unbuttoned, unzipped her jeans, and pulled her underpants partly down so that her belly showed. Wesley was telling her what to do. She lay back and spread her legs again, opening her blouse and holding her breasts together with her hands. She knew he could see her. The good feeling between her legs started again. Her body rocked and she gasped. She felt she was melting inside, and she wanted more. Where was Wesley? She longed for him.

She was incapable of reflective, deductive, or abstract thought. A new message came to her and she was absolutely certain it was from Wesley: he would be late, but he didn't want her to be alone, so he was sending a very good friend to stay with her. He would come later. She smiled with a lovely expression on her face, and held her breasts together again. She opened her legs wider and the good sensations returned. She closed her eyes. She could feel something penetrating her, and she came, and came again.

Sandy Sydney crossed the few steps between them, but didn't touch Melissa, remembering how that other woman had fallen apart. Flimsy bitch. Or maybe she did something wrong. All these new powers were a pain to figure out. Sandy stooped and told Melissa to open her shirt and display herself. She'd have to figure out some way to touch her without burning the crap out of her.

Melissa opened her eyes, and said, "Sandy. How nice to see you. I thought you were gone." No memory, no discernment—totally bewitched.

Sandy replied, "I was just playing a game. Just like we are playing. Do you like the game we've been playing?" Melissa smiled, nodding happily.

"Good girl, Melissa. Now we're going to take a walk to a special place. We'll play more there. I'll show you how I really play."

So Melissa walked next to her, as simple and innocent as a two-year-old. They walked in the shadows and on secret paths. The whole way,

Melissa felt happy and safe. She was sweet and compliant, skipping and dancing with joy.

A thought came to her mind, such a good, happy thought: she would like to be with Sandy for the rest of her life; whatever Sandy wanted to do with her was fun and good. Only Sandy existed.

Sandy Sydney smiled. They would stop every once in a while and Sandy told her to take off more of her clothes. She tickled her all over. Melissa thought that was so funny. She loved Sandy—she would do anything for her friend.

"Call me 'Mommy!'" Sandy said, and Melissa obeyed. Finally, they got to a cute little cave, and Sandy said, "Take off your shoes and socks, Melissa." That was all she was wearing by then. Melissa laughed because Sandy was breathing really hard, with big, big breaths.

"Good little girl, Melissa." she said. "Go in the cave; we're going to play for a while, then we'll go see my friends."

43

MARK AND THE others bustled around, taking the furniture from the central court and setting up a new camp on the Rim near Grandfather's lean-to. Almost as one, the Numenon staff had developed a great dislike for Will Duane, their overdone camp, and the corporation for which they worked. The mine Will wanted to foist on the Indians was a big part of it, but every one of them had some other beef with Will over some sleazy thing he had done.

Mark was helping Gil drag the big lounges out for them to sleep on. Mark looked up and watched one of the Indians drive a golf cart carrying Rich Salles into the Numenon camp's central court. Rich staggered out of the cart and sat down at one of the tables. He put his face in his hands and didn't move. Gil and the others clustered around him; something really bad must have happened. Mark walked over with Doug, whose guards trailed behind them.

"I can't believe it," Rich said brokenly. "I can't believe it. She was all burned up. She was on the ground. I found her in the canyon. I was painting." He'd mutter and then be silent. His face looked as if there was a rubber band pulling his features back. His body seemed like quivering rock; his shoulders reached for his ears. "I can't believe it ..."

Mark's mind was pulling up everything he learned in graduate school. He was the only one who knew anything about psychology. Clearly, Rich was traumatized.

Four stages of trauma. Let's see. First stage, denial and shock. They're quiet. Can't talk much.

Rich was in stage one: he needed help and support. Mark turned to the others. "We need to be with him. He's had a shock. Can somebody get a blanket?" Rich just sat there. Mark spoke to him, "Rich. We're here with you. If you feel like—"

Screams ripped open their hearts, jolting them, shattering any illusion that all was well. They put their hands over their ears, doubling over at the horror at the sound. It was Melissa. The cries came from a point behind them, farther east, somewhere in the Badlands. The most awful part was the realization that the sounds weren't physical; their ears weren't hearing them. Melissa's soul was screaming for them to help her.

They ran to the Rim and looked over the edge, as though the screams would leave a tangible trail. The shrieks stopped as abruptly as they began. They realized the most likely reason for their stopping, and ran even harder toward their source.

Then, everyone saw it: light, like a flash of lightning, so bright that it was visible even in daylight, burst from a point perhaps a mile and a half away as the crow flies. Twenty or thirty flashes occurred, but they bore no thunder. These stopped as abruptly as the screams.

"Oh, no!" Rich jumped up and cried. "Not Melissa!" He ran crazily. "Get a fire extinguisher!" He ran toward the distant spot. Seeing his extreme reaction spurred them. Delroy grabbed two fire extinguishers and a blanket. Doug grabbed a long rope. His guards and all the others followed him, racing along the Rim, trying to remember where they'd seen the flashes. They could see mounted men galloping across the plain from the horse corrals. Two were in front, followed by a posse of about ten.

Doug looped the rope around his shoulder and took off like a gazelle. He was almost as powerful a runner as Will. His guards couldn't keep up, but followed doggedly. They were all rescuers now. Because of the Bowl's circular shape, running along the Rim to the spot where the light originated was a much shorter distance than reaching it on the plain below, where the cliffs and rock formations spread out. The runners would then have to reach Melissa from the cliffs above her. The cliffs were twenty to thirty feet high in some spots, but they had a bird's eye view of the maze formed by the canyons. Anyone approaching from the plain would have to penetrate the labyrinth.

Melissa's screams ripped Wesley's soul. He stood by the line shack with Bud Creeman. He gave Bud a look that said, *If she's hurt, I'll kill you.* Wes sent out a mental call to the horses, *I need a brave, fast horse.* He didn't have to say why, the horses had seen and heard. They knew it was Melissa, and they loved her. They charged toward Wes, their eagerness to help showing in their speed.

First to arrive was a gnarled horse, the color of a mouse. It was covered with scars and as rough as the desert. The horse slid to a stop. If ever a horse was made to run, it was this one.

The animal snorted and half reared, and Wes swung up just as a similar horse arrived for Bud. They began the race to save Melissa, if she could be saved. They both knew what happened to Lisa Cheewa. They both knew what the abrupt end to Melissa's cries could mean.

The horses headed out at a dead run. A group of additional animals found riders as the spirit warriors followed Wes and Bud across the plain. Clouds of dust marked their progress. It was three hard miles to reach the base of the cliffs. From there, who knew how long it would take to find Melissa? How far into the canyons was she? Where was she in the maze?

The blue lights that flickered during Wes's martial arts exercises blazed now.

*

Bud felt almost as energized himself. *It's my fault; I should have watched her better.* He knew this was crazy, he had watched her. She must have snuck off. But he also knew how he would feel if Wes had let something happen to Bert. Bud felt awful. He'd deal with that later. Right now, he wanted to kill whoever hurt Lisa, and God forbid, did the same to Melissa.

If anything happened to her, Bud knew he'd have to fight Wesley; and he knew who'd win. Bud didn't care. He deserved a beating.

44

U P ON THE Rim, the runners watched the horsemen cross the plain. They seemed to move so slowly. Jon could hear the hard breathing of the others and feel the stitch in his side from the running. They moved out as fast as they could, but the distance seemed to lengthen as they covered ground. Melissa's silence was terrifying. Since the initial screams, there had been nothing to indicate she was still alive. Doug surged out ahead of them, followed by the two Indians, Jon, and then Gil.

Jon was surprised by Doug's tracking ability; he had already reached the point on the rim opposite where the light flashed. Several fingers of high land projected into the plain from that point; a wrong choice could cost Melissa her life. Moving between the fingers like a hunting dog, Doug suddenly stiffened and chose the projection to the left, the east-most finger and the least obvious choice.

He jogged along the top of the canyon, seeming to sniff the air below. Jon thought Doug looked like a bloodhound. From where they were, they couldn't see the riders who were moving along the base of the cliffs, hidden by the land's raised brow. *How will we ever find her? A rat couldn't find its way out of here.* From the upper vantage point, he could see how canyons often had hundreds of projecting fingers, these reached for other canyons, dead-ended, forming a maze of tunnels. He could see caves everywhere; it was a labyrinth.

Doug charged into the maze, undeterred. The others held back as he ran down one dead-end finger after another as though drawn by a magnet. He tracked back and forth for quite some time. Finally, he jumped a small gully and slid down the cliff face to the canyon floor. They heard him moving among the fanning fingers of the canyon. He stopped. Jon heard him saying in his mind, *Bring me a blanket. Tell the others to go out to the canyon edge and guide in Wes and Grandfather. No one else. People should stay away. I've found her.* Tears flooded Jon's eyes. He took the blanket and slid down the cliff face. He was utterly unprepared for what he saw.

Wes and Bud reached the cliff face. Which of the canyons should they take? From their vantage point it was impossible to tell which would lead to the source of the flashes. Wes got off the panting horse and ran back and forth between the canyons. He finally selected the easternmost and went down it at a slow jog. Bud stayed at the entrance, waiting for Grandfather.

Grandfather and Elizabeth were first to arrive, traveling in a souped-up golf cart. Other riders followed quickly. Bud gave the two horses to them and jumped into the cart. It moved slowly up the canyon. Other trackers explored side canyons for clues he might have ignored. Wes was tracking one person: Melissa.

Wesley made a single long whistle; he'd found something significant, but not Melissa. The golf cart rounded a corner. Wesley was standing outside a well-hidden cave. The cliff wall opposite the cave opening looked as if an explosion inside the cave had torched it. Worse: the rock was splattered with blood and what looked like shredded flesh and bone. The golf cart pulled up.

"Don't touch anything, *anything*. Including Melissa, if she's in there," Grandfather said. "A demon's flesh or blood will infect you if you touch it." They went in.

Elizabeth shone the light from a heavy electric lantern around the cave. Like the canyon wall, the cave's walls were blackened by fire and splattered with blood, scraps of skin, and bone. Melissa's socks and shoes were heaped in the entrance. Wes winced. There was no sign of Melissa.

They shone the light on a piece of human jaw stuck in the cave wall; the jawbone was covered with fair skin, and three teeth were embedded in it. On the other side of the cave, a strip of scalp with long blond hair was plastered to the ceiling. They didn't think any of it was from Melissa. Where was she? Wes left the cave and sprinted up the canyon.

Grandfather and Bud entered the cave. "Look," Grandfather said, pointing to the shred of skin and piece of jaw. As they watched, the long blond hair drew up into itself, thickening and shortening. The strip of skin did likewise, moving slowly like a slug. Soon, both skin and hair were thick, coarse, and black—they might have come from a wild boar, or a demon. The piece of jaw made a similar metamorphosis: the teeth turned sharp and yellow, and the skin and flesh coarsened like animal hide. It moved and shivered, as alive as anything on the planet.

All around them, the drops of blood and shreds of flesh were turning black. All were moving, coalescing at a central point. Grandfather motioned for Bud to leave. Once outside, Grandfather stood in the cave's doorway and extended his hand. He made a slight motion and flames shot from it, incinerating first Melissa's shoes, then the entire interior of the cave. Satisfied he'd burned any flesh to ash, Grandfather turned to the canyon wall behind him and did the same, finishing by etching symbols around the cave opening and on the canyon wall.

"I've sealed the cave to spirits and demons. Sandy Sydney will not be able to regenerate here," Grandfather said, looking around. "Each shred of the demon's body can produce a complete new demon. The creature is not dead. The flesh in the cave doesn't amount to a whole corpse. Sandy Sydney is out there, rejuvenating herself.

"You know what Melissa did, don't you?" Grandfather asked them, grinning.

"She blew her head off," Bud answered.

"She sure did! Blew her head right off! She did it better than a trained spirit warrior!" The old man was pleased with Wes's prospective mate. The cave showed no sign of injury to Melissa. Grandfather knew that while the demon was not dead, it was in no condition to carry Melissa away. It would be a few days before the fiend would reappear. So, where was Melissa? Why didn't she make any noise?

A whistle from Wes told them he'd found her. The golf cart inched forward. Jon stood by the entrance to a very small blind canyon, barely five feet wide; Wesley was next to him, motioning them back. Doug stood next to them, holding a blanket, with Jon behind him.

Grandfather joined them, telling the rest to go back down the trail and give them privacy. He had no idea what condition Melissa would be in. The four of them walked quietly into the canyon. It twisted, extending perhaps fifty feet into the cliff wall.

Melissa was huddled at its end. The soft red rock wall bore marks from her hands where she had attempted to claw her way out of the canyon. She was curled up in a ball on the ground and rocking softly. Her hands and forearms covered her head. As they came closer, she trembled but did not acknowledge their presence in any other way. Blood covered her hands and forearms up to the elbow, and she was naked. Wesley wanted to go to her and hold her, but Grandfather shook his head.

"She could still be dangerous. Let me try." The old man knew that Melissa was as capable of projecting deadly energy as Wesley or himself. Will Duane had told him what she had done to hurt Doug back at Numenon. Her powers were evident, even then.

Chanting softly, Grandfather walked slowly toward her. They could all feel a rustle of menace from her as he grew near. He said something to her in a Native American language and she relaxed; when he touched her, she went limp.

"Hand me the blanket," Grandfather said. Wesley stepped forward with it, wrapping it around her and holding her to him. Her head fell back and he buried his face in her neck, kissing her.

"No! Don't!" cried Grandfather. Blood covered Melissa's mouth, chin, and neck, bathing the entire front of her body. Wesley was smeared with it now, as well. Grandfather shook his head: this is what he had been afraid of. Demon blood would infect them both. "Get into the cart. Don't touch the blood. We have to get them into the healing cave right away."

Wesley carried Melissa to the cart. Grandfather jumped in and Bud drove to the healing cave as fast as he could. Melissa sat, eyes open, apparently seeing nothing, hearing nothing, and certainly responding to nothing.

"What's the matter with her?" Wes asked; this was worse than if she'd been screaming and hysterical.

"Could be a spell," said Grandfather.

Elizabeth added, "Or shock, trauma, or something worse—she's dissociated. Did you say she had memories of some sort of abuse?"

Grandfather replied, "She's been sexually abused, very badly. She has no memory of it."

Elizabeth nodded. "That's it. Her memories are breaking. Hopefully we'll get her to the cave before they blow."

They rushed into the gathering darkness, reaching the cave as night fell. The spirit warriors had set up security at the cave's mouth.

Will Duane ran up, ashen. "Is she okay?" he asked.

Grandfather shook his head. "We won't know for hours. We'll let you know what happens. Leave us alone now. If you want to do something, pray for all of us. The demon is still out there."

With that, Grandfather, Elizabeth, and Wesley disappeared into the cave with Melissa.

The Numenon crew had gathered at the mouth of the healing cave. They had seen Melissa's bloodstained face and staring eyes—what had happened to her? Rich Salles was close to collapse, having had two traumas in one day. First he had found Lisa, and now this. Jon was right behind him; since 'Rique's death, Melissa had been his closest friend. Would he lose her, too? The rest were reeling.

Will's leadership asserted itself automatically. He said, "Let's get back to the camp site and have a meeting."

Will Duane took control. No matter how disillusioned they might be with him, everyone trusted his judgment under fire. He dispatched Delroy and Hector to light the tiki torches, and jumped in, calming everyone.

"I'll airlift everyone out of here tomorrow at first light if there's any more danger to us. Until then, no one should go anywhere alone. We move and act as a group. This is our base and we are a team. We won't know how Melissa is for some time. She's with Elizabeth and Grandfather; she's got the best care we can get her here. Let's get on with the evening until we know something."

Tyler Brand drove up in a golf cart. "Grandfather will be speaking after the evening chant. He'll put some perspective on what's happened. Elizabeth is examining Melissa now. She and Grandfather will heal her, and she'll spend the night in the cave." The professor looked around the group, a compasionate human being rather than the scary warlock he'd seemed before.

"Don't worry," Tyler said, putting his hand on Will's shoulder. "I've seen Grandfather work miracles. She'll be all right."

Will was close to tears. His voice was hoarse when he spoke. "Thank you. I care a lot about Melissa."

45

WILL STOOD OUTSIDE of the circle formed by the motor homes watching his employees talking. He said earlier that they were a team; that wasn't true. The MBAs blended in seamlessly with the drivers and Jon. Will was excluded from his own people and no one noticed it but him.

The night was as beautiful and romantic as the previous one. Will looked out over the moonlit plains. A balmy wind blew in from over the desert; sounds of coyotes and night animals broke the silence. Behind him, who knew how many more than four thousand people hummed and clucked, socializing and living their lives, forming a happy network, going from tent to tent chatting and laughing.

He looked up at the sky. He'd never seen so many shooting stars. He walked away from the Numenon encampment, throat tight, and found a flat rock some distance away. *Here I am at Grandfather's spiritual retreat, just like Marina wanted me to be. Except none of the pieces add up.*

Will looked back into the Numenon compound. Everyone had gone to the chant, which was cranking up in the Pit. He could hear the voices going strong. Grandfather and Elizabeth still were healing Melissa.

There was nothing to do but wait. He couldn't wait. Will slipped into the *Cass*, noticing that Jon had painted over the name *Ashley III* on all of the vehicles' sides and replaced them with a nicely lettered *Cass*. He'd asked him to do it earlier, and Jon had gotten right on it.

His daughter, Ashley Cassandra Duane, preferred the name *Cass*. He persisted in calling her Ashley because Ashley was the sweet little girl she had been as a child. Cass was the foul-mouthed drug addict who had cursed him the last time he saw her and would probably die. He loved his daughter in spite of what she'd become, so he'd renamed each of his series of RVs the *Ashley*.

Will put on his last set of clean running clothes. He was so tired that the muscles under one eye were twitching. His face felt drawn, and his legs were leaden as he headed out on his third run of the day. The moon made it light enough to see—pretty much. He'd stay on the Rim; that was an easy run.

He liked the way he felt when he was revved up, putting out his maximum performance. It was a high. When he got upset, both his mind and body sped up; that's where he was that evening, going ninety miles an hour and feeling like shit. He couldn't slow down until he knew Melissa was okay.

In his mind's eye, he could see her the first day she walked into Numenon. She wore an expensive suit. Her powerful, almost manly walk reminded him of his daughter when she'd been healthy. Everything about Melissa reminded him of Cass—Cass as she might have been. He loved Melissa as the daughter he'd lost and for herself. He saw the vulnerability in her that no one else acknowledged. Melissa returned his feelings, Will knew. He was a father to her, the father that she wanted. People sensed their relationship, and thought he was sleeping with her. Never.

Now he might lose Melissa, in addition to his Cass. He needed to run. He could run past the pain. Run past it and shut it down.

Will finally reached the state of euphoric hyper-drive he sought. He was soaring when he stumbled on a pebble on the edge of the Rim. He bounced, then skidded, and finally tumbled over the brink, rolling and sliding thirty feet to the plain below.

He lay still and silent. No one knew where he was. No one was looking for him.

46

"DID YOU LIKE Grandfather's talk today?" Carl kneeled in front of Andrea, shoving his face into hers. He had a long scar from his forehead to his jaw. His nose had been broken and spread all over his face. The tattoos crawled up his neck from under his shirt as though they were alive. Her lips began to quiver. Carl bellowed, "Did you like Grandfather's talk?" He had returned from burning her things in a rage.

"Yes," she quavered.

"Then why did you lie to him?" She scrambled to get away, but he grabbed her arm.

"I didn't lie to him."

"You didn't tell the truth, either!" Carl's roar destroyed her remaining defenses.

"I was going to go back and tell him. I made a mistake. I was going to tell Mr. Duane. I was wrong." Tears. "Please …"

"You're scaring her, Carl," 'Fonzo said.

"You ought to be scared," Carl shouted at her. "Do you want to end up burning up everyone you touch? Do you want to be like her?" By now, the whole camp knew what Sandy Sydney had done to Lisa.

"No! I don't." The tepee swayed around her. She felt faint. When Carl and the others got back from burning her stuff, they had taken her and 'Fonzo to the other side of the Bowl, near the Numenon camp and Grandfather's hut. They were in a tall, pale tepee, all soft skins. It looked very old. Spirit warriors clustered outside, but just Carl, 'Fonzo, and she were inside. She thought they were going to kill her.

"I didn't do anything wrong," she wept. "It was a mistake."

Carl laughed. "I don't think it was a mistake at all. They picked you on purpose. You're just the kind of," he spoke several Indian words that sounded very nasty, "they look for. Tell me what happened with Enzo Donatore."

She gasped. How did he know Enzo's name?

"Tell me."

She told them everything. About the graduation trip to Europe that her parents had given her, Diego finding her at the Alhambra, the castle and how awful the people had been at dinner, and Enzo making everything okay. More than okay.

Both men watched her like snakes at a gopher hole, with their glittering dark eyes. Dark skin. Black hair. Fierce and terrifying.

"He offered me a job and gave me some money to help him." She pressed her lips together.

"How much money, Andrea?"

A look from Carl and she told him. "$300,000."

"You don't come cheap, do you?" He chuckled. "I bet you really wanted that dough, didn't you?"

She couldn't talk, he was so overpowering. "Well, uh … yes, but I didn't see the harm. Everyone cares about money." She was panting, realizing that her future at the Meeting, and maybe her future, period, depended on what she said. "Everyone says … Well, I've never had any real money." She licked her lips. "Enzo said Grandfather wasn't a genuine shaman, just a nice old man fooling people. He said that everyone here was scamming."

She looked from face to face. "But what he said isn't true. I could tell when I met Grandfather. He's wonderful. But something had me inside." She clutched her chest. "I couldn't tell him the truth. Do you understand?

"I tried, but the words wouldn't come out. It was like they were stuck here." She touched her throat and stammered, saying, "Uh," a few times before choking out, "I'm really sorry. I didn't mean ..." Figuring that she was dead anyway, she told them about the supermodels throwing up and waiting for her reports.

"They're back on the road?"

"I think so."

Carl shouted something to the warriors outside. She could hear people moving around, and then leaving.

"Andrea." When her name came from Carl's mouth, it sounded strange. "Tell me the truth, as much as you can see it. You wore clothes from his castle?" She nodded. "Did you eat or drink with him?"

"Yes, dinner. I didn't eat in the dining room, everyone there was so mean, but later, Enzo and I ate by ourselves."

Carl's face grew grimmer. "And you drank with him."

"Yes, wine. I've never had such good wine." Her lips curved happily, thinking of it. "The more I drank, the better I felt, and the clearer I could think." Carl let out a ragged breath. She frowned. "That was fake, wasn't it? There was something in the wine. A drug or something." Carl didn't answer.

"Did he touch you?"

Her face flushed. "He ... he held my hand and kissed it."

"Did you fuck him?"

"No. I wanted to. I wanted ..." She felt so full, so open, a pod about to burst and release seeds all over. She had wanted him to touch her everywhere. She couldn't hide it from the two men, or cover up what her body wanted. Her cheeks flamed.

Carl shot a look at 'Fonzo. "You okay?" 'Fonzo indicated he was.

Carl grabbed her so fast that she couldn't cry out. He had her by the shoulders, shaking her. "You stinking little bitch, you're too stupid to know what you were getting into. You were too greedy and stuck up to know you're lucky you're not dead. A couple more days, and you'd be screwing whoever he pointed you at. You'd end up like Sandy Sydney." Carl screamed at her in his language for a while and then shoved her so hard she fell over.

Andrea lay on her side on the tent's hide floor. No one had ever spoken to her like that. It was true. When she had been alone in her tent, she had wanted to have sex with everyone. Her body demanded it. And her dreams at night, her body rising and falling ... sensations. Release.

"Help me! Please." She pulled herself up and grabbed at Carl. He pulled away. "I don't want to do all those things." Images of moving bodies, arms and legs intertwined, filled her mind. Thrusting. "And I don't want to be the way I was when Diego found me. I was snobby and I did want money. I ..." She looked from Carl to 'Fonzo and back. Wailing, she said, "Please. I don't want to die."

"That makes more sense than anything else you've said. I'm going to let you go—to him," Carl indicated 'Fonzo with his head. "You do everything he says, and I mean everything, an' you may get through the week alive." He stuck his face in hers again. "Your friend in Spain has just figured out that he's lost his new," he said another Indian word. She figured it meant whore. "He will come for you, sacred Bowl or not."

Carl turned to 'Fonzo. "You up for this?" 'Fonzo nodded.

"Okay. I'd better marry you before I get back to work," Carl said.

"Marry us?" She was aghast.

"Yeah. Usually Grandfather does it, but he's busy. You're going to need it in a while. You're soul mates."

47

GRANDFATHER AND ELIZABETH hustled Wesley and Melissa into the deeper regions of the cave. Speed was of greatest importance. Wesley already had the glazed, drunken look of one penetrated by a demon. Much less of its blood had touched him than Melissa, but he seemed to have fewer defenses against it.

"It's his depression," said Grandfather. Melissa moved easily, totally compliant with the wishes of anyone around her. Blood covered her face from the nose down, drenched her throat and chest, and ran down her body. She looked as if someone had thrown a bucket of the stuff on her.

Elizabeth didn't think she had sustained any injuries. "She must have bitten Sandy Sydney before blowing her head off. I'd bet that's all demon blood."

They reached their destination: several mineral pools deep in the cave. The caves beneath the Mogollon Bowl were ancient. This cave complex was one of the most venerable. Inhabited by the Ancestors for thousands of years, it went on for miles. Its ponds had healing properties of all sorts.

Elizabeth and Grandfather headed to the most strengthening, most purifying, most healing one of them all.

When they got there, they put the electric lanterns down and Elizabeth pulled out a couple of pairs of latex gloves. Rushing water poured into the pool's bowl from above, flushing its contents down a narrow tube in its bottom. Several such bowls existed in the cave.

"Take off your clothes," Grandfather said to Wes and Melissa. Elizabeth hustled the couple into the pond while Grandfather removed one glove. Aiming his hand at the pile of clothes, he torched it just as he had the cave. When the clothes were ashes, he used the flames to blast them into the flush hole.

Elizabeth began her work. She was on a flat ledge level with the pool; Melissa and Wesley were in the pool next to her standing neck deep. Elizabeth examined Melissa's mouth, face, and torso.

"Nothing," she said to Grandfather. "It was all demon's blood. But the way they are acting is weird."

Normally, soul mates, having touched as long ago as they had, would be almost uncontrollable seeing each other naked. These two acted like drugged two-year-olds who hadn't noticed the other. Even washed off, the demon blood seemed to affect them.

They had no towels, so Grandfather and Elizabeth marched them naked to the living area of the cave. The ponds they left glowed slightly with phosphorescence, the light of the lanterns triggering their luminescence. The cave walls also lit up with a ghostly glow. Melissa and Wes walked docilely, without objection.

Elizabeth looked at the naked Melissa as she walked ahead of her. She had a perfectly shaped, slender torso, lovely slim legs, and rounded buttocks. It was her breasts that Wesley would worship. They protruded in a way that made them seem more appropriate on a fertility goddess or a wild animal than a young woman. Her nipples turned upward, as if defiant and proud. They were burgundy tinged and contrasted sharply with her skin. *She should drive Wes wild, if he ever wakes up and looks at her.*

Conversely, Elizabeth knew Wes's body quite well, having stitched up portions of it almost every year. He had a long scar on his left knee from a colt running him into a fence. The wide, thick scar on his right forearm was from getting dragged roping. Wes seemed to beat himself up on purpose, given the number of collisions with barbed wire and cattle and horses' hooves she'd patched up at the Meeting. But she'd never seen a body as perfect as his, scars and all. Only Elwin's came near. She yanked her mind away from memories of her ex-husband.

They finally reached the cave's main chamber. The main bed was made up in the middle of the room. Two smaller beds were set up at the cave wall. Someone had brought clothes for Wes and Melissa, and a cooler of food. Elizabeth pulled out two sweatsuits and underwear.

"No wounds at all," she said to Grandfather, helping Melissa put her clothes on. "I don't think the demon touched her physically. Psychically, yes."

When Melissa was dressed, she sat on the bed, silent and staring. She made no attempt to contact any of them, keeping her eyes down and away from theirs. They left her alone while the process inside her unfolded. Soon, Melissa had wrapped the bed's quilt around her. She sat hunched, looking warily to each side. Fear vibrated from her. Grandfather motioned for Elizabeth to move away from her.

Grandfather, Wes, and Elizabeth sat at the table. Jon had brought some food for them. They ate silently, while observing Melissa from the corners of their eyes. Wes was in a strange state. He was in the room, but just barely, and not himself. He's in shock, Elizabeth realized.

Melissa didn't appear to know they were there. The way she used her hands, moved, and sat; it all indicated a young girl, not even a teenager. Any noise made her start, and she became more agitated as time went on. She got off the bed, quilt around her, and stood in front of the rear opening the cave, the exit to the pools and other areas.

She withdrew to the sidewall where she could watch the whole space. She hunched over, the quilt wrapped around her and flopping over her head, rocking back and forth. As her agitation peaked, her mind began calling, *Help me. Help me. Mommy, Daddy. Please help me, Mommy.* The utter desolation in the voice tore into Elizabeth. Then Melissa was silent.

Elizabeth whispered, "No one helped her. No one ever came."

Melissa heard the whispered message. The impact was instantaneous: she flew back against the cave wall like a rag doll tossed by a giant. Her heels dug into the ground as she tried to scramble away from something invisible that was attacking her. The blanket around her fell open, and her legs spread wide, pulled up, and bent at the knee. Her hands drew back as though being held over her head.

Her body began to move, its cells releasing the knowledge of what happened. Her pelvis rocked and tilted and vibrated; her whole torso shook from the power of her attacker's thrusts. Melissa screamed in earnest as her body released its secrets: she had been raped and raped, more times than anyone would ever know.

She screamed. Terror ricocheted off the walls. Her shrieks pummeled the listeners. Melissa's desolation and pain washed the cave, striking their ears like lashes from the inferno. Wesley curled up in the corner and shuddered. Knowing what someone had done to her was brutal for everyone. Brutal for Melissa remembering and feeling it; brutal for the others to know it was possible.

Melissa's body movements slowed and Elizabeth whispered to her, "Can you see who it is?"

A tiny voice spoke, "It's Rob Courtney. He lives behind us. Oh, no!" It all began again. This time her cries were, *Please don't hurt me.* Still, her body discharged its horror. Melissa gagged, retched and spat, her head and mouth moving in what could only be oral rapes.

Her body finally stopped moving. Elizabeth and Grandfather put her on the bed and laid her on her back. Elizabeth wiped Melissa's face and covered her up again. She had done plenty for one session, but she could do more.

"It's Elizabeth," the doctor whispered. "Do you remember me?" A nod. "You're doing really good work. Do you want to do a little more? It would help you." The head shook no. Elizabeth sighed. Oh well. "All right. I'm going to help you come back. I'm going to touch you. Is that all right?" Melissa nodded her head.

Elizabeth kneeled on one side of the bed and placed one hand on Melissa's breastbone, the other below her navel. She prepared to summarize what happened with the child and balance Melissa's energy, removing as much residual trauma as possible. This didn't happen.

The instant she touched her, visual images began to flow. Melissa's healing process was nowhere near complete; her distress was so strong that the mental images were projected into the middle of the room where Wes and Grandfather could see them, too.

They could see the young Melissa at her parents' home. Her younger brother and sister were sleeping in their rooms. She came down the stairs, a reedy pre-teen, and walked into the bright kitchen.

He was there. Terror flooded the cave as the shock of the looming figure registered.

He was six foot two, two hundred and fifty pounds to her hundred. Bright red hair fanned out from his head; it shone like a halo in the light behind him. His ham-like forearms were covered with curly orange fur. At first, his face was blank, blacked out in her memory, but Grandfather touched Melissa and the face appeared. He was about twenty-five years old with a red stubble beard. His coarse features had an unmistakable sadistic expression.

He held a hunting knife in one hand. With the other, he grabbed Melissa and pulled her next to him, holding the knife to her throat.

"Let's go downstairs and play," he said, the knife firmly at her throat. Once there, he locked the door and ordered her to strip, commenting on her body as she did so. "Come over here." Melissa started to scream and the knife went to her throat. He made threats that closed her throat forever: if she screamed or told anyone, he'd use the knife instead of his fingers on her body, and then go up and do it to her little sister, who was seven.

"Now let's play harder." The three watched her memories, appalled. As time went on, the memories changed, appearing to come from a vantage point outside her body: scenes floated in the air, by the ceiling. The mental pictures were detached and held only visual information.

By that time, Melissa felt very little, physically and emotionally. Her body had its own set of memories: it held and remembered all of the physical sensations.

Her attacker talked to her continually, taunting her. "Is this how you Jew girls like it? Put it in your mouth, you little Jew-bitch."

Wesley withdrew. How could anyone do that? He saw why she hated her parents so much. They didn't help her at all. Not once. They didn't even know what was happening.

A scene from the family breakfast table hovered above the bed. Sun streamed in the large windows of the well-designed, modern home. Her father was reading the newspaper.

"Look at this, will you?" he said. An article announced that Rob Courtney, son of Senator Fillbrook Courtney, had been arrested for burglary. He had been in trouble with the law for theft and sexual offenses since he was a teenager—facts covered up by his famous father. "He's been our neighbor for years! He could have broken in here. Someone could have been hurt."

With that revelation, Melissa relaxed and appeared to sleep.

Elizabeth said, "Some session."

Grandfather sighed. He still had to address the assembled Meeting that night and give them some explanation about what had happened to Lisa.

"Well, we'd better get to work," he said. Elizabeth nodded and went over to Wesley. "Come lie on the bed, Wes. You need to be healed."

Grandfather and Elizabeth reached inside their patients and cleaned up as much spiritual debris as possible. Grandfather reached directly into Melissa's body and pulled out shame, guilt, unworthiness, fear, anger, compulsions, and phobias. He yanked the ugly growths out by the roots and threw them on the floor. A crawling black mass soon stank up the cave. He turned around and incinerated it as he had the contaminated clothes.

Grandfather lifted Melissa to the spiritual heights she had reached playing her violin the night before, to the bliss that belonged to her. She deserved it, having faced the greatest terror in the world. Before leaving, Grandfather stroked her face, thinking, *So beautiful, with so much more pain to endure.* It would all erupt again, and need excising and healing again, perhaps for years. *If I had you alone for a week, beautiful one, I could heal you.*

He wouldn't be able to devote that time to her at the Meeting. "I'll do my best, my great warrior, and for your husband, my son, Wesley." He kissed Melissa's head. Grandfather walked out of the cave chuckling. "She blew that monster's head off!"

Elizabeth did much the same thing with Wesley. She saw the mass of depression inside him had grown in the one day since Grandfather had healed him. She was very clever with depression; she was able to trim it back even farther than Grandfather had. She raised him to the heavens, and left with Grandfather, staggering with exhaustion.

Wesley's soul opened to the light, showing himself to the Great One as he was, with no attempt to hide anything. At first, he felt only love, encouragement, and peace after Elizabeth's healing. Acceptance of Melissa. Forgiveness. Gratitude.

But other sentiments lurked inside him: thoughts unformed, feelings unexpressed. Less noble reactions to what he'd seen, dark currents that quailed from consciousness. The One called forth these poisons and made them spill their venom.

The One said, "Look at all your truth, Wesley. Open yourself so that you can heal."

Wesley did, acknowledging a few things.

Melissa would need healing for a long time, years most likely. She'd have symptoms and flashbacks like she'd just had—he knew that from his own traumas. He felt angry and robbed.

His bride, his perfect soul mate, had been so defiled that it revolted him. He had been raised from the church's give-away box. He'd had second hand everything all his life. Now, he had a second-hand wife.

Rage filled him below the bliss Elizabeth had instilled. He raged over his soiled bride, raged at her attacker. Raged at the world where such things took place.

The One penetrated this tangle of feelings and thoughts, holding it in a crucible of love and understanding. Wes received an instantaneous message—a wordless infusion of meaning, delivered whole into his depths.

The Great One said, *See your wife as I do: perfect, whole, and unblemished. Nothing happened to Melissa's soul. That is as perfect as the instant I created her. See her with My eyes.*

In less than a flash, Wes saw Melissa as the Great One did. The One knew no differences between nationality or color: all children were the same. Wes knew that he would lose friends over his wife, but he wouldn't lose anyone who'd seen the truth.

He looked at Melissa sleeping and felt no shame. *She has done nothing wrong*, the silent voice prodded him. And look what she did even though she was damaged. First in her class at Harvard, and then one of Will Duane's top employees. She lived a model life, even for Silicon Valley.

Wes watched her sleep for a while. He lay close to her and held her in his arms. In the horror of the afternoon, he had forgotten what it was like to be near her. Holding her was like drinking nectar. He lay down with Melissa, intoxicated. He hoped he'd be able to sleep. He'd never break his vow of celibacy.

They are a beautiful couple, Grandfather thought as he left the cave. Great warriors. If they can't last until I marry them in the morning, then so be it. Wes looked like an angel, his face soft and relaxed next to Melissa's. The corner of the shaman's mouth twitched. Wes had no idea what lying next to Melissa all night would be like. His desire would grow so great in a few hours that not consummating it would be torture.

48

G RANDFATHER WALKED UP to the Meeting stage like Ben Hur, his presence booming through the amphitheater. The crowd had kept on chanting and dancing until he got there, and the Numenon musicians joined in at the end, as they had the night before.

Grandfather listened to the combined music a moment, motioning them to continue playing. *It's strange music, but very beautiful.* What he had wanted was happening. They were coming together. He raised his hand and a hush fell over the crowd.

"Most of you know that evil things have happened today. You saw the helicopter and saw people rushing around at dusk. Two women were attacked by a demon." When he said, *demon*, a grumble of disbelief went through the crowd.

"When I say 'demon,' I mean 'demon.' It disguised itself as a woman from Numenon, but it was a demon. You don't have to believe me. But I saw its true flesh and blood, as did others. Scales and tusks like a boar's. One of the women it attacked blew its head off!

"But the demon is still alive, even without a head. It is out there, healing itself and waiting to attack again.

"Will Duane is not to blame. He told me that he thought Sandy Sydney was dangerous; he said it the first minute I met him. We did not take him seriously enough." His gaze raked the crowd.

"If you want to leave tomorrow, I understand. Before you go, you need to know why demons came to this Meeting." He surveyed the crowd, deadly serious. "They are here because what we are doing can rock the world. If the Numenon people and our People come together, we can heal centuries of hatred. We can change the world.

"The devil trembles in fear of what we are doing. When the foundation of the universe shakes, it cracks the core of evil and demons come out. They do what demons do: stop change, stop love, stop growth. They kill.

"Your own demons know what is happening. The demons who live inside you and poison you; they know what's happening. Do you know your demons? Hatred, anger, sadness, blame, envy, jealousy, greed, and fear. All of them may be talking to you this week. You'd better be ready." His face was grim. "I know all about inner demons. I was almost devoured by them. I didn't know the danger came from here." He touched his chest.

Grandfather hesitated. Every year, very early in the morning, the Great One came to Grandfather and told him what to do in the Meeting. This year, the One commanded him to give a management seminar. And he was supposed to tell all the secrets he hadn't before.

"This year is the last Meeting, so it's a time to say what hasn't been said. Here is a secret ..." He bent over, a finger to his lips. "Some of you wonder why I use ideas from other people and talk about things that most shamans don't. This is the reason," he whispered, but everyone heard it. "I've been to the white man's college. More than that: I've been to graduate school." Gasps went up.

"I am a guinea pig. Do you know what they are? Kids' pets? Little animals to experiment on. When I was stolen from my family, the Indian schools wanted a really smart Indian to show how we could be tamed. And trained. That was me. The guinea pig." He patted his chest.

"I was so smart they sent me to a seminary in Berkeley. I would be trained to be a Christian minister." He grinned, the wildest grin in the world; the crowd was silent and open-mouthed.

"I studied Christianity like I was supposed to during the day; but at night, I studied what they didn't know about. I studied other religions. I studied a man named Karl Marx. Have you heard of him? When I read Marx, I felt that he spoke the truth.

Grandfather stopped and closed his eyes. He began to nod his head rhythmically and chant a few guttural syllables; the Great One was coming to him. He picked up a rattle and began shaking it; he was becoming lost in a trance.

Abruptly, he came back. "The Great One says I must finish my story. I read Marx. He said that the poor people are good and that the rich create all the evil in the world. We needed to rise up and kill the rich and make a new world. Because of Marx, I hated anyone who had anything. I only liked poor people. I saw the world through glasses marked 'hatred.' I was in danger of my hatred eating me.

"My favorite professor asked me, 'Does your hating the way things are change anything?' I said, 'No.'

"He replied, 'That's right; it poisons you. You do no good for anyone when you are full of hate. You don't see the world as it is.' That was true. I gave up my hatred, hatred that came from the ideas of a man I didn't even know. I was happier. I might have stayed in Berkeley, in that world.

"But I found out something about my family and walked away from the white man's world. It had nothing for me." He chanted again; the state was taking him. "I came to the land of the People and walked into the desert. I didn't care whether I lived or died. I offered my soul to the Great One. I walked and walked. Finally, I fell down.

"When I woke, Great-grandfather was there. He took me to his hogan, and I began to learn the truth. Great-grandfather showed it to me in living flames. I owe all that I am to his Teaching. So that is my story. When I gave up everything and had nothing, only then did I begin to learn what reality is.

"I must dance now. It has been too long. Now it is time to dance." Grandfather began to dance, moving rhythmically, nodding his head, moving his arms. He held rattles in each hand.

He chanted, "Hey-o, hey-o, hey-o," as he went far inside himself, deeper and deeper. The deeper he went, the more radiant he looked. His brilliance shot around the Bowl, igniting others. A drummer started to play, a very simple, austere percussion. No one else danced; they just watched Grandfather.

People began to nod their heads and sway, joining the ecstasy. They couldn't be alive and not feel it. Something profound was happening. Grandfather continued to dance quietly, rhythmically, inhabiting every molecule of his body. He was just there, dancing worship. And the Great One was there, too.

49

THE MEDICAL TENT looked like a Japanese lantern from a distance. The Bowl's decrepit electrical system was working perfectly, for the moment. When she entered the tent, Elizabeth found Will Duane unconscious on a stretcher in the middle of the floor. She took over, moving efficiently.

She had the warriors lift the unconscious billionaire onto an examination table. Elizabeth sent everyone out of the tent but Kangee Phillips, one of the warriors, and went to work. Will Duane had a nasty abrasion and contusion on the left side of his forehead; his unconsciousness indicated a concussion. His hands, elbows, and knees on both sides were badly abraded; his lower left leg was also scraped and bloody with a few cuts that required stitches. She suspected his left ankle was sprained or broken. She didn't know about internal injuries.

"Kangee, cut off his shoes," she said. As Kangee sliced Will's left athletic shoe neatly, Elizabeth smiled. He could have cut the clothes off anyone in the crowd and they wouldn't have noticed. Kangee was an expert with a knife.

Elizabeth dressed Will's wounds with Kangee's assistance. She didn't bother to hide what she was doing when she scanned Will's ankle and skull; all the warriors knew what she could do with her hands.

When she said, "Nothing's broken," Kangee nodded, accepting her words. He helped her as she cleaned Will's wounds, made a few stitches, and bandaged what needed it.

Will Duane smelled; he'd been running very hard. "How many times did he run today?" Elizabeth asked.

"Three times," Kangee said.

"How long each time? How far?"

"About five or six miles."

"Did he drink water while he was running? How did he seem when he ran?"

"He drank before and after running. He seemed strong, but like he was running from something."

Elizabeth shook her head. Running eighteen miles on a hot day? He could do it if he was a conditioned runner and hydrated properly, but why? She made a mental note to add that to the file she'd started on Will. It included the clinical records Marina had given her.

She agreed with Marina's diagnosis. It was hard to believe: the richest man in the world, who had all the planet's medical resources available to him, had gone undiagnosed and suffered for sixty-two years. How blind could people be? Including people with MD behind their names.

Will started to regain consciousness as Elizabeth finished. She put a cast on the ankle, extending it to his knee; it was badly sprained, but not broken. It didn't need a cast, but this crazy man would be off and running tomorrow if he wasn't tied down. Next time, he might kill himself.

"Kangee, could you watch him while I talk to his people?"

A small crowd stood outside the tent. Elizabeth pulled Betty aside. "I need to find out some personal information about Will. You've been closer to him than anyone. You can help me treat him properly. Would you answer a few questions?"

"Certainly."

"Does he have periods where he seems very happy and intuitive? Extremely active and productive?"

Betty smiled. "He's that way all the time."

"To the extent that he seems out of control, driven by something?"

"Yes, he does. When he's been under stress, or if he's lost something he loves, there have been times when he seemed to go into orbit. Now, for instance."

Elizabeth nodded. "How about his sex life? From what you know, is he very active, moderately active? Inactive? I'm asking for clinical reasons."

Betty hesitated. "Well, I don't know if I should talk about that."

"I need it to make a diagnosis. It's privileged information. No one else will know."

"All right. The last two years, he's been very restrained. He was dating a woman. They split up a few months ago." Betty's eyes filled. "He's had a very hard time since. I've worked for him for so long; I can't say I like everything he does, but he's been suffering so much." Her voice trailed off.

"Thank you. That helps a great deal." Elizabeth smiled sympathetically. "I need to ask more for diagnostic purposes. What was his sexuality like before he was dating this woman?" Elizabeth knew very well who she was. Marina Selene was a good friend and colleague. She was the one who suggested Will's diagnosis. And contrary to what everyone thought, Marina hadn't slept with Will.

Betty grimaced. "He was horrible. He pursued women constantly. He'd woo a woman, bed her, and throw her away. He'd shower her with flowers and gifts afterward, but he'd discard her, no matter how nice the packaging looked. I know about this, because I ordered the flowers and all the rest. Will came across as very smooth and sincere, but he was a sex machine."

Elizabeth nodded again. Exactly as she expected. One more question. "Is he really as brilliant and creative as they say?"

"He's twice as brilliant as people know. He could run all of Numenon by himself, but there isn't enough of him." Betty smiled sadly. "That's why I've stayed with him all these years. Being around him is the most exciting thing in the world. But if you had to live with him, he'd drive you crazy." She wiped her eye. "I guess I care for him more than I know."

"Betty, you've done the only thing that will get Will the help he needs. I think he has an illness that has gone undiagnosed his whole life."

The doctor led Betty to the others. "Well, it's late. It's been a big night and tomorrow will be a big day. Let's get some sleep." Elizabeth was surprised when they didn't move and kept looking at her expectantly.

"What about *Melissa?*" Jon asked.

Elizabeth had forgotten her ordeal earlier that night. "Oh! She'll be fine, Jon. The demon didn't hurt Melissa as much as she hurt it. Grandfather and I were able to help her. You can talk to her tomorrow. Wes is with her now. I expect that she and Wes will get married in the morning."

"What!" exploded Betty. "Melissa still intends to marry Wesley? She doesn't even know him."

Elizabeth nodded. "It's something that happens often here, Betty. People who are meant for each other meet and marry. I wouldn't be surprised if it happens to more people in your group." Elizabeth thought she might as well warn them. The mating frenzy wasn't over.

"But people who've just met? Who come from completely different backgrounds? It's immoral, and will certainly lead to divorce."

Elizabeth moved closer and touched her shoulder, sending as much healing energy into her as she could. Betty relaxed and softened.

"None of the hundreds of marriages Grandfather has performed here have failed. No divorces. This is the eleventh year. What other group has a record like that?" Elizabeth addressed Betty. "Trust me. Wes and Melissa are meant for each other. They've had a rough start, but they'll get through it."

Betty relaxed. "I'm exhausted," she said. "I'm sure you are too, Elizabeth. Let's call it a night."

50

I T WASN'T A night for Elizabeth. Will was awake and groggy on the examination table. Elizabeth stood in the tent's doorway, half in, half out, hardening herself. She would do her professional duty. Period.

Elizabeth knew Will was her soul mate: she'd known it since they first shook hands. She'd held the knowledge at bay. That she was able to do that was evidence of her power as a spirit warrior, plus she had had lots of things to think about to distract herself. Knowing that the real reason this would be the last Meeting was Grandfather's imminent death, the demon attacks, and healing Melissa and Wes were perfect diversions.

Elizabeth didn't want to meet her soul mate. Meeting him would require a large change in her life, inner and outer. She had a few issues to deal with concerning her ex-husband. So she "forgot" what she knew about Will.

How would she handle the arousal that inevitably accompanied touching one's beloved? The same way she'd handled her sexual feelings for the thirty years since her husband walked out. The same way she got through medical school with two little kids: stuff it and work harder.

She turned slowly and approached the examination table, lips tightening. She would do her duty, as a professional and as Grandfather's student. That her loathing of her patient as representative of corporate culture was a bit sharper than it might have been, Elizabeth noticed not at all.

"Will, I need to examine you. I use a technique that Grandfather teaches. It doesn't hurt, though you will feel our energies touch. May I go ahead?"

The great and powerful Will Duane looked up at her, blue eyes filled with terror.

"You don't have to, Will, but I'd like to know what happened so that I can help you." Before doing a psychic exam, she wanted to make sure that Will didn't have any internal injuries that had escaped her because he had been unconscious. Also, he stank. He needed a sponge bath. She got a basin and towels, and gritted her teeth.

His naked body was draped with a sheet, which Elizabeth lifted a portion at a time to bathe him and palpate his torso. The famously randy Will Duane would not look at her; she couldn't tell if he was more embarrassed than she was.

The doctor was able to see what a very good-looking man Will was. His chest had a thin mat of white hair. His pectoral muscles were clearly defined, as were his abdominals. He had no excess fat.

Most thirty year olds don't look like this. You're a real stud-muffin, aren't you, Will? Hostility streaked through her. At the same time, her hands tingled where she'd touched him.

She continued her examination, inevitably removing a particular portion of the drape and confronting Will's penis. Flaccid, thank God. She'd seen many penises professionally, very few personally. They always looked pathetic like that, lying there as if they didn't know what to do.

She felt profoundly sad after scanning his interior life. Will clung to her like a child when she was with him psychically. She felt the depth of his need to be connected, to be loved. She felt his conviction that he was unlovable, inadequate, and no good; she felt his anger and pain, his need to strike out, to compensate.

She knew the skills he'd developed, the high performance machine he'd made himself, to hide his pain and fear. She felt the depth of his spiritual poverty. Will Duane was a human mess—and he knew it. He cried to her wordlessly, *Help me! Help me, please.*

When Elizabeth was done, she called the two warriors in from outside. They lifted him, unresisting, to one of the cots. She tucked him in like a baby, simultaneously wanting to kiss him goodnight like a child and run for her life.

Elizabeth went to bed in a nearby cot, too tired to grumble about its hardness. She had to stay with him because of his head injury. As she went to sleep, an image haunted the doctor: it was young Will Duane, a sweet six-year-old, abused and traumatized. She'd seen him when she was inside Will's mind. The child looked at her and his eyes melted her heart.

Elizabeth was very good at keeping the army of men who would woo her at bay; she could resist Will Duane, even if he was her soul mate. Even with his physical attractiveness and money, his behavior had been so reprehensible that Elizabeth gagged thinking about it.

But the child inside him … Will Duane she could reject, but she had no defenses against that poor child. Elizabeth said, *Yes! I'll help you,* to that little one the instant their eyes met, deep within Will Duane's soul.

She was dozing when she felt a small, soft presence next to her cot. Will's snoring from the other side of the tent attested to his location and the fact that he was alive. It wasn't Will who was standing next to her cot. It was the child; he had come to her. She moved over in her bed and opened herself to him. The child slept with her, a disembodied soul clinging to her for his life.

Elizabeth felt the tiny Will Duane enter her body and twine himself around her being. His soft cries as he released the pain within himself kept her close to tears. She held the child tightly, and loved the tiny boy as well as she could with the heart of a mother.

This child needed her. That she needed him as well was harder to admit. Elizabeth had been alone for far too long.

51

MELISSA AWOKE IN the middle of the night, roused from sleep by persistent groans. She sat up, struggling to remember where she was. The events of the previous day tumbled in her brain like clothes in a drier from hell.

"Wesley!" He wasn't in the bed next to her. "Wesley!" she said urgently.

"I'm over here," an anguished voice replied. Melissa crawled across the bed. The cave's walls had a phosphorescent quality that reacted to movement. She could see Wesley curled up in a ball on a bed by the cave wall. He was clutching his knees to his chest and moaning with pain. She went to him.

"Wes! What's wrong? What's the matter?"

"I've been up for hours. I hurt so bad; it won't stop. Can't you help me? Please?"

"Oh, Wesley, yes. What should I do?"

Wesley gasped and clutched his knees to his chest more tightly. "Just go over there on the bed, Melissa. Take off your clothes and lie down. Open your legs. Let me, please …"

"What!" Melissa slowly and furiously articulated her message. "I've had a really, really bad day, Wesley. I need to get some sleep."

With a strength she didn't know she had, she hauled him over to their bed. She shoved him down and said in clipped tones, "Now-shut-up-and-go-to-sleep. We'll deal with this in the morning."

With that, she did "what the Chinese guy taught her" to him, as hard as she could. It barely had an effect. So she did it again, just as hard, and then again. When she was finished, Wesley was barely breathing, but looked happy. Melissa was so stirred up that she couldn't go back to sleep. She had to "Chinese guy" herself. Two sets of snores filled the cave.

At seven the next morning, Grandfather checked the cave. He wanted to see how the couple was doing. He fully expected them to have "broken training;" he'd never seen soul mates spend the night together and not be intimate. The old man was shocked when he entered the cave—they had not had sex. The energy in the space was as bland as a baby's. They'd done what no one had ever done: kept their pants on. What warriors!

"Wesley. Melissa," he said to the sleeping forms. They didn't move. They were out cold.

He looked around, stroking his chin. They were chaste; they hadn't violated the Rules. This put a whole new spin on things. He'd have to consult with the Ancestors and the Great One. He went outside and looked at the sun. He had a full day. They'd have to be married by ten if they were going to be wed that day. He knew once Wesley woke up, he couldn't last until night.

Grandfather left, shaking his head. How did they do it? Not since he and his wife were married had anyone done it.

This was cause for celebration.

52

"ARE WE REALLY married?" Andrea sat on a cushion wearing an exquisitely beaded buckskin dress. The fine skin was so pale it was almost white. Elaborate patterns of blue beads covered the top. She touched it in wonder. "It was so nice of them to let me wear this. It looks really old." The remains of a Native feast lay on a tray next to her.

'Fonzo stripped the meat from a bone with his teeth, reclining by her side. "We're married according to the tribe. Carl's marriages are recognized by them. But it's not Christian or legal with the county. That means you can get out of it if you want."

"What about you?"

"Nope. I'm chained to you forever."

"That doesn't seem fair." She looked for napkins. She didn't want to wipe her hands on the beautiful dress.

"Here," he handed her his grotty handkerchief. "It's better than nothing." She had thought he was an ugly man when she first saw him. He was very dark and his jaw was misshapen. His nose was like a beak. Plus, he had terrible scars down his face. But he didn't seem ugly lying next to her. He seemed just regular. He regarded her more intently as time passed.

✗ "What do we do now?"

"Hang around until we go crazy with lust, then jump each other." 'Fonzo picked up the dinner tray and shoved it out the flap-covered opening of the tepee, saying something to the men outside. They laughed, a conspiratorial male laugh. They sounded as though they were inside the tepee; its skin walls provided no privacy.

"What do you mean, crazy with lust?" But she knew all about the "attraction" soul mates would feel. The briefing materials Enzo had given her talked about it. "We don't know each other."

"We know each other well enough. What do you feel when I touch you?"

She blushed, hating the way she turned bright red when embarrassed. Nothing had felt so good as him touching her.

"That's cool," he said, and pointed at her flushed face. "I wish I could do that. I'm too dark to get all pink." But his face had turned a swarthy red. He couldn't totally hide his feelings. He moved closer to her, propping himself on one elbow. That semi-insolent grin was on his face. "You said you didn't know me. So get to know me. Ask me whatever you like. Fire away."

"Okay." She thought for a moment. "What did you think of me the first time you saw me?"

"I thought you were a snobby white bitch," he said, his smile disappearing. "And that you had the hottest body I'd ever seen. What did you think of me?"

"I thought you were rude and disgusting. Even the worst street people in Berkeley weren't as awful. And spitting that stuff into the fire …" She made a face.

"That's why I get laid so much. A lot of women get off on that." He was making fun of her. "But I gave up my plug yesterday. 'Cause of you."

She hadn't seen him take the round tin out of his pocket recently. "That's very nice of you," she said.

"Yeah, it was. I'm about to die of nicotine withdrawal." His hands shook, but she couldn't tell if it was put on.

"Well, I'm sorry, but it's better for your health. You can get cancer from smokeless …" He frowned. "All right. I won't lecture." She was flustered. Might as well ask the questions that really bothered her. "Are you homeless?"

"Nope. I got a really nice home—a 1985 Ford Econoline van. I fixed up a stove in it. Mattress on the floor. You an' I can go jammin' any time. Y' have to be careful about the cops is all, an' how long you park in one place." He watched her intently.

Andrea tried to mask her horror. "You live in a van?"

"I just said that. What else do you want to know?"

"Why are we together? It doesn't make sense."

"Maybe I'm one of those frogs you gotta kiss."

She sat up and tried to run for the tepee door. He grabbed her and sat her down next to him on the cushioned floor, holding on to her. His eyes sought hers. They were absolutely black, like lasers. He seemed to understand everything.

"Don't you know me?" She couldn't break his gaze. She did know him. He saved her from the Gila monster. He saved her from Enzo. He held her and it felt wonderful. He didn't care that she was afraid of everything and saw a shrink and looked terrible when she cried and took medication and thought she was stupid even though she wasn't. She didn't mind that he knew all of that.

"Yes, I know you." They were lying next to each other on the cushions.

"Do you want to know why I look the way I do and why I was acting the way I did when you first saw me?"

"Yes."

He looked more attractive as time passed. He was clean and smelled good. He'd taken his shirt off, which added to her anxiety. He was very thin, but the way men in magazines were, where all of their muscles showed. His smooth brown skin disturbed her. She wanted to touch it. It seemed such a contrast next to her whiteness. All of this was bizarre.

He seemed to be arguing with himself, but made a decision. "Okay. I'll tell you what happened. You can't say anything until I'm done." She could feel him distance himself from her so that he could talk about what he had to say.

"I'm a college graduate. Surprise you, Berkeley?" It did, but she'd said she wouldn't talk. "Yep. Tribal college. Not Harvard, but a bona fide credentialed, four-year college. I majored in creative writing." He laughed. "I wanted to be a novelist. Now there's a field where you can make a good living." 'Fonzo snorted. He seemed to be a well of bitterness.

"You know what else, Berkeley? I was married and had a kid. What do you think of that? Stinking ol' 'Fonzo Ramos had a family; a whole family. I had a mom, dad, sister, brother, wife, kid. All of it." He stopped. She thought he might run out of the tent, but he finally went on.

"Never go to a graduation on a reservation, Berkeley. It may kill you." He broke eye contact. "I picked up my diploma with everyone at the ceremony. Cap and gown. Big deal. We went to someone's house for a party. We were all drunk when we left; everybody but the baby.

"I was driving. We were doing about ninety-five when the front tire blew. Bam!" He made a loud noise and then raised his hands. "Just like a bomb. The car rolled five times in the center of the freeway. Nobody had their seatbelt on.

"I was the only one who lived. In five minutes, I went from a college graduate with family and a future to an ugly piece of shit with nothing.

"It was my fault. I killed all of them."

She wanted to say, *No, the tire blew*, but she could see he wouldn't pay any attention.

"I got these. He pointed to his crooked chin and the scars on his face. "They fixed my nose pretty good." He turned his profile to her, showing her a classic Indian hawk nose. "But the rest ..." he shrugged. "I got some burns on my back, too." He turned his back to her and she saw the scars.

"When I got out of the hospital, they'd all been buried. Everyone on the reservation hated me. I got a can of gas, poured it all over our trailer and set it on fire. Whoosh!" He raised his hands like an explosion again. "All gone. I hit the road. Picked up something for the trip." He made a movement like taking a swig out of a bottle. "Picked it up and didn't put it down until I met Grandfather. I've spent a lot of time lying in gutters, Berkeley." He looked at her, blazing. "Aren't you glad you married me?"

She didn't know what to say. "That's awful," was all she could muster.

"I gave up drinking when I met Grandfather, but I'm still an alchie. I will be all my life. I stay with Grandfather as much as possible. I've been to most of the Meetings. Grandfather has me stay at the back of the Bowl to keep a lid on things. Some people bring booze. Mushrooms. You know. They want to whoop it up, fight, get loaded, out of Grandfather's sight. I keep that from happening."

"You were working for Grandfather when I first saw you?"

"Sort of like Carl. He's been in prison. He's the slasher/rapist. Heard of him?" She nodded. "Scares people to death. And so do I. I work for Grandfather the rest of the year, too. In prisons, with drunks. Not much of a salary, but I've got my van." Those piercing black eyes again. He reached out and touched her breast, his hand skittering over the patterned beads.

Her eyes widened and she pulled away, but it was hard to go far while lying next to him.

"I've wanted to do that since I first saw you. You've got incredible tits. Do you like that, Andrea?" His hand kept caressing her, finding her nipple through the beads and circling over it.

She tried to sit up, but he wouldn't let her. She struggled and finally sat up. "If we're going to do this, we need to discuss our sexual histories. I mean, going to bed with someone is like going to bed with everyone they've slept with for five years." Her breasts felt heavy. The one he'd touched tingled. Between her legs ached. "This is serious."

'Fonzo regarded her, amused. "Okay, Berkeley. How many men have you had? Five hundred? A thousand?"

"Four and three-fourths."

"This month, or in your life?"

"In my life."

"What! You went to Berkeley. No one at Berkeley has had four and three-fourths lovers. And how do you do three-fourths of a guy?"

"Well, we were really into it, but I looked down. He had herpes. I saw the lesions. I jumped up and left. But don't worry, I didn't get it. I went straight to a clinic."

"You walked out on a guy while you were doing it?" A grin spread across his face.

"Yes. STDs are nothing to fool with. Some can't be cured. Like herpes, and AIDS. They can cut viral loads down to immeasurable levels, but the disease is not gone."

"You know a lot about sexually transmitted diseases."

"Oh, yes." She pulled her brows together and sighed. "I've studied them. I guess I'm a little bit like I am with spiders and snakes about them. Probably I'd have had a lot more sex if I wasn't terrified."

'Fonzo looked like he was enjoying this conversation immensely. "Was it any good? The four and three-quarter fucks. Did you get off?"

"There's a lot more to sex than getting off."

"No, there isn't. You fuck and you get off. As many times as possible."

"How many women have you had, 'Fonzo?"

He blew out the air in his lungs. "I don't know. Before I got married, after my wife died. Since I've been living in my van. I don't know, Andrea."

"That's it. We're not doing anything until you've been checked out. You could have something contagious." His hand shot out and grabbed her wrist. He was too fast.

"I have been checked out. They do medical checkups on us before the Meeting. Elizabeth examined me. I'm clean as a whistle. Besides, I haven't been with anyone for a long time." He grinned at her. "Except for a few old friends who give me a freebie every once in a while."

"You go to prostitutes?" Her eyes were as wide as her mouth.

"No, they come to me." She struggled to escape. He raised his voice. "Andrea! Think! Why would they come to me?"

She thought. "Because you're better than the men who pay them?"

"I make them feel good. Most of them haven't felt anything for years."

His hand snaked under her skirt, between her legs and then inside her. The buckskin dress hadn't come with panties.

"Oh!" She cringed when she felt him touching her, but he didn't stop. He used two fingers inside and his thumb in front, rolling them over and over. He kept finding spots that felt better and better. She struggled, but finally gave up. His other hand was on her breast. His eyes raked her up and down.

"Do you like that, Andrea? Are you feeling something?" He paused. "You're a little virgin girl, aren't you? You've never come with a man. Have you by yourself?" She shook her head. "I'll fix that." His face was flushed. He kept looking at her body, up to her face and down to her knees. His hand moved all that time.

She couldn't believe what she was feeling. "Oh, 'Fonso. Stop." The sensations got too much for her. Her breast felt like it was going to melt. His hand was wet and slippery. She felt like she was approaching a cliff.

"No stopping, Andrea. I've wanted to do this since you walked out of that tent. You are not going to get away, and I am going to do everything I want to you."

The first time she came, it surprised her. Nothing could feel that good. She wanted to do it again, but her wetness disturbed her.

"Let me take the dress off. I'll get it messy."

"No, Andrea. Leave it on. Get on your hands and knees." Her eyes went wide. "I'm not going to do anything weird to you. This is traditional. I want to take my smart, white wife the way my Ancestors would have."

She put her rump up and he tossed the dress's skirt over her back, stroking her bare buttocks and flanks.

"Nice, Andrea. Creamy." He stroked her hips and butt cheeks and bit her softly. Then she felt his hand and fingers inside again until she was bucking and moaning. "This is the rest of your life, baby." His voice sounded flushed, the way his face had been. "Glad you married me?" He kept making her come; she couldn't stop him. She never wanted him to stop.

He drew his body away from her and pulled his fingers out. She could hear him breathing hard, but he didn't say anything. He entered her. She tried to bolt when she felt it, but he grabbed her around the waist with both arms. "I'm not three-fourths of a man, Andrea. I'm a whole man. You won't get away from me."

Once he was inside she couldn't speak or think or do anything but push back against him. He wasn't like the four other men she'd known. He didn't lie on top of her, squishing her, while he rammed away. She didn't just wait until it was over, she moved with him. He went fast and slow and seemed to know what she wanted before she did. It was like they were dancing. He used his hands at the same time, on her breasts and belly. He made her cry out. When she felt him getting close, it excited her more. She shoved herself against him.

"Oh, 'Fonzo. Keep going. Oh, shit. Oh, God. I'm going to die." He bit her neck and collapsed on top of her. She didn't care who heard her scream.

They laid next to each other, naked. The dress had been carefully put to the side long before. He had his back to her, knees drawn up. She thought he was sleeping until she saw his shoulder shake.

"What's wrong, 'Fonzo?" She touched his shoulder and looked into his face. Tear tracks streaked his cheeks.

"It hurts is all." He grabbed her hand and rolled onto his back. He put his other hand on his chest, rubbing it. "I didn't know how much it would hurt."

"Did I hurt you?" She would never hurt him.

"No. The opposite." His face screwed up and he stuffed down sobs.

"'Fonzo, what's the matter? Can I help you?"

"You are helping me. It's been a long time, is all."

"Since what?"

"I felt anything. Since I was happy. You're right, Andy, there's a lot more to sex than getting off." He stroked her cheek. "They used to call me Al before. I'd like you to call me that."

"Al? For Alfonso?"

"Al. That was my name before Ginnie and Maggie died. And the rest of them …" He pulled his knees up and covered his face with his hands.

She sat silently and let him weep. He wasn't like the men she'd read about in magazines, stiff and controlled. He wept freely. She got his handkerchief for him.

He pulled her down to the mat. "Kiss me, Andy."

She wanted to say, *My name is Andrea*, but she didn't want to be snobby Andrea any more. She kissed him.

"Words are in my head again." Al lay on his back gazing at the tepee's poles. He smiled. "I thought they were gone."

"Words?"

"Yeah. When I was writing, I practically had to fight them off. But I don't think I'll write the words in my head now." He grinned, mischievous.

"Why?"

"'Cause they're mostly about your ass and how I feel when I'm inside of you. But I expect some other words will come along."

53

ENZO LEANED OVER the see-stone, his palms spread on its granite setting. He gazed at the gray fuzz it projected, and cursed. The stone could not penetrate the aura of the Mogollon Bowl.

Andrea had turned. He couldn't see her, but he could feel her will flip-flop in his gut. She had turned against him and blabbered everything she knew. His head ached and bright halos formed around the see-stone and everything else in his lair.

He turned to his laptop and typed a bit, hitting Enter decisively. There. Just a little taste of what it meant to spurn Enzo Donatore.

His face contorted and he threw his head back in a roar. The sound shook the castle's stone foundations. He could feel his offspring stirring in the dungeons. Not yet, my pretties, but soon.

He roared again as he realized what else Andrea's defection meant.

She was the fourth one to escape him! First that Duane slut, dried up and half dead by the time she fled, taking her bitch of a daughter. He could see Cass Duane sitting in a basement full of nodded out junkies. The daughter hadn't done too well. Sandy Sydney was the third defector. She wasn't gone for sure, but close enough. To lose another one!

The news would rocket around the castle, traveling on the ethers. Most of his people were psychic; they didn't need to bother with ethers. Everyone in the castle who'd been there long enough to get the real scene would erupt with joy when they heard of Andrea's defection. If *she* escaped, maybe they could, too. He'd have to enforce discipline even harder. Work, work. That's all she'd been.

Sweet Andrea with the big tits would find out what it meant to cross him. How should he punish her? Ah. He would curse her. He closed his eyes and whispered.

"I curse you and everything you touch. Your work will yield pain and poverty. Your eyes will see only ugliness. Your mind will think thoughts of darkness. Stinking sores will cover your body. Monsters will be born of your womb. Everyone you love will die a gruesome death. I will pursue you and drag you into eternal torment.

Enzo amused himself thinking about what he'd do to Andrea when he got his hands on her. Unfortunately, he couldn't do any of it if she remained in the Mogollon Bowl. Or around that fake, Grandfather.

She could escape him if she stayed in safe areas, but eventually, she'd slip out and he'd get her. She would pay. Everyone she loved would pay.

Thinking about revenge might be sweet, but how was he going to get Will Duane? Where was his Plan B? He screamed at the see-stone. "Show me! How can I destroy Will Duane?"

The stone abruptly whitened and threw out light. Its crystal images spun rapidly, then settled on a huge house with perfect proportions, its surfaces a combination of rough rock edges, smooth stucco, and bands of bright stainless steel. The contemporary mansion nestled into the hill, landscaped and groomed like a palace.

What was the see-stone telling him by showing him Duane's house? Well, he could see *it*. Duane might be out of striking range, but his house wasn't. What could he do to a house? Blow it up? Bug it? Poison it?

He saw all the paramilitary operatives Duane had planted around the grounds. Could he do something with his staff? Turn them? Hannah

Hehrmann, Duane's Chief of Security and a former Israeli commando, walked across the driveway. Could he turn her? Unlikely.

The stone jolted away to reveal another building. Enzo cursed again. The Numenon International Headquarters in Palo Alto gleamed in the California sun. More of the same, prize-winning architecture hailed as a masterpiece by the experts. His eyes swept the brilliant green lawns, the parking lots. The boardroom. The stone had taken him inside.

Four people sat in the magnificent room, papers laid out on the sleek wooden table that filled much of Numenon's most important meeting room.

"Frank, we'll have to execute it fast. If he finds out about it, he'll come out fighting," said Ric Chao.

"We'll have the jump on him, and we can fight, too," Frank Sauvage said. "We've been gathering facts, making a good case. We'll be able to present them to the Board this weekend—or sooner. He won't be here to defend himself."

"We really must do this. He's too erratic to continue as CEO," Mel Buckman added. "It's a sad situation. Something I thought I'd never see when I signed on."

"I agree. I have nothing but good feelings for Will," Sarah Belson confessed. "He's built an incredible corporation, but with his continued whims and peculiarities—the 'retreat' he's on now, for instance—he's a liability to the corporation. I feel very sad saying that, I've been with Numenon my whole career. But we need a change."

"Will needs to go. We'll give him a golden parachute, maybe even a platinum one," Frank Sauvage smiled. "But his time has come and gone."

Enzo smiled broadly. See, that was how things worked. Just when you're most hopeless, the universe steps forward and gives you what you want. He could see Sandy Sydney's mark on all the men; they had been her "clients." They would turn into what she was soon enough. Sandy had given them to him. Maybe she wasn't so bad, after all. He turned his attention back to the boardroom.

"We've got almost everything we need. And we're not doing it to him, his craziness is doing him in. Going to a retreat with Indians! How crazy can you get? Do you know what it's cost us?" Ric Chao's hostility practically dripped from his mouth.

"He's the majority stockholder, CEO, and Chairman of the Board. He made Numenon. *Can* we oust him?" Sarah questioned.

"All we need is the Board's vote. And we can get it. Let's go back to work." Frank closed his briefcase. "We'll meet again tomorrow. I've got some leads to check out."

Enzo sat back, basking in the fundamental righteousness of the universe. He didn't have to do anything and Duane would be ruined. Duane would be destroyed as he basked in the Bowl surrounded by his favorites, thinking he was safe. Enzo could destroy his life without touching him.

Of course, if he could mangle Duane physically, that would be even better.

54

ELIZABETH'S EYES SHOT open. She fumbled by the side of her cot; her watch's illuminated dial told her it was four thirty a.m. It was the third time that week she'd gotten up that early.

Shit! Shit! Shit! She was in the menopause—that's why she woke up so early. And had energy bursts and hot flashes that left her sheets soaked.

Elizabeth had never had any problem with being female. Her body's functioning hadn't hampered her one bit through medical school or her career. Long ago, her mother had told her, "One day, my period just stopped. That was it." Elizabeth expected menopause would be the same for her.

It wasn't. She was on a handful of hormones to tame the symptoms. Most of the time she could sleep until six a.m. Getting ready for the Meeting and the trip to the Mogollon Bowl had tossed the balance she achieved out the door, hence her early wakeup.

Elizabeth snuggled into her unyielding cot. The sound of Will Duane's soft breathing from a nearby cot reminded her of the small child who had come to her in the night.

She let her mind roam, forcing herself to stay on the bed; she needed to rest her body if nothing else. The day would be busy—and she was going to ride that afternoon if it killed her.

Elizabeth normally worked herself silly doctoring people at the Meeting, and then went off to her family's ranch in southeastern Oregon for a week. She hadn't ridden since she went home for Christmas. It was the longest time she'd been away from horses in her life.

I am what I am because of a horse. Elizabeth recalled the image that had haunted her since 1964. The back end of the horse ... She and Elwin were at the Cheyenne Round-Up, the biggest rodeo in their part of the world.

When it happened, she was twenty-three years old and Mrs. Elwin Bloodstone. She had two babies on the ground, and many more to come, most likely. El was a bareback bronc rider. Elizabeth and Elwin had their own trick-riding act. They put on an impressive show, two gorgeous Indians riding amazing horses. Her mom took care of the babies back at the ranch.

Elizabeth could remember the first time she saw him. Elwin Bloodstone was the most beautiful man she'd ever seen. He pulled into her family's ranch on a spring day and asked if they were hiring. He acted cautious; he was a half-breed and not welcome in some places.

She still could see the look on Elwin's face when he realized that the ranch was owned and run by Indians. He hadn't known that he was walking into the most prosperous, prestigious American Indian-owned ranch in the west. Their land extended as far as the eye could see. They were the Lewis family of the Diamond Bar L Ranch, near Remedy, Oregon.

Elizabeth was Native American royalty. The youngest child and only daughter of the richest Indians in the western States (in those days before casinos), she had been seventeen when Elwin Bloodstone drove his old truck into the Diamond Bar L. The year was 1958.

El was a bronc rider and ranch hand from Texas. He didn't own a pot to pee in, but he did have a guitar and a voice to go with it. Her father gave him a job after he saw the young man work an unbroken horse. He worked it a new way, gentling it with long sensuous strokes of his hands. Elizabeth was mesmerized by those strokes and his hands.

Lying in her cot in the dawn in 1997, listening to Will Duane snore, Elizabeth remembered how she'd felt when she was seventeen and in love for the first time. She couldn't eat. Couldn't sleep. She'd be up first thing, busying herself around the horse corrals.

Elwin Bloodstone cut through her like butter. There was no seduction. He didn't take her virginity; she threw it at him. Elizabeth slipped around like a cat, making herself available whenever and however he wanted.

They were married when she was three months pregnant. Gordon Lewis could not tolerate his daughter, his iron angel, giving herself to a penniless half-breed drifter. Gordon Lewis hated Elwin Bloodstone with his entire soul. So did everyone else in the family, but her.

And there it was in her mind's eye, what she wanted to forget but could only remember: the cruddy old horse trailer, Buzz's spotted white butt on the left side, a rough buckskin on the right.

She must have known. Why would she be carrying her gun? The rumors about Elwin started almost immediately. He went off to do some rodeoing a couple of months after they were married. Why not? He could earn some money and she couldn't ride, being so pregnant.

The rumors came back before Elwin. "More brown babies should be showing up around here," they laughed in town.

Elizabeth didn't believe what she heard. El was so wonderful when he got home, the kindest, gentlest father. And the best lover.

El continued to rodeo. Not only was he winning, he was starting to get bookings to play and sing at rodeo dances. Elwin was becoming a celebrity and a heartthrob.

When Elizabeth saw what was happening, she kicked butt—her own. She got it down to the size it had been pre-baby. She was twenty years old, the mother of two, out on the rodeo circuit. Her mother watched the babies while Elizabeth watched her husband.

Elizabeth got a reputation of her own. If there was anything Elizabeth Bloodstone could do better than ride, it was shoot. She'd enter fast draw contests and win them. She'd do sharpshooter demonstrations and leave people astonished.

She watched Elwin like a hawk and he was faithful as long as he was in her sight. Which brought Elizabeth back full circle to what happened and why she was where she was today.

She had walked quietly through the rodeo grounds to the parking area where the trailers were kept, her pistol hanging down by her side. Dust splashed her new boots, but she didn't care. She didn't notice the people running when they saw the big gun. The world seemed quiet and still that afternoon. Very peaceful. Slowed down.

The rodeo was over. She was ready to leave and couldn't find Elwin. She knew where he was; she'd seen him smiling with that bleached blond. When she found him by the woman's old brown trailer, Elwin was pressed up against her. Her back was against the trailer's rear door.

Elwin's tongue had to be halfway to her navel, Elizabeth could see. His hand was on her breast. The other woman's curly yellow hair stuck out from behind Elwin's sleek black mane.

Elizabeth walked up, as silent as only she could be. When she was at point blank range, she said, "Elwin, I told you I'd kill you if I caught you like this again. I expect you know I will."

People stopped around them. Elwin backed off the blond so that Elizabeth could see her competition. The woman was pretty, in a cheap, used sort of way.

She meant to kill them both. For the first time in her life, she choked. Her hand jerked as she fired. The bullet missed them and fired into the trailer. It hit Buzz-saw, her beautiful Appie horse. She'd given Buzz to

Elwin as a wedding present. The bullet hit him in the left buttock next to the tail. She could see him buckle in the trailer; his pelvis was broken—he was ruined, unfixable. A living dead horse was leaning against the trailer walls. They were all that was holding him up.

She screamed. "I shot Buzz! Oh, God! I shot my horse!" Elizabeth doubled over. Someone took her gun and Elwin and the woman tore off in the chippie's truck and trailer rig.

That was the last she saw of Elwin Bloodstone.

"The worst thing I've ever done," Elizabeth whispered, "was shoot that horse. He was worth fifteen of Elwin and his little whore, too."

That's what the woman was, as it turned out.

Elizabeth went home, but couldn't stay there. Everyone in the Bonheur Basin knew; she felt them laughing at her. Her husband had left her—Elizabeth Lewis, the Indian princess—for a bleached blond, white prostitute. She had shot her own horse over it.

That was the beginning of her rise to fame and glory. She moved to San Francisco with the boys, and then down to Palo Alto. She ran away to school: first to San Francisco State, then Stanford, then Stanford School of Medicine. And on to my medical practice and working for my People. She earned her master's in Public Health and all the honors just came along.

I am what I am because I shot my horse.

Elizabeth got up. She was so depressed she could hardly move. Will Duane still slept. She walked heavily into her own tent to get dressed, and sat at the dressing table looking into the mirror.

Just get me through one more day. A tear ran down her cheek. She couldn't hold anything back; everything hurt. Grandfather was dying. Her dearest friend was leaving her. She forced herself forward. She would do her work, no matter what.

Her meeting with Will Duane in a few minutes was the most important professional meeting she would ever have.

Elizabeth knew what she had done on the Reservations with the limited dollars at her disposal. She'd had an enormous impact on morale and people's lives. What could someone with real wealth do if he committed it to her People? What if he committed it to living in a way that reflected human values? Will Duane could change the course of history.

He had to be brought on board. She also shared her friend and fellow healer Marina Selene's conviction that Will was treatable if the core of his illness could be reached and healed.

She dressed carefully, as it would be the last chance to spruce up for quite a while. Wes and Melissa's wedding would undoubtedly follow her meeting with Will Duane. Then Grandfather's talk. One of the Numenon people was supposed to be speaking, and she wanted to hear what he had to say.

Her new red silk blouse looked good. It was western style and had matching silk fringes across the front and back yokes. She wore a tiered denim skirt, low-heeled boots, and the silver Concho belt Wesley had made for her. She peered into the mirror, trying to do something with her face.

I'm so fat! So fat and old. Her shoulders sagged as she stopped brushing her hair. *And I'm tired. What have I really done with my life? What have I changed?* She leaned forward to keep her tears from staining her silk blouse.

Never fails. Every time I wear silk, I end up crying.

She gave herself a silent pep talk. *This is menopause thinking in your head, Elizabeth. It's due to hormones. You've lived a good, productive life. Your children are fine people. You are a success.*

But I'm so alone, drifted up from her depths.

"I want to die," whispered Elizabeth. "I'm so lonely, I want to die."

55

ELIZABETH WALKED BACK into the medical tent as Jon arrived with breakfast for Will. He said, "I brought breakfast for you, too, Dr. Bright Eagle."

"Thank you very much, Jon. Call me Elizabeth."

Her heart grabbed seeing Jon, just as it had when he walked into her office in Palo Alto. When Jon Walker had come into her office a few days before, she knew he was "positive" the minute she touched his hand.

"Jon, I need to talk to you today. Perhaps after Grandfather's lecture?" Jon stared at her, looking as though he knew what she had to say. Elizabeth sent out a psychic message to all the warriors to keep an eye on him. He shouldn't be alone.

Jon stumbled away.

Elizabeth sat at the table Jon had set up, complete with an off-white table linen, crystal, and creamy china stamped with the Numenon logo in gold. Will was eating an omelette with all the trimmings.

Show time—almost. She prepared to give her spiel, but the food tempted her, as it often did.

Will watched Elizabeth eat. *There's a woman who likes her food. None of this anorexic bullshit.* She was beautiful with her rounded face, sparkling dark eyes, and high cheekbones. And proud. No doubt that she was a warrior. She sat like one.

He liked what she was wearing. The fringes and tiered skirt. Her gray hair was tied up with a red bow. The bright red of her blouse matched the bow, both warm and cheerful. Will felt better that morning, though he couldn't say why.

Breakfast was a pleasant interlude. They got to be together and relax before Elizabeth began. She had something important to say to him, he could tell. She wheeled him away from the table toward her desk and bookcase. An office area. She examined his abrasions and changed his dressings. "Good. How's the ankle?"

"It hurts."

"It will hurt; it's very badly sprained. You're lucky that you're alive, Will. Do you realize that?

"Given what happened, I need to talk about my clinical observations of you right now. I have some ideas that might make your life better. Do you have time?"

Will had nothing but time. He was stuck in a wheelchair.

"Will, you know that I scanned your psyche last night. I know pretty much everything you shared with Marina."

He jumped. "You know Marina?"

"We're very good friends. We work together all the time. She's a brilliant healer."

"I didn't know you knew Marina. No one said anything about that."

"She called me about you the minute she found out you were coming here."

"Did she say that she wanted to see me? Or missed me?"

"No, Will, she did not. She won't be seeing you in person again. We've decided that your relationship with Marina isn't healthy."

"We've decided? Who's we?" He glared at her.

"Grandfather and me. And Marina."

"Too bad for me. It's not like I don't have a stake in this. I don't suppose you got a medical release to talk to her about me. I don't remember signing one."

"Will, I'm not here to argue about Marina. We have some serious issues to discuss that will affect the rest of your life. I think you may have a medical condition that affects how you feel and behave. It can be controlled with medication, and treatment can make life much easier for you."

"What are you talking about?"

"Your life. Let's talk about how life is for you, Will. How it really is, not the glossy public version. For instance, what were you thinking about when you went running last night?"

He scowled and drummed his fingers on the wheelchair arm, as though he wasn't going to say anything, but then he burst out, "Did you know that my staff have set up a new camp next to Grandfather's lean-to? They hate me so much they won't sleep in the same campground as me." He had no intention of telling her that, but the words just flew out of his mouth. He didn't even know it bothered him that much. It did.

"Your own people exclude you?"

"I'm excluded from my own life. I can make a big show at a conference, but when it comes down to it, no one likes me."

"Okay. What I would do if I were you is listen to me as though your life depended on it. Because it does. I think you have an affective disorder. That's a mental disorder that affects mood. The disorders are a family. They run on a scale from almost normal to a tendency to mild-to-severe depression. That's on the low side. On the high side, individuals can have a mild elevation of emotional state followed by a mild low. In others, extremely elevated moods alternate with crippling depression, indicating a true bipolar disorder. A person with a bipolar disorder can be come psychotic at both the low point of his depression and the high point of his mania.

"The disorder we think you have is 'hypomania.' It's sort of dimmed-down mania. A person with this disorder doesn't get so manic that he becomes delusional, but he moves pretty fast."

"What are you saying? That I'm crazy?" His voice rose again. "I didn't get where I am because I'm crazy."

"Hypomania is the one mental illness with a positive side. Some of the brightest, most creative people in history have been hypomanic. The disorder tends to strike the smartest, most intuitive, inspired people. Artists, writers, genius types. Politicians, even Presidents. Successful business people. Even CEOs in Silicon Valley."

Will made a disparaging gesture with his hand.

"Do you ever feel down, Will? Depressed?"

"Christ! I'm down all the time. I have so many problems that an ordinary person would collapse just hearing them. But I don't give in. Feeling lousy is what made me who I am. That, and my father telling me I'm worthless. Feeling lousy and worthless made me the richest man in the world." He glared at her, having no idea why he was telling her all this.

"It's amazing what forms our lives, isn't it? Do you know how I got where I am? I killed a horse," Elizabeth said. "That made me who I am today." He wanted to hear more about the horse, but she pressed on.

"Do you ever feel irritable, Will? Do you explode at people?"

Will felt an explosion building right then. "No. I could blow up fifty times a day, between the office and home, if I wanted to. I don't. I wait until I'm calm, then I deal with my people. I get mad, but I control it."

"That isn't what I've heard, Will. I've heard you described as volcanic and terrifying. I've been told that feeling your rage would mark a person for life."

"Who told you that?" He raised out of his wheelchair. "It's not true. I'm known for being fair."

"And demanding."

"Who told you that about my temper?"

"I have patients, Will. Sometimes they talk about work related issues that affect their health. Stress, for one thing."

"My *employees* are talking about me?"

"To their doctor. It's their right." He wanted to question her further, but she went on. "Do you feel irritable? Do things bother you?"

"*You're* bothering me. What you're asking is none of your business." If she hadn't been a doctor and an attractive woman, he'd scream at her. Will shifted in his wheelchair, grabbing the arms. His knuckles turned white.

"I need to know if I'm to help you.

You're annoyed with me right now. Do you feel irritable other places? How about at work?"

"Of course I'm irritable. I work with morons who can't do a day's work. I have to tell them how to do everything, stroke their egos, pat their asses. I'll have a deal cooking, and they want to go on vacation. If I say no, I'm the bad guy.

"When I've got something going on, a new product line, a merger, anything, I take off like I've got wings. I've been like that my whole life. Whenever I have a big challenge, I seem to speed up and get through it. I sleep about four hours a night. I can work harder and faster than anyone. And I have visions. I might as well tell you that since you're playing Sherlock Holmes. I have visions that tell me what to do. I see lights and things ... Wonderful things. They're always right. I guide Numenon by them. That's why I'm so successful."

"And you've never lost?"

He sat back. Marina. Kathryn. Cass. And that time that he wouldn't tell anyone about. He'd called Betty from the house when he was so upset and she'd called the doctor. They'd put him in restraints, kept him in his room. Kept it a secret. His Board of Directors couldn't know he was hospitalized. That asshole psychiatrist they got for him kept talking about his complexes and family structure. He stuffed him so full of drugs he couldn't think. Will scowled.

"You fit the syndrome perfectly. You're a classic case. In addition to being brilliant, creative, and a workaholic, you have a layer of chronic depression and are subject to periods of hyper-activity and euphoria. You have religious-type experiences. And you suffer from hyper sexuality. I've heard that from a number of people. Your appetite for sex is prodigious. Will, those are the symptoms of hypomania. The good news is that your condition can be controlled with medication and psychotherapy. It's treatable. Thousands of people are doing well with medication—they function just fine."

She went to her medicine chest and gave him a tablet and some water. "I'm starting you on a low dose to see how you tolerate the drug. We can increase it later in the week, if all goes well. We'll talk every day, or more if you need it. You could be feeling great by the end of the week. It's not optional, Will. Your life depends upon it." She nodded at his leg in its cast. "I don't want you to hurt yourself anymore."

Elizabeth got up and stood next to him. She put her hand on his shoulder, but jerked it away like he was a hot flame. That instant's touch felt better than anything had in his life.

He savored the feeling her hand had left. She was marvelous. Tough as nails. Everyone was afraid of him, but she wasn't. She was as smart as he was. And she was beautiful. Will had hope for the first time since splitting with Marina. He smiled at her, his face soft.

"I'll see you in a few minutes, Will. It's time for Melissa and Wesley's wedding." She left the tent.

Did the lingering pleasure in his shoulder mean anything?

56

WHEN HE MADE eye contact with Elizabeth Bright Eagle, her expression told Jon that his HIV test was positive. He staggered off. She let him go without a word of kindness or support. He felt a few seconds of shock, and then …

Goddamned sons of bitches. He got on the golf cart he'd commandeered to take Will's breakfast to him. The Indian driving the golf cart pulled away and looked at him wide-eyed. Jon didn't care.

How can they require blood tests? *That's got to be illegal!*

As they drove to the Numenon camp, Jon's fury settled on everything, but mostly the state of the Indians' campground. *Look at this dump!* These people have no couth. He couldn't even think about the stinking porta-potties.

And *Big* Doctor Elizabeth! What a great physician! No doctor in San Francisco would let a patient walk off after learning he was positive.

Jon was in such a rage that he didn't notice the four or five golf carts following them, or the other carts converging on the Numenon camp. He continued to silently vent his anger. They're Neanderthals.

By the time they got to the campsite, he realized that he was infuriated and he knew what to do about it. When he was angry, nothing gave

Jon as much pleasure as using a knife. He'd get into a rhythm working with his knives, cutting up vegetables into fine pieces, skinning poultry, deboning meat. The clicking of the knife on the cutting board, the movement of his hands, seeing the shredded product on the other side of the knife brought a peace that he hadn't found elsewhere. He'd chopped his way through love affairs gone bad, telling his parents he was gay, and 'Rique's almost continual affairs.

As he entered the court, he saw a bunch of gigantic warrior-types lounging around, looking at the camp and its decor. They were making fun of it! That set him off more. Jon didn't find it remarkable that he could hear their thoughts as clearly as the spoken word.

A gust of wind blew eddies of dust over the Bowl. Jon shouted. "Mark! Jeff! Get to work on those tables!" They jumped to, cans of spray cleanser and cloths swishing. "We've got to stay ahead of the dust! We are not savages!"

The warriors looked at him.

"Listen you people," Jon half-shouted. "Get over here." He marched to the edge of the Bowl, not looking back to see if his entourage was following. They did follow and ended up looking out over the spectacular desert scene. In the morning light, colors were not yet bleached by the harsh sun. The sky was pale blue, the rocks and mountains moody shades of brown, rose, cinnamon, and mauve.

"It's beautiful!" said Jon vehemently. "It's serene. Simple. Magnificent. Now look over here."

Jon took the whole troop, thirty-four people by now, to the inside edge of the Numenon camp, overlooking the main campground. It was teeming with chaotic life. "Now, what does that look like?"

"It's uglier than sin," he continued, with his litany of the main camp's ills. "Look at those cooking fires all over. Someone could get burned. The smoke is in everyone's eyes.

"Why don't you organize a central cooking area?" He was earnest now, not angry. "I'll help you, if you like," he found himself saying. "This afternoon."

Marching back into the camp kitchen, Jon busied himself preparing for his "chop." He pulled out his knives and sharpened them, then went through the menus he'd planned and set up the vegetables so that he'd chop them in order of use, and set out the meats in the same order. He moved his knives and a few cutting boards outside to one of the serving tables.

He was slow getting into it, making a few desultory whacks at carrots to start. Everyone gathered round.

"Why are you here?" he asked the assembly.

A guy in a blue shirt replied, "Elizabeth told us to make sure you were all right."

Jon flared. "Did she say why?"

Blue shirt shook his head. "No."

Jon was puzzled. He'd been broadcasting his HIV status far and wide with his thoughts. They were all psychic; why didn't they know?

The guy continued, answering Jon's question. "We do a thing called, 'pulling the shades' for personal subjects. Elizabeth pulls some nice shades for her patients." He smiled. "We care about people, Jon."

The way the blue shirt dude said this was very kind. Elizabeth sent all these people to watch out for him. She did care. He teared up for the first time that day.

Which pissed him off. Damned if he'd cry in front of these goons. He took a few hard whacks with his knife, finally getting into chopping. As he loosened up, memories started flowing. Rage boiled in Jon as he remembered.

What a stupid, whack!, stupid, whack!, stupid, whack! Whack! To think that 'Rique should be dead. He was forty-two. Whack! Whack! Just barely middle-aged. Whack! It wasn't fair! Whack! Yeah, it was true. Whack! They'd gotten the virus from what they did. Whack! Whack! But how many straight people lived lives just like his and 'Rique's? Whack! Whack! Lots did—he knew that working at Numenon.

Jon's knife was flying. His hands were a blur. The chopping sound filled the air. The formerly bored spirit warriors were riveted. Skill with a knife was highly prized by their community.

Kangee Phillips—the master knifeman—arrived, summoned to watch the knife artist. Jon didn't notice. He kept slicing, chopping, skinning, deboning, dicing—you name it—as quickly as people could bring him the meat and vegetables from the kitchen. He switched knives from hand to hand, working just as well with each.

"Look at him," Kangee said to his neighbor. "A warrior."

Looking up, Jon found sixty or seventy people watching him. He was as high as a kite and crowd. Having gotten their attention, he began to chop for real. He chopped with a knife in each hand, changing knives like lightning; he sliced little animals and people from vegetables, did fancy cuts for garnishes, juggled knives, and made them dance upright along the table. As a grand finale, Jon tossed one knife over his head high in the air. He caught it with one hand—behind his back. The crowd burst into applause. Jon laughed and bowed.

Bud Creeman had joined the group, his eyebrows raised. He pulled Jon aside. "You are what they say."

"What do they say?"

"You're a spirit warrior. We want you to join us. Grandfather said yes."

"What does that mean?"

"Mostly, it means you're part of our family. You're a student of Grandfather's and you follow his teachings and rules. You also come to our special trainings. It's very hard, but if you can do that," Bud nodded at the table where Jon had chopped, "you can do our trainings, no sweat."

"I'm not one of your People."

Bud nodded. "We have a number of warriors who aren't. You'll be part of an elite group that will love you all of your life. You'll learn how to live—and die—well."

"You know I'm gay, don't you? My partner just died of AIDS. I'm HIV positive."

Bud nodded. "Grandfather follows the old ways. Before the Europeans came, many of our tribes recognized that some people liked their own sex. These are called 'two-spirited' by some tribes." Bud looked earnestly at Jon. "The rules are the same for everyone."

Jon nodded, easily. Gladly.

Bud tugged at his ear. He was supposed to remember something. Watching Jon chop wiped it right out of his mind. What was it? He was almost ready to ask Jon what it was, when he remembered. "Oh! I'm supposed to tell you that the wedding is in fifteen minutes! We have to hold it down by the cave because Sandy Sydney's still loose. It's safer down there."

"Fifteen minutes! I can't do a wedding in fifteen minutes!" Jon shrieked.

"Doesn't have to be fancy," Bud said.

Jon glared. "Yes it does. She's my best friend." He looked around the camp. "Can I use all these people?"

"Yes."

He ran into his motor home and came out with the megaphone. "All right, *people*. We are doing a wedding in fifteen minutes. *My* kind of wedding." He looked around. "I'd like the ceremony to be in front of the Chinese screen. You, you, you, and you, pick the pieces of the screen up and carry them to the cave in the golf carts. Set them up in the middle of the cave. Let's do it, people. We're warriors!"

Palm trees were soon descending over the edge of the rim, heading to the spirit/healing/wedding cave below; the Chinese screen tottered with them, each cart with its own section.

Jon was in the middle of making canapés when Bud came back, saying, "The wedding's late—you've got about ten more minutes."

"Oh, good. That will give me time to bake a cake," Jon snarled.

57

A HUGE INDIAN, WITH tattoos covering all the skin that Will could see, came to take him to the wedding. He was the guy who had picked him up when he was running that first night.

"I'm Carl Redstone." His voice was deep and resonated in his chest. He nodded at Will, but didn't offer to shake hands. He half-lifted Will into a golf cart and loaded the wheelchair afterward.

They headed along the Rim to the path that went down to the horse area. It was familiar by now. Will's brain felt fractured. The session he'd had with Elizabeth had shaken him. He was mentally ill. Or had a "disorder." He did. He knew it. Will groaned. Had he achieved what he had because he was brilliant, or mentally ill?

The giant stopped the cart. "You okay?"

"My ankle hurts."

The thug leaned over and put his hand on Will's cast over the ankle. He felt a pulsation, the pain lessened. Another, and it was almost gone.

"What did you do?"

"It's something I can do. Most of us can do it, some."

"Could Elizabeth have done that?"

"Yeah. She could heal it all the way if she wanted to. She fixes broken bones."

"Why didn't she do it?"

"Prob'ly because she thought you'd kill yourself if you could run around." Carl started to drive off.

"Wait," Will said. He could see the Bowl behind him. The campground was as busy as ever. "Shouldn't everyone be going to the wedding? Wesley's really important."

"Yes, they should." Carl ground his teeth and gripped the wheel tighter.

"They're snubbing Melissa and Wesley's wedding?" Will was appalled.

"Yeah. That's what they're doin'."

"Because she's white?"

"And with you."

The wedding was in a fair-sized grotto in front of the cave's opening. The grotto had thirty-foot high, red rock walls all around, except for a narrow entrance. It was as safe and secluded a place as you could find outside of a bomb shelter. Jon had worked one of his miracles on it. It looked like a wilderness country club. Will smiled.

He'd gotten that huge coromandel screen down there. It was the first thing Will saw when Carl wheeled him into the area. Jon had set the screen up in the middle of the open space, with its back toward the entrance. The wedding would take place in the middle of the grotto. That made sense; the bride and groom would be coming from the cave. The procession would move from there to the altar. They could retreat to the cave quickly if they needed to.

Carl shoved Will's wheelchair toward the opening in the cliff face. Will heard him grunt. Hard going. He looked down. The grotto's floor was swept and raked. Jon's doing, undoubtedly. If it hadn't been swept, pushing the wheelchair would have been impossible.

When they got to the grotto's rear wall, Carl stopped by the cave opening. Elizabeth came out. Will felt a little disorientated seeing her.

"Will, Melissa wants to speak with you. She's just inside."

Carl pushed his wheelchair through the opening and then exited, along with Elizabeth.

Will could see Melissa standing a bit farther into the cave.

"Are you all right, Melissa?" He was instantly protective. She seemed tiny and fragile to him, even though she looked beautiful, wearing a pale blue dress trimmed with lace. Her normally large eyes were huge, their whites gleaming and misted with tears.

"Yes," she answered, but it was a quavering "yes."

"Do you want to stop this, Melissa? I'll go out there and—"

"No. It was just so fast. I'm ..." Her tears bridged her lower lids. She leaned forward so they wouldn't mark her dress. "So much has happened."

"Melissa, if you want me to, I'll shut this down right now."

"Oh, Will. You're so sweet." The tears kept coming, distressing her more. "I don't want to mess up my makeup. I don't have a hankie."

He handed her his. "Keep it." Will inhaled hard, his eyes boring into hers. "If he hurts you, if you need any help, call me. I'll be there in a minute. Do you understand?"

"You'll take care of me." The corners of Melissa's lips turned upward the tiniest bit.

"You're goddamned right I'll take care of you." Will's feelings rose like a flood. She moved closer to him and put her hand on his shoulder.

"I think it will work, Will. I love him. I really do." She sniffed, looking up at him. "I've never felt like this with anyone."

"Okay, but if he gives you trouble, you call. If you need anything, ask. Everything I've got is open to you."

She laughed. "I don't need that much, but I wanted to ask you something."

"Anything."

"Would you give me away?"

"What?"

"At the wedding. Would you walk me down the aisle?"

Will's heart grabbed and, for a moment, he thought that doctor was wrong about it being healthy. It settled down and he realized he was moved to the core. "I'd love to. There's nothing I'd rather do." He'd been holding her hand. Will raised it to his lips.

"My girl." He smiled. "When I saw you in the hall for the first time at Numenon, I thought you were my daughter. Then I realized you were the daughter I wanted. Smart, strong, beautiful. And healthy. I love you, Melissa."

"I love you, too, Will. I think of you like a dad. My dad's a nice guy, but he's not you."

"We need to get going," Elizabeth's voice resounded from the cave opening.

Will lifted Melissa's hand in a courtly gesture.

Carl entered the cave and propelled Will out of the opening. They waited for Wes and Grandfather to emerge.

Will's throat tightened. This was probably the only time he'd get to escort a young woman—any sort of daughter—up the aisle. His eyes filled and he blinked, trying to blink his feelings away.

Palm trees were arranged on both sides of the tall screen. In front of that was an altar. Part of it was ordinary: a podium that they used for presentations. The edge of a book peeped over the top. The Bible, Will supposed. The rest was most unusual: a buffalo skull, and other ceremonial items that he didn't recognize, were arrayed in front of the screen.

In the back, which was really near the enclave's entrance, all the tables they had brought were covered with clean white cloths and spread with appetizers. The fragrance of spiced coffee emanated from a huge silver urn, and banquet-sized containers promised more delicious drinks. A large umbrella shaded a huge wedding cake with a crystal swan sitting on top of it. Will wondered where in the hell Jon had gotten it. It was probably the closest Jon could come to a depiction of Grandfather's totem, the crystal eagle—which everyone in camp seemed to be talking about.

Jon was hovering around the hors d'oeuvres, looking more nervous than Will felt. More and more people came, dressed in the most amazing ways. Shirts with ribbons all over. They were wearing restrained versions of their pow wow regalia.

Good, they're dressing up for the wedding. More people came. Still more entered. The area in front of the cave was jammed. But only a relative few could fit into the confines of the canyon. Were many waiting outside?

Once the grotto filled, Grandfather and Wesley stepped out of the cave, blinking in the light. Bud Creeman walked up as Wes's best man. They moved up the aisle to the altar. Will watched Wesley, not knowing what to think. The man was spectacularly beautiful. The tests they'd given him showed him to be brilliant. But Will would always see him almost naked and shooting lightning bolts. Would he be a good husband for Melissa?

Wesley had his hair in a ponytail, with several large brown and white feathers attached. He wore four silver and feather earrings in one ear and two on the other. His shirt and jeans were black, befitting a spirit warrior, but his shirt was trimmed with a riot of ribbons in every color. They streamed from his shoulders and the shirt's yoke. He looked wildly festive.

Will was at the cave mouth next to Melissa, ready to walk her up the aisle. He saw people oggling her and took a better look at her dress. She wore a mid-calf length, pale blue silk dress with an off-white lace petticoat showing beneath it. The dress's long, flowing sleeves were trimmed with the same handmade lace. Breathtaking.

She moved next to his wheelchair, pale and looking worried.

"Melissa, are you sure you're okay?" he asked.

"I'm fine, Will." Her huge eyes teared up. "This means a lot to me, you being here. I love you, Will."

Will's heart quaked. He whispered, "Remember, anything you need, ask me. No limits. If you have any problems with Wesley, or anyone, you come to me."

Jon started music on Melissa's minuscule sound system: a slow, classical guitar piece in perfect taste. She clutched Will's hand, looking at him for reassurance.

"Just ask, Melissa, just ask." And then he let her go.

"Friends. We are here today to witness the marriage of our dear brother Wesley and his bride, Melissa," the shaman began. "Last night, I had a dream. I saw that they will be very, very happy. They will have a wonderful marriage and many children. They will be leaders in the world, and they will do more for our People and the world than most of the rest of us put together."

Grandfather's dreams were never wrong, and the crowd inhaled to cheer. He held up his hand to stop them. "I'm not saying that it will be easy," the old man said, turning to Wes and Melissa. "Many of those I have married have had hard times. But those hard times have produced the greatest learning and the greatest marriages. And the greatest spirit warriors—and you will be the greatest of the greatest!"

He was silent and closed his eyes. When he looked up, he was in an ecstatic state. "I don't approve marriages. All I do is recognize who's correct for each other, and they recognize it themselves. I've felt the energy and connection of these two people and it is perfect. Melissa and Wes are soul mates. They are joined at the deepest levels." He nodded with eyes closed a few seconds.

Grandfather turned to Wes and Melissa. "No one is forcing you to marry?"

"No," each of them said.

"Is there any reason these people should not marry?"

There was a rustle, but no one said a thing.

Grandfather kept talking. Rings. A Psalm. "The heavens tell out the glory of God, the vault of heaven reveals His handiwork.

"Now we start the Native portion of the wedding." Grandfather beamed. A quilt was wrapped around the couple.

People exclaimed: "His mother made that." "It's beautiful." "That's why Rose Silverhorse didn't come. She knew Wes would get married." "She could never stand losing her favorite."

Will watched, remembering his own wedding. Grace Cathedral, with its carved stone towers and Episcopalian correctness, was packed. Nob Hill had never looked better. Inside the church, lilies hung in cascades, looped in wreaths. Exploded from vases. Fell from Kathryn's bouquet. The air was thick with their perfume. Kathryn was a dream, a very expensive dream in an ivory peau de soie gown. They went to the Club afterward. She didn't get drunk until the reception was almost over. He didn't get what that meant, somehow.

Words and sounds. Grandfather raised a pipe. He passed it to Wesley and Melissa and then to Will. The old man sang. The sound was heartbreaking. Will's heart was breaking. When Wes kissed Melissa, tiny blue whirlwinds of energy swept over their bodies. People jumped back, fearful of electrical shock.

Will never saw it coming. After the ceremony, Betty approached him from the crowd.

"I've arranged for someone to take me to Las Cruces. I'll be flying home from there." Her face looked so tight, he was surprised she could speak. "I've spoken to John. We're going to try again, and get it right this time. We'll be moving. I'm giving my notice." Her eyes filled.

He coughed, more of a choke. "Well, we've had a good run, Betty. Longer than most marriages. I appreciate what you've done for me." She kissed his cheek and was gone.

"I'll see you get the platinum retirement plan," he called after her.

58

ANDY AND AL headed up the handicapped ramp that had been pulled out of the *Cass's* underpinnings and knocked. Andy was panting as she stood there, she was so scared. This meant her whole life. Would Mr. Duane forgive her when he knew what she had done? Would he let her keep her job with Numenon?

Carl came to the door.

"Can we talk to Mr. Duane? It's important."

"He's feeling bad. His secretary quit." Carl started to close the door, but Andy put her foot in the opening.

"Tell him that I was hired by *Enzo Donatore* to spy on him."

"Who said that? Let her in," Will's voice boomed from the interior of the *Cass.*

Andy barged in, followed by Al.

Will sat blinking at her. "Who are you?"

"Andrea Beckman Ramos." She held out a hand. He didn't take it.

"Enzo Donatore hired you to spy on me, and you're telling me about it?"

"Yes. Because I'm not going to do it." She looked at Al and Carl. "They saved me, or I would have, though."

"Why didn't you tell me, Carl?" Will turned to him. Carl's face went blank.

"That doesn't matter," Andrea interjected. "What matters is that I would have been on my way to becoming Sandy Sydney if they hadn't saved me. And I might have gotten some of the information Enzo wanted."

"What are you talking about?"

"Can we sit down?"

Will waved his hand at the *Cass's* luxurious leather banquettes and lounge chairs. Andy sat, followed by Al and Carl.

Will faced Andy, looking like an attack bomber, even in a wheelchair. "Tell me what this is all about? Start from the beginning."

She talked about her encounter with Enzo. "When he found out I had a job with Numenon—"

"You work for me?"

"I just got hired as an Analyst 1. I haven't started yet. When he found that out, he said a lot of really bad things about you. He gave me $300,000 before even starting. Well, he started with $100,000, but I bargained him up." She shot a look at Will, who looked faintly amused by what she'd said.

"Anything else?"

"Triple my Numenon salary and benefits, and a new BMW." She hung her head.

One side of Will's mouth turned up a tiny bit.

"I took a negotiation course." She looked at him through her eyelashes, feeling scared. "I heard you liked people to take it."

"Did he touch you, Andy?" Will's voice was gentle.

She told him about that.

"After Al saved me, I kept wondering why he didn't ... have sex with me. He could have. I couldn't resist him." Her voice faded. "But I realized when I got here with the supermodels—"

"Who?"

"He flew me to New Mexico on a corporate jet. Two campers and a truck met me. They were full of people who looked like supermodels." She posed like one of them. "They got really sick when they got close to the Bowl. I was so stupid." Her eyes misted. "When I got here, I could see that Grandfather was real. And then things fell apart. Al saved me. If it weren't for him, I'd be … gone."

Andy's nose began to run, as it did whenever she wept. "I'm sorry. I didn't know. I had all these dreams of a wonderful life …"

"You have nothing to be sorry for. He's done the same thing to people who've been around far more than you," Will said. "Come over here."

One wall of the Cass was covered with elegant cabinetry. Will pushed a button and the doors retracted, revealing a compact but very powerful computer lab. Will wheeled himself over to the wall, and pulled a flat shelf out of the front of the unit. It had several built-in keyboards. He powered up the computer system.

"Stop!" Andy cried. "Turning it on will fry it. It did my laptop. Willy Fish fixed it. It's burnt and melted, but it works. I tried it."

"Willy Fish. Who is he, Carl?"

"I'll bring him over."

The computer screen lit up. Will hit some keys. "Okay. Tell me if you saw either of these people at the castle."

A beautiful black-haired woman appeared on the large screen. The screen divided into a large image in the middle with smaller images of the woman arranged around it. The veins under her skin and the minute shadings of her face were drawn clearly against her fine, blue-white skin. Her eyes were an even deeper blue than Will Duane's, and as magnetic. Her hair cascaded to her shoulders. She was in a garden, smiling. That image faded and one of the others from the surrounding screens took its place. She was riding a horse, playing with a dog. In a ball gown. Back in the garden.

"Did you see her?" Will asked.

Andy shook her head. "No, she's so beautiful that I would have remembered her if I did." Andy kept her eyes on the screen, rapt. "I've never seen a movie star that beautiful."

Will pushed a button. Another face appeared, younger and not as lovely at the older woman's. A dark haired young woman with intense blue eyes. Her eyes were more focused than the other woman's. More aggressive. She was Will Duane's daughter, anyone could tell that.

"You didn't see them?"

"No, but they could have been somewhere I didn't go. The place was huge. Who are they Mr. Duane?" Andy asked.

"They're my wife and daughter. Ex-wife. Would you like to see them after Enzo got to them?" He didn't wait to see if they said yes.

The screen filled with Kathryn Duane's face. A scarf covered her thin hair. Blue-black shadows rimmed her cheeks. Her face looked like it had collapsed into death's head. Another image came up; she was getting into a limousine, her straight skirt hanging against shrunken buttocks.

The younger woman's image appeared. An emaciated shell, half her head shaved, her scalp tattooed with a Chinese dragon. It flowed down her neck and arm. Her lips and nose were pierced many times. The piercings were rimmed with red flesh; they were infected. Her eyes looked as dead as her mother's, circled hard with black eyeliner. A decorated tree in the background and garlands of greenery said it was Christmas.

"That's what Enzo Donatore would have done do you, Andy. That was my ex-wife the last time I saw her, years ago. And my daughter. That was last Christmas. Cass was at my ranch in Montana at Christmas. I don't know where she is now."

"That's what he wanted me to find out—where they are—or, if I couldn't find that out, if you knew where they were."

"So you can leave now, and tell him what he wants to know."

"No, first I'd need to get into that," she indicated the bank of computers, "and pull out a few other things he wanted."

"What?"

"The plans for the Ranger VIII, and your new mega computer." Another nod at the bank of computers. "He'd probably like to have the plans for that, too."

Will bridled. "You've got a lot of nerve coming in here."

"I thought it would be worse if I didn't. Now you know. Oh, he also wanted some *vitae* on you and your wife and daughter, and the—"

The super computer began flashing red lights and emitting a wailing noise.

"Shut it down! It will be destroyed," Will cried.

"No, it's not that." Andy sat at one of the keyboards and began to type. "That's a hardware malfunction." She typed furiously. A diagram like an electronic maze with all sorts of pathways appeared on the big screen. A line ran through the middle the maze's corridors, as though it were seeking something. A circle with a cross through it appeared and the line ran into it and stopped. The image changed, showing a blow up of the interior of the computer at the targeted spot.

"Okay. There it is. I can fix that. Do you have a paper clip?" Will didn't move. The red light kept flashing. "If I don't fix it, the machine *will* melt down." He rummaged through a drawer.

"Here."

Andy unhooked the computer's front cover module and pulled the machine forward. It slid easily on a shelf. She pulled up a side panel and looked inside, typing with one hand and glancing at the big monitor. Images appeared on the screen at a greater resolution. "Hmm. Do you have a someone with a PhD in computer science here?"

"No. I have three MBAs."

"What did you bring them for? They're useless. I'll do it myself. I need a ballpoint pen." Andy dove in with the pen and a paper clip. Moments later, the red light stopped flashing. The target-like circle on the maze faded away. Andy stood back, then typed a bit more.

"I just reprogrammed it. It will be fine for the rest of the trip. You should have someone look at the design when you get back. The way the hardware's put together shows the problem. There should be more space between—"

"How do you know all this?"

"I've been messing with computers my whole life. Other little girls played with Barbies, I rebuilt motherboards. Getting my MA was easier than what I was doing on my own. By the way, you need better security," Andy said. "While I was working, I could have pulled off everything Enzo wanted."

Will stiffened. "You can do that?"

She nodded. "The thing's a sieve." Her brows knit. "I need to check something." She pulled up a screen and typed. "Oh, my God. Look at that." It was a bank statement with a zero balance. *Her* bank statement. "He took all of my money."

Will had pushed his wheelchair away from the computer and sat studying her.

She guessed what he was thinking. "Do I still have a job a Numenon?"

Those blue-laser eyes focused on her. "Talk to me at the end of the week."

"I know," she wilted. "I'm dishonest and a person of bad character. I'm a spy."

"A reformed spy. I think you had bad judgment, which is just as damaging." Will seemed to grow about three feet as he sat in his wheelchair. "If you use what you found out here against me, if you ever steal from me, or betray me in any way, I will see to it that you won't work anywhere on the planet. If you hurt me or anything of mine, I'll kill you."

Both Al and Carl stepped toward Andy at that one. Will raised his hand.

"You need to know that, Andy. And so do you, Al and Carl. I don't fool around. I will kill Enzo Donatore because of what he did to my wife and daughter. And I will kill anyone else who hurts anything of mine."

Will turned abruptly and stared at Al. "You're her husband, right?" Will scowled. "If she wasn't honest, she'd have taken what she wanted and be on her way back to Enzo. She's not going to do that. She's going to run to you." He pointed at Al. "Keep an eye on her and see that she doesn't get into trouble.

"Get out of here, all of you. I want to take a nap. You, too, Carl." He touched his forehead as though he had a headache.

They walked out the door and stood on the landing.

"Well, that was fun," Al said. "Are you glad you told him, Andy?"

59

A T THE OPENING to the grotto, a messenger from the Pit awaited Grandfather. The old man was shocked; it was Paul Running Bird—and he hadn't attended Wesley's wedding.

"Everyone's getting restless, Grandfather. The People have been waiting for half an hour."

Grandfather hadn't seen much of Paul after he gave the Numenon people the map that could have gotten them killed. He must have been slinking around, hiding. Good. He deserved to be cast from power. He probably deserved to be thrown out of the Meeting, but the Great One hadn't told the shaman to do so.

Grandfather knew how miserly the attendance at Wesley's wedding was. The tight space in the cave grotto created the illusion of a big crowd, but given that almost four thousand people were at the Meeting, the couple of hundred who came was an insult to Wes and himself.

Grandfather frowned. He knew if Wesley had married one of the People, they would have been forced to have the wedding at the Pit. Everyone in the Bowl would have come. No one would be hounding him to leave the wedding to give a talk—they'd all be making merry with the happy couple.

"You really should come, Grandfather, people are talking," Paul whined.

"Oh, I'm sure they are, Paul. Go tell them that the wedding party is wonderful and that they are invited. If they don't wish to come, I will be there when I arrive. They should wait quietly and enjoy the beauty of the Bowl. Or people can leave and do whatever they want. They'll know when I get there."

As Paul left, Grandfather motioned to Kangee Phillips, the master knifesman and one of his most trusted spirit warriors. He was known to have a memory so good that the warriors said he would remember everything an elephant forgot.

"Repeat my message," Grandfather commanded. Kangee did, word for word. "Follow Paul. See what he says to the crowd. Remember it. I'll ask you to tell what you remember at the right time."

The band struck up, playing their best and loudest. Soon, everyone was doing some sort of Native American/California-native dance rendition. It was a good wedding, for those who were there.

Melissa and Wes were cutting the cake. She was unraveling, Grandfather could see.

Time to end the party. He waved the couple back into the cave and turned toward the golf cart. Grandfather sighed. His problems were stacking on top of each other. The insubordination of the People, undoubtedly egged on by Paul Running Bird, was one difficulty.

But there was another situation brewing that he hadn't imagined. It might be a serious problem to the whole Meeting. Or maybe it wouldn't affect anything. But maybe it would. Should he tell everyone about it?

His jaw clenched as he bounced along in the golf cart as Kangee drove.

When he and Rebecca married, Great-grandfather told them that they had been given a gift from the Great One to reward them for being exemplary warriors. It was a secret gift, given only to those of Great-grandfather's lineage. Given very sparingly. In fact, he and Rebecca were the only two people who'd received it, that he knew of.

Until now. As he married them, the One told him that Wesley and Melissa had been granted the same gift. It had a name, a name so deep and ancient that even top spirit warriors couldn't pronounce it. He could hear it in his mind in Great-grandfather's voice, but he couldn't say it.

In the Great One's world, the act of procreation was elevated to mystical levels, to spiritual and physical ecstasy. It took the souls of the couple involved to the depths and heights of the universe, and brought them face to face with God. The act created new beings, holy beings fit to live in the One's blessed domain.

What Wesley and Melissa had been given was that in its highest form—for twenty-four blessed hours, the Creator would take them to the deepest realms of sensual existence. It wasn't just sex, it was a tableau of what human sexuality could be, unfolding, spiraling downward, touching the Divine at deeper and deeper levels.

They would start out making love like any honeymooning couple. Their intimacy would bring them to states usually known only by the blessed souls of history. They would be quiet for a time, and then their intimacy would deepen more, and more, spiraling downward and upward until their union and exultation reached the core of existence.

When they reached the core, the silken shroud separating the world of creation from the Divine would tear open. The effulgence of God would pour over the lovers. They would be lost in the substance of love, the substance of being. They would merge with God, nothing less.

Grandfather remembered this very well. Having experienced it, no one could forget. That is why he and Rebecca had remained married, though they couldn't live together. They were eternally a couple. Because of those twenty-four hours, he had never taken another woman in the forty years they'd been separated.

What Wesley and Melissa would receive was a gift for the entire planet, human and nonhuman. When Melissa and Wes reached the depths of existence, the universal fabric would break. Living water would burst forth, filling the universe with blessings. Dry lakes would fill and polluted rivers would throw off their contamination. Endangered species would reproduce. Barren women would conceive.

Children born that night would be the best and finest that people could produce. Wes and Melissa would be blessed above all creation for the rest of their lives.

So they had to complete the journey. The planet depended upon it. He couldn't stop them even if he wanted to, the Great One had begun the process.

He sighed deeply. Why did he have this stupid Meeting? It had gotten so out of control because Paul Running Bird had disobeyed his orders and opened that website about him and the Meeting. When he told Paul to take it down, he put it on his own website, made information about the Meeting into a "chat room" that was "password protected." It was safe, Paul said. Only Native spiritual seekers would find it.

Grandfather didn't understand what "password protected" meant, other than that it didn't work. The four thousand people attending this ridiculous last Meeting were due to Paul's programming skills and the *Internet* calling in the flotsam and jetsom of his world. He should have stopped Paul before he set up his site in 1995. But maybe it already was too late when he found out about it.

Plus, he didn't know about the gift the Great One would bestow on Wesley and Melissa. It had a negative aspect. Well, it didn't need to be negative, but he suspected that it would be in this crowd. The experience spread to others. Great-grandfather had sent Rebecca and him miles into the desert when they received the gift. As far as they'd gone, when they returned to Great-grandfather's camp the next day, people approached them with huge grins. They made ribald remarks. He realized that the others had felt what he and Rebecca felt.

As Grandfather thought about what was coming, the potential for disaster grew. He didn't know most of the people at this Meeting. Oh, he knew his warriors well and would trust them with his soul. They were pure and disciplined and able to handle themselves no matter the temptation. The warriors were about five hundred of the four thousand in the Bowl.

Quite a few others—maybe a thousand—he knew because they'd attended previous Meetings or he'd healed them. Or he'd visited them in jail. They were on a spiritual path and were self-controlled, when they remembered. Seeing the Great One was not a major goal for any of them. They wanted to be like him, as long as it wasn't too hard. They had attended the Meeting primarily to see friends and be part of his group. They wouldn't be able to withstand anything.

The last group, perhaps twenty-five hundred people, were complete strangers. He'd never met them; they'd never been to any other of his events. They were spiritual tourists, called by Paul's website to see the great shaman at his last Meeting. They'd collect an experience, something to tell their friends about. They'd see flashing lights or manifestations in the sky and think they were almost as developed as he was. If they didn't see anything, they'd gossip and tear down everything he said. Tear *him* down.

The Rules called for everyone to be celibate this week. He didn't think that too hard. The warriors were supposed to be celibate all the time if they weren't married, though he did give some a "special dispensation" if not having sex was too hard.

But the tourists were there to look and take; they considered refraining from *anything* a terrible and unjust punishment. He knew this from sitting in the Pit with them. From smelling them and hearing their thoughts. They were beasts. They were his People, of course, but they were exactly like all people of all races. Only the best would rise to the top and embrace the life of the soul.

He sighed again, biting his lower lip in consternation.

"Are you all right, Grandfather?" Kangee asked again.

"Yes, my son. I'm just thinking about the wedding." That and everything else that might transpire. Wesley and Melissa would spiral ever inward. The Gift would bring interludes that no one could imagine, things that seemed crazy. He remembered thousands of dancing girls whirling around him on his night. All of them were his wife. Who knew what the Great One would give Wesley and Melissa? Who could predict it?

And who could predict what would happen with the tourists and strangers came in contact with the couple's energy? He could feel their vices as he walked through the Pit: rage, sloth, viciousness, lust, hatred, the desire to destroy. Whatever the tourists held closest would come roaring out.

Should he tell everyone what was coming? Should he tell the People to leave the Bowl for the night? Could four thousand people pack up and leave for a few hours? Where would they go? Sandy Sydney was still out there, stalking.

Thinking seriously and considering as many facets as he could, Grandfather decided it wasn't his problem. *He* didn't give Wes and Melissa the gift, the Great One did. He would have to trust the One to handle what happened.

He would keep Wes and Melissa in the cave for the full twenty-four hours. That might help. He knew that they wouldn't get to the deepest portion of the gift until the end of that period. Everything else would be a warm-up. Maybe people would be sleeping by then.

He sighed again. Why should such a glorious thing cause problems?

60

PAUL RUNNING BIRD felt a resurgence of righteousness when he got back to the Pit. True, he may have made some mistakes that put the Numenon party in danger earlier, but what had their illustrious guests contributed to the Meeting? Nothing. The pretentious motor homes parked on the hill were a mockery of Native American values.

Most of them, the ones who mattered—Will Duane and his three executives—hadn't attended any of the scheduled events, flagrantly breaking the Rules.

What did Grandfather do about that? Nothing. He'd thrown a girl who wasn't in the Numenon party out of the Meeting earlier. Doug Saunders had been involved in whatever she'd done. Why wasn't *he* tossed out?

"It's so typical," Paul said, almost to himself.

"What?" people asked him. The crowded Pit seemed to amplify his words.

"Grandfather says one thing, and does another. The Rules apply to us, but not Will Duane." A group turned to listen to him. "This isn't really an Indian retreat. Grandfather mixes up so many traditions, he teaches *stew*." Everyone laughed at that.

"This Meeting will be a 'management seminar.'" Sarcasm dripped from Paul's tongue. "That Numenon driver is supposed to teach us *psychology*." He rolled his eyes. "Why should we have to listen to that crap?

"Why do we have to listen to that? 'Because the Great One told me so.'" He aped Grandfather's speech. People around Paul cracked up. "No one listens to it. Will Duane and his friends don't even show up, but we're breeching the *Rules* if we skip that shit.

"I can hardly wait to see what the old man has planned for the rest of the week. Economics? Yoga? At least that Mark asshole will be done today.

"Next year, *I'll* put together an authentic gathering—now that Grandfather is *finally* retiring."

"Wow. That's great, Paul. Put me on your mailing list." "Me, too." "Yes, put me down."

He went to his tent to get some paper and pens. He returned to the Pit as Grandfather arrived.

Paul didn't feel anything was wrong at first. The old man walked to the front of the amphitheater, sniffing, almost like he was getting the scent of the crowd. That was easy; the crowd was so hostile Paul felt it like a slap. Not a slap directed at him, though. When Grandfather assumed his cross-legged position on the buffalo robe, he smiled pleasantly at the crowd and said, "How are you this morning?"

Sullen silence greeted his words, with a few boos breaking the stillness. The old man seemed to like that, as though he would enjoy a tussle. "You didn't wait here all this time, did you?" That brought a chorus of resounding boos. "You didn't have to. You were free to go." More boos.

From way in the rear, Willy Fish, roused to a frenzy, shouted, "You tol' us to stay here til you came."

"I said that? I wasn't here. How could I say that?"

Willy called out, "You sent Paul Running Bird to tell us. He's a spirit warrior."

"Paul?" Grandfather craned his neck, looking for him. "Paul, you and Kangee come up here. You, too, Willy." A few moments passed as they climbed up on the stage. That's when things began to turn ominous to Paul.

"Paul, what did you tell these people?"

"Just what you told me to say," Paul replied, leaning away from the shaman as though he was contaminated.

Grandfather nodded. "Ah. We'll see. Are you a spirit warrior, by the way?"

"No."

"Did you tell these people you were?"

"No."

"I see." The old man turned to Willy. "Why do you think he's a spirit warrior?"

"He looks like a warrior. He runs the Meeting." He crossed his arms over his chest.

The shaman nodded and said, "Paul, you have done more to keep this Meeting running than anyone. I appreciate all that you've done over the years." He clambered to his feet and hugged Paul in front of everyone.

"Maybe I haven't praised you enough for it, but I thank you now."

Paul beamed. He was finally getting the recognition he deserved. His chest swelled and tears flooded his eyes. Maybe everything would be all right.

Grandfather sat on the robe again and crossed his legs, seeming to expand as he did so. He was stern and terrifying when he spoke next. "But all that you've done, doesn't make you a warrior."

He turned to Willy Fish.

"Willy Fish. Why was I late?"

"Because Wesley was getting married."

"Do you know Wesley?"

Willy brightened. "Oh, yeah. He's really nice. *He's* a warrior."

"Do you like him?"

"Sure."

"But you didn't go to his wedding. Why?"

Willy's face darkened. Willy cast a glance at Paul, who started to speak for him. Grandfather raised his hand. "I want Willy to speak."

Willy mumbled, "He married a rich white woman. He's a traitor."

Grandfather looked at him. "How is he a traitor?"

"He'll go live in her fancy house."

"Now that he's married, Wes will go live with his wife—that makes sense. Is it her fault that she's wealthy? Is she wealthy, by the way? Does anyone know for sure?" Grandfather looked at the Numenon crew and picked out Doug, the only executive in attendance.

"Is Melissa rich?"

Doug shook his head no, and replied, "Not for where we live. Plus, everything she's got, she's earned herself. She's honest and she's good to people. And, God, is she smart."

Grandfather nodded. "Wes married a very fine woman, who's worked for everything she has."

The crowd was still simmering softly, but was chastened. Grandfather turned to Willy Fish and to Paul. "Tell me, do my dreams predict the future?" Both nodded.

Grandfather looked over the crowd and said, "Would it matter to anyone that last night I dreamed that Wesley and Melissa would do more for our People than any of us? More than me? Would you have gone to Wesley's wedding if you knew my dream?

"I love Wesley. It would hurt him if he knew that his good friends didn't go to his wedding because of his wife's color and who she is— when they don't really know who she is."

He turned to Willy Fish. "Willy, what was the message I sent when I was late?"

Willy puffed up with indignation again. "Paul told us you said we should sit here in the sun. You would come when you felt like it."

Grandfather looked at the crowd. "Did you hear that?" Some nodded. "I didn't say that. Paul said that and you believed him. Is that right?" They nodded.

Grandfather went on. "Everyone knows Kangee Phillips, don't you? Would you trust what he said?"

The crowd's "Yes!" moved across the Pit. If they hadn't seen it in action, they all had stories about Kangee's memory.

Paul Running Bird's face registered terror as Grandfather asked, "Kangee, would you repeat Paul's words, and show us how he said them."

Kangee walked forward a few steps with an air of self-important authority. He stopped in the middle of the stage. As he repeated Paul's statement, his mouth tightened as though he was eating something sour.

"Is that the message you received?" Grandfather said to the silent crowd. "That's nothing like what I said. You see, our minds carry the seeds of our downfall."

Paul sidled to the edge of the stage, his face bright red. This was going all wrong.

"Stay, Paul."

"I didn't do it on purpose, Grandfather; it's what I heard."

"I know, Paul. Our minds color what we see and hear. At Wesley's wedding, I read the beautiful Psalm nineteen. The psalmist says, 'Who is aware of his unwitting sins? Cleanse me of any secret fault.' What we just saw through Paul was the working of his mind. It was an unwitting sin. He did not know he was distorting my message."

The old man raised his eyes to encompass the crowd, deliberately dropping Paul. "How many of you would have gone to Wesley's wedding party if you had received the actual message I sent?" Whistles, yells, and hands went up. "How many would have gone if they knew more about Melissa and my dream?" The crowd was almost silent, but every hand went up.

"You can't be a warrior if you are a slave to your secret faults," Grandfather continued. "You can see people all around you exploding with love and visions and dreams and wonder why you don't get them. You blame me or the Great One, when the fault is yours. You don't get the fruits of spirit because your secret faults have not been rooted out."

Rage exploded inside Paul. Grandfather had revealed everything about him—he'd never had a vision, never had any of the experiences everyone talked about. He jumped off the stage and started to walk away.

"Stop, Paul, or leave this Bowl and never come back."

Paul spun to face him. "You're picking on me."

"No, Paul. I'm doing what needs to be done." He leaned a little closer to Paul. "Do you remember when the Numenon group got lost?"

Paul's eyes bugged out. "Oh, yes, I led Willy and Bud on an expedition to find them. We brought them in."

Grandfather nodded. "The Numenon people gave me this." He pulled a sheet of paper out of his pocket and unfolded it. "You faxed them these directions to the Bowl."

Paul went white. "I don't remember that."

"Really? Anyway, the map says they should go over here." Grandfather pointed to the map and held it up to the crowd. "Instead of taking the center road. What you told them to do would get them lost, Paul. Why would someone who cared about me and my work send our important guests a map that would get them lost?"

"My assistant sent it." Sweat broke out on his brow as Grandfather revealed more.

"Is your assistant someone I know? Can he come up here so that I can talk to him?"

"No. He's not one of our People. He's never been here."

Grandfather nodded. "Ah, I see. If your assistant has never been here, how could he draw a map without your directions? Why would it be signed with your name? I know your signature."

Paul ran to the first row of the crowd.

"Paul. Stop," Grandfather commanded.

Paul turned. "I don't remember what I put on the map. My office was busy when I faxed it to them. I never meant to get them lost, or make everyone mad at you, or hurt Wes, either."

Grandfather turned to the crowd. "This is a secret fault. Paul has taught us a lesson, let's give him a big hand."

Paul smiled sweetly, feeling his stomach churn. He locked eyes with Grandfather. The son of a bitch did it. He humiliated him before the whole Meeting. Humiliated Paul Running Bird, who founded and kept the Meeting going for eleven years. He hated that sanctimonious old turd.

Grandfather had shoved Paul over the edge.

Paul slowly left the Pit. He acted cool, but he burned inside with humiliation. This was the last disgrace he would endure at Grandfather's hands. He wouldn't wait until the Meeting was over. He would destroy the old man this week. Now.

The heavens opened. Light didn't fall on him, or exhaltation. An idea came. An idea that would change everything. He had his first spiritual experience as his relationship with Grandfather ended.

Something huge and more wondrous than an old shaman came to him. He didn't know who it was, just a brightness smiling at him from the inside. A power separate from Grandfather's tired platitudes. A power that was the real thing.

Once he'd felt that power, people turned toward him.

"Hey, Paul. The old man really shafted you."

"Who knows what he was talking about? Secret faults? What does that mean?"

"What you did wasn't so bad. So what if they got lost?"

"I don't think they should be here at all. And look how Grandfather favors them. Have you seen Will Duane at anything?"

Paul walked through the crowd and people quietly approached him, reaching out to him. Something had changed.

61

"THEY'RE HERE?" ENZO barked into the intercom in his office. He hadn't left his desk since he felt Andrea betray him.

"I have them in the vault where you ordered," Diego's voice returned via the speaker.

"I'm coming. Don't warn them."

Enzo whirled away from the see-stone and headed deeper into his personal quarters. He ran through the dimly lit clubroom with its commodious chairs and wrought iron furnishings. The door to his bedroom was open; the shadowy fringes of chains hanging from the bed's black leather canopy were barely visible. He loped out the rear of his chambers, and down the stairs.

His feet slapped a terrifying rhythm. He dropped lower beneath the castle, turning and turning as the staircase wound into the mountain. Trickles of seeping moisture oozed down the stone walls. Rustles and scratching noises from deeper within the stone told him his children were awake, clawing at the floor and trying to escape. Rubbing their beaks along the walls. They were hungry and wanted out. He'd unleash them in good time.

"Ah!" he said as he threw open the heavy wooden door to the dungeon. "You're back from your triumphant mission! What do you have to tell me, my lovelies?"

The five of them were huddled in the back of the cell, not looking like supermodels any more. Although they weren't restrained, they didn't move. Their eyes darted around the rock chamber. This rock wasn't cheery and buff-colored like the castle's upper floors; it was dark, and stained with rust-colored streaks accumulated over centuries. Metal implements were stowed in wall racks and chains capped with manacles hung from the walls. A fire burned in a round iron vessel in the middle of the room. The fire popped and embers shot toward the ceiling.

"Oh, you're afraid, my darlings?" Enzo pulled a branding iron out of the coals and examined its glowing end. "I promised you rewards you cannot imagine if you succeeded. All you had to do was deliver that little idiot, watch her for a week, and then bring her back to me."

"It was hard," Rollo said. "We got sick."

"*We got sick,*" Enzo mocked his voice. "Of course, you got sick. You should have stopped farther away from the Bowl, imbecile!" He slammed the red-hot end of the brand against the cauldron, bending it and notching the vessel's wall.

"Oh, please don't hurt us," pleaded one of the women.

"You don't want me to hurt you?" She shook her head. "Then why did you fail?" He swung the iron rod at the glowing red pit. The crucible flew over, bits of charcoal and burning embers tumbling across the floor. The models pulled together, moaning.

"You had the best navigation systems, the best surveillance equipment, and you let the stupid twat get way!" He began swinging the brand in every direction, dislodging the torture implements from the wall. "She went over to them, with you practically there."

"We *weren't* right there. It was a long way to the Bowl—"

"Shut up! You let a bunch of Indians chase you in a truck. They would have caught you if I hadn't broken their axel. You had to call for my help from a gas station, like tourists!"

"My people do not call for help. They do not run!" Enzo threw back his head and roared. "You will pay."

He screamed into a speaker, "Diego, get down here and flog these idiots."

Back in his office, Enzo bent over the see-stone. "See!" he commanded. "See!" The stone went straight to the Numenon headquarters and focused on Duane's enemies. Lovely. He'd have a few tidbits to advance their cause soon. Sandy Sydney's influence on them was growing daily; he could see their demonic nature as they plotted to depose their leader.

The stone skipped to the impenetrable mist around the Mogollon Bowl. He saw a flash on one side, but it disappeared in a heartbeat. Sandy Sydney. Given the good work she'd done at the Numenon headquarters, he wasn't so angry at her. He might even forgive her if the men she had infected performed.

Enzo sat and studied the stone. It still couldn't penetrate the Bowl's power. But the people inside the Bowl could extend themselves to him. He'd forgotten the relish with which humans longed for what was bad for them. They grasped for more and better and different. They would do anything to satisfy the bellies of their desires.

He understood them so well. Humans were vicious little animals, differentiated from himself and his whelps only by strength. He was more powerful than anything in existence. Humans knew that. That's why they built all those silly churches and temples, trying to ward him off.

But they couldn't. He was infinitely patient. Humans carried his seed inside themselves; it waited to burst forth and grab and destroy. He had a feeling that what he and the old shaman taught about a supreme power wasn't so different. Except that *Enzo* got it right. Evil would triumph.

Enzo gazed at the see-stone, a wonderful insight coming to him. If that Indian was already seeking him, more of the humans in the Bowl probably wanted him, too. Their tendencies would create an entry into the Bowl for him and his spawn.

When he had that thought, he felt a gentle movement like a feather touching his skin. A burst of light followed, and then an opening. The one he'd felt before was reaching out to him. This was someone who shared his values and goals. Someone who wanted what he offered: everything.

Enzo could see him in his mind, not through the stone. A handsome Indian chap, gray-haired. Looked like a banker. "What's your name, dear fellow?"

"Paul Running Bird."

"And how can I help you, my man?" He could feel Paul's mind searching and groping, looking for a Teacher who would satisfy his expectations.

Enzo projected a beautiful brown face with almost black eyes into Paul's mind. The vision was a dignified, middle-aged man. Paul's face registered idiotic happiness as he had his first revelation.

Enzo spoke to Paul. "What do you want, my friend? I can help you." His voice was deep and rich.

"I want recognition for what I am," Paul answered. "I am a modern-day shaman with a message for everyone. I don't want to wait for people to recognize me. I want to lead the Meeting. I want all these people to love *me*. Now. At this Meeting."

"Of course, my friend. I'll lead you step by step. I'll come to you and tell you what to do. You must do what I say, or all will be lost." Enzo kept himself hovering in Paul's mind, fading softly until just his smile remained.

Enzo slapped his hands on the granite slab holding the see-stone, and laughed.

Running Bird wanted to be a shaman? Oh, he would be a shaman. Miracles? Prophecies? Visions? They'd swarm over Paul and everyone around him. He was the go-between he had been looking for.

If Paul wanted an Indian chief as his mentor, Enzo would deck himself out with feathers and paint, and a peace pipe, too.

62

ABOUT FOUR HUNDRED miles of glacier separated them. Wesley sat on a bench by the rock table in the cave, his face in his hands. Melissa sat on the other side of the cave looking at her feet.

He thought there was some correspondence between how you worked a horse and how you dealt with a woman. At their wedding reception, he could feel that Melissa was close to cracking. The minute they got into the cave, he let her go and backed off. He could tell she had an edge, a comfortable distance, like a horse. If he got any closer than that edge, she'd get nervous. If she were a horse, she would have to move away, and maybe kick as she ran by. Who knew what Melissa the person would do if he pushed too hard?

"Are you okay?"

She shook her head. "No. I need to be alone."

He couldn't do anything about that but leave the cave, and he wasn't going to do that. The warriors out there would laugh at him, walking out on his bride.

He went back to thinking about horses. If he left a fine horse alone in an enclosure and didn't threaten it, it would eventually come to him out of curiosity. He could put a hand out and touch the animal. Once

Wes had a hand on a horse, he could catch it. He'd send some of that healing energy into it, and it would gentle down.

"Melissa, I love you."

Melissa looked up, face tense and distressed. "I love you, too, Wes. And I don't know what to do." When Wes started toward her, she pulled away. "Please, just give me a few minutes."

"We don't have to do anything, Melissa. I just want to hold you."

"But I can't do that. I can't."

Wes sat on the bed with his back to her. Melissa could hardly breathe: he'd removed his shirt. He was so beautiful. His shoulders made a broad horizontal stroke. Under them, his back curved down to his hips. He was wearing his jeans; she couldn't see his buttocks. She could see expanses of smooth brown skin and curving muscles. He reached around the back of his neck and loosened the tie binding his hair. It dropped in a cascade.

"Take off all your clothes and lie face down. I'll give you a massage. I'm really good at it," she said pertly, pretending that her lungs were working properly and her legs weren't threatening to collapse. She turned around while he stripped. When she turned back, he lay on the bed on his stomach, hair falling to each side of his neck.

A half-naked Wes was more than she could handle. She'd seen his back and top half when he was sitting there, a quarter of his body. Seeing all of him—his back bisected by his spine, the curves of muscles on the backs of his arms, his thighs, the swell of his buttocks rising from the small of his back—was too much for her. He had dimples above his butt! No one could look like that. She put her hand to her chest.

Their wedding quilt was draped on the bed; she picked it up and covered him, exposing his back above the waist. She put oil on her hands and rubbed them together, warming the oil as her massage therapist always did.

All of Melissa's psyche was working, as it does in everyone, all the time. One thing it noted, far below her awareness, was how little hair

Wes had on his body. He had no halo of red curls or disgusting body hair. No pink skin, nor swine-ish blue eyes. He was small and fine-boned, with hardly any fat on him. Nothing like … Something far below her surface relaxed. He was different from … Her hands were white against his darker skin. Such soft skin. Its texture was so fine. Wes was safe. She was safe with him here, in this room.

"I love you." She kissed his back.

Wes gasped when her lips touched him. "Melissa," he whispered.

63

MELISSA COULD FEEL the energy currents of a horse very easily; on Wes, they were absurdly clear. His muscles were perfectly delineated, like an anatomy chart. He was beautiful. More beautiful than his body were the currents of light running through him.

She wanted to pause and just look at him, a quarter of his body at a time. But Melissa would finish the massage she'd started, because she'd set out to do it. That's how she was. She worked like a professional, shoulders, then arms ... lovely muscles. The long scar below his elbow, like the skin had been rubbed off. How did he get that? He had a lot of scars. What had happened to him? Was ranching dangerous?

Her palms rested between his shoulder blades, directly behind his heart. She felt something: a shadow, as if something had been removed, but the outline remained. Like someone had gotten up off a carefully made bed. Melissa could see the shadow of sadness all around Wesley's heart.

Who he was changed as she tuned in to him. He wasn't the terrifying, gorgeous Wesley, naked on the martial arts field with blue lightning all over him; he wasn't the crazy, equally terrifying man running around the cave screaming as he had been when he woke up. And, especially, he wasn't the person who was in the cave last night who witnessed her shame. Melissa remembered everything now, and knew he'd seen what happened to her, and heard her screams.

This man under her hands wasn't an interloper. He was Wesley, with soft skin and pain and grief around his heart. He had his own horrors, which she didn't know. Wesley, who was like her, fighting his demons, a man who hurt and cried. She could feel his tears. This was her mate, her soul mate, given to her to love. Her eyes moistened. She touched him tenderly, completing her massage. She removed the quilt and saw the shallow dimples above his buttocks. Ran her hands over them, and the backs of his thighs. Slowing down. Looking and feeling, textures and colors. Scents.

Her universe became her hands and their connection to him; her breasts, their seeking tips, the triangle linking her hips, and the triangle that ended between her legs. His body, her hands ... the flow between them. She was getting to know Wesley. Her Wesley.

He lay on his stomach in the bed, floating in bliss. A brilliant halo of white and gold fanned from his head, blinding him. Through the glare he could see the blurred outline of a beautiful woman, her long hair flowing out in all directions, streaming in the light. Wes thought she was the White Buffalo Calf Maiden, revered as a goddess by the People. She was speaking to him, telling him how wonderful his life would be.

"Wes. Wes. Turn over on your back and I'll finish your massage."

He was surprised to hear her voice. "Melissa? Was I sleeping?"

"You blissed out. Turn over." He could barely move. As she massaged him, he'd learned she could do so much with her hands. She'd explored him for what seemed like hours, touching him absolutely everywhere, except where he wanted her to touch him the most.

Wes rolled over onto his back. The quilt covering him was gone. He looked up at Melissa. She stood, staring at his crotch, hands raised, motionless. She looked at Wes. His black eyes grabbed hers.

"I don't know what to do," she whispered. He didn't answer her, just reached down and touched himself slowly, showing her how he liked it. Melissa watched his hands, and then hers replaced his.

"Is that right?" she said.

He flushed, then shuddered when it happened; she stared as though the moment was frozen in time.

He gazed at his bride. She'd taken off her clothes, all but the necklace he'd given her. He held out his arms to her and she lay down next to him. That was easier than looking at each other. She felt so wonderful next to him, naked.

"Can I touch you? Just touch you?" he said. She squirmed and acted like she didn't want him to touch her. She looked away. Wes let the energy flow out of his hands. He was a healer; something came from his hands that stopped her squirming. She looked blank and couldn't move. He made her feel only his hands. The only sound was her breathing and his. Her legs parted, as though she couldn't stop them. That's when he started touching her the way he wanted.

Wesley sat up and studied his wife. Her hips didn't look that wide, until he saw the way they curved out from her tiny waist. Her shoulders were like porcelain, so white. He liked her breasts; they seemed so big next to her small frame. He caressed them, the energy flowing from his hands into their softness; her nipples were burgundy-tinged and so, so sensitive. She responded to his touches, breathing deeper and raising her chest to him.

He bent down and kissed her nipples. They had a delicious texture and sweetness. Melissa gasped. He kissed her, putting his hands on her body; very quickly, he was learning to use healing energy for something else. She couldn't resist him: he was gentling her like a green filly. He placed one hand on her to keep her calm, and used the other to explore and stimulate her. She'd let him touch her anywhere now, and she opened herself to him, spreading her legs. Her breathing lengthened as she relaxed into his touch. He kept going, doing what he wanted. Going deeper, and farther.

Wes felt her stiffen and try to pull away when she felt his fingers inside her body. He paused and let his energy work. He watched her, liking being in control. *Let it happen. You're okay*, he reassured her with his mind. He kept talking to her as he intensified the movement of his fingers. She looked into his eyes and he kept smiling at her, keeping the energy and movement in his hand steady.

He could feel her wanting to run, but he wouldn't let her. Her pelvis moved by itself; he held her tightly, and she shuddered as her body released. He prolonged her orgasm much longer than it would have lasted naturally. He loved watching her while she came, mastering her.

They lay together, Wes kissing her softly. "You're so beautiful, Melissa," he whispered. Their bodies were pressed together, moving slowly. Very soon, Wes found himself inside her. It was the easiest and most natural thing in the world. They both stopped moving when they felt it.

He would have never imagined being inside her would feel so good. Inside Melissa, inside his wife, was where he belonged. Nothing blocked it, in his mind, or conscience or anywhere. What they did was right with all of him, all of her, with the universe. They loved each other and were married, and what they did was absolutely pure. He was home.

Wes wanted to thrust as hard and fast as he could. Something in him said, *Go slow, Wes. Go very slow. Just let it happen.* Grandfather always told him to go in the direction that seemed hardest—that would be the most satisfying in the end. So he went very slowly, inside of Melissa, joined with her. Something was happening.

"Do you feel it? You're moving."

She nodded, looking into his eyes. "Yes. I'm kissing you, Wes, with my body."

They were loving each other; it wasn't even sex so much, it was love that was being released. Wes realized how much he loved Melissa.

What they were doing was sacred. The open, warm light inside Melissa expanded. Wes rocked into it.

Something said, *Wait. Give her time. Let it happen.* He kept reassuring her, holding her hips to him. She was getting scared again, frantic; something was building that frightened her.

Wes said, "It's all right. Don't be afraid." At the right time, he rocked harder, just once.

Melissa exploded, crying out and moving her pelvis spasmodically. Wes felt the warmth inside her flow all around him. She opened up and rolled like a wave, flowing and flowing until nothing was left. Wes's hips started to move by themselves. He called out her name when he released into her body.

They lingered in the perfection of their mating, falling asleep in each other's arms.

64

"I WANT THE TRANSITION to be as smooth as possible." Will sat at his desk in the *Cass*, talking to Alan Morris, CEO of Recomtrex, Inc. on his cell phone. Numenon was merging with Recomtrex, or "gobbling it up," according to some of the financial columns.

Alan Morris sounded bewildered. "You're saying that you want to reduce our labor force using natural attrition, rather than laying everyone off at once? But Jim Billinghorst called Monday saying that after the merger, you were going to lay off almost eight thousand employees."

Jim Billinghorst had called Recomtrex to tell them thousands of employees would be laid off because Will had told him to do it, or he'd be fired. But Will had changed during the time he'd been at the Mogollon Bowl.

"That was a misunderstanding," Will said. "Jim didn't hear me right. I called him from the jet. Lots of noise. We've redone the numbers and attrition looks doable."

"Really?" Alan sounded truly flummoxed.

"I'll be home Saturday. We can go over the paperwork next week. I'm sure we're going to have a good working relationship, Alan."

Will was dialing Jim Billinghorst to tell him about the changed policy when his NumoPhone turned itself off. It didn't run out of juice, or crash; it carefully shut down. Will tried to turn it on. A message appeared on the screen that read, *Attempting to activate this device will cause irreparable damage.* He turned to the super computer on the wall.

The screensaver on the computer's huge screen—that day's *Wall Street Journal*—carefully folded in on itself as though someone was putting the newspaper away. The screen became bright blue, then black. The machine made a click and turned itself off. Will stared at it. He could hear the satellite dish on the roof pulling back into its bay and the cover deploying over it.

Will knew not to touch anything. What Andy had said happened to her laptop was chilling enough. He didn't want to see the super computer smoking.

He wheeled his chair over to the door, planning to ask Carl what happened. But he already knew. The Mogollon Bowl had decided it was time for him to join the party. It was Wednesday. He'd stayed in the *Cass*, working for four days, and flagrantly ignoring the Rules. His grace period was over.

He needed to go to the scheduled events like a good boy. That was okay. Mark Kenna was going to be speaking pretty soon. Mark had shown a great deal of promise when they were driving in. Will wanted to see if he could qualify for a higher employment level than a driver.

Will could see Carl out in the court with some other warriors.

As he reached to open the door and call to Carl, his body jerked and threw itself backward. He thrashed, out of control. The wheel chair tipped over and he fell out, landing on the floor.

"No!" he cried. "No!" His hands gripped his head. Images careened inside it. He screamed at what he saw. "You can't have it."

Carl dashed in and grabbed Will under the arms. He dragged him to his bedroom and hoisted him on the bed.

"Oh, God, they're going to take it all." Will felt like he'd walked into an explosion. The floor seemed to be flying up in pieces around him, along with images of brilliantly designed buildings, boardrooms, and power. A life was destructing. Will's life.

"They're taking everything." Carl put his hand on Will's forehead. "Can you see it, Carl?" He nodded.

Will could see them in the boardroom. Sauvage. Chao. Belson. Sarah Belson was against him? Who else? A dozen. They were forming so fast.

"I've got to get back to Palo Alto."

"Does your phone work?" Carl asked.

"No."

"This won't work either." Carl indicated the *Cass*.

A flash of horror bathed Will. "I can't get back to the office? Oh, God. I'll lose it all."

"Don't you have it in stocks or something?"

"Yes, I'm the majority stockholder in Numenon. But I also have my own money in an SPE. *That* will kill me. Not the money, but what the feds will think I'm doing with it." Carl looked lost.

Will shook his head and ran his fingers through his hair, trying to think of a way to explain complex financial mechanisms so that Carl could understand. "SPEs are Special Purpose Entities. They're like corporations inside a corporation. But they're not corporations—usually they're partnerships or trusts. They're for insiders only, no stockholders. They're legal, but they don't show up on the main company's books." Will met Carl's bewildered eyes. "I know that sounds fishy, but it's permitted by law.

"I've wanted to get into the oil business for a long time. I kind liked the image of being an oilman." Will flicked his wrist, a disparag gesture. "A few years back, I went to one of those countries aroun Caspian Sea to buy a company and almost got myself killed.

"Then I discovered that I didn't need anything but paper. notes, futures. Much safer than trekking around in the Midd' created an SPE. It gave me lower interest rates, and tax advantages. Mostly, it shifted risk on to Numenon."

Carl sat quietly, listening intently.

"I thought I'd clean up, but I didn't. The values of my investments kept falling. Numenon had to pledge more shares to cover the loss. The stockholders got nervous, and that has made Numenon's price shaky recently. That's probably what got the revolt against me going.

"I was going to handle it before I left, but it got crazy, getting out of Palo Alto. I thought it would be okay for a week, but what I just saw ..."

"How were you going to handle it?" Carl seemed as though he understood what Will was saying perfectly.

"I was going to buy out the SPE. Own it outright and pull it out of Numenon. The risk would be mine and Numenon would have no exposure."

"How much would that cost?"

Will frowned, considering the question. "I can buy everything for 500, between that and 900."

Carl's brows drew together. "Thousand?"

"No, million. That's doable."

Carl's jaw dropped and his eyebrows spiked up.

"Yeah. I've got that on hand, but I have to set up the buy-out and paperwork with my attorney and transfer funds. I can't do that without the computer. If they find that SPE outstanding, they'll say I'm not just incompetent, I'm a thief."

"Maybe Andy could do something," Carl said. "She's really good with computers. Maybe Grandfather could get the satellite to work."

"Where is she?"

"She's with Al. It's their wedding night. Could it keep until tomorrow?"

Will felt the muscles in his shoulders tighten. "I suppose. They don't know that I know what they're planning back at Numenon." Will wouldn't relax until Andy had sewn things up, but he could let her have her wedding night. Maybe. He chewed on his finger, something he hadn't done since he was a kid.

"What's going to happen?"

Will's head dipped forward. He rested his forehead on his hand. "They're going to fire me. They're collecting evidence of my incompetence. The SEC and Attorney General will come after me. And they'll get me. That's what I saw." Slow tears ran from beneath Will's hand. He glanced at Carl.

"I created the largest company in history and ran it for forty years, making more money for more people than anyone. And creating more jobs. A bunch of shitheads that couldn't make a can opener are going to throw me out."

"Can they do that?"

"Oh, yeah. They can demonstrate I'm too volatile to run Numenon. I've given them plenty to work with. I have a bad temper. I blow up. I scream and yell and curse. They'll find people who say I harmed them. And maybe I have. They'll look at everything I've done since I was twenty-three. They'll find what they need. They don't even need the SPE, but that will clinch it."

Will gasped, his ribcage pumped in and out without his willing it. "This could be the end of me. Not my money, *me*. I don't know if I can stand it. They'll take my reputation. The way people see me will change." A sob escaped him. He put both hands over his face, fishing for his handkerchief and using it discreetly.

They sat silently for a long time. Will felt good around Carl. He'd felt that way from the time Carl took him back to the Numenon camp in the golf cart. Will could feel him healing his tattered soul just sitting in the same room. Carl knew about prophetic visions. Will didn't think that he understood all of what he was talking about financially, but maybe he did. Carl understood what it meant to Will.

Will understood something, too. The first day he'd been at the Meeting, he'd put his hands on that horse. He'd heard the words, *Why did you come here? You need something that's here. Find it or you'll be dead in a year.* The words had shocked him. He'd mulled them over constantly.

Will had identified one thing he needed: a tribe. He needed people who cared about him near him, and he needed to care about his companions. He needed bonds as tight and unbreakable as the warriors'. He *would* die if he didn't get that. He hadn't found community anywhere in his life, but he felt it here, with Carl. Maybe there were others, too. Maybe he needed to find out more things about himself, but he needed to do this first.

"Carl, would you like a job?"

"Will you be able to hire anyone if you get fired?"

Will laughed. He hadn't thought he ever would again. "I have a bit put by. I'll still be worth close to fifty billion."

"What do you want me to do?"

"What you're doing. Stay with me. I want you to watch my back. It's going to get rough when we get back. There may be a lot of news coverage. Rumors about me. Hell, the *truth* about me. Carl, I was a real cock hound. Whores, everything. For years. The only thing I didn't do was orgies.

"And then the feds. I don't think I've broken the law more than any other CEO in Silicon Valley, but maybe I have. If I have, they'll find it. They'll paint it as bad in any case. You need to know that about me."

"I was in the penitentiary. Steurke, for a life sentence. But ..." Carl recited the litany of his past.

"You were released when it turned out that the evidence against you was bad. You served nine years," Will responded.

"You knew."

"Searched the Internet. Do you want a job? We could call it security. Do you do anything else?"

"I'm a chef. I went through the Culinary Program in the penitentiary."

"Are you any good?"

"Yes."

"Okay. You're a chef who also does security. Will a hundred grand be enough? You can live at my place. I've got lots of room in the house and three guest houses."

Carl's mouth opened and closed several times, but he didn't make a sound.

Will spoke again. "I need you, Carl. I'm not good at saying stuff like this. But I need you, and I need people. I don't want to be alone any more." He knew his vulnerability showed on his face, but Will couldn't hide it.

Will thought about the home he'd return to, dread running through him. He couldn't live alone in his 15,000 square foot architectural masterpiece any longer.

He couldn't live alone.

65

MARK WAS UP on the stage speaking again when Carl half-carried Will to the Numenon section of the Pit. The wheelchair wouldn't work in the gravelly dirt. Will sat on a wood plank in the front row. The other four drivers sat next to him. Will could see Jon up in the camp doing something in the kitchen. The MBAs had disappeared. He hadn't seen them all week. Well, he knew where Melissa was.

He got a bunch of dirty looks from the other Meeting attendees as he made his way to his seat. He had been right; he needed to be a good boy from now on. Carl got dirty looks as well, because he was with Will. Okay. Time to jump in and wow people.

Elizabeth abruptly approached from her seat a bit farther down the front row. "How are you feeling, Will?" she asked in a whisper.

"I'm fine."

She gave him a thumbs up sign and headed back to her seat. A couple of people glared at her. He turned his attention to Mark.

The driver had his flip-chart on a tripod. He'd drawn a big oval in the middle of a large pad of paper. The oval had lines cutting it into three pieces horizontally. A couple of dashed circles and a bunch of dots floated in the center of the oval.

"These dots—the measles, as Grandfather put it earlier—represent subpersonalities. Those are parts of your personality that have developed into almost separate people inside of you."

The Bowl convulsed. Its surface rippled for a while and settled down into an uneasy stillness. People exclaimed and jumped up. Living on the San Francisco Peninsula for most of his life, Will had been through many earthquakes. The Loma Prieta quake in 1989 was the biggest he'd experienced. That was 7.1 on the richter scale. Big enough to knock down sections of the Bay Bridge and part of the I-880 freeway in Oakland. Whatever just happened was bigger than that. Will didn't think they had earthquakes in New Mexico.

He looked at Grandfather, who looked around, jaw slack. Despite the quake, none of the sunshades covering the Pit had fallen down. The benches hadn't collapsed. No one seemed very upset. The old man looked at Mark and waved him to continue.

"Subpersonalities develop to make daily life easier. You can be a student one minute and act the way a student is supposed to act. You can go to a job interview and know how to do that. You can know exactly what to do without figuring it out every time.

"Problems arise when one subpersonality takes over. The glamor girl movie star thinks she *is* her beauty. When it starts to fade, well, we've all read about older stars who fall apart. Other examples exist: body-builders who pump so much iron they look like cartoon figures. They *are* their muscles. These acts keep them from knowing who they are and from growing as human beings."

"Mark, give me one practical application of what you're talking about," Will interupted. He thought that Mark had a future above his status as a driver, but this was so boring he couldn't stand it.

Mark responded easily. "It has a twofold application. Most people are run by their subpersonalities and don't know it. Take the obnoxious professor who thinks that people without PhDs don't exist. He alienates everyone, but he doesn't know it. If he knew what a jerk he was being in his 'I'm smart' act, he could act differently and get better results. When you know your favorite subpersonalities, you can step back from them and respond to what's really happening."

"You can be more effective by knowing this stuff," Will paraphrased.

"Yes, at work and everywhere. There's more; it's impossible to get to the Transpersonal Self if you think you are your muscles, or your brain, or your success."

"What's that … *Self?*" Will had thought that Mark had something to bring to the party. Looks like he didn't.

"I talked about the Transpersonal Self before you came." Mark moved to the oval and touched its top. "This is where the human being touches the divine. Experiencing that is the goal of human life. It's way more important than being effective at work." Mark turned to Grandfather, whose face was lifted to the sky—a beatific expression bathed it.

Will looked at the old man and felt as though he'd been struck. Something radiated off of the shaman, a measurable force. He felt giddy with happiness just being around him.

But that wasn't the point. "That's really nice for Grandfather, but how would you run a business like that?" Will asked.

Mark took a deep breath. "Who do you think is the most effective person here, other than you?"

Will looked down the line and stopped at Elizabeth. "Elizabeth."

"I agree. Elizabeth, would you like to come up here and do a demonstration?"

"Will it hurt?" Everyone laughed.

When the doctor jumped onto the stage, the crowd greeted her with a roar of applause. The People loved Elizabeth. She swaggered toward Mark. Will smiled. Doing a demo with Elizabeth might be more than Mark bargained for.

"Hi, Elizabeth, I'm Mark Kenna. We haven't really met." They shook hands. "What I'd like you to do is talk about your life."

She opened her mouth to speak, and the air seemed to grow brighter. Glowing figures appeared in the sky above the Bowl, spanning the horizons. They were surrounded and partly hidden by sparkling mist, but they were definitely naked. The bodies moved slowly, kissing.

"Stop that!" Will jumped up, landing on his injured ankle. He yelped in pain, then flopped back down and yelled from the bench. "Stop that! That's *Melissa! You can't show her like that!*"

Melissa was wrapped around Wesley, loving him with tantalizing gentleness. Like the really hot love scenes in good movies, Will couldn't see anything too explicitly, but what he could see was blistering. The passion, the exquisite bliss, the rapture on their faces. He had never had sex like that, only dreamed of it.

He looked around the crowd. People's faces reflected that same awe. Everyone could feel what it was like to love with nothing held back. The scene lingered above, beguiling them, seducing them, showing them what life could offer, if only they dared to commit like that.

And then the catcalls started. "Whoa-ho, Wesley. Doin' great." "Atta way, Wes!" "Go for it!" "Boy, is she *hot.*" The crowd burst out with ribald comments. None were from the spirit warriors.

Granfather leaped to his feet and shouted, "Everyone! We are going to leave. Pack up your camps, we will leave now. The Meeting is over. We are going home."

The crowd kept staring at the sky and shouting encouragement to the newlyweds, paying no attention to the shaman. The sky gradually dimmed to its normal hue and the figures faded from sight.

"We must go," Grandfather insisted. "We cannot be here. I do not know what may happen. You must go for your safety."

After Wesley and Melissa's images disappeared, the group turned its attention to Grandfather. "How did you do that?" "What was that?" "Was that really them?"

"My friends, Wesley and Melissa have been granted a great gift. They are so pure and such good warriors that the Great One has graced them with ..." Grandfather was forced to explain the sacred gift.

"They must complete it. It is a boon for all of the world. Barren women will conceive. Dying species will regenerate. Droughts will end.

"But we need to leave. They are too close to us. I do not know what will happen next. The gift continues for twenty-four hours."

Will looked up on the stage. Grandfather, dazzling and frazzled both, stood by his buffalo robe, emploring his followers to leave. Mark held on to his flip chart as though it could take off. Elizabeth stood, mouth slack, staring at her Teacher.

"What is this, Grandfather?" she asked. "I've been with you thirty years. You never said anything about this."

"You didn't tell us when we came, either," Will said, disturbed. This was a breach of contract. They were supposed to have seven days at the retreat and had only had ... How many days had they been there? He'd been in the *Cass* working. However long it was, it wasn't seven days. He'd spent a ton of money getting his people there. He intended to get what he'd paid for. "You should have told us this could happen."

"I didn't know about it, Will Duane. The Great One didn't tell me. The One probably didn't know until Melissa and Wesley were wed."

"What's going to happen?" A racous voice rose from the crowd. "More like that? I'll stay for that." The voice became a swell. "We'll stay!" Everyone seemed infected with joy. They laughed. The Pit was becoming a four thousand-person party.

"No! Things you can't image will happen. This is just the beginning. We must go. Wesley is a fine warrior and so is Melissa. Spying on them is wrong." Grandfather began to role up his buffalo skin. "We will go."

"I took my vacation time to come here." The complaints began. "Where can I go? And what can I do for *three* days?"

"This is the last Meeting. You haven't healed my arthritis."

"It took almost a week for me to drive here. I'm not going to leave."

"Why should we leave? That picture didn't show that much." The images in the sky had been hot, but not R-rated.

Everyone wanted to stay. Grins sprouted everywhere. People hugged each other. Couples hugged each other. And kissed.

That was exactly what Grandfather wanted to prevent. "Everyone, go back to your tents and begin packing. We will leave now. The Meeting is over."

The crowd's new, loving mood dissolved as Grandfather attemped to shoo them toward the campground and their belongings. Boos resounded. "Why should we leave?"

"We don't have to leave," said Paul Running Bird, as he leaped onto the stage. "Grandfather and his people can go. *My* people will stay. I'll lead us in our own Meeting." Paul was changed. His hair was a bit longer on top, its forelock falling forward in a manner similar to James Dean's. He looked rebellious, cool, and authoritative at once. His hips seemed narrower and his shoulders broader.

"What!" the shaman cried. "You have no authority to run anything. This is the Great One's Meeting. Great-grandfather and the One are behind all I do!"

"I have my own ancestors, and my own teachings. I found them here, over there." He waved toward the outer edge of the Pit. "I had a vision when I was sitting quietly. *My Chieftain* is behind everything *I* do." Paul stood proudly, raising his sculptured chin and looking noble.

"My people will stay and finish the Meeting. Grandfather and his people will leave."

"Never! You will *never* lead the Meeting! The Great One created the Meeting and the Great One will see it finished!" Grandfather was so furious he made little hops from one foot to the other. "We will stay!"

"Oh, good." Paul sneered. "We'll divide the Pit right down the middle. Or maybe you won't need that much space when my people come to me." He opened his arms in a gesture of welcome.

Will stood up carefully, aware of his ankle this time. He motioned Carl to assist him in standing.

"That's enough," he spoke loudly and firmly. Everyone looked at him. "There's one Meeting, and it's Grandfather's. He runs the show. We go or stay as he says." He paused and looked around. They stared at him, silent, and then looked to Grandfather, accepting his authority. Will smiled. Being the richest man in the world still meant something.

"Paul, could you come over here? I need to speak to you."

Paul jumped off the stage and approached Will, looking wary.

"Come over here and talk to me. I don't bite." Will smiled enticingly.

Paul slipped over. Will motioned him closer. He looked charming until Paul was in whispering range.

"Paul, you're a lying snake. You knew exactly what you were doing when you sent us the bad map. I've thought you were trying to undermine Grandfather, and now I know you are. Grandfather's the boss. Shut up about leading anything. If you don't stop this bullshit—starting now—I will destroy your life. You know I can do that, don't you?"

Paul blanched.

"Yes. I see that you do. Apologize to Grandfather and get out of my sight. I don't want to see you again. Or hear that you're organizing anything."

Paul gave him a hateful look, and slunk into the crowd. He didn't apologize.

Will turned his eyes to Grandfather, who stood in the middle of the stage, arms raised. The shaman spoke loudly. "If you want to stay, we will continue with the Meeting. I don't know what may happen. It could be dangerous. I think we should leave.

"If you want to leave, do it. If you stay here and something happens, remember that I warned you. You do what you do at your own risk." He motioned the people to leave the Pit and go home. A couple hundred did.

Elizabeth had been standing on the stage, waiting to do whatever exercise Mark had in mind for her. When Grandfather dismissed everyone, she stepped back, forgetting she was on a platform. She gave a little cry as she went over the edge. Carl caught her and set her on her feet.

"Are you all right?" Carl asked. Will hobbled over.

She had tears in her eyes. "That was so awful. Paul has no right."

"You need to lie down," Carl said.

They looked in the direction of the camp headquarters and her tent. All four thousand people in the Meeting seemed to be heading there.

Will saw her slump. Her camp must be a nightmare. The noise of the crowd. The doors of all those porta-potties slamming and their smell. Who could sleep through all of that? She must be exhausted.

Carl asked on her behalf. "Can Elizabeth take a nap up at your camp?"

"Certainly!" Will responded. "Why don't you move up for the rest of the week? Betty's motor home is empty." He felt like someone had hung Christmas lights on him.

"Well, I suppose I—"

Carl answered for her again. "She'd love to. Elizabeth, you go take a nap. I'll have the guys bring your stuff up while you're sleeping. Go, Elizabeth." He shooed her along.

Elizabeth looked over her shoulder toward the main camp as she walked up the rise to the Numenon camp. She was halfway up when she turned and called to Carl. "I was planning on going riding this afternoon. Would you ask Bud to get Crème Puff in for me, Carl?"

Carl stared at her like she was insane. "Crème Puff?"

"Yeah. I really miss ol' Puffy."

66

PAUL WALKED QUICKLY and resolutely away from the Pit. He kept his face impassive, but shook like he had a corked volcano inside. He'd destroy Duane, not the other way around. Not watching where he was going, he ended up near the back of the Bowl. Chu and his crowd looked like they'd started the party already.

Chu waved to him, holding out a bottle. "You want some?"

"Not now. Later. Where's 'Fonzo?"

"He married some white bitch. They're shacked up over there." Chu waved his bottle toward the desert.

"I saw him with Grandfather and Will Duane earlier. I thought he might have moved into the main camp."

"You saw him with Will Duane?"

"Big as life. He supposedly was in Duane's motor home, too. With his *wife*. I think he reports to Grandfather."

"'Fonzo is a stoolie? He tells the old man what we do?"

"I'm sure he does. Probably has for years."

Chu unleashed a stream of profanity more offensive than Paul knew existed. He smiled. That would fix 'Fonzo's wagon. He wanted to fix as many people as he could.

Paul headed for the least occupied area at the rear of the camp. He found an open area and stumbled, landing on his knees, praying instantly. *You said I'd run this Meeting. You said you'd help me.*

His Chieftain's gentle, smiling face appeared in Paul's mind's eye. He heard his voice, silently. *I said I would guide you step-by-step. I didn't say to jump on the stage and try to take over. You may not be able to attract everyone in the Meeting, but I promise you that you will have enough followers to start your own movement. The people joining you here will spread your fame. Be prepared, Paul. You will be famous and rich.*

Paul felt much better. *What about Will Duane? He said he'd destroy me.*

The Chieftain laughed, a robust, masculine sound. *Don't worry about Will Duane. Within a week, he'll be a has-been.*

"Really?" Paul was so delighted that he spoke out loud.

Yes, indeed. Forces are moving to annihilate him. He'll get what he deserves. But I must instruct you on what to do. You will only reap your reward if you do what I say. I want you to sit cross-legged right where you are. Turn your back to the center of the Bowl. Pay no attention to the crowd or anyone who approaches you. Do not look at them or speak to them. Do you remember any of Grandfather's chants?

"Yes."

Sing one quietly for a time, ten minutes if you can judge the time. Then sit silently with your eyes closed. Sit up straight and put your hands on your knees. Breathe steadily. Do that for four cycles: chant then sit quietly, chant ... Four times.

Do not speak to the people who cluster around you until you have made four cycles. Then you may speak to them. Tell them your experience with me. How you met me, what I look like. That I come from an ancient lineage, but not Grandfather's. Invite them to join you, doing exactly what you've been doing. I will give you—and them—spiritual experiences beyond your dreams.

Paul, my darling, you must do what I tell you next. This step is very important. See that circle of rocks outside the Bowl?

"The big one by the parking lot?" Paul asked, as he pointed at it.

Yes. When I tell you, and not before, take your people there as fast as you can. Run as though you were running for your lives. Stay within the circle and don't come out until tomorrow. Do not come out of the circle no matter what you see or hear. Doing this exactly as I say will give you your fame and destroy Grandfather. Can you do that?

"Yes, but will anyone come to me?"

Leave that to me.

67

THEY SLEPT FOR a while, wrapped in each other's arms. When Wes awoke, he felt as if someone had attached a fire hose to the base of his spine and turned the water on full blast. Closing his eyes, he saw it as a white light. It gathered strength as it moved upward, a force more powerful than the atomic bomb. The sensation wasn't painful, but it was very intense.

"Melissa! Do you feel that?" he whispered.

"Yes. I think it's what Grandfather told us about. Just let it happen."

The light and power rose slowly up his spine. As it hit certain points, balls of light ignited on his backbone, exploded inside him like spinning wheels. He could see lights and colors, taste delicious flavors, and hear beautiful sounds as each spinning wheel activated.

"Do you see it, Melissa?"

"The lights and music? Yes. All the way up my body."

The movement worked in tandem. At each inner explosion, the corresponding part of her body vibrated with his, and the vibrations' energy moved back and forth between them, producing almost unendurable bliss. They rocked back, brows raised, mouths slightly open, unable to move.

When the white light reached his heart, it seemed to explode. He felt himself a tiny figure, in a huge red rock cavern. He could hear a powerful lub-dub, lub-dub, lub-dub and watch the wall pulsate with each beat. He was inside a heart. His heart.

As far as he could see, walls of red stone glistened in the light, shot through with flashing veins of gold and silver and sparkling gems. Wes shivered. He walked into the cavern, marveling. After a short while, he discovered a crimson sea that lapped against the stone shore. The sea glistened in the soft light, extending into the cave's vast reaches.

Wesley put his hand into the liquid. It was blood. He was at the wellspring—the source—of the river of blood that runs below the earth and supports it. The walls of the cavern were blood-stone, the People's blood turned to stone.

Wind blew off the sea of blood, calling to him. Wes stepped into the red ocean and it bore him up. He walked across it. All around, he could hear the voices of his Ancestors, singing and calling, rejoicing at his coming.

White bone rose abruptly from the scarlet ocean. The island was a buffalo skull. The skull rose before him, hundreds of feet from front to back, glowing white against the red. Wes fell to his knees.

Trembling, he put his forehead to the holy surface and prayed. The wellspring of the blood of his People existed in his heart, and in the center of that was a sacred altar. All of it was him.

A great warrior stood at the far end of the skull. His bonnet sported so many feathers that Wesley could not count them. They were two and three deep at the top, with wings falling to the ground and trailing for yards behind him. Each feather testified to a brave deed in battle. Each feather was six feet long.

The chieftain looked just like him, but this man was a god. He was many times Wes's height and massive, beautiful beyond any man Wes could imagine.

The chieftain bent down. Wes saw light glinting from between his teeth, out of his eyes, from his skin. The giant held out his hand and Wes stepped onto it.

Wesley peered into the giant's face. It looked just like his face, but Wes was afraid to say it was him. The warrior/god laughed.

You are afraid to know the truth, little one? I am your own true Self. The giant stroked him with a finger, continuing to talk with soundless speech.

This night is your reward. Look, the chieftain said. *Greet your bride.*

Wesley's skin crawled and his eyes grew wide. Melissa was coming to him, her heart wide open. Melisssa was seated on a white lotus in an ocean of liquid pearls. When Melissa's glittering sea lapped against the lotus, sounds of violins and stringed instruments filled the cavern.

The goddess of Melissa's heart was in all white. Her hair was decorated with opals and white plumes. Her face was lit with an expression of rapture and desire. She was coming for him, the lord of her heart.

When they touched, their oceans merged like fireworks. Melissa's brilliant white sea shot across his deep blood red one, forming an explosive lattice. The red and white intermingled, but neither disappeared.

Wesley's god-like host assumed a cross-legged position. Wes felt the goddess come to her lord and lower herself upon him, wrapping her legs around his body.

He felt the pleasure of that joining with every molecule of his being. He thought that this was a vision, a spiritual experience, not a physical one. But he became aware of his body; he was sitting cross-legged facing Melissa. He could feel himself deep within his wife and she could feel herself holding him tight.

They were joined in soul and body, swaying back and forth, in ecstasy.

Their rapture was beyond human knowledge. The bliss surged and flowed, raising them ever higher. When their bodies could stand no more, the feelings and sensations ebbed and gradually ceased.

A deep tone echoed throughout the wedding cave. Blue light filled it. Their bodies were interlocked; she straddled him. From the base of Wesley's spine, and the base of Melissa's, soft-edged columns of blue light rose higher and higher, spinning in a spiral around them. The spirals interacted, encircling and rising far above their heads. The couple was conscious, but neither could move.

When the double spiral reached the cave's ceiling, it began to play, rocking its hosts back and forth, tossing them, touching them, frolicking. The intertwined lights swooped and danced.

When Melissa and Wesley approached exhaustion, the double helix raised itself to the cavern's roof. Jet black eyes glittered at the end of each coil. Two long, forked tongues shot out to sample the air.

Wesley's eyes widened: mystical snakes were wrapped around them. Wesley was not too afraid; his People revered snakes. These had to be safe. The reptiles raised themselves to their highest, forked tongues testing the air. The serpents whipped their hoods open. They were cobras.

Now Wes was horrified. Deadly cobras had come to their marriage bed. Melissa steadied him with her thoughts. *Don't move, Wes. It's okay.*

With that, the cobras struck with astonishing speed. Wesley's cobra bit him on the base of his neck. Quick as lightning, Melissa's did the same.

The lovers fell onto their marriage bed, lifeless.

68

J ON'S EYES WERE drawn by movement overhead. Melissa and Wesley's images filled the sky. Jon plopped down on one of the teak chairs. He couldn't look away. They were so beautiful.

Jon crumpled. He and 'Rique were like that in the beginning. Jon looked around frantically. The others were returning from the talk and he was losing it. He ran for the motor home he shared with the drivers.

Clutching his knees to his chest on the RV's couch, he tried to keep it together. 'Rique died six months ago. Okay. They had loved each other. He was HIV positive. He would get AIDS. He would die. Deal with it.

He looked through the window into the courtyard and saw the beauty of the camp. The beauty of the world. He was leaving this place. A massive tide of grief knocked him flat. He pulled out his handkerchief and let it flow.

"Jon! Jon Walker? Are you in there?" Jon looked out the window. A group of Indians, no, more like a *delegation* of Indians, stood outside the RV.

"Yes?"

"We're here to take you to the group kitchen."

Jon had forgotten about their stinking kitchen. "Why don't you keep doing what you've been doing?"

His visitors looked offended. "You said you'd help us."

Jon sucked in a breath. A chef's work was never done. He sniffed and tossed his head as he joined the Natives.

"This is where we thought the barbecue pits should go," said one man.

"Yeah, this will do." Jon began giving orders, directing the set up of an outdoor kitchen for thousands. He realized maybe he was hasty in being so critical of the camp's cook-it-yourself arrangement; it was messy, but effective.

However, the Indians charged ahead. Jon faded as the leader, collapsing into his own thoughts. His admirers flocked around him. He smiled and waved them off; his mood was falling rapidly.

He kept fantasizing about Wesley. That scene over the Bowl had triggered something. He imagined Wesley loving him like that, feeling the closeness, the sweetness of true love around him.

Stop it! You're still grieving for the love of your life. Wesley just married your best friend. You love Melissa. Wesley's not gay—he doesn't even like you. You're HIV positive—you could kill him. Stop it.

He looked up to see that several large barbecue pits were almost done. Aisles between the pits were ample for people working around them. People were bringing over tables and chairs for a communal dining area. It had happened all by itself—Jon hadn't done much of it. People were talking about cooking shifts and planning the dinner. He was mystified by how well things were flowing. *It's almost as if they've done this before.*

Jon jumped when a crazy-looking old lady thumped toward him in a walker. People stepped back as the white-haired woman approached; she was obviously the eldest of the Elders. He'd never seen so many wrinkles.

Her eyes were set in her head at slightly different angles. Her head jutted forward and she looked at him sideways. She was spooky.

Is she a witch? Jesus, she's scary.

The old woman smiled. "I am Avalina Cocina," she said in a raspy voice.

He didn't like the way she eyed him. Fey, that's what you'd call her. Touched.

"You are beautiful, Jon Walker. You should find Benny Silverhorse."

"What!?"

"You should find Benny. He is a two-spirit like you. You could make each other happy. My Rose would stop crying." Avalina smiled. Her teeth—the ones she still had—were crooked and yellow. "Rose Silverhorse is Benny's mother. And Wesley's."

Jon's skin prickled when he got it. Wesley had a gay brother. He spun to face the old lady. "*Wesley's* brother is *gay?*" He stared at her, as though Wesley's brother was hidden in her eyes. This was impossible—dreams like this did not come true.

Avalina smiled with her crooked mostly missing teeth. "Oh, yes, Jon Walker. We have two-spirits, too. And dreams do come true. Benny is prettier than Wesley. You would like him. He is sweeter, too. Like a melon."

"Where is Benny?"

"No one knows." Avalina shrugged. "He ran away six years ago. For four years, he wrote to my Rose, one time a year. She has heard nothing from him for two years. She cries and cries. No one can find him. You should find Benny. You will make yourself happy and make my Rose smile again."

"How old was he when he left?"

"He was fourteen. He ran away with an old white man. They went to a city."

Jon stammered, "Had Benny been ... in cities before?"

Avalina shook her head. "He lived on the ranch with his brothers and sisters and mother. And his father. He had never been to a city. He was a good boy."

One of the men who had been setting up the kitchen came over. "I need to take Avalina to rest now," he said to Jon, deferential to both of them. He picked up the tiny lady and someone else took her walker. She put her arms around the man's neck and looked back over his shoulder. Her gaze pierced Jon again.

"You should find Benny. Then you will be happy."

The onlookers turned their attention to Jon. Seeing his confusion, one of them said, "Avalina Cocina is a Holy Woman, almost as great as Grandfather. She gave you an order—four times. You must do what she said."

Jon watched Avalina depart. Benny Silverhorse seemed like the answer to his prayers; but it was so stupid. A fourteen-year-old gay Indian kid who'd lived on a ranch his whole life running away to a city? He'd be twenty now. Still a kid.

If he was alive, he had to be a hustler. That's the only way he would survive. Did these sweet people know anything of the life awaiting Benny?

Benny Silverhorse had probably stopped writing because he was dead. A beautiful boy with nothing else going for him would end up a prostitute, or in pornography. And he was probably an addict. AIDS would find him before Jon could.

Find Benny! Jon shook his head. The person who Avalina knew was dead. Even if his body was alive, Benny's soul would be ruined by what he had to do to stay alive.

Jon knew more than that. Benny might have disappeared in places that his People couldn't fathom. Benny could vanish into a gray existence outside society. If he was beautiful enough, he could be a concubine or slave to some wealthy collector. He could be the property of some club.

Jon could try to find him, but why? Getting him free would be impossible. Jon's mood plummeted.

"Howdy. Y'all might not know me." A tall man who looked like he'd stuck a watermelon under his shirt approached Jon by the food prep area. He had half-circles of sweat under his arms that reached almost to his waist. "I'm Tribal Police Chief Elmo Gregg. I popped in to talk to Mr. Duane when y'all were comin' in. I just wanted to tell you it was seriouser that I thought."

"What's more serious? Why are you telling me? Why don't you tell Will?"

"Well, I did talk to him, as I said. An' I tol' that driver, Mark, is it? But I don' think either of them got the picture. Lena can paint the shit out of all your pretty RVs in a night. She'll want the big one most of all, Mr. Duane's."

"Who's Lena?"

"The chief's daughter. Went off to art school and went plum wild. Ran away. Her daddy had to chase her all the way to Seattle to find her. Know what she was doin'?" Jon shook his head. "Hanging off freeway bridges, paintin' the concrete sides. She called it 'urban art.' Her daddy and the authorities called it vandalism.

"We had an incident last night out in the parking lot. I wanted to give you a heads up."

"Why me?"

"Seems like you're the most sensible of the bunch up there. What she did was real pretty, though. Big rose, eight feet across, kinda day-glo, with kachina dancers all around it. A piece of art on a Winnebago."

Jon could see the *Cass* painted with roses and whatever else a young girl might think was cool. He was horrified. "Okay, I'll watch out. I'll get everyone to watch out."

"An' I wanted you to know that I'm on the job. Me an' the tribal police. We been watchin'. Can't show ourselves on account of Grandfather and the spirit warriors and the tribal council and the chairman. Turf war." He shook his head. "Plus the finance chief. They want Mr. Duane to finance the casino in the worst way. We aren't part of that. But we got your back: out of sight, but on the job."

The Indians wanted Will to finance a casino? This place was making him crazy. "Uh, thanks."

"We'll be there if you need us. Can I watch you chop?"

"If you want."

People were clamoring for him to begin a chopping demonstration. They'd set up a table and cutting boards. There must have been fifty knives laid out. He allowed himself to be led to the board. A kind-of-clean, white cotton apron was tied around his waist. A huge crowd gathered.

The image of Wesley rose before him, with a haunting figure behind it.

Benny Silverhorse. Sweet as a juicy melon. Benny would be twenty now, seven years younger than Jon; light years older, most likely. The sweet face taunted him. Energy leapt into Jon's hand. *It's not fair!* The knife moved faster, harder. Whack! Whack! Whack! The crowd pushed forward to watch. A buzz of comments flew up around them.

Jon threw tid-bits of vegetables to the watchers, tossed and caught his knife, as animated as he had been that morning. The image of Benny came to him again.

No! No! Leave me alone. The knife moved faster. He railed at the vision silently. *Go away! You're not going to save me. Nothing can save me.* Sweet Benny; he was grasping at straws.

No! Whack! *No!* Whack! Benny could save him. One more romance would protect him. Death couldn't come to a man in love.

That's not true. Jon continued chopping, fighting with himself. He wanted the peace that came to him when he used a knife. The silence in his mind. As though by magic, the stillness he sought arose within him.

All that existed was him and the knife and the motion of his hand. Out of his pure stillness came two words: '*Rique knew.*

He slammed the knife onto the board. He felt the impact, but was too shocked to make a sound. When he raised the blade, the end of his left index finger flew off, landing in a bowl of fruit.

Jon screamed, blood exploding from his fingertip. It spurted rhythmically, following his heart's beat. Ruby splatters covered the meat on the chopping board. People jumped up to help him. Some reached for the fingertip.

"No!" he shrieked. "Don't touch it!" He wrapped his finger in his apron, squeezing it tight to stop the bleeding. The pressure didn't stop anything. He looked at the blood-soaked table in front of him in horror. His blood could kill.

He let go of his finger and picked up the cutting boards, throwing them, the food and the knives he'd touched into a garbage can. Blood spurted again, fanning out on the ground.

"Don't touch me!" He tied up his hand with the crimson apron again. Death was right beside him. He sobbed and didn't try to hide it.

He felt a soft touch and looked up. Grandfather's kind eyes met his.

Grandfather wrapped his arm around Jon and whispered in his ear, "Jon, we're going to walk over to the camp headquarters. I'll help you there."

Jon bent over and held his hand tightly, the injured finger wrapped in many layers of apron. Grandfather walked to the chopping area and picked the end of Jon's finger off an apple. He tossed the apple in the garbage.

Once in the cement building, Grandfather held Jon, who was unable to speak. He finally whispered, "I don't want to die." Grandfather stroked him, his touch having an hypnotic effect.

"Let me see your finger."

"It will bleed again."

"No, it won't." Slapping the severed end of Jon's finger onto the exposed fingertip, the shaman held it for about fifteen seconds.

Jon felt pain, then warmth, and then bliss radiating from his finger. He looked at the fingertip. Though bloody, just the finest scar marked the place where he'd sliced himself.

"It's healed!"

Grandfather smiled. "Now for the rest of you."

Jon's eyes widened. "Can you?"

Grandfather shook his head sadly. "I can't heal the virus, but I can help your soul."

A golf cart and driver appeared as if by magic. Grandfather and Jon climbed in and took off. Jon's finger was healed, but his body shook so hard it seemed as though it might fly to pieces.

They went along the Rim, then down the switchbacks to the flat land where they kept the horses. The driver turned up a deep canyon and zigged and zagged through rock formations. They rounded a bend and stopped.

"Get out and take off all of your clothes," said Grandfather.

"What?" Jon was dazed. Grandfather seemed as if he spoke from a great distance.

"Do as I say."

Jon complied. His clothes were splattered with blood.

"Stand back." Grandfather stretched his hand toward the pile. Blue flames erupted from the palm and incinerated the bloody garments.

"Okay, let's go over here."

They walked through a narrow opening in a rock wall into an setting that looked like it came from outer space. High cliffs surrounded a solid rock grotto. Not a leaf punctuated the red rock. The undulating stone floor stretched out for acres. Hot springs dotted it. Steam rose everywhere. Some pools were higher than others. Water spilled out of them into lower ponds. Springs burst into the air, creating natural fountains. This was a wonderland.

"These springs are all over the Badlands. Will Duane and your friends know nothing about the springs, and you will not tell them. Get in the water." He indicated a nearby pond with a gesture of his head. Grandfather stripped and followed him. They sat on an underwater ledge.

The instant the shaman sat next to him, Jon's head fell forward and tears ran down his cheeks, hitting the water like balls of pain. He wept, plummeting deeper into grief. Grandfather made no move to stop his fall, not a pat or a comforting word. Jon cried until his anguish ran its course, but didn't disappear. He floated on a plateau of misery.

"What did you come here to tell me, my son?" Grandfather said softly.

"'Rique *knew*." The words prompted another proxym of tears.

"Knew what, my son?"

"That he was HIV positive. He already was positive when we got together. I lived with him for four years. We did *everything*. He *knew*. He called me *Querido,* dear one, knowing what he was doing could kill me.

"He showed me lab tests saying he was negative. He must have faked them. He *lied* to me." Jon's chest rose and fell. "I don't understand how he could say what he did and do that … But he loved me, I'm sure of it.

"I don't understand." He looked at Grandfather, beseeching. Something about Grandfather made talking about his deepest secrets easy. "When he was dying, he said that he didn't tell me because he didn't want to change anything between us. In what we did. He didn't want to go through treatment. He knew how hard it was. He wanted to keep the life he had until he got sick and died.

"He didn't seem to care what he had exposed me to. I don't know how many other people he gave HIV." Jon dropped his forehead into his hands. The surface of the pond broke into concentric circles as tears fell. He looked at Grandfather. "He was never faithful. Not for three days. If anybody even slightly attractive was around, 'Rique would seduce him.

I pretended I was his loving partner, but it wasn't like that. I was so jealous, all the time.

"If 'Rique was with someone, I couldn't stay home thinking about what he was doing." Jon shrugged. "I got around almost as much as he did." He shot a glance at Grandfather. "I didn't want to, but I couldn't stand knowing he was with someone else.

"All the way to the end, I acted like I loved him. Everyone thought we were the perfect gay couple. I went to the hospital every day, sat with him. Fed him at the end. We did love each other, but we weren't soul mates. I see real soul mates here; we weren't like that.

"His funeral was a circus. Everyone in the design world from San Francisco to New York to *everywhere* came. He was a hero to so many communities. He did all the society people's homes—and yachts and offices. He was Latino. He was gay. A dozen guys threw themselves on his coffin and claimed to be 'Rique's *querido*.

"He left me everything he had. I think it was an 'I'm sorry. I love you.' Big fucking deal. He killed me." Jon's eyes narrowed and rage erupted.

"I want to *kill* him. I wish I'd never met the son of a bitch."

Grandfather looked at him impassively. "So you cut your finger off instead."

Jon nodded. "Now. At home, I do a lot things that could get me hurt. My therapist said I was a masochist and sex addict. So I quit going to her."

"Your therapist is right. What do you want to do now, my son? You've come to a place of healing."

"I want to live. I'll do whatever treatment is available. I won't be like 'Rique. I've got to get a new job. Will won't want me cooking for him. No one will."

"What else do you want?"

Answering that took Jon a while. "I'd want a real relationship like 'Rique and I supposedly had. I want to be faithful. I don't know if I can do that. 'Rique and I weren't so different." Jon sighed.

"So 'Rique might not have been the one to give you the virus?"

"No. It could have been anyone." Jon turned his face away from the shaman. "I want to blame 'Rique, but I'm the one who did it.

"I've never told anyone that." He shot a shy glance at Grandfather.

The old man chuckled. "That is why you came here. To find the truth and be healed."

"I know I'm a sex addict and masochist. But I keep having this crazy idea. Avalina Cocina told me I should find Benny Silverhorse; she said we would make each other happy. I don't know how to make anyone happy, including myself. Or if thinking about him is healthy for me."

Hope reared it's head. "Is Benny so gorgeous, Grandfather?"

Grandfather appraised Jon. "I saw him last when he was fourteen. He was more beautiful than any boy I have ever seen, even Wesley. I could see that he would become even more beautiful as a man."

"Avalina said I should find him. She said we would be happy."

Grandfather's eyes were sad. Jon knew instantly that the shaman knew of Benny's probable fate. "You would have been very happy, had you met six years ago. But you did not."

"Is he dead?"

"Often, I can tell when one of my students has died. I feel it." He touched his heart. "But not Benny. If he lives, he is hiding in the shadows."

Grandfather's chin dropped and he wiped at his eye. He hummed a few syllables of some chant.

"Should I try to find him?"

"Why?"

"Avalina Cocina told me to. But I don't know why."

"You should know why. When you know why, you should find him. But you shouldn't try before you know your real reasons. Maybe you shouldn't try at all. Don't find him because you think sex will save you. Most likely, Benny is dead. He may have the sickness you have."

Grandfather was silent for a long time. Finally he spoke again.

"Do you wonder how that woman, Sandy Sydney, was able to do what she did? She used the sacred energy for evil. Some people don't believe in the dark side, Jon Walker. Some people see evil as just lies or a place where the light is blocked. If evil were that, Sandy Sydney couldn't have used the energy to hurt others. I have never had a student go to the dark side. But Benny … I fear he may have turned. I can't feel his energy."

The shaman was silent for another long spell. Then he said, slowly, "I trained Benny especially. I knew he would have a hard life. I knew he was a two-spirit from the first time I saw him. He was four. I trained him how to defend himself. When he got older, I trained him much harder. He was with me from September to June the year he left us. He ran away from me and went home because I trained him so hard. He is a greater warrior than Wesley. Do you understand?" Jon could remember lighting flashing from Wesley's body. He nodded. "If he lives, Benny is very dangerous. He is *angry*, Jon Walker, more angry than anyone I've known."

More silence. "He could be dead, but I don't think so. He could be in trouble. That, I think is true. He could be a servant of the Dark Lord. Only find him if you're ready, Jon Walker. If you find him, it won't be just a love affair to take away your pain. Finding Benny could kill you. *Benny* could kill you in an instant."

Jon stammered, "'Rique came to me when I was driving here. He said I had two years to live. He said I wouldn't suffer …"

"If your friend came back from the other side to tell you that, you should trust him. You will not suffer."

"But two years! I'll only be twenty nine."

Grandfather ducked under the water and came up beaming. "How lucky you are! Two years! There is so much you can do!" Grandfather let out a whoop. "What I could do with two years!" He looked at Jon conspiratorially. "I will die in a few months."

"And you're still doing the Meeting?"

"Of course. I wish that I could do more. Heal more people. See my friends come into their own. Praise the Great One. But, oh! The glory of where we will go. I've been there. When I had my heart attack, I went to the other side and saw its splendor. I saw my daughter and old friends. But the Great One threw me back here. He said I had more work to do." Grandfather smiled at Jon conspiratorially. "Let's keep my death our secret. People get so upset—I haven't told anyone. Well, Elizabeth knows."

"What should I do for two years?"

"You should listen to your heart. You will know what to do."

69

H E WAS THE light. He was limitless space. He was the song of the universe, the sound of love and devotion being born. He slept, cradled by the Great Mystery, satisfied in heaven's arms.

"Wess-lee." The Mystery's voice awakened him. "Wess-lee. My Wess-lee." The Great Mystery called him. He separated himself from the boundless peace and took form. The outline of his body appeared against the living water. And then his body was flesh and he was in it.

"Wess-lee. Come to me," the Mystery called.

Wess-lee looked at his arms, long and roped with muscle, covered lightly with black hair. They had looked like this when he was young. His legs were also the same: shorter than his arms and more muscular, with the same black coat. His torso was compact and his belly divided by bands of hard flesh. He felt his face and head. His forehead sloped back and his chin receded. Hair covered all of his face but his muzzle. His mouth opened in surprise.

"My dear, Wess-lee. I have made you as you were on earth."

Wess-lee looked toward the brilliant, shining source of all that exists, the Great Mystery.

"I have called you, Wess-lee, because this is a night of miracles. What have you wished for more than anything?"

He didn't dare hope, but yet he did. "That Mee-lisa could come to me."

"And so she can."

The hair on his back prickled and stood erect. Mee-lisa was his first wife. She was the wife he'd never forgotten, killed in her youth by the great shaking and fire, killed with their only child in her belly.

The beautiful Mee-lisa ... his heart had longed for her. They had loved each other more than all the stars in the sky, the blades of grass on the earth, the drops of rain flowing to the rivers.

Wess-lee looked around frantically. Where was Mee-lisa? She had not been allowed to come to the abode of light when she died.

Compassion flowed from the Great Mystery. "I could not bring her here, Wess-lee." The Mystery explained. "I did not mind her killing her first husband. He beat her and caused their infant to die. But when she killed every man, woman, and child in his village as well as him, that was too much." Wess-lee's eyes widened. She hadn't told him that.

"Her time of separation has passed. She can come to you."

Wess-lee jumped to his feet, looking around.

"No, my dear one, it is not so easy. She was a dangerous woman. You must make sure that she is reformed enough to live in my realm. If she is, you may bring her here. On earth, this is a miraculous night; you may claim her tonight, and only tonight."

Wess-lee kept looking around. The Mystery's kingdom had no entrance and no exit: nothing but light. How could he find Mee-lisa?

"I will show you the way, my dear one, but I must talk to you first." The Mystery paused, as though trying to find a way to say something. "Many cycles of hot and cold times have passed since you lived in flesh. Thirty thousand years have gone by since the cave bear."

Wess-lee's hands flew to his head. He felt the jaws of the great bear crush his skull. He felt the pain once again, pain he had escaped when it happened by leaving his body forever.

"Yes, my dear, you remember how you died. Do you remember the rest of it, how you came to me, and why?"

Images of that time came to Wess-lee. The band was struggling to survive. The shaking had come again, and the fire exploded from the mountains. They went to search for a safe new home. When they found the new cave, they had praised the Great Mystery.

Unfortunately, the bear that lived there came back. Wess-lee could see himself from high above in that other time, drawing the enormous bear deeper into the cave, away from the others. Saving his people. He gave his life without a thought.

"Your sacrifice pleased me, my dear one. You have won the right to visit Mee-lisa and bring her here, if she is not dangerous. Your body from the old days is gone, but I will put your soul and image into the body of one of your descendants. His name is Wesley. He and his wife are enjoying their wedding night. Her name is Melissa, and she is the descendant of your wife Mee-lisa. You must find her inside Melissa and bring her out."

Wess-lee wrestled with what the Mystery was telling him.

"You need to find Mee-lisa inside her descendant and bring her home, here, if she's safe to be here." The Mystery stroked Wes-lee's head. "It's hard to understand, my dear one, but this is the only way it can be done. Tonight is special on earth, a night where heaven touches the ordinary world. Things are possible tonight that won't be possible again.

Wess-lee started to stand, but the Mystery bade him stay. "There's more for you to do in the future time. You must teach Melissa and Wesley to love the way you and Mee-lisa did. Such abandon is pleasing to my eyes. You need to do something else. You need to teach Melissa to fight."

Wess-lee considered that. Mee-lisa had been a good fighter when he knew her. He rubbed his jaw. What could he teach her descendant that Mee-lisa's blood hadn't already taught her?

"Little Melissa is dangerous, Wess-lee, if she is angry or afraid. But she needs more power than she has now, if she is to survive and save her people. She needs more skill."

"Is something bad going to happen?" Wess-lee thought of cave bears and the shaking that knocked down mountains.

"Something bad is happening right now, and more will come. She must be prepared for the part she will play.

"The new world is very different, my Wess-lee. What the people of your time knew naturally, the new people have forgotten. I said that thirty thousand years have passed since you lived. I know you don't understand numbers, but as many hot and cold times have passed as there are stars in the sky. You will find the new world strange and repulsive."

Wess-lee's brows knit. He scratched his chin.

"I have given you a hard task, my darling. Can you do it?"

Wess-lee nodded, and then disappeared.

70

WESLEY WAS STILL sleeping; Melissa could see his form in the bed and hear his snoring. Seemed odd to hear such an elegant man making such primitive sounds. Melissa looked at him with adoration. She could see their future stretched out before them, a wonderland of romance, fabulous sex, and spiritual experiences. She got goose bumps recalling his lovely body and all they had done.

She had never felt so free in her life; no trace of the trauma of her abuse remained. She could remember what happened to her when she was a child, but it didn't impact her in any way.

"I'm alive for the first time. I feel wonderful!"

She wore the necklace Wes gave her and tied a big flower-print silk scarf with long fringes around her waist like a sarong. Melissa felt very sexy as her bare breasts bounced while she got out plates and silverware. She found a note from Jon in one of the coolers.

Girlfriend –

Grandfather left these carafes of liquid slime for you, labeled #2 and #3. You had #1 with lunch. Grandfather said to tell you the drinks are part of "the experience." Drink #2 is for

"When you want to go on to the next step." And drink #3
is for "When you want to come back." He said you'd know
what that means.

Well, girlfriend, duty calls. Don't do anything I wouldn't
do.

Jon

She poured herself a glass of #2. The drink looked and smelled like guava nectar, with a subtle difference she couldn't name. Sipping it, she thought, *Mm. Really good. Well, I'm ready for the next step.* She'd put out some salads, barbecued quail, a rack of lamb, and some wedding cake—how did Jon come up with the cake?

She looked around the cave. Lanterns provided some light, but the stone seemed lit by its own warm phosphorescence. I like this cave woman stuff, she thought. All I need is my cave man.

Wess-lee felt himself tumbling, dropping ever downward. He felt a thump! as he re-entered his body, and then unendurable, crushing pain. Images of his last moments on earth returned quickly—and stopped him from crying out. The bear might still be nearby.

"Wesley? Are you awake?" He groaned. "Wes? I've got dinner ready."

Wess-lee heard something sounding like his name, and a woman's voice mispronouncing it. He froze. No hunter would show himself unless he had scouted the area first. Plus, Wess-lee remembered that the Great Mystery had told him that the wife of his descendent, in whom he would find Mee-lisa, was very dangerous if she was angry or afraid. Would he frighten her?

He began to reconnoiter without letting her see him moving. He touched the skin he lay upon. He had never seen such a thin skin; it was made of something like spider-web, put together in squares. Over him was a thicker skin, very bright colored, brighter than the brightest birds or flowers. Wess-lee shivered.

What was this thing covering him? He wanted to bite it and tear it a bit to investigate it, but he did not want to make the female mad. He pulled at the skin below him. Beneath it was a truly terrible bed. It was not made of branches or soft grass. It was covered with a slick, shiny skin that reminded him of a snake's belly. It had patterns on it and strange marks. He knew it was a Holy Marking, a charm put on this bed by a holy man. It looked like "S-E-R-T-A." Wess-lee would remember this holy charm. It might save him in this strange world.

Beyond the bed, the cave looked normal, but just at the first glance. Fires held in strange shiny containers ringed the wall. The paintings on the walls were the modern type that Wess-lee didn't like. He could feel the Spirits in the cave; it was a good place. Many holy men had prayed there, many offerings had been given to the Great Mystery and the Ancestors. He reached out and recoiled—repelled.

His arm was hideous: slender and long, with weak, thin bones and a tiny hand. He was almost hairless! Wess-lee was deeply shaken.

"Wesley? Are you okay?" she called to him. "That was a really powerful experience, wasn't it? It was Tantric sex, I've read all about it. Don't be worried. It was just a Kundalini manifestation." She walked over to the bed. "Are you okay?" She put her hand on his shoulder and peered into his face.

Wess-lee saw her and hid under the coverlet. *O Great Mystery— protect me!* Never in his life had he seen such an ugly creature: hairless white skin, a huge protruding forehead, giant bulging eyes, a big chin, and a wide, flabby mouth.

The horror of his predicament sank in. His Mee-lisa was in that monster, and he had to find her there. He recalled that in life, you would often get what you wanted, but not the way you wanted it, or when you wanted it. Most often, you got what you wanted when you didn't want it any more. Things had not changed.

"Wes. What's the matter?" He could feel the concern in her bizarre voice.

Using all of his courage, he peered from beneath the covers. She was just as ugly on the second look. Wess-lee had faced saber-toothed tigers, lions, bears, and predators of all descriptions. He was a brave man—but he felt terror in this strange place. He had to stay—his only hope of finding Mee-lisa was by being with this woman. He gazed into her eyes. Their expression said that she was concerned about him.

He groaned and put a hand on his head.

"Oh, do you have a headache?" She took his hand and pulled him from the bed. "Was all that too much for you?"

Wess-lee looked down at his naked body and almost jumped back into bed. He was just as ugly as this woman—his legs were way too long. He had tiny, scrawny limbs. No hair. No muscle to speak of at all. His organ was ridiculous; how could a man make babies with that tiny thing? He looked at the woman. No wonder these two were mated. They were so ugly, no one else would have them.

A barrage of words flowed from the woman's mouth. It was worse than all his other wives together. He followed her, smelling food. He wanted to eat, but first he had to do something. He walked along the wall of the cave, sniffing the air.

She screamed, *"Wesley, what are you doing?"* She ran to him and grabbed his hand. She dragged him into a nearby chamber with one of the flush holes in it. "There's the toilet—you go there."

Wess-lee sniffed the air and smiled approvingly. Others had used this place for this purpose for many years. He finished and turned to the woman. She led him back to the table.

"I can't believe you peed in the cave."

At the table, Wess-lee immediately knew the cause of the problem with these people: the food. He picked up a quail and examined it. A bird he caught would cover the table. Of course these people were scrawny. He ate the quail in one bite, bones and all.

She looked at him, the whites of her eyes showing all around. The woman leveled another barrage of words at him. They hit like hailstones, forcing him to retreat inside himself.

"Wesley, wasn't that an incredible experience? That was Kundalini. It's an energy that the Hindus say is coiled at the base of your spine, waiting to be awakened. When it is activated, it climbs up your spine, purifying and energizing you spiritually. And remember the lights along our spines? Those were chakras.

"Did you know they can give you incredible strength? Oh, of course you do, you're a spirit warrior! It's just a different system, Wes, nothing to be afraid of.

"Are you okay?" He was holding his head. "I've got some aspirin." Wess-lee followed her with his eyes. He liked the way her hips widened out from her waist. The skin made of flowers she wore was very interesting. He wanted to chew on it. Her breasts were horribly misshapen, but he found the way they bounced beguiling.

"Here, Wes, try this. Grandfather sent us this drink for when we want to move on to the next step. Might as well, huh?"

Wess-lee smelled it. It was a special drink made by holy men for young girls on their wedding nights. It made them more receptive and relaxed. The drink was not something for men. He looked at the hideous face before him; maybe he should try some.

She said, "Take the aspirin, Wes," and shoved them into his mouth. He gagged them down. "You're having a rough time, aren't you?" she said, leaning on his shoulder.

Wess-lee stiffened. He felt the same pleasure at her touch as he had at Mee-lisa's. This woman did have his wife inside her. But where?

She filled the thing she held in her hand again and drank it. Two drinks of this nectar would make the women of his clan receptive to a tree stump. How much would this woman take?

She looked into his eyes and Wess-lee could understand what she meant from the feelings coming from her. She was telling him that she liked mating with him, that she loved him.

Wess-lee found the poor ugly thing sweet. She took his hand and, once again, Wess-lee felt the wonderful flow of pleasure that made him love Mee-lisa past death. He lifted her hand to his mouth and softly licked it.

"What are you doing, Wesley? You're acting so weird." She shook her head began to talk again as though she'd never stop. "That huge cavern with the ocean, Wes, is the heart chakra. That's where we went, Wes! We saw the god and goddess of our hearts merging in love in the heart center."

To his surprise, she reached over the table and did something to his face. It was a very strange kiss; closed lips with almost no use of tongue. A horrible thought occurred: what if he had to mate with this poor, sad creature to reach his Mee-lisa? Wess-lee groaned.

"Does your head still hurt, sweetie?" She got up and found some "Horse Piss" left over from their wedding reception. "Try this. It might cheer you up." She kept drinking the #2 nectar. She moved her hips as though she was a female wildebeast in heat, as though she wanted to service a herd of males. The drink had worked.

The woman continued speaking. "Well, anyway. When the Kundalini rises to a certain level, the heart is activated like that." She paused and looked at Wess-lee. He stared back, opening his mouth; a huge, satisfying belch rolled out.

"Wesley! What is the matter with you?" She looked annoyed. Wess-lee was worried; he had made her angry by doing a natural thing. Women were always like that. He had to pass gas, too, but the Great Mystery had warned him several times not to make her mad.

One thing Wess-lee knew about women was that they hated it when you passed gas. It was such a simple thing. So natural, yet they said, "Wess-lee, didn't your mother teach you anything?" They always brought his mother into it.

Wess-lee had hoped that humanity had progressed since he died, but the woman's reaction to his belch told him it hadn't. He would have to hope and pray for the day when a man could fart in peace in his own cave.

Melissa peevishly continued her tirade. "I know your mother taught you better." See, she brought his mother into it.

"Remember the cobras? The cobra is the symbol of the Kundalini, especially the blue cobra. The Hindu deities are often shown with a cobra over their heads."

She never stopped. Wess-lee had never heard so many words. He finished one carafe of "Horse Piss" and went back to the food storage device by the wall for another. He touched the device in awe. What was it made of? Neither bone, nor hide, nor wood. It was cold inside. The container was a miracle.

The woman kept talking as he caressed its surface. Inside he found the golden liquid he sought, and more of the #2 liquid for her.

Wess-lee studied the Holy Markings on the cover of the storage vessel. He would remember "I-G-L-O-O." The symbols might save his life. Wess-lee carried the carafes back to the table. The woman's ceaseless talk irritated him to distraction; he wondered if he could just cuff her a little to make her quiet. Would this make her scared or angry enough to be dangerous?

"The cobras bit us. The ecstasy was so intense that we both passed out. Well, in Hindu thought, if you see a snake in meditation, it means you're really progressing. If it bites you, that's really good."

She poured another glass of the nectar and leaned over, pushing her breasts together with her elbows and smiling pertly as though she wanted to haul Wes-lee back to the bed. "This stuff is an aphrodisiac. I've had two carafes of it, and I'm ready. Come on, baby, it's our wedding night."

Wess-lee contemplated strangling the woman. His language was very simple, consisting of a few hundred words, many sacred symbols, signs, and grunts. Mostly, his people communicated through touch. When he touched a person, they connected psychically; he could usually read their thoughts, see the images there, and feel the feelings.

The woman before him was hopeless. Words, words, words. If he choked her unconscious, he'd have a chance at contacting Mee-lisa once she passed out. He looked up and noticed the unmistakable expression on her face: the female wanted to mate with him.

Wess-lee had faced many challenges. The cave bear was less repulsive than this woman. He poured her some more of the 'Opening' drink and took a healthy swig himself. She took his hand. He understood that message and took another gulp straight from the carafe. It didn't make her look any better.

The female led him back to the bed, smiling and swinging her hips. When they got to the bed, she pulled the flower-skin from around her hips. Wess-lee's spirits sank around his ankles. Looking down at himself, he could see that his spirit was not the only thing that had sunk. How he would do what he was supposed to do, the great warrior did not know. He heaved a sigh and got into the bed. Where was Mee-lisa?

"What's the matter, Wes? Are you sick? You really don't seem yourself. Let me feel your forehead." She touched his forehead. "Maybe we should have Elizabeth in to see you. I guess we could ..." Her mouth was off and running faster than the fleetest antelope, endlessly droning into his ears.

At Melissa's touch, Wess-lee burst into tears.

71

ELIZABETH AWAKENED FROM her nap. She sat up and looked around the RV's bedroom. It felt safe and snug. She got out of bed and looked in the mirror. Her hair had come out of its bun while she slept. She fixed it. Peering at her face, Elizabeth realized she looked better than she had before sleeping.

The doctor perked up even more when she noticed the sunlight streaming through the windows. She still had time to ride. Sticking her head out of the motor home door, Elizabeth saw the guards and a pile of her things.

"Great!" she exclaimed. "Bring my stuff in. Put the guns on a golf cart, and," she pointed to the kitchen area, "my bags in here. If you could put my saddle and horse stuff in a golf cart, I'll haul it down to the barn."

Thanking them, Elizabeth threw her things in the drawers of the motor home's bedroom. She liked her space neat and organized.

Elizabeth pulled out her jeans. Somehow, they looked small. They'd fit the year before. Grimacing, she pulled them on.

They were like leotards. She looked at herself in the mirror, horrified. Could she have gained that much weight? Elizabeth tried to suck in her tummy. Could she go out in public like that? It was that or not ride. What about the shirts?

Elizabeth went through her shirts. They looked small, too. Only the red one looked like it would work. She bought it less than a month before. She tugged her shirt around her breasts. She could hardly button it.

I look like a hussy. Elizabeth thought as she gazed the mirror. *Well, no choice. If I want to ride, this is all I have.* She put on her boots and slipped her belt through the jeans' loops. She wore a tooled leather belt and a trophy buckle she had won at a rodeo a million years ago. Every time she wore it she thought of Elwin.

Turning on her heel, she grabbed her hat and burst out of the door. She had bought her new hat as a joke. It was a bright red, ten-gallon hat. It was made of felt and had a wide, rolled brim. The hat was a Western stereotype—and all the rage these days, with the crown sticking up more in the back than in front. Elizabeth had stuck two eagle feathers in the hatband. She kept it on with a horsehair tie-down with cute fringes on the ends. Over-the-top horsy chic!

She piled into the golf cart, hoping that none of the men scattered around the Numenon camp noticed her tight clothes. It didn't work. She could hear every one of them catch his breath as she drove the cart across the courtyard.

She heard someone whisper, "That is one built woman!"

Elizabeth headed toward the stables, passing Will Duane's sleeping form on one of the lounges. On impulse, she stopped and got out, approaching him quietly. Will was so nice to let her stay in the motor home, and she had been cold to him that morning. She tapped his shoulder.

"Will—wake up. It's me, Elizabeth."

Will slowly opened his eyes and peered at a figure bending over him.

"Do you want to ride down to the horses with me? We can talk and you can see me ride." He blinked, as though he hadn't understood her words. Elizabeth repeated her invitation.

"I'd love to," he replied, hobbling to the golf cart. One of the warriors folded his wheelchair and put it in the back. "Let's go."

"Let's watch Gil work a horse," Elizabeth said when they got down to the corrals. "I've heard how well he's doing." She looked at the sun. "There's plenty of time for me to ride afterward." The place was swarming with people. Most were clustered around a big round structure with high solid walls.

"Gil? A horse?"

"Gil Canao. Your Gil. He's a very nice man. I met him when you first got here and he hit his head. He's been here every day working with Bud."

Will was nonplussed. He hadn't seen the Filipino MBA since they'd arrived. He was working horses?

"You can learn a great deal from horses," Elizabeth went on. "About mastering fear and being assertive, but not using any more force than you have to. Bonding with another creature so that it trusts you. Grandfather approved Gil's working with Bud. That's why you haven't seen him much."

Nice if someone had told him.

"Bud said that he's learning amazingly fast. He's going to work a horse in the round pen." She looked at the round structure with eight foot high wallls. A scaffolding ran around the top so that spectators could watch what was going on in the pen. Bud Creeman was up there, calling into the enclosure.

"Okay, Gil, nothing fancy now. You're a beginner and that's a wild horse."

Will looked at Elizabeth. "Gil's in there with a wild horse?"

"Bud wouldn't let him in there if he couldn't handle it." She looked at the pen and back at Will. "Unfortunately, you can't get up there to watch him, but there's a peephole in the door. You can get an idea." She pushed Will's chair to the peephole and helped him look in.

"My God! Get him out of there." Will's eyes bulged. The animal was enormous. It ran around the edge of the circle, blasing air out of its nose.

"Okay, Gil," Bud called. "You just want him to run around a few times in each direction and get him to stop facing you. Use that thingy to motivate him." The thingy looked like a fishing rod with a bunch of strips of plastic bags made into a pompom tied at one end.

Will watched as Gil did exactly what Bud instructed. In minutes, Gil was standing in the middle of the pen next to the horse. It arched its neck and looked at him while Gil stroked its neck.

"Want to put a halter on him?" Gil indicated that he did. Bud tossed out directions and encouragement. In a few more minutes, Gil was walking the horse around the pen on a lead line.

"I can't believe I saw that." Will shook his head. Gil was the weakest member of the MBA team. Yes, he was first in his class like the others. Yes, he was very productive and a super hard worker. But he didn't have the chutzpah—the balls—to make it in the boardroom. Will had invited him to the Meeting because he had a feeling Gil had something special, if it could be brought out.

Gil slipped out of the pen and saw Will and Elizabeth sitting in the golf cart. "Hello, Elizabeth." He turned to his boss. "Will, we need to hire Bud."

"Why?"

"I've been working with him this week, and I've never learned as much in any management training course as I have with Bud and the horses. We need to hire him."

"As what?"

"A management trainer. What Bud does is fantastic, Will. You won't believe what he can teach—the person as much as the horse. Self confidence. Assertiveness. When to step back so you don't get killed."

Will had been looking for an excuse to hire Bud Creeman since he saved his life on their way in. And look at Gil! A few days with Bud and he looked like he could take on Frank Sauvage. Or the devil himself.

"Okay. We'll hire him. You do the deal. Start at 100K, keep it as close to that as you can. Full benefits package. Housing at my place. Tell me how you do."

"He's got a wife and will have a baby very soon."

"Give him one of the guest houses." He turned to Elizabeth. "You're still going to ride?" She nodded.

"Bud's catching my horse. He's over there." Elizabeth started the cart as the earth began to ripple again. Everything around them jerked up and down, shuddered and shook. Will thought the quake rolled longer than the previous time.

"Are there earthquakes in New Mexico?" he asked.

"Nothing like this. Grandfather said it's because of Wesley and Melissa," Elizabeth said. "We shouldn't worry about it. There's nothing around here to fall down."

Not to worry? He'd be knocked off his feet if he wasn't in the cart.

"I'll get Puffy, and we'll be off." Elizabeth smiled. He didn't know she could look that friendly. "You can watch me saddle up, Will."

72

WILL LISTENED AS Bud and Elizabeth talked about her ride. The cadence of their voices sounded like they were from another country. Looking around at the dark horsemen and their mounts, he realized he was in a foreign territory.

Bud approached Elizabeth. "He hasn't been ridden since you rode him last year. Are you sure you're up for this?"

"Bud, I just slept for three hours. I'm up for a trip to the moon."

"Well, Puffy may give it to you. He's all yours." Bud stepped back, shaking his head. "Give me your address, in case I need to forward your mail."

Elizabeth indicated her guns in the back of the cart.

"You're going out to the bluff where we shoot?" Bud asked. "That's ten miles away. That's a long ride at this time of day." Bud looked up at the sun, followed by Elizabeth.

Will's gaze trailed after both of theirs. He sat in his wheelshair, feeling like he'd been dropped in a culture as foreign as anything in the Far East. But this was the West and the world of horses. He guessed that it was about three in the afternoon, but it felt like two a.m.

"You'll have enough light to get there and back," Bud said, frowning.

Now that the golf cart was stopped, Will could get a better look at Elizabeth. She looked like she'd come from Las Vegas. Skin tight clothes—and that hat! He looked around the stable yard. There were a lot of people there. Had they noticed her tight clothes?

Yeah, men were sneaking peeks and pretending they weren't. Even Bud was affected. Everytime he looked at Elizabeth, he blushed. Will would like to look at her all day. She seemed to realize what everyone was thinking. Elizabeth hustled around the cart and pulled her saddle out of the back. She wanted to get out of there.

More aspiring horse masters appeared, not wanting to miss Elizabeth riding that insane horse. She chatted with Will as she got her bridle and the rest of her horse stuff out of the golf cart. She disappeared into the tack shack's depths, emerging with a lariat, thick halter, and lead line. Leather gloves protected her hands. "I'll go catch my horse and be right back," she said, with that beguiling smile.

Will was thunderstruck. Elizabeth was the most fascinating woman he'd ever met. Roping. Riding. Shooting. He didn't know what to say to her. He felt hopeless and helpless, stuck in the damned golf cart with his ankle throbbing.

A giant crash coming from the corral behind him jarred him alert. He swiveled in the cart, looking at the corral wall. It was taller than he was, and had rails made of heavy lumber. The posts were big, too. Will didn't know a lot about construction, but that corral was obviously made to contain something very large—and powerful.

Bud and the onlookers ran to the fence. Will wanted to get closer, even it was only to witness Elizabeth's death. Choking from the dust, he piloted the cart to the corral and peered into the enclosure. The biggest horse he'd ever seen crashed into the fence directly in front of him. He recoiled, horrified.

The horse careened around the edge of the corral, never slowing, and never swerving. It was like a black and white Molotov cocktail. The blasting sounds coming from its nose sounded like roars.

"That horse is crazy! Get her out of there!" Will yelled to Bud.

"Oh, I reckon I wouldn't try," he answered. "She'd kill me if I tried to stop her. She'll have Puffy caught in about a minute." He turned to the other guys and said, "Watch this. You'll never see nothing like this."

Will watched as much as he could, closing his eyes at the horse's worst assaults. "*That's* Crème Puff?" he asked Bud.

"Yeah. Elizabeth's got kinda a sense of humor about what she names her horses." He grinned at Will.

Will heard Elizabeth say, "Good, Puffy. That's a good boy." The sweet talk continued and the hoof beats were abruptly silent. It took a while for the dust to settle, but Will could finally see Elizabeth feeding Puffy carrots and petting his face.

As casually as if this was how she caught her horse every day, Elizabeth petted her way up his neck and put the halter on.

"Good boy, Puffy." She worked with the horse a few minutes, getting him to heel and stay, the way their dog trainer had when Cass was little and they had a dog. Maybe the horse wasn't so dangerous after all.

Elizabeth said, "Open the gate." The minute the gate opened a crack, Puffy took off at a run, making his getaway.

When he got to the end of the rope, Elizabeth stopped him, yanking his head and body around with one expert motion. She stroked him some more, then walked him back and forth through the gate until he acted like a well-trained dog again. Elizabeth walked Puffy around the stable yard. The illusion of training disappeared fast; the horse began jumping and blowing up at every little rock and bug.

Will sighed and shut his eyes. Elizabeth's show was too intense for him. When he looked again, he saw that Puffy was saddled and watching Elizabeth like she held the key to heaven. She put her rifles in scabbards on each side of the saddle and placed the saddlebags full of ammunition behind the saddle, tying and clipping them on.

Elizabeth had been talking to Bud, turning to face him as she put on her chaps. She must have had them since she was a little girl: their fringes reached just below her knees and their leather was worn almost through in places. Elizabeth's back was to Will. The doctor first buckled the chaps around her waist and then bent over and reached through her legs to secure little ties that kept the chaps on.

Her derriere was directed at him. As she bent over, her thighs and buttocks made the most bountiful horseshoe shape. She was warm and round and luxurious. No scrawny, shrunken butt—stroking her wouldn't be like touching a dead chicken. So many of the women he'd been with were like that. Elizabeth was warm, like delicious prime rib, dripping with life and succulence. He also realized that the impotence that had been plaguing him since he split with Marina would be cured by the right partner. Elizabeth.

She turned and spoke to him, every word a benediction. "I'm going to do some shooting. I'll be back by dark." As she talked, she put two ammunition belts over her shoulders, wearing them crossed, Bandeliero style. The leather belts pressed her enormous breasts, which were jammed into her tight blouse.

She looked at him carefully, then walked over to him and whispered, "Your medication is in my purse, right there." He could see it in a little cubby in the cart's dashboard. "If you need something for panic while I'm gone, take one. How are you doing?"

Will shifted in his chair, grimacing, glad that he was seated so she couldn't see the bulge in his pants.

"Things are going to get better, Will, you'll see."

She walked over to Bud and Puffy. He watched her mount and ride off as though he was watching the parting of the Red Sea.

Elizabeth stepped up on that huge horse like a feather. She landed in the saddle the same way. Waiting a moment, she indicated to Puffy that he could walk forward.

That's when Will panicked. He whispered, "Bud! Should she be riding that horse? Maybe you should send someone with her in case there's trouble."

Bud shook his head. "Oh, I guarantee there'll be trouble with Ol' Puff. But there'll be worse trouble if I interfere. And no, I don't think she should be riding that horse. She's not twenty years old, an' she don't ride broncs every day. I don't suppose anyone could tell her that."

They stared at Elizabeth's receding back. Her erect carriage was as magnificent on a horse as it had been every other time he'd seen her.

"Oh my God!" they exclaimed at once. Puffy exploded. Hooves, legs, head; spinning, twisting, leaping—flying through the air as he bucked harder than any horse could. Will saw four feet of air beneath his hooves, and that was on one of the little bucks.

"She'll be killed!" Will shouted.

Bud shook his head. "I reckon she can last ten seconds, Mr. Duane."

Elizabeth pulled Puffy's head up and got him moving forward. She turned him in a circle, galloping fit to challenge a Triple Crown winner. She ran in a circle for a while, and then she headed him out straight into the desert. Soon, all they could see of them was a fast moving column of dust.

Will watched it with tears in his eyes.

73

THE MINUTE MELISSA touched Wesley's forehead, images from his mind flowed into hers. A Neanderthal-type face looked back at her, the inhabitant of her husband's body. She recoiled and tried to leap away. Before she could, Wess-lee grabbed her and held her close to him, placing his hand on her forehead. A wave of relaxation overcame her. Limp, she heard her Wesley's voice in her head.

Melissa. It's okay. I'm here.

Trembling, she thought back, Wes … There's a cave man inside of you …

It's okay. He's one of my ancestors. He's supposed to teach us something. The love of his life is one of your ancestors. She's inside you somewhere. It's got to be part of that thing Grandfather told us about. He didn't say our ancestors were in on it, but they must be.

It was too much—all that had happened, and now there was a cave man inside Wesley looking for his mate inside of her. She wanted to go back to Palo Alto and join a woman's group. She longed to howl in despair, but she was too relaxed from whatever that caveman was doing to her. She had taken a lot in the past few days, and now this. She was cracking, the way a bowl of Jell-o would crack. She didn't have enough backbone left to do more than jiggle.

Wess-lee saw it and began to stroke her. As he touched her, the ancient cave man learned of her abuse, her family, and her achievements. He saw her world and was appalled. It was full of noise, dirt, grime, and pollution; many, many people, all crowded together.

Beholding it, Wess-lee was close to hysterics himself. What a horrible place the earth had become. He couldn't understand how the Elders would allow the filth and smog. The modern tribal leaders must be degenerate.

He petted the little waif softly, making purring noises in his throat. He needed to heal this poor little wretch; that, clearly, was one reason he was there. When he reviewed Melissa's world, he saw that she was not any uglier than the rest of her people.

He lay quietly with her for quite some time, letting his energy flow into her; healing her and relaxing her, she slipped into sleep. He felt something once again: this strange woman was part of him. The energy flow between them was as intense as with any of his wives, close to his experience with Mee-lisa.

He discovered something else. He liked touching her peculiar, pale body. Once he got used to her, he found her attractive in a bizarre way. Wesley's body, the body he was occupying, found Melissa very attractive—that was for sure.

Wess-lee roused Melissa, letting her see images from his mind while she was relaxed. She needed to get to know him. The half-asleep Melissa was able to tolerate seeing Wess-lee's physical form with his slanted forehead, chinless, ape-like visage, powerful arms, short legs, and muscular, hairy body. With all that, he was a human, not an ape.

He showed her his world: immense trees, plants she'd never seen or imagined, and huge, carnivorous animals. A life of perpetual danger; volcanoes, earthquakes, floods, violent storms, hungry predators, and other humanoids competing for food. He stroked Melissa softly and let her absorb the facts of his life.

He told her his story with mental images.

"Mee-lisa's inside of me?" her tiny voice warbled. "I don't think so. I didn't go to Harvard to—"

He silenced her and let her into his mind.

"I can see her," Melissa said, amazed. "She's smaller than you but looks the same. She has *blond* curly hair. It's all fluffed up here ..." Melissa indicated the front of her head. "She's got a cavewoman pompadodre! And curls down her back." Melissa's nose crinkled. "She's covered with *tattoos*. But they're pretty. Sort of." Melissa was nonplussed. "She looks *hip*. That's my ancestor?" Melissa paused. "She *is* my ancestor. I can feel it."

When she realized what Wess-lee told her was true, Melissa's thoughts became louder than thunder. They were as loud as the noise a mountain made when it exploded. They pelted him like the rain during a monsoon. And words! He held his head.

"Oh, my God, Wess-lee! Do you realize what an incredible anthropological find you are?" She shouted, popping out of the relaxation he had induced. Super-charged energy—brain waves—fizzed from every pore along with her words.

Her thoughts followed, hyper-energized: *The implications are amazing! Psychic contact with pre-historic man. The geophysical, as well as the biological, implications! It's proof of life after death, reincarnation, and the transmigration of the soul. We've got to study you!*

Nothing could think so fast or with so many words, but Melissa's mind kept accelerating. She'd consumed almost three carafes of the #2 nectar. She was becoming crazy.

"My God, Wes." Her energy screamed through Wes-lee as she shouted, *"We can make a fortune. This could be a TV movie. A bestseller! The implications are ... Jeez, I can see spreadsheats in my mind. We'll be set*

for life." She paused, thinking, before bursing out with, "I need to call my mom and have her get the Smithsonian in on it."

Melissa stopped abruptly. "How will we separate you from Wess-lee for scientific purposes? *Can* we separate you? Can people see him, or am I the only one?"

All of her MBA training and everything her parents had taught her was kicking in, when she stopped abruptly. Wesley was screaming at her.

"Stop thinking—you're killing him!" Wesley shouted. Only then did she notice that Wess-lee's body was writhing and he was gasping for breath, barely aware of what they were saying.

"Your thoughts are too much for him. Stop it, Melissa. You're killing him."

The number and volume of Melissa's words slowed immediately. "If he died, would you die, too, Wesley?" Her expression said she knew the answer.

"He wants to find Mee-lisa," Wesley said. "He thought he had to have sex with you to do it. We look really ugly to him, Melissa."

She grabbed the quilt and covered herself. "Oh, no! I always thought I was ugly. Only since you and I, Wes, have been here ..." She peered at him. "Is that you, Wes? Who are you?"

"I'm Wes."

"Where is he?"

"He passed out."

"Oh, God. I'm so ugly that a caveman thinks I'm hideous and doesn't want to have sex with me." She began to sob. And didn't stop.

Wesley didn't know what to do, but Wess-lee did. He tenderly held her, stroked her softly, learning how she felt about her body. He put one hand on Melissa's forehead and the other at the base of her skull.

Engaging his healing powers, he nodded. The problem was clear. The front part of Melissa's brain was many times larger than it needed to be. That accounted for all those thoughts and the rapid speech.

"Wesley?" Wess-lee asked. "Can I make the front part of her brain not work? I will let what she really needs work, so she can walk and find the toilet. She will have a much better disposition."

Wes replied, "No! She needs her brain. I love her the way she is."

Wess-lee nodded sadly. This explained the state of the modern world. Too much thinking, not enough thought that mattered, and almost no acting on that thought. Still, she needed that huge brain to survive her dreadful life.

He allowed his energy to pulse through the lower part of her skull and neck. There was the rest of the problem. Her lower brain stem and more primitive mental functions were hardly operational. She undoubtedly could barely find her way home. That's where she could be healed. Wess-lee let his energy flow, and soon she stopped crying, her whole body relaxed.

She slept, perhaps for just a few moments. When she awoke, Wess-lee peered at her through Wesley's eyes. He had his hand on the back of her head.

She looked at him breathlessly. Wess-lee knew his effect on women. He was magnetic, many times more powerful than Wesley. Her chest rose a bit and her hips moved. She was attracted to him.

"Do you still think I'm ugly?" she said.

He shook his head. He spoke to her wordlessly, *You are beautiful for your world.* Energy continued to flow through his hand; her body relaxed as though she was melting. He continued speaking into her mind, *I want to explore you. Wesley is part of me, and I of him. And you and Mee-lisa are the same. We are all part of each other. I want to find Mee-lisa in you, and you in you.*

"You mean with *sex?*"

He nodded.

"You won't hurt me?"

No.

When Wess-lee felt her assent, the energy in his hand changed. In seconds, Melissa's breathing deepened. She looked at him, eyes darkening and widening. Her chest moved toward him. Wess-lee smiled, she didn't look so ugly to him now. When he put one hand on her breast, she arched her back, moving her hips with his caresses. He smiled again, kissing her softly.

When he kissed, Wess-lee used his tongue and lips much more than Wesley had. Melissa pulled away from the animal-like contact. But then she began to kiss him the same way—wildly excited. He touched the back of her skull occasionally, activating her primitive brain centers. Every touch brought her out more. Drops of sweat formed on her upper lip.

Wess-lee made small sounds to show his pleasure as he touched her. His hums and grunts and small noises were almost continuous. Soon, Melissa was making them with him. Wess-lee liked this woman. She reminded him of Mee-lisa. He kept his hands on her and intensified his energy. He wouldn't stop until she was his, body and soul. She would be his mate.

74

AFTER ELIZABETH RODE off, Bud noticed the strangest thing. When he'd come out that morning, maybe three or four of the mares were in heat. This was odd, since he hadn't noticed any yesterday. The mares in heat were in a good, standing heat—that usually takes a few days to develop.

Judging by how they were acting, the mares should be bred right away to get pregnant. That was weird, but not too weird—mares pastured together tended to cycle together.

Then there were Bud's own thoughts. Ever since he'd seen Wesley and Melissa up there in the sky, thoughts of Bert drifted into his head from nowhere. They drove him crazy and almost had gotten him hurt with the horses. This was not how he usually was. He was usually peaceful inside.

Today, nothing was normal, and it was getting to be more abnormal by the minute. He didn't need to think about Bert; her sister Roxy and the doctors were taking good care of her back at the camp. Their baby wasn't due for another two weeks.

Bud looked out at the herd again, and damned if half the mares weren't in heat. It was downright embarrassing if you hadn't seen it before. There they stood, squatting and peeing, squealing and raising their tails, ready for action. This was truly impossible.

Tyler Brand and a bunch of warriors pulled into the stable in golf carts. Swirls of dust rose around them. Tyler looked as pissed off as Bud had seen him. He stood by his cart and surveyed the equine orgy in the field. "*What* is going on?"

"You can see it." Bud waved at the pasture.

Tyler stared for a few moments and exhaled hard. "Grandfather ordered us out on another patrol. We're supposed to find Sandy Sydney." The slump of Tyler's shoulders said he didn't expect any more success than he'd had previously. "I've been on four patrols so far. I don't know what Grandfather expects. She'll materialize out of thin air?" He looked at the way the mares were acting again and shook his head.

"Saddle up all the geldings," Tyler said to the warriors. They took all the geldings they had—a smart move. "If you've got any kids around here helping you, have them drive those carts up to the Bowl. I think they'll need them more up there than down here." The professor sighed again.

"Someone saw Sandy Sydney west of here in the desert—she's a huge vulture with a misshapen head," Tyler said. "Watch out, Bud. She's fast and can cover a lot of ground. We don't know where she is."

"I'll keep an eye out." Bud waved slackly as they rode off. His fantasies of Bert returned full strength. Only to be cut short when he remembered Bert's situation. She was up in the camp, lying on a cot in their tent. He knew that carrying an eight and a half month pregnant woman to the Meeting was a mistake. Even Grandfather was worried when they drove in, poor Bert jolting across the desert in his old truck. Neither of them wanted her to come.

Bert had been unswayed by their protestations. "The baby's not due for two weeks. If it comes early, Grandfather or Elizabeth can deliver it." She was such a spirit warrior that she would brave anything rather than miss the last Meeting.

Once she got to the Bowl, Bert felt awful. She'd been lying in their tent most of the time, fighting cramps and backaches.

Thank God, they were next to Elizabeth's camp and the medical tent, and all the other doctors' campsites. Bert was safe, surrounded by people who could help her. Plus, Grandfather had told her sister to stay with her the entire Meeting. Roxy was a third year nursing student, practically as good as a doctor.

Bud sighed, his sweet darlin' Bert looked like a whale. He'd never seen a pregnant woman that big. But Bert would be okay. She was in the middle of the Bowl with lots of help.

After Tyler and company left, Bud leaned on the fence rail by the tack shed, watching the spectacle in the field. He felt something on his foot and looked down. Damned if a couple of mice weren't doing it on his boot. "Get outta here!" he yelled, kicking hard. The mice flipped into the air, landed and resumed what they'd been doing.

Bud looked around. What was going on? Everywhere he looked were mating creatures: birds fell out of the sky, ground squirrels rolled over in heaps, mice cavorted, unnoticed by the rollicking desert rats around them. Bugs humped each other unashamed. Even scorpions danced gingerly, loving each other their own venomous way. Bud had never seen anything like it.

"Oh, no!" Bud yelled. "Don't do that!" Grandfather had said they might "experience some of what Wes and Melissa were feeling." But this? Every living creature was on fire.

The stallions had noticed the mares. They'd brought six of them in to be trained that week. They were pacing frantically in their corrals, posturing and neighing, *I'm the one for you, baby!* at the mares. The whole bunch of them had worked themselves into a lather. Several stallions were launching themselves at the corral walls, trying to jump out.

Bud couldn't stop what was happening. The mares responded to the stallions' calls, moving in closer, turning their hindquarters to the studs and making displays of female flesh usually only seen in red-light

districts of major cities. Not only that, the mares that hadn't been showing were also coming in heat. He was surprised when Gil Canao tapped
his shoulder.

"Do they do this very often?" he asked, wide-eyed.

Bud wanted to hug Gil. He was the only person who'd stayed to help
him.

"I'm sure glad you're here, Gil—"

Their talk was interrupted by a thunder of hooves. They turned in
time to watch the big black stallion that Wes had ridden neatly clear his
corral wall. The rest were planning on following him. Some would be
able to jump the high fences, others wouldn't. Those who failed would
get hung up by their hind legs—they could be badly injured.

"Gil, we gotta let the rest of them out. You open the gates of those
two corrals; I'll do these three. Stay out of their way, they may blast out."

Bud and Gil accomplished the task in jig time and stood there
watching the resulting frenzy. The stallions just jumped in. They did not
fight over mares as they normally would; they cooperated. By this time,
all the mares were in heat, about a hundred or so. With six studs. Gil
stood with his mouth open.

"Do they usually do that?"

Bud couldn't speak. Who could stop the tide? Only one horse
remained unaffected: Bunny, the disgusting black mare that had stepped
on Gil's foot and slobbered on him when he started with the horses. She
obviously wasn't in heat.

Chores done, Gil asked Bud, "Would you mind if I go back to the
camp? I'd like to call Gabriela." Gil opened his mouth as though he'd
remembered something. "I need to talk to you, too. It's about something
important."

Bud regarded him. This was the most promising of the students: he
asked to be excused, helped him until the end, and worked his tail off.
Bud grinned at Gil's filthy, green-slimed shirt.

"Sure. Say hi to Gabriela for me. We can talk later. I need you to do something for me. Can you drive those carts back up the hill for me?"

"All of them?"

"Yeah. Any other interns down here to help?"

"No, they're gone." Gil stared at the carts. "I know what I'll do." He very quickly hooked the carts together like a train.

"That's cool, Gil. I didn't know you could do that."

"I was a caddy at a golf course back home." Gil took off for the main camp in the first of six carts. Looked like a bunch of beetles.

Bud walked over to the tack shed and, flicking a pair of mating flies off one of the cups, had a drink of water. What was happening seemed almost Biblical; a plague of some kind. He didn't know if it was good or bad.

The sky turned mauve and coral over the Western horizon as the sun headed for its night's rest. Thunderclouds amassed in the mountains. Lightning and thunder shattered the silence. They sounded almost like drums.

"Gonna party tonight, party tonight ..." He hummed the classic rock 'n' roll song. "Won't be long now until I can go see my sweet Bert."

When he thought of his wife, he remembered her curvaceous figure before she was pregnant. Bud's brows furrowed, recalling her huge belly. How was Bert on this weird evening?

75

"STOP! WE DO not do that!" Grandfather pulled couples apart up in the Pit. "You feel what you do because of Melissa and Wesley's gift from the Great One. You are feeling some of their bliss. But this is the Meeting. We keep the Rules." People were hugging and kissing, only slightly more restrained than the frolicking horses.

"Stop! We are going to leave. Pack up your things. We are leaving now!" The shaman wished he'd insisted that they go that afternoon. Now was too late, but he had to try. "We must leave."

No one paid attention to him. His arms dropped at his sides. What a great mistake this Meeting was. His last Meeting. How would his life's work be seen by those in the future if it ended the way it was heading? Whatever happened would be reported all over the planet the minute people returned to "civilization" and the Internet.

Increasingly, he didn't know the people he was pulling apart. They were new attendees, lured by Paul Running Bird's magnificent and forbidden website.

Carl Redstone joined him in patrolling, relieved of his duties with Will Duane since he was down at the barn.

The shaman could hear screaming and shouting from the back of the Bowl, bellows that could only come from brawls. Chu and his hoodlum friends had broken out the booze early. What else did they have? Mushrooms? Meth? The crowd seemed to gravitate toward Chu's territory, drifting like the tide. Things were sure to go downhill. But how far?

"Carl—find the spirit warriors! Send them to the back of the Bowl. We must stop this!"

Carl charged off to find his fellow warriors and Grandfather went back to trying to keep order. "Stop that! We will keep the Rules!"

Grandfather jumped when someone tapped him on the shoulder. He turned to see a familiar face. "Elmo Gregg! What are you doing here?"

"Pretty much the same as you. I got the Tribal Police out in force, tryin' to keep a lid on this thing. Ain't working, though." Elmo held his high-crowned hat to his chest. Threads of sweat-slick hair ran across the top of his head. "This thing's about to get outta control."

Grandfather nodded in agreement. "I have sent for all of the spirit warriors." His jaw was set and tight.

Elmo grabbed his hat by the brim and worked it around with his hands. "I was kinda hopin' you'd do more'n that."

"What?"

"Bring Wesley out from wherever he is and have him clean up this mess. I heard he's a one-man army."

An amorous threesome staggering toward the campgrounds jostled Grandfather before lurching on.

"Fifteen minutes of Wesley an' all this would be over." The Tribal Police Chief looked like he might drop to his knees and beg.

Grandfather pulled himself up to his full height, almost five feet. "No. He must stay where he is. He must complete what he's doing. The whole world depends on it. He *must* stay with Melissa."

Elmo gulped. "Okay. You're the boss. But I'm tellin' you as the Police Chief for more years than I had any sense to be, this is gonna get worse. A lot worse. Wesley could clean it up, no problem."

"Wesley cannot come out. He *must* stay where he is."

"Well," the Police Chief sighed, "if that's it, that's it. You might what to think about what I said in a while. Wesley could stop it."

Grandfather watched Elmo's slim form walk into the crowd. He was almost skinny, if you saw him from the back. Was he right? Should he pull Wesley up top? *Could* he pull Wesley out of whatever state he was in? Grandfather knew the Great One's gift had barely begun to manifest. It would be dawn before it reached its fullness. It needed to complete itself for the world to be blessed.

Was it so important that Wesley and Melissa complete what they'd started? Yes.

More importantly, could Wes stop what was going to happen? A niggling thought lurked deep in Grandfather's mind.

Could his beautiful warrior stop an avalanch? Or would he be destroyed like so much burning straw?

76

LIGHT FILLED THE chamber, blasting into corners and crevices, exposing things that were better left in darkness. The see-stone quivered, broadcasting radiance. Enzo had never seen it so excited.

He was riveted to the stone, grasping the granite table upon which it stood with both hands. The entire Mogollon Bowl was pulsating with … something. Some energy. He couldn't see what was going on, but whatever it was had weakened the Bowl's power. He could destroy it completely, if he was lucky. Sandy Sydney was hovering around the crater's edge, hoping to get in.

"Diego, bring the children up," he called to his brother.

"The *children*?" Diego sounded aghast.

"Yes, the children. I asked for the children; I want the *children*."

"All of them?"

"As many as will fit in this room. The others can stand on the stairs."

His offspring crowded into his office, looking around with voracious interest. He seldom released them from the castle's dungeon and crypts. Other than a hiss or two, they were silent, beautiful children. Those who favored his wife had slithered in, legless serpents. All were black, but some showed diamond markings. The offspring who looked like him moved with admirable quickness, their long legs capable of covering ground relentlessly. All the youngsters had red eyes and glittering black scales.

"I've brought you here to wish you well on your first mission. You are to go to this place," he pointed at the area indicated by the glowing stone, "and destroy everything there. Take a good look at these humans." He waved a hand and holograms of Grandfather, Will Duane, and Andy Ramos hovered above the table. His enemies. "Capture them, but do not kill them. Hold them for me.

"These humans have harmed me. All of them should be dead, but *I* will kill them." He looked over the crowd of reptiles, glaring. The room was jammed, as was the stairway almost down to the dungeon. All the kiddies could hear his voice. Their hearing was as acute as his.

"You are to travel here." He pointed to a map of the world that appeared on the wall. An arrow traveled from their castle in Spain to the Mogollon Bowl in New Mexico. "Are there any questions?"

They were hesitant, knowing what he would do if they irritated him. "You need to know things! ASK QUESTIONS!" He pounded his fist on the table, cracking the granite.

"How do we get there?" one of them said hesitantly.

"How do we get there?" he jeered. "How do you think? How do you travel?"

"Under the ground?"

"Of course, moron."

"It's a long way."

"Then you'd better get started." He wanted to rage at their stupidity, but he wouldn't. He would stay under control.

"Do we leave now?"

"Yes. I'll signal you when it's time to burst out. You hear my voice anywhere, yes?"

"Yes, Daddy," the chorus resounded.

"When I give the signal, come out. You can do anything you want to the humans."

"Anything?"

"Anything. But I want those three alive. *I* get to kill them." He pointed to the holograms. The images of Grandfather, Will Duane, and Andy Ramos now hung by their necks, dead.

"When do we stop?"

"When they're all dead." He considered the possibility that they might run into trouble. "I'll give a signal if you should come back. And do it smartly if you hear me hiss."

"Are you coming, Daddy? And Mum?"

He smiled at that one. He was bold, whoever he was. They should have given the children names. But there were so many of them. Who could remember what the little snots were called?

"I may come, and your mother. Now off with you. Carry out your assignment. Stay underground. Remember, I'll signal you when to jump out."

"When will that be, Daddy?"

"Could be any time. Get going!"

77

THE CAVE WAS a different place. Night ruled with purple shadows as deep as musk. Twinkling blue lights shot around the darkness like hordes of jeweled fireflies. While the lights spun, spirits and Ancestors clad in blue light hovered near the cave's ceiling and applauded the act on stage—two human figures reclining on a velvet field. Blue and silver painted their valleys and mountains, their shadows and highlights.

A man and a woman sported on a soft bed. Silver luminescence defined his buttocks as he drove himself into her flesh. Wrapped tight around him, her long legs jerked.

The show had begun simply. Wess-lee had kissed Melissa. Very soon, she lay on the bed, arms over her head, covered with sweat and moaning. Wess-lee explored her mouth and face with his lips and tongue, opening her every pore to his essence.

As he loved her, the Ancestors touched him, marking him with the tattooing he wore in his life. Wes-lee's body was tattooed with primal motifs. His face was bisected: one side black, the other red. The ancient Wess-lee had been massively adorned, as befit his stature in the clan.

Humming softly, he claimed Melissa's body part by part. Wess-lee claimed her shoulders, her breasts, and her armpits. Claimed her belly and thighs for himself. He savored her odors, inhaling deeply, taking in her perfume. She cried out in rapture as he touched her. Wess-lee gazed upon her with love. He would teach her and her husband what they needed to know of lovemaking. And hopefully Mee-lisa would appear at the end.

Wess-lee worked his way down Melissa's body, sniffing and licking. As he explored her, he did what he needed for her to attain her fullness. Wess-lee taught Melissa all the sounds to make to hold the pleasure when the sensations grew too intense. She learned very fast. Finally, he placed his hands on the insides of her thighs and willed her to relax as he reached her most sacred part. She did so, looking at him hopelessly and helplessly. Her legs fell open.

Wess-lee didn't stop. He pushed her harder and more. Sweat burst from her body and she clawed the sheets with her hands. And he kept going. Her eyes rolled back; Melissa was lost in bliss. She stayed there, vibrating from head to foot.

Wess-lee wanted to bond the couple for their lifetimes, not tear them apart. So he instructed Wesley every instant. Wesley was with her at least half the time. Wess-lee kept Melissa in screaming delight until she reached the level of surrender he wanted.

Finally, Melissa's eyes showed she was complete: she had no more boundaries, no more resistance. She was his totally. He could do whatever he wanted with her. Wess-lee did not mate with his women until they reached this state. Lazier men would have done it earlier and missed her fruits.

When he claimed her, she responded beautifully. Wess-lee pulled Wesley in, showing him how to change rhythms and positions. He showed him all his favorite movements and what they did to him and the woman. When he was finished, Wesley and Melissa were sound asleep, holding each other.

The Ancestors wanted to touch Melissa, leaving marks such as he had on his body. He thought to wake her and ask permission, but he wanted to see her body decorated the way Mee-lisa's had been. When they were done, she was transformed. Her left breast was almost covered with a bold black mandala. A smaller mandala centered on her right nipple. Primal motifs covered her right hip and both shoulders. Her face was marked with delicate patterns across the cheekbones and down the nose.

The cabaret turned and pulsed, an amusement out of time and space, both school and pleasure palace. Wess-lee had taught the young lovers everything he knew. The two people who had entered that cave that morning were gone. Mature sexual beings remained.

Still, Wess-lee was disturbed. Where was his Mee-lisa? As he despaired, Melissa woke up and caressed him as he lay in Wesley's body. She got up and walked over to the ice chests, the tattoos on her naked body alluring.

Wess-lee found Melissa fascinating. Her moods changed like quicksilver. Now she was haughty, nasty—and very sexy. She rummaged in the ice chest and found something—a small bottle of the #2 liquid Grandfather had made, all that was left. Melissa downed the bottle and threw the empty container into the chest. She stalked off to the bathroom, her arrogance reminding Wess-lee of the big cats of his world.

A few moments later, she walked back toward her man. Rounding the corner into the main cave, she felt dizzy. She stopped and held her head. Rumbling, crashing noises rang in her ears. The earth began to move beneath her feet. She could hardly stand up. The shaking!

A roar engulfed her as rocks and boulders began to tumble everywhere. Her band ran in terror—running for their lives. She could see them ahead of her. She couldn't run as fast as the rest; her huge belly held her back.

Horror flashed through her as flames erupted. Burning rock spurted from the ground where she stood, claiming her instantly. She felt no pain, as the molten lava incinerated her and her unborn child.

As she died, Mee-lisa cried, "Wess-lee—Wess-lee!"

He flew from the bed and grabbed her, holding her to him and comforting her with soft sounds.

"Mee-lisa, Mee-lisa!" His beloved had come home.

78

ONCE HE STOPPED trying to kill her, Puffy settled down. Elizabeth rode him into the desert at a slow, rolling lope. Her lower back, lumbar 5 to be exact, ached. The disk had a slight bulge that was working on becoming a herniation. That was the wage of so many hours spent at a desk. It took all her concentration to ride Puffy. He was so spooky that only by being absolutely centered could she calm him enough to ride.

He reacted to everything she did: move a hand or foot, clear her throat, anything. Why had she put on those damn spurs? She didn't intend to make him buck. She wanted to turn and wave goodbye to … to Will, though it cost her to admit it. She forgot that she could neither turn nor wave on Puffy. Both were outside his "allowable movements from riders" range. So was grazing his side with a spur.

He damn near dumped her. No one was near enough to see how close it was. The ammo belts made her top-heavy. Normally—well, when she was thirty-five—she could have ridden that bit of bucking, but at age fifty-six, weighted on top, she was lucky she didn't lose a stirrup. That's all it would take.

She knew all about Puffy. His body told his story. He was a papered horse, the tattooed registration number on his upper gum said that. It had been obscured by someone else's handiwork with a tattoo gun. Whoever had bred him had tried to erase the number. When they found out how Puffy was, they had trailered him out to the desert and turned him loose. His illegible tattoo made sure that he couldn't be returned. She sighed. Puffy's ears flew back like she'd hit him.

"Easy, Puff. I'm not going to hurt you." Whoever had owned him would have been kinder to put him down. But she knew how hard that was to do. She couldn't put him down, either. He was magnificent. Twelve hundred pounds of equine perfection. His muscles bulged and his tendons were like steel rods. His coat was a riot of black and white, like a painter gone crazy.

Why did she do things like this? She did them all the time. The minute she got to the Bowl and reconnected with the guys, she had to prove she was the toughest of them all. She'd never shot a gun with Puffy around; she knew she'd scare him to death. She planned on leaving his halter on and tying him to a tree when they got to the arroyo.

That brought her up short. There were no trees out at the bluff where they shot. She couldn't ground tie or hobble him. He did neither.

Elizabeth made a snap decision. She turned east and headed back into the darker part of the Badlands. There was a bluff a little farther than she'd intended to go that had some junipers strong enough to hold Puffy. She would go there. It wouldn't take much longer, and she could still get back before dark.

She rode down a wide trail, crossed a dry streambed, and zigged and zagged up a canyon, knowing exactly where she was. She had done this kind of cross-country riding almost since birth. She was an expert tracker and had a great sense of direction.

Elizabeth looked up in the sky and saw Wesley and Melissa making love, exactly as they had been that morning. She gaped at the vision. The agony she had felt, but couldn't express in the Meeting, welled up. She started to cry. And couldn't stop.

Puffy switched his tail and crow hopped, his small bucks giving her warning of what he would do if she gave in to her feelings. "Okay, Puffy. I got it."

She did have it, too. The reason she could ride this horse and no one else could was that she'd cracked the animal last summer. The key to the horse, the way to get into his heart and mind, was his fear. Big, strong, and tough, Puffy was scared of everything. When he got scared, he blew—harder and wilder than any horse she'd known.

Elizabeth chirped to him, heading deeper into the wilderness. "Come on, Puffy, we're almost there." It was darker in the canyons. The shadows affected her thinking. The danger that riding such a horse in such a place didn't occur to her. Having ridden all her life, Elizabeth knew that if Puffy felt her power and leadership slip, his fears would assert themselves. If she remembered, she paid it no mind.

She reached the streambed and bluff she was seeking, and swung off her horse. When she tacked him up, she'd left Puffy's halter on, slipping the bridle under it. She attached the halter's lead line to her saddle with the saddle's ties. They always left the halter on back at their ranch in Oregon. If you were out working on the range, you never knew when you'd have to tie your horse to handle an emergency.

No one who knew horses ever tied them by the reins—only Hollywood cowboys did that. She undid the lead rope and tied Puffy's reins securely where the lead line had been. She had come out to shoot for a very specific reason: shooting worked for her when nothing else did. Or it had that other time.

Elizabeth looked around the edge of the creek and found the biggest tree she could. It was a dead juniper, probably hundreds of years old by the size of its gnarled trunk, but only eight feet high. You could probably tether an airplane to it without it budging. Bared, gray branches stuck out from the trunk like petrified hands.

She tied Puffy to the main branch and loosened his saddle a bit, thinking about where she'd set up to shoot in the dry stream bed. She knew exactly why she was out there: she needed a miracle.

Having figured out where she'd shoot, Elizabeth reappraised Puffy's situation. The juniper would hold him. The juniper's roots would be wide, if not deep. Better get cracking. She lifted her saddlebags off, draping them over one shoulder. She winced as her back reacted; they were so heavy—what was she doing?

She stopped to pat Puffy, and put him in a light trance with her touch. "Stay here, Puff. I'll be back." She removed the rifles from their scabbards and walked around the bend in the creek bed and out of Puffy's sight. She hoped the arroyo would muffle the sound so that he didn't get too scared. It didn't matter anyway. She'd tied him so that he'd never get loose.

The sand and gravel of the creek bed radiated the day's heat. She could feel it through her boots as she walked along with her explosive load. She knew why she was there, but suddenly, it didn't seem like such a good idea. Neither could she abandon the plan. She was trapped, pulled in. Going back to a previous time, repeating something. Mesmerized, she found the place she wanted.

Elizabeth set up her guns, memories flashing around her. She was back in 1964. Elwin had left her a few months before. She didn't grieve, nor did she fall apart. She didn't cry or moan: she got mad. She was at war with herself and the universe.

But she had handled it, following the same type of urge that pushed her right now. She loaded up the ranch truck with her guns and the bullets she'd made at night out in the barn. She stuffed the camper with her sleeping bag and food, and set out to their shooting range. The bluff was just like this, soft limestone and miles of it.

She shot for four days. The holy number—she didn't know that then. Elizabeth had set up her guns methodically, the way she did in her sharpshooting act. She began firing, all those years ago. She saw only one thing: Elwin. She saw him smiling at her, waving at her, holding his arms out to her; she saw him every way she could.

And then that blond floozy would be there, and they'd be doing it, right in front of her. Every round she shot, every bullet that left her gun, was leveled at him. She shot until she ran out of ammunition. It wasn't enough.

Enraged, Elizabeth began to fire into the bluff. She could hear Puffy thrashing and pulling at the tree, panicking and trying to escape. Soon, she couldn't hear him any more, she couldn't hear anything but the sound of her gun and her memories.

Long ago, her Grandmother Bright Eagle had come to her on the fourth day when she was totally empty and had nothing left to shoot. She looked up, out of ammo, but nowhere near emptied of the hurt and rage. She had nothing, not even hope.

They stood on the bank across from her, all of them, where she'd seen Elwin's face. Grandma Bright Eagle, and all the others. Her Ancestors, her warrior kin, all those gone to the other side. They stood there, hundreds of them, looking at her.

It was her first vision. It wasn't an ecstatic vision—it didn't make her high. Her relatives looked at her. They said she was in for a hard road. But she had a road.

In that long ago vision, Grandma said, "Don't worry, little one. You have a great future. Go forward." Grandfather was there, too. That's when she first saw him. He said, "Come to me. You will find a way."

The vision came when she was so desperate that she could only look up, not think or even wish. A door opened up, and she went through it.

That's what she was hoping for this afternoon: another door. A turning point. Even though she had gone through the door after that first vision and become a credit to her people, the pain never went away.

Long ruby shadows fell. It was getting dark and she didn't know where she was. Elizabeth groped to get control of her mind. Where was she? She had been shooting. She could see her rifles and pistols scattered. Yes. Shooting. The pain roared up again, it wasn't finished with her yet.

Elwin ran off with a prostitute and divorced her.

What did that make her? Revulsion welled up as she looked down at her enormous breasts and fat thighs, her wide belly. Elizabeth clawed at herself.

"He liked her body better than mine," she howled. She wanted to die—death would be a relief.

Blood streaked her face and darkened her nails where she'd scratched herself. She had no release; no relatives on the other shore. No door.

Wait … something revealed itself. Yes. The way out. The door opened.

Her pistol lay on the ground before her. She picked it up slowly, feeling its holy weight. She'd found the way out, after all.

Elizabeth lifted the pistol and placed the barrel into her mouth.

79

THE MOST TERRIBLE workday of Bud's life was ending. Everyone had slunk back to the camp, leaving him alone at the stable, doing his duty. He prepared to count off his duties again when he realized the sun was down and it was almost night. Something was wrong.

Elizabeth.

He was supposed to go out and follow her before it got dark—what was wrong with him? All he could think about was Bert.

He looked around. Tyler and the guys weren't in, either. Mr. Duane must be sleeping in the line shack. The horses were still at it out in the pasture. He scanned the corrals. The only horse left was the disgusting Bunny, the worst horse in the universe.

He grabbed a halter and went out to the mare's corral. He couldn't remember if anyone had actually ridden her. She smelled bad and had a scaly skin disease that looked contagious. Between that and her disposition, everyone left her alone. The mare did have white-haired marks on her back from old saddle sores—she must have been ridden at one time.

Bud noticed something else: she was the only mare not in heat. That figured—what stud would want her?

Saddling Bunny was the perfect end to the day. She pulled back when he tied her to a hitching rack. Almost pulled it out of the ground. He had to hold her lead line with one hand and saddle her with the other. She tried to step on him at every turn. She slobbered and blew snot all over him.

Deciding where to put his saddle on her sway back was not a problem: he put it up on her and let it drift to the lowest point. That's where he set the cinch.

Ol' Bunny saved her best stunt for last; when he got her saddled, and started to step up on her, she staggered and fell over on him. Bud was fast, but Bunny was almost faster.

He kicked her belly. "Get up, you …" No words were bad enough. "I need you to find Elizabeth. I don't like you any more than you like me. But you will get up and behave or I will shoot you right now."

The rage in his voice must have done the trick. Bunny stood up and proved to be not only broke, but well trained. He missed the switch of her tail that said, *I'll get you later, you son of a bitch!*

They did pretty well for a while. He headed toward the bluff where Elizabeth was supposed to be shooting. He got almost all the way out there, thinking about Bert off and on, losing his concentration, when he looked at the low cliff and realized she wasn't there.

Bud was an expert tracker. He seemed to track by feeling the essence of a person, not by any trail signs at all. Elizabeth hadn't been here all day. But that crazy horse of hers had, he could tell that. If he couldn't tell it by the lingering feel of the horse, the wrecked trees, scarred boulders, and drag marks told the tale.

"That crazy Puffy must be pulling a tree!" Bud marveled. "That means Elizabeth must have tied him up. Why would she do something that stupid?" He wasn't the only one losing his mind. Everything came clear: Elizabeth was out there in the desert, on foot, and no one knew where.

Something else came to Bud: a sense of imminent danger. Something was stalking Elizabeth. He knew what that something was: Sandy Sydney, in whatever form she might have now. He had seen Lisa Cheewa's injuries and had no doubt of the demon's capability. He groaned, turning Bunny around.

This time Bud paid attention to his tracking and sensed Elizabeth's essence. He got back to the point where Elizabeth had taken the Y in the trail. He let Bunny stop for a moment. He had no choice, she was attending the call of nature. He was fully on duty now; thoughts of Bert did not intrude. Elizabeth was in danger. So was he. He had to find her.

Bud let Bunny finish peeing, then urged her forward. A light dawned—that was the third pee she'd taken since they turned around. She wasn't coming into heat, was she? *Not now!* Bunny wouldn't move. She raised her tail and let out a tremendous whinny—there was no mistaking that she was saying, *Come and get it!*

"Come on, Bunny! Let's go!" Bud kicked her hard enough to stove in another horse. He took the rumel, the rawhide quirt on the end of his reins, and swung it over her shoulders and back again. An over and under. That was normally enough to turn an ordinary horse into a Triple Crown winner. He did it again and then, again.

Bunny would not move. She began dancing around like a girl at prom, whinnying and carrying on, lifting her tail and squirting white stuff like every mare in heat does.

"Oh, Bunny, why now? Don't you know this matters, girl?" He had been thinking the old mare wasn't so bad. She was about to teach him otherwise, and that what's important to a human isn't important to a horse.

Bud could hear something out in the desert. Another horse. Damn it! Some wild stud out there was answering the call. What could he do? He tried kicking her again with no luck. She was in the grip of something bigger than both of them: love. Bud sat in the saddle, trying to figure what to do. He never heard it coming.

"Owww! Owww! Shit! Let go of my leg, damn you!"

Bud took his hat and beat off the enormous mammoth jack donkey that had grabbed his thigh with its filthy yellow teeth. "Oww!" His leg hurt louder that he could yell. The jack backed off, looking to attack his rival for the favors of the fair Bunny from another angle.

Bud gasped, "Where did you come from?" It was the biggest, ugliest, meanest jack he'd ever seen.

When the jack charged again, Bunny whipped her butt to face him. The donkey reared up, planning to kill Bud with his front end and breed Bunny with his hindquarters. Bud saw those teeth and hooves coming at him. He shucked off Ol' Bun faster than he had when when he won that calf-roping championship a few years back.

Bud hit the ground running and was fifty yards away when he turned back and yelled, "You coulda' let me get my saddle off!"

The jack paid him no mind, he was busy scratching his chin on Bud's saddle horn. When he finished, he got off Bunny and let out the loudest jackass laugh Bud had ever heard. "Hee-haw! Hee-haw! Hee-haw!" He backed up a few steps, bucked high, and then ran off into the desert with Bunny at his side.

"Damn it!" Bud cursed. He watched her deliberately smash his good saddle into cacti as she ran.

Meanwhile, Bud had a problem. He was on foot in hostile territory. Elizabeth was in immediate danger. He had to find and help her. Something else was coming to him on the psychic Internet—Bert needed him. The baby was coming!

80

SHE FOUND HERSELF sitting in the sand of the creek bed, the barrel of her pistol in her mouth. She was poised to squeeze the trigger.

Death was an easy squeeze away.

Light, clear as water, was there. Just clarity. Nothing fancy, no thunder and lightning. Just the transparency in the bright air of this creek bed in the desert. Alone. Is this how she wanted to end her life? Time moved slowly; every instant took a year in that space of clarity—luminous clarity. Nothingness. Just awareness. Was this how she wanted to end her life?

Elizabeth withdrew the pistol from her mouth. Her hand drifted to her side, still holding the weapon. Its muzzle rested on the sand. She realized she was ill. She made a choice: she wanted to live. She wanted to heal.

She did everything as it occurred to her, one step at a time. Her mind wouldn't hold thoughts. She just saw what she needed to do in the next instant. She was a danger to herself. Elizabeth opened her pistol and emptied it of ammunition, throwing the bullets as far as she could. Her guns were scattered about. She emptied their ammunition and found the remainder in her saddlebags. She threw it all around the draw, as far from herself as possible.

She had to get home. This time of clarity would fade and she would want to die again. She looked around; long shadows covered everything. She had no idea where she was, no memory of riding in. Nothing. Puffy. She rode Puffy there. She had to find Puffy. The draw was empty, she looked in every direction, up and down the dry creek bed. Elizabeth didn't know where he was; she didn't recall how she'd gotten there.

She put her pistols in their holsters and buckled the belt around her waist. An ageless wisdom told her not to leave her weapons. Something in her told her that the enemy could get them if she abandoned them. She looked around in the dim light. She could see where she had dragged her way into the creek bed.

Elizabeth struggled out the same way, hauling her rifles. When she rounded the bend where she had tied Puffy, her heart sank. He wasn't there. Not only wasn't he there, most of the scruffy juniper tree she'd tied him to wasn't there. A big hole in the sandy soil showed where he had pulled it out.

"Oh, no," Elizabeth cried. She looked around. The clarity was leaving, her mind was going into the blackness again. She looked around, whispering, "Oh, God, please help me!" Nothing; just the silence of the empty desert.

Elizabeth could see the drag marks where Puffy had high-tailed it with the tree. He would go back to the camp. She followed Puffy's trail, a rifle under each arm. Nothing looked familiar. Elizabeth began to cry again. Glimmers of the images she had seen that afternoon appeared in the night sky. She and Elwin were making love in the stars. "Please. No more. Please."

Elizabeth struggled along. She would not leave her weapons and they grew heavier and heavier as she traveled. Her mouth grew parched as she walked, panting. The sound of her breathing filled her ears. It was completely dark. She couldn't see the trail Puffy had left any more. The soft avalanche of confusion was setting in again.

More than anything, she wanted to check her guns for the bullet she missed. She wanted to go back and find just one bullet. But she couldn't. She'd set it up so that she couldn't kill herself.

She had been given a gift of clarity for a moment; now it was gone. She was ill. The desert grew cold. She shivered. She hadn't thought to bring a jacket. Her water was in the saddlebags—which she'd left behind.

"They'll find me in the morning," she was able to realize. "I'll be all right. They're the best trackers in the world. Maybe they'll find me tonight. I'll just stay here. They'll find me." She put her rifles down and sat by them in the dirt. She was so tired. Just a little nap, just a little sleep, and she'd be all right.

She was awakened by the cold. It wasn't something outside her—it was seeping into her heart. Dread filled her. Something was out there. White cold terror flashed through her body. Whatever attacked Lisa and Melissa was out there. She could feel it stalking her. The shaking began in her depths and worked its way out to her limbs. She couldn't stop it.

"I've got to get control." She willed her body to relax. To stop shaking. And it did. She willed her mind to relax; she slowed her breathing, she became very still. Motionless and soft. Relaxed. Elizabeth sat there, quiet and motionless. Time stopped.

Violent crashing noises brought her to her feet. She grabbed a rifle, intending to use it as a bat. Something gigantic was heading straight toward her, toppling everything in its path. Birds flew out of their cactus homes as the saqueros were knocked over. Small animals rushed past. Elizabeth prepared to meet her doom. Her jaw was relaxed and her brow smooth. She would fight until she died.

Dust flew up, blocking her vision; the popping brush obscured the underlying noise almost until it reached her. It stopped with a final crash. Elizabeth looked into the darkness: the trail she was on was surrounded by scrub brush and cactus. She heard the creature's breathing—snorting blasts—and footfalls. Those were hooves!

"Puffy? Is that you?" Elizabeth crept toward the sound. Sure enough. His white-ringed eyes were visible in the dark. She walked up to him and he snorted and pulled away. "Oh, Puffy." She examined him. "Oh, my poor baby. Look at you." He was scratched and cut to hell, but nothing that wouldn't heal, nothing that would slow him down. He still had his saddle, bridle, and that very stout halter and lead rope. Half of the tree she'd tied him to was there, jammed in the scrub—that was the best knot she'd ever made! She started laughing.

"Oh, Puff. Were you too scared to find your way home?" She tightened up the girth slowly. He spooked and snorted, still acting the fool. She gingerly walked up the rope tied to the tree to loosen the knot. She found she couldn't: Puffy had pulled it so tightly that the knot might as well have been welded. Her knife was in the saddlebags.

What was she to do? She was trapped in the desert with the only horse in the universe too stupid to find its way home. She wanted to cry, but had to hold it together to calm this damn horse; she knew he was dangerous. Why did she ride a horse like this? Why did she do things like this?

The menace she'd felt returned; it was real and it was stalking them out in the darkness. Her rifles were twenty feet away. She wouldn't leave them. She couldn't let go of Puffy for fear that he might break loose again. She couldn't lead Puffy to the guns; the rope tying him to the tree was jammed in the underbrush. She couldn't go anywhere. What to do?

She was losing hope when something deep inside her spoke. It said, *Unsnap the lead rope at his halter.*

The way out was so obvious. Elizabeth backed Puffy a step, and unsnapped the bull snap that had held him all afternoon. The rope dropped to the sand. He was free, and so was she. She led him away by the reins, laughing as she did so.

"Look Puffy, that's how you get rid of things that chase you. You unsnap them and walk away. It's so simple." She was slightly hysterical. "That's all I had to do. All I had to do was let him go and walk away."

She started to weep, leaning on Puffy's shoulder. She put her arm over his neck and let the tears fall. Puffy turned his head and nuzzled her. He began to groom her shoulder with his lips, just as he would another horse.

"Do you like me, boy?" Elizabeth said. "Get me home, Puffy. Get me home." Her hilarity vaporized, replaced by sadness darker than a skull's eye socket.

Her clarity receded again. Sludge and darkness replaced it in her consciousness. Fear. Elizabeth had just enough time to put her rifles in their scabbards on the saddle. She remembered to take off her spurs before climbing onto Puffy. She was awkward and banged him with her right foot while swinging it over. Miraculously, he didn't buck.

"Take me home, Puffy," she whispered, starting to shake again. Her lucidity vanished the moment she hit the saddle. She grabbed the horn, sobbing, leaning first to one side, then the other. The reins hung slackly on each side of Puffy's neck, useless to stop or guide him.

81

BUD WAS IN a real fix, stuck out in the desert with his wife calling to him on the one hand, and the woman he admired most in the world calling on the other. He hit his hat on his leg a few times to relieve his tension and then put it back on his head. He set off down the path Elizabeth had taken, whispering into the wind, "Bert, honey, there's doctors and people back there to help you. Elizabeth don't got no one."

He hoped Bert could hear him. Bud loved his wife more than he knew a man could love a woman. He walked fast, trying to sense where Elizabeth was. This was the right direction. When the lights started flashing in the distance, he upped it to a run. There had been lights with the attack on Melissa: flashing blue lights like electricity. Sandy Sydney was attacking Elizabeth!

Bud felt helpless. The flashes were far away. They were getting closer, but he would never get there in time. Elizabeth was probably already dead. He ran faster. He would probably die, too; he had no weapons. He'd seen Lisa. He couldn't let that happen to Elizabeth, nor to anyone else.

Bud ran as fast as he could in boots and spurs. His breath ripped and raged through his chest. He was fat and out of shape. The sounds of his own breathing filled his ears—that and the thunder. The evening's thunder sounded louder tonight.

He wanted to cry. Beautiful Elizabeth dying like that! That damn Sandy Sydney! Damn her to hell! The thunder in the mountains expressed his anger.

Bud vowed, "Elizabeth, if she hurt you, I will kill her." More thunder seemed to applaud him. Bud stood up tall and—jumped back three feet, faster than he knew he could.

Puffy damn near ran him down! The thunder had kept him from hearing the horse's hoof beats.

"Damn! That horse is fast!" he exclaimed as the animal shot past him and up the trail, heading for the camp. "He has to be going seventy—I've never seen a horse run like that! Son of a bitch!" Bud didn't usually swear, but, God bless it! That was Elizabeth holdin' on to that gelding's back!

"Oh, Puffy! I never knew you were such a good horse!" He started walking back to the camp, so choked up he expected to be crying like a baby any second. "I never seen the like. That crazy horse ran faster than the devil woman! He saved Elizabeth when no one else could!"

Bud walked along, half sobbing and rejoicing, until he became aware of something. He was still out there. Puffy had outrun Sandy Sydney, not killed her. She'd already shown she liked Indian flesh, maybe she liked male Indian flesh, too! He took off at a run, nowhere near as fast as Puffy, but certainly faster than you'd expect a chubby horseman wearing cowboy boots.

A huge explosion behind him motivated Bud more. "Oooh, lordy. That must be the ammo. She's got Elizabeth's guns!"

Bud was a sweaty mess when he made it into camp. Will Duane was circling the stable yard in the golf cart. He had one hand on the wheel and the other around Elizabeth's shoulder. Her head was on Will's shoulder and she was weeping. A miracle had occurred.

The real miracle was that Puffy was tied to the golf cart and being led around by it. In normal times, Bud would have expected the horse to be dragging the golf cart, not the calm scene before him.

Clearly, something had happened in the desert.

"Mr. Duane! Is Elizabeth okay?"

Will stopped the cart the minute he heard Bud.

Puffy snorted and turned around as Bud advanced toward him.

"Good, Puffy. Good, boy," Bud approached the gelding gingerly. Amazingly, Puffy acted like any other horse. He touched him. Bud untied Puffy and led him over to Will Duane. "Is she okay?" he asked quietly of Elizabeth. Will nodded and stroked her shoulder.

"I think so. Physically, anyway."

"What happened?"

"I was asleep," Will said. "When I came out of the shack, it was dark. There was no one here. The horses were going crazy. I took the golf cart to the stables and Puffy came flying in with Elizabeth on him. He stopped by the tack shed and Elizabeth got off. She was crying so hard she almost couldn't stand. I got the golf cart over there and she climbed in."

"And Puffy didn't spook?"

"No. Elizabeth said, 'Puffy's got to be walked. He'll die if he isn't walked out, he's run for miles.' She was too upset to do it, so I said, 'Fix my ankle and I'll walk him.' She fixed my ankle." Will's eyebrows rose about up to his hairline. "I couldn't believe she healed me. But she couldn't get the cast off without tools and I couldn't lead him with the cast, so I tied him up and walked him with the cart."

Bud turned to Puffy and stroked his dried-sweat encrusted neck. "You're some horse, Puffy." He buried his face in the gelding's neck. "You saved her, Puff. You saved her for all of us."

Will nodded, eyes filling. "Elizabeth's bringing him home with her. I told her she could keep him at my place. I've got a barn. Puffy will like it."

Now that he'd found Elizabeth safe, reality hit Bud: Bert needed him! Also, Sandy Sydney was around. They'd better get back to the Bowl, pronto!

They set out across the dark mesa in the cart, Bud driving, Elizabeth in the middle still crying softly, and Will on the other side with his arm around her. That cart was moving at a pretty good clip—it acted like it was turbo-charged. The vibration coming from the Bowl was weird; the place felt really off, strange. Bud accelerated. Something was wrong.

They were at the foot of the cliff when the screaming started. What was happening up there? Where was Bert?

82

SANDY SYDNEY WAS having a really bad day. She'd finally gotten her equipment in working order after her "accident" with Melissa—and she would settle with that little bitch before the week was up—when more troubles arose. When she had the "accident," Sandy had quickly dematerialized outside the cave and then rematerialized in a canyon a few miles away.

Not having a head proved to be a problem. No senses: no sight, hearing, smell, taste. All she had was touch. Not having a brain made thinking hard, and with the inability to use logic, Sandy ended up taking the first live body that came along.

That's how she wound up in this putrid, stinking, filthy, foul-minded, flying piece of crap: a turkey vulture. It was first on the disaster scene, a mistake that buzzard would never make again. Fortunately for Sandy, the vulture was female. Having to live in a male vulture would add insult to injury.

So, she shape-shifted. With no directions, no support: all by herself. Wounded. Alone in the wilderness. Who could do it perfectly under those conditions? After three days, she'd finally mastered "vultureness" and could fly. She'd also redone her human head fairly well in a conceptual way inside the vulture—without a mirror!

Sandy was pissed. She couldn't get out of the vulture; she didn't have all the moves down. She was stuck in this low status life form. Sandy wanted to be an eagle, but they would have nothing to do with her. Even a coyote would be better than a stinking buzzard. Their lifestyle and table manners! Their conversation. What they ate.

That afternoon, Sandy discovered the turkey vulture's one redeeming feature: they had the most exquisite sense of smell. They could smell better than any animal on earth. The delicate perfume of that girl's blood wafted across the desert, as desirable and delectable a scent as its owner was a morsel. But that excursion didn't work out. The woman with bleeding saddle sores turned back to the barn.

She went to Elizabeth's shooting gallery looking for fun, found the ammunition and piled it together. She looked around for guns. She almost had the shape-shifting concept down. If she had a gun, she could shift into its shape. She could be a regular killing machine—that would be a professional first.

Blowing up the ammunition was all she could do. Sandy found she could greatly amplify the bullets' power. Then she was forced to take a detour; the vultures were gathering to the east. She finally became aware of her vulture body; she was consumed with lust. Her eyes burned with passion.

She shot eastward.

83

WESS-LEE CARRIED HER back to the bed. He held Mee-lisa as she reentered bodily life, remembering and experiencing her death and its trauma. She shook and clung to her husband. He made sweet little noises to comfort her, stroking her softly. Melissa and Wesley were thrown to the rear of consciousness as their ancestors took control of their bodies.

"I am here to tell you something." Wess-lee spoke their language. Mee-lisa looked at him, not voicing her hopes, but sitting very erect. "Have you learned your lesson, Mee-lisa?"

"Yes!" She leaned forward and clung to him. "Being away from you was worse than all the fire and shaking in the world. Worse than all the cave bears. I almost died from sadness. And I thought and thought about what I did." She told him about her first husband and what happened, which she hadn't done before. "It wasn't wrong to kill my husband, but killing all his band was wrong." Wess-lee nodded. That was what the Great Mystery had said. "I will never kill like that again. Only to eat and if we are attacked. I will be good forever."

Her teary eyes and beseaching face told him that her words were true. "I believe you, Mee-lisa. Your time of waiting is over. You can come with me into the golden world."

She shrieked and jumped upon him, practically rolling out of the bed in joy.

Wess-lee held his mate. She relaxed in his arms, looking at his strange, small body. "You look ugly, Wess-lee, but I don't care. I waited so long, wanting you. You could look like a wart-hog. You could look like anything."

Wess-lee began to kiss her and hum. He stroked her softly and nibbled at her skin. She breathed more deeply. Soon, they were making love. He spoke to her in ways she understood.

"Mee-lisa, I don't know how long we have in these bodies. When we are with the Great Mystery, this pleasure will not be open to us. This is our last time. We must share everything we have to share."

Wesley and Melissa were awed as Wess-lee and Mee-lisa loved each other. It was slow, rapturous, and breathtakingly beautiful. Wes and Melissa's ancestors were so bonded, each gave the other his whole heart, her whole soul. There was no coyness or game playing or flamboyance. Wess-lee just gave himself to Mee-lisa and pleased her with everything he had. She did the same.

It's like watching God. At the end, when Mee-lisa and Wess-lee peaked, Melissa was moved to tears. *They're ancient and they love each other so much. Can I say the same?*

I'm going to love Wesley for the rest of my life and for all eternity. With all the stops out. With all of my heart. She looked up at Wesley, deep inside Wess-lee, and said, "I love you." The words came back to her.

Wess-lee was pleased. He had found Mee-lisa and assured himself that she was not a danger to anyone. He'd loved her body and soul. And, true, he'd enjoyed her descendant a bit. Now all he had to so was teach little Melissa how to fight.

"Wess-lee wants to know if you know how to fight," Wesley interpreted.

"No. Except if you consider what I did to Doug fighting. I don't remember what I did. Oh, yes, and I blew the demon's head off."

Wess-lee nodded. That was a good start.

"He's going to spar with you and see if he can get whatever you did going again."

"Why do I need to fight?"

"He doesn't know. The Great One said you needed to."

"When am I going to need to fight?" She was thinking in terms of holding her ground in the vicious hallways of Numenon.

"The Great One didn't say."

"This week? Here?"

"He just told Wess-lee to teach you to fight."

The sparring was a failure. The Wess-lee/Wesley/Mee-lisa/Melissa combination had been run pretty near every way it could. They were too bonded to work up much aggression. Wess-lee looked around the cave. He wanted to go home. How could they get little, too-smart Melissa to fight?

Mee-lisa knew. Taking control of her host's body, she stalked toward Wesley, eyes glinting. She kneeled and took his organ in one hand, expertly pumping it until it stood upright. She put Wesley's cock in her mouth, and began pleasuring him.

Mee-lisa flew back as Melissa took back control of her body.

"Get away from my husband," Melissa shrieked, pulling away from Wesley and facing the wall. She tore at her chest, as though trying to dislodge Mee-lisa from within.

"If you touch my husband, I'll kill you." Melissa was enraged. Her soul flew upward, out of her body, creating a being made of energy like the one that had appeared over Wesley in the martial arts exhibit. Her powerful display was a crackling Amazon whose almost transparent frame bristled with muscle. The apparition could only reach the roof of the cave, which she banged against, discharging sparks and small bolts of lightning.

Mee-lisa smiled. You will be able to grow much larger if you need to, she communicated to her host. And you'll be able to fight anything.

"Get out of me. I'm *done* with you." Melissa charged around, screaming at an invisible enemy.

Wess-lee wanted to leave, but he couldn't leave little Melissa feeling the anger she did. He made soothing noises and held her, lifting her onto the bed. He laid down with her and stroked her until she relaxed. He embraced her, nuzzling her neck. And then he was finished with her.

He felt himself separate from Wesley and stood next to the bed. Mee-lisa had pulled herself out of Melissa. The two stood watching their descendants sleeping, peaceful and innocent as infants or angels. Their world might be horrible, but good existed in it with people like this. Maybe they would solve some of its problems.

Wess-lee looked at Mee-lisa. He could see through her as though she was made of water. She was a vision, but real. He loved her curls and tattoos and beautiful face.

"It's time to go," he said. She smiled back at him and took his hand. The roof of the cave opened, revealing the light of the Great Mystery all around them.

Wess-lee and Mee-lisa drifted up into the great awakening, together at last, finally unfettered, going to their own true home.

This time, it would be forever.

84

"YES!" ENZO JUMPED to his feet and clapped his hands. At last, it was happening! He couldn't see into the Bowl, but the humans inside could reach for him. And they were! Hundreds of them, wanting release from Grandfather's terrible, repressive rule.

"I want to screw my best friend's wife!" This came up from any number of people. He felt them lifting their hands and souls to him. The party in the Bowl was really cooking.

Enzo responded, "Do it! Do it my darlings! Fuck them all. Fuck their sisters, too! Fuck everyone!"

The cries rose to him. "My brother-in-law is an asshole. I'd like to carve him up." Or beat the crap out of him, or kick his face in.

"Do it! The rules are: no rules! Kill, maim, destroy, steal—*do whatever you want!*"

"I want to get loaded. *Really loaded.*"

"Certainly, my lovely. Go to the back of the Bowl. They're dishing it out. *I'm giving them more! Whatever you want!*"

More pleas. "I've hated her since third grade. I'd like to punch her black and blue. I'd like to stab her with scissors!"

"Do it! Do all of it! You don't need my permission! Do whatever you want, all the time."

And they did, moving out to satisfy their wishes.

Enzo threw his head back and roared, waking everyone in the castle, including the dead. Diego ran into the room.

"Look, Diego! They're doing it! They're reaching for me!"

Diego looked into the see-stone and saw the haze over the Bowl thinning. He could see perfectly in some areas. The fog dispersed as he watched.

"Humans are exactly as I told you. Greedy, stupid, vicious, and unable to follow anyone's orders. But they'll follow my orders after this night is done."

"They're killing each other," Diego gasped.

The party had become a riot.

"Loose the children!" he shouted. *"Children! Get out here, you little bastards! Go to work!"*

As Enzo screamed, he grew taller. His arms and legs bulged, his shirt split down the back. His pleasant smile was replaced by a beak studded with three inch fangs. His flesh thinned and shiny black scales surfaced. Claws studded his three-toed feet and sharp blades rose from his spine. His reptilian form emerged, making him a deadly, unstoppable murder machine.

"Let's go," he growled, red eyes flashing like lasers. "Get up here, children." More of them streamed from the dungeon. He was surrounded by hundreds of small versions of himself. "Travel as fast as you can. When you get there, do whatever you want. Kill! Maim! Destroy!"

Before he left, Enzo composed his features into those of the Chieftain and called to Paul Running Bird. "My darling, move your people to the place I told you *now*. Look what is coming ..."

He let Paul see his children rising from the desert floor. Hordes of them. Black scaled, mouths dripping venom. They tore into the unarmed

People, biting off heads and limbs, tossing them. Playing. And then they discovered the women.

Paul jumped up and screamed, "Follow me. Monsters are coming. Run!" He ran full tilt toward the circle of rocks Enzo had shown him. Paul didn't look around to see the hundreds of people running with him. *His* followers, produced by carrying out the instructions his Chieftain had given without question.

Enzo smiled, watching from the see-stone. They might be the only ones who survived.

85

"WE DO NOT do that here!" Grandfather shouted. The old man was beleaguered and alone. All around him, couples, triples, quadruples, and more gave up any pretense of propriety.

This was God's party night, he realized. The night that the Great One erased the rules. What was happening was the reason Great-grandfather had him and Rebecca go so far away from the others on their wedding night.

They were at ground zero, right above Melissa and Wesley. People would remember this night all over the world. Statisticians would ponder the unexplained blip in international population figures in nine months. Demographers would be amazed. Grandfather knew this because that's what had happened when he and Rebeca experienced their twenty-four hours of heaven. It was an exceptional night to be conceived—or to die.

He climbed up on the stage, telling the musicians to go to their tents. They were busy being ardent with their admirers. Hence the lousy beat. He could see better from the stage. Yes, everyone at the Meeting was affected.

Grandfather looked down from the platform as a sea of elderly ladies converged upon him. White heads topped with hopeful, lined faces struggled toward the stage. Avalina Cocina led the mob. He stared at his long-time followers in amazement. What were they saying? He listened to their querulous voices.

"Oh, Joseph! I have loved you for so long! You are so beautiful! Oh, Joseph, I will make you so happy." Avalina's speed was surprising, considering she was piloting a walker. "I've always known we belonged together. It's not too late."

The old women massed before him in front of the stage, their white hair shining. They beckoned him with knobby hands, holding their sticklike arms aloft. Crooked smiles promised sweetness, gaping teeth and all.

Oh, no! They want me—that way! He had no idea how many older, and not so much older, women were massed before him. They seemed to be in love with him. He shouted, "I love you all. You are my sisters."

They were attempting to climb up onto the stage, when Carl pulled up in a cart at the platform's end. "Get on, Grandfather!" The old man sprinted into the cart and Carl gunned it out of the crowd.

Carl and Grandfather fled. The old ladies followed, a tottering horde.

"Everyone! We are going to the Ballroom! We will have a wonderful party there. We will keep the Rules! We will dance and sing! You will love the Ballroom—it is a huge cave the warriors use. It is very safe."

Grandfather and Carl rode around trying to whip up enthusiasm, but there wasn't much. A small group of wannabe celibates assembled behind the cart.

The blast rocked the cart and knocked everyone in the Pit flat. It came from outside the Pit, somewhere in the rear of the Bowl. Carl and Grandfather craned their necks to see what had happened, but a fog of ... something ... prevented it. The air became gelatinous and disgusting.

After the explosion, a grinding roar arose from the back of the Bowl. They couldn't see what caused it, but the sound rolled forward, entering

the Pit, fouling everything. The sound made them nauseous, and more—
it made them wild. People screamed and held their ears.

A different type of flood swept across the Bowl and the ground
heaved. Drunken energy leaped across the buckling earth. Hostility and
aggression flamed like torches, spreading over the crowd, overrunning
everything. Screams of rage mingled with the grinding sound. The orgy
became a riot as lovers turned upon each other.

"Run!" called Grandfather. "They're going crazy! Get us to the
Ballroom, Carl!" Women jumped onto the cart, grabbing at Carl.
Grandfather bellowed, "Get your hands off him!"

All the warriors working together couldn't stop the venomous surge.
Recruits for the celibate party in the Ballroom were no problem now.
People who'd been loving each other got up and ran behind the golf
carts, trying to outrun the madness. More carts appeared as warriors
helped the elderly and infirm.

"To the Ballroom! To the Ballroom!" everyone shouted.

Looking back, Grandfather watched the clouded atmosphere clear.
Black forms emerged from the Bowl's rear and galloped over the backs
of the maddened humans. Broad spiked backs, mottled skin, gleaming
red eyes. Beaks with huge, jagged teeth. The creatures bounded toward
them like panthers. Muscled arms raised swords and clubs as they ram-
paged across the Pit. The people screamed and ran.

86

ANDY SAT UP and pulled her sleeping bag around her. Even though they were honeymooning, Al had insisted they move to the back of the Bowl so that he could keep the hoodlums in line. As the afternoon waned, it seemed a worse and worse idea. They started rioting and Al had left the tent, trying to stop them. She sat there and anxiously waited for her husband to return.

Someone was yelling. It was the mean guy who owned the Gila monster, Chu. And other voices. She could hear Al bellowing back. They weren't backing down as they had before. She could hear the crazy, out of control quality of their voices that signaled intoxication.

The yelling stopped and something more intense began. Quieter, with occasional explosions of sounds. Like a crowd of men were egging someone on.

"Oh, no." She jumped out of the bag and put on the clothes the women of the Meeting had provided her. She yanked up her jeans and threw on her shirt and shoes. Andy stepped through the opening of the tent.

The air glowed orange. Andy ran toward the campsites at the edge of the Bowl. Something was dreadfully wrong.

A ring of men were clustered around something on the ground. They growled like animals, not even human. The ring writhed and contracted as whatever was inside it struggled to escape. Shouts and curses filled the air like the cinders and smoke of the Oakland fire. She was almost there when she realized what was on the ground.

Al. They were kicking him.

"No! Stop! Stop that!" she screamed, running at the men. They turned to look at her. Some of them pulled back so that she could see. Chu stood over Al. They'd all been kicking him, but Chu was up closest, aiming at Al's head with his steel-toed boot. He stepped back so she could see his handiwork.

Al's face wasn't recognizable as a face. When Chu kicked him in the ribs, it made a dull thud. No snapping of ribs. They'd already broken them all. Blood soaked through his shirt. He didn't move.

"Watch this, bitch," Chu pulled his foot back, aiming at Al's face.

"No!" she shrieked and ran toward the knot of … thirty men? She didn't know how many.

At her scream, Al moved, turning his head and rolling away. He was alive! Because he'd moved, Chu kicked his shoulder and back, not his face. She could hear bones crack.

"You have to stop!" She was very close when she noticed them staring at her. She looked down. Her blouse wasn't buttoned right. Part of her breast showed. They turned toward her like a single organism.

"You want a real man, you white bitch?" Chu bellowed.

They turned on her, fanning out so that she couldn't get away. Andy spun and ran as fast as she could toward the main camp. Everyone seemed to be gone. The center of the Bowl was a huge party with bonfires raging. She could hear drunken laughter and screams. Clumps of men fought. What was happening? She had no time to wonder; they were right behind her.

Andy was nimble and quick, dodging around tents and camps. She should have been able to get away from a bunch of drunken maniacs. But they were maniacs. They kept chasing her when normal guys would've quit.

She got a stitch in her side, but kept running. She knew what would happen if they caught her.

"Come on, bitch. We won't *hurt* you. We jus' wan' a taste," Chu slurred the words, chucking them out between gasps. He was closing fast. The camp headquarters, the two derelict cement buildings, were up ahead. She ran toward them as if they offered some hope of safety.

"Stop or I'll beat the crap outta you." He was less than ten feet away. She screamed, and then screamed again as she was tossed off her feet.

The earth moved like it was a carpet that a giant had picked up and shaken. She fell, skidding and rolling, not knowing where the men were. Andy crawled on her hands and knees, heading for the headquarters, trying to get her feet under her. She finally stood and looked over her shoulder.

Something was climbing out of the ground. Huge things like … monsters. Black monsters with scales and red eyes. Long reptilian tails. Ten feet tall. Taller than that. Huge. They clawed their way out of the earth and looked around. Their eyes lit up at the motion in front of them. The men who had been chasing her were rolling around, too drunk to get up or see the danger.

One of the black things picked up one of her pursuers, held him to its face and made a horrible noise like boulders screeching together. The others repeated it. Laughing. The monster twisted the man's head off and threw it. They waded in, tearing the mob to pieces.

Andy took off twice as fast as she had run. If she could make it to the headquarters, if she could just get inside.

87

J ON STEPPED OUT of the motor home for some fresh air. He looked between two of the vehicles at the amphitheater directly behind the Numenon camp. The moon lit the scene perfectly. The Pit was a tapestry of moving flesh. He saw Hector Carrillo heading for a circle of rocks beyond the stage—Hector and a bunch of Indian women, arms interlocked.

People in the Pit began to wave at him. Lots of people. He could see them easily; the Pit was within shouting distance of the Numenon camp. Men who had been kissing other men passionately broke off and turned toward him. Jon realized that there was a generous gay population at the Meeting. About ten percent of the crowd was gay, just like everywhere since the beginning of time.

Several hundred people were waving at him. Jon waved back, smiling. People beckoned to him to join them. He shook his head, no. He couldn't do that any more. That didn't stop them—the whole community began to stream up the hill toward him.

"No!" Jon shouted. "Go back. I can't. You can't! I'm HIV positive! I'm positive!"

A rush of something hit him in the face, knocking him down. There was an explosion at the back of the Pit! A horrible noise came from the other side of the Bowl. It made him sick to his stomach. It made him feel like fighting.

Jon struggled to stand erect. When he looked up, the crowd that had been running up the hill with so much bonhommie had changed. Scowls and curses replaced smiles. His erstwhile admirers shot up the hill like rut-maddened, enraged elks. Fear shot through Jon. It didn't take a genius to see that they intended to rape him. Down below in the Pit, he saw Grandfather jump off the end of the stage and take off in a golf cart with Carl. People followed them. The ones who didn't follow Grandfather went at each other tooth and nail.

Jon spun and ran into the courtyard formed by the motor homes. A crowd of Indians still hung out in the Numenon camp. "Run! Get out of here!"

"Why?"

"Look!" Jon pointed at the edge of the Pit. A crowd of crazed people screaming, "Jon! Jon!" was clawing up the hill. Behind them, a riot raged.

"Get in the RV," Jon yelled to the Indians. He sprinted for his mobile kitchen. "Grab what we'll need for overnight."

They piled into the motor home en masse, snatching what they could on the way. Pads from the lounges, the plastic chairs. Jon locked the doors the instant they closed, horrified by the enraged looks on his people's faces as they charged up the hill.

Jon looked around wildly. The only way out was along the Rim. He'd have to cross the camp's central courtyard. To his right and in front of him, he could see Grandfather and a caravan of golf carts heading to the path that led down to the horses. He couldn't drive down that path in the motor home, but he could stop at the top. They wouldn't chase them, would they?

As he tried to make sense of what was happening, the earth buckled. Those who were standing were thrown against the RV's walls or onto the floor. He grabbed the steering wheel or he would have been tossed off of the driver's seat. Something horrible filled the air, something worse than anything he could imagine. Barely able to sit up, Jon saw *monsters* leap into the camp, attacking the people who'd been intent on attacking him.

People were running past the vehicle, trying to escape. Jon and the others watched hopelessly as the demons began tearing up the Numenon camp.

Jeff Block ran from his motor home to their rear door, barely making it. The warriors let Jeff in and slammed the door shut.

"Oh, my God! The motor homes!" Jon cried. He grabbed a bunch of keys hanging from his belt. The keys to the other Numenon vehicles had been left in his safekeeping. He hit the auto-lock buttons, locking the motor homes. Scaled, venom-slobbering demons surrounded them, scratching at the windows with razor sharp claws.

Jon swiveled his head and saw they were attacking his Chinese screen—tearing it apart! He floored it, driving across the Numenon camp. They could not ruin that screen! 'Rique had given it to him. Dull thuds marked the path of the massive vehicle through the demons. Some bounced off; others fell under the wheels. Sickening thumps said they'd run over them.

"Get the screen!" Jon screamed when they reached it. Warriors jumped from the rear entrance and grabbed it, swinging its panels to keep the monsters at bay. The instant they were inside, Jon took off, heading directly toward Grandfather's lean-to. Doug Saunders stood beside it. Another necessary stop to let Doug in, and they joined the crowd backed up at the Rim, trying to make it down the hill. Behind them, they could hear the Numenon camp being ransacked. Jon looked in the rear view mirror and saw demons he'd run over getting up. They had to be dead—he'd run over them. But they were up and raging.

Grandfather's group of golf cart-borne refugees had already disappeared down the path, followed by many people on foot. Jon perched at the top of the Rim. He couldn't drive the RV down there; it was impossible. The machine would roll and tumble down the cliff at the first switchback.

The wedding tepee was next to them. It had been toppled. Two huge women were trying to fight off a crowd of enraged drunks who had pulled a pretty girl out of the fallen tepee. They had her on the ground and had pulled off her jeans. Her panties were shredded. The girl was screaming and fighting, but could only lose.

"Leave her alone!" yelled Jon.

Doug jumped out and took on the whole bunch. He grabbed the leader and punched his face. Jon could hear the bones crack, and see the face's shape go soft. But Doug was overpowered. He would have lost had not the rest of the warriors poured out of the motor home, and grabbed the girl. Doug kept slugging away.

The warriors shouted, "Get out of here. More are coming."

Once in the motor home, the girl continued to scream and fight. She didn't seem to realize she'd been saved. Doug jumped back in with the warriors behind him.

"Get her to the Ballroom, Jon. She needs Grandfather."

Jon swung his head around to see Doug take the girl to the rear of the motor home. He began speaking in softly in a language Jon hadn't heard. Doug held the girl as though he knew her well. As Doug stroked her soflty, the pretty young woman's cries turned to heaving sobs. Finally, she sniffled softly. The two big women who'd been with her helped her dress. Doug kept talking to her, softly.

The thugs who'd been attacking the girl charged the RV, throwing themselves against the windows. Jon looked back and could see the demons closing in on them.

Eyes bulging and rimmed with white, Jon launched the huge vehicle over the Rim.

88

LEONA BRAND STOOD on the Rim where the trail to the horse facilities branched off. Where was Tyler? The sun was setting and there was no sign of him.

This is so typical. The most important thing they had to do at the Meeting was ask Grandfather for help saving their marriage. But what does Tyler do? Run around the desert playing the mighty warrior.

Leona wore a tiered velvet skirt and silk blouse, ready for the big party Grandfather had promised that night. She was going to make Tyler notice her if she had to set her hair on fire. Except he wasn't there.

Leona turned to go back to their tent. Their encampment was solidly in the middle of the campground, demonstrating their oneness with the People. They were next to Elizabeth's tent, and the gigantic medical tent. All the doctors' and interns' campsites. And Bert and Bud Creeman's camp.

She almost ran into Bert's sister, Roxy, who dashed out of Bud and Bert's tent. She looked very anxious. "What's the matter, Roxy?"

"Do you know where Elizabeth and Bud are? I think my sister's in labor."

"They're down with the horses. I was just over at the path. I didn't see anyone coming up."

"Bert's been having contractions for hours. I'm afraid the baby's turned wrong." Roxy's face was stiff with fear. "I don't know what to do."

"Go back to your sister. I'll go over to the medical tent and get a doctor. Have you delivered a baby, Roxy?"

Roxy shook her head. "No. Third year nursing students don't do that. I've assisted, but I've never done it by myself."

"Okay. You stay with Bert. It could be false labor."

Leona dashed into the camp and was shocked. Bonfires raged everywhere and people danced and frolicked. On the hill, those ne'er-do-wells who hung out in the back of the Bowl were raging drunk. She could see fistfights. People were necking, groping, rolling around all over the place.

She found the doctors and interns easily. They were standing—sort of—in front of the medical tent. They were locked in a group grope and acted as inebriated as everyone else. She decided not to bother them; they weren't in any condition to practice medicine.

Leona crept back to the tent where Bert and Roxy waited. An orangish light filled the air. They were smack in the middle of the camp, with no easy escape route. Cowering in the tent as the day waned, Roxy, Leona, and Bert kept the electric lantern off, not wanting to call attention to themselves. Bert Creeman was exhausted, both from the rigors of camping at such an advanced stage of pregnancy and from having had contractions all day.

Bert had a severe lower backache and cramps between her contractions, which were coming every ten to twelve minutes. As time passed, they realized that help was not coming. Roxy readied herself to deliver her niece or nephew.

Bert's face was lined with tension and pain. She clutched a knitted baby blanket in her hands, something she had made for the baby. She was in control, barely, whispering, "I wish Bud would come."

They felt something like an explosion, and everything became a thousand times worse. From the fights and cries of anger all around, from the sounds of what could only be rape, the three women realized they were in real danger. Grandfather's voice no longer rang out, nor could they hear golf carts. They heard people screaming and running. Growls and terrible noises that sounded like rocks grating together punctuated the humans' cries. And then it got quieter and the shouts were farther away. The snarls died down, but they'd hear one occasionally, a horrible reminder that danger hadn't passed.

They needed to move. Bert's contractions had stabilized for the moment. If they could get a golf cart, they could get out of the Bowl and find Grandfather.

"They leave golf carts behind the Headquarters to charge. I'll see if I can find one," Leona whispered.

She peeked out of the tent opening. The Headquarters was a few yards behind the tent where they hid. Their camp was too close to the Headquarters. Tall black creatures that looked like dinosaurs stood next to it, making repulsive noises and waving clawed paws. They seemed to be joking. Leona craned her neck and surveyed what she could see of the rest of the camp. The dinosaurs were all over, tearing things up with their talons. Red eyes flashed and scales glistened. What were they? Reptiles? Monsters? Demons?

She and the other two women were helpless where they were; all the beasts had to do was slash through their tent to get them. They would do that, and soon.

Leona looked around. The brutes had roared and swept their claws and tails from side to side, laying waste to the area between the Headquarters and the back of the Bowl. Leona leaned out a little father to see what options they had. To the West, in the direction of the path that went down to the horses, things seemed quieter. The demons had already passed through and done their worst. As far as she could see, bodies littered the ground. But the monsters were gone.

She could see a few tents standing. Leona pulled back into their tent.

"We have to leave. The demons are moving this way. Over there," she pointed, "almost everything's leveled, but they're gone. I think you'll be safe while I get a cart. Bert, can you walk a little way?"

Bert indicated that she could. Leona and Roxy got her up and out of the tent. Looking from side to side and stumbling over bodies, they half carried Bert a long way, much farther than Leona had intended. Bert grimaced when the contractions came, but she didn't cry out. They knew not to make a sound.

"This one looks good," Leona said. They'd found a decent-sized tent that wasn't filled with dead bodies. It was much closer to the Rim and the path to the horses. She stepped inside the tent and helped Roxy guide Bert in. "You stay here and I'll ..."

She couldn't move, or speak. It was as though some obscene power had taken over her body. Her eyes stared in the direction they were · pointed when the freeze began. Leona could see the other women; they watched her from the same horrified paralysis. Bert slumped to the floor of the tent and then fell on her side. Even if her muscles didn't work, gravity did.

Leona had no idea what was going on. All of this was supernatural. Whatever caused the riot must have been playing with them. Everything was silent, and then she heard voices and the sounds of horses. Men were circulating around the Bowl, calling out people's names.

"Leona! Where are you? Can you hear me?" It was Tyler, searching for her. He kept shouting, "Where are you? We can save you."

She couldn't answer. All she and the others could do was listen to Tyler and the warriors searching and calling out. They exclaimed over what they saw, cursing. And then they stopped and she could hear them riding away.

A little while later, the sound of engines said the men had gone to the parking lot and gotten vehicles. They called to each other as they loaded wounded people into the cars and trucks. Tyler called to *her.* The out-of-the-way tent she had selected was too hidden for Tyler and the others to notice.

Leona tried to scream, or move, or make noise. *Tyler, we're here. Help us, please!* She couldn't pull in a deep breath to yell or even weep properly. It was as though the devil had put the Bowl on pause. There was nothing she could do.

Silent tears ran down her cheeks as the engines revved and the rescue party headed to the trail going down to the horses.

No one would save them.

89

TYLER AND THE search party reined their horses to a stop at the top of the path and looked around in horror. The wedding tepee was knocked down. The campground was leveled and ransacked, with collapsed tents everywhere. Not a living soul was in sight.

They'd run into remnants of a mass exodus at the bottom of the switchbacks. He could see larger group in front of them, heading across the plain. He questioned a few.

"What happened? What is everyone running from?"

"Monsters! Demons!"

"They had claws and red eyes!"

"They're killing everyone!"

This was the stuff of nightmares and horror movies. Tyler couldn't believe his ears. But he believed the terror of the people around him. "Where are you going?"

"We're going to the Ballroom. Grandfather's up ahead," someone pointed. He wasn't wearing any pants. Tyler should have gotten the picture. He got it when he reached the top of the switchbacks.

Nothing moved. All most of the tents were torn down, people's belongings strewn all over, with the bodies. It was a massacre.

"Ride over to the Numenon camp. See what you can find," Tyler ordered. "The rest of us will fan out and," his voice faltered, "look for survivors." They could see bodies littered about, none moving. What happened here? Where was Leona?

"Keep in sight of each other. Whoever did this may still be here." This was an eerie pause, just a pause. Tyler had the feeling that whatever did this was just out of sight, getting ready to attack again.

Supernaturals. They had to be something like what attacked Lisa. They'd been looking for them out in the desert. Damn it! They were *here*, in the Bowl!

"Hello? Can anyone hear me?" He rode slowly through the camp, calling Leona's name. Calling the names of friends. No answer. He found his tent, collapsed and empty as were all the tents around it. They were slashed to threads. The things had claws. If the monsters caught any-one, they killed them. Bodies lay all over. He got off his horse and led it through the ruined camp; he needed to check the bodies. Would he find Leona?

Tyler bent down and touched a man. He jumped back. "Phew!" The stench of alcohol was overwhelming. "They're drunk!" he shouted to the others. There must have been thousands of people there—all passed out, drunk! Who could have brought enough booze to do this? It must have taken truckloads.

When Tyler stumbled over a head, he realized they weren't all drunk. The head lay there, eyes wide, mouth open, face slashed. One of the slashes had taken the head right off of its body. He didn't recog-nize the man, nor did he find his body. He looked more carefully at the random piles of people and saw missing limbs and gutted trunks. He turned someone over and discovered his chest was a gaping hole, his heart removed. Corpses littered the ground as often as drunks.

The others were discovering the same, and more. Knots of bodies told the rest of the story—a mass orgy had taken place.

Where was Grandfather? How had this happened at the Meeting? Where were their wives and loved ones? Tyler was heartsick, hoping he didn't find Leona in some tangle of drunken flesh.

They led the horses, covering the camp on foot. The horror of what had happened hit them harder and harder as they realized how many people—men and women—had been brutalized. They lay singly and in groups, terrorized and bleeding. Some moved and moaned as the rescuers passed.

"Help me, help me," a man called. All smelled of alcohol.

What could they do? There were ten warriors, and thousands of people who needed help.

"Tyler! Over here!" one of the guys called from the Pit. A group of elders had been trampled. Avalina Cocina was among them.

Tears filled Tyler's eyes. He put his ear to Avalina's chest. She was alive—they were all alive. Barely. They were so *old*. Who could do this to old people? Why hadn't Grandfather made sure they were saved?

Tyler turned to the men. "Let's get our cars and load them with injured people. We'll drive them to the Ballroom. The doctors will be there. We'll move everyone who's hurt." He didn't have to say, *And let's make it quick.*

The place felt out of kilter, spinning, like the earth could open and disgorge more evil at any time. A sound like the grating of stone on stone kept everyone's nerves raw.

While the others headed to the parking lot to get their cars, Tyler rummaged around and found the medical tent. It was collapsed. The drugs like painkillers and morphine were missing, but antibiotics and bandages were there. He threw them on a tarp to pick up later.

Where was Leona?

Tyler found a woman who had obviously been gang raped toward the middle of the camp. No passed out demons were in evidence, just men he'd known as long as they'd been coming to the Meeting.

Tyler looked at them in disgust. He marked their faces, wanting revenge. All his years with Grandfather, all his study of philosophy, and poof! Civilized morals were nothing to the primal feeling the destruction aroused.

Tyler wanted to kick their skulls in, swinging his boot to, "This is for that woman! This is for bringing booze here! This is for insulting Grandfather! And this," the biggest kick of all, "is for Leona."

Where was she? Had they hurt her? Despite his primitive impulses, his warrior training kept him from acting. Grandfather would handle revenge.

Tyler yanked himself away and rode his horse across the Bowl to the parking lot. At least he could pick up the wounded. Something moved in the corner of his eye. He thought he saw a female form beckoning to him. She was so erotic, she stopped him in his tracks. For one horrible instant, he wanted to follow her.

He could see someone was camped in a ring of big boulders beyond the edge of the Bowl. Cheery firelight shown on the cliff walls above the encampment. Hopefully, whatever happened in the Bowl missed them.

The stupidity of being out there by himself dawned on Tyler. He found his SUV, unsaddled his horse and smacked it on the butt. "Get out of here!" The animal took off, heading back to the desert, its home.

"That's it! Let's get back to the camp!" Tyler jumped into his SUV and caught up to the others. It was an easy drive in this direction; the parking lot was just outside the Bowl. All they had to do was make their way over the slight rise the way they had when they arrived. He spearheaded the rescuers with the other men fanning out in their vehicles. Operation mop-up had begun.

They didn't take as many wounded people back as they wanted to. The feeling of imminent danger was twice as strong when they returned with the vehicles. They felt like the monsters were just out of sight. Still, they filled the vehicles; people who needed medical help were tightly crammed into the warriors' trucks and SUVs.

"How far did you get?" Tyler asked a warrior returning from reconnoitering the Numenon camp and beyond.

"I got into the Pit, but not past it. I picked up these people." He indicated his full truck bed. "There's a lot more, but I didn't have room." He stopped speaking when a surge of malevolent energy shot around them and the grating sound returned. The earth would open again, and soon.

"Let's go!" Tyler led the retreat—which ended up in a mad run across the plains once they got down the switchbacks. Lights flashed into the sky from the Bowl; whatever had been after them wasn't done.

"You did your best, you did your best," Tyler repeated to himself. He had all the bandages, all the medicines. And an SUV full of moaning people who needed them. Fortunately, Grandfather and the rest had already escaped.

Where was Leona?

90

LEONA JERKED WHEN the paralysis ended; it left as sudddenly as it had come. She was so stiff that she had to wring her hands and shrug her shoulders to move. She picked her feet up one by one and stamped them. Only then did she feel as though she could walk. It was pitch black. Noises of rioting were far away.

"What happened?" Roxy cried, rubbing her hands together. Leona could see the whites of her eyes glinting in the darkness. "I could hear Tyler searching for us." She put her face in her hands.

"I don't know, Roxy. Everything that's happened is impossible. But we can move now. I'm going to find a cart before it happens again." Roxy wiped her eyes.

"Roxy, we can cry later. Take care of Bert." Bert lay on the tent floor where she had fallen. Her eyes were closed and she appeared to be asleep. "If I get a cart, we'll have to leave fast, so be ready." Her lips tightened.

"If I'm not back soon, wake Bert up and *drag* her to the path. Get down to the mesa and follow Grandfather's trail. Don't wait for me."

"Leona," Roxy's face said what she couldn't with words—don't die, Leona, come back.

"I won't take any chances. I've got to go." She slipped through the tent's opening.

Leona darted back toward the Headquarters, hiding wherever she could. The Bowl looked like one of those medieval paintings of hell. The moon illuminated fist fights raging only a few yards away. The participants were too involved with each other to notice her. Piles of bodies looked like a giant had thrown them.

Behind her and far in the distance, Leona thought she could see a few people disappearing over the Rim to the horse facilities. That's where they'd go if she succeeded. Leona picked her way through the bodies and devastation. When she got to their old tent, she knew she'd been right in moving Bert and Roxy. Their tent and all those around it had been destroyed and ransacked.

Leona crept through the tangle of porta-potties to the rear of the camp office. No carts sat there charging. The area was empty, except for a pile of bodies in a heap to her left. And something was going on behind the cement office building. Leona peeked, and jumped back behind a porta-potty. The grating noise and shadows of of reptilian heads cast by the moon said demons were back there.

A golf cart carrying more monsters pulled up between her and the building. The creatures looked like a cross between bikers and dinosaurs—they had shiny black scales and red eyes. Their hands ended in claws and curved tusks stuck out of the sides of their snouts. One wore a feathered bonnet, a tremendously significant and valuable piece of pow wow regalia. Others had scarves and hats. They must have pulled trophies from their victims. The grinding noise must be their speech.

Leona Brand could see them yakking and laughing in their horrible way. One of them had a square bottle, which he emptied. He belched. The others laughed.

She saw movement out of the corner of her eye. 'Fonzo's—no, he wanted to be called Al—Al's new wife, Andy, sprinted toward the camp headquarters. Could she find safety in there? Was there anywhere that was safe?

Should she try to help her? Leona had her own problems. She was hiding behind a porta-potty with the only golf cart in sight occupied by demons. She had no way back to the tent, and no way to get the golf cart. She couldn't call to Andy without bringing the monsters down on her. If she perished, so would Bert and Roxy, and the baby. Leona remained silent.

Something caused an uproar among the demons behind the headquarters. The ones in the cart jumped out and joined them. Leona dodged forward to a portable toilet closer to the cart—and the monsters.

A woman began screaming. Leona thought it must be Andy. The screams continued, horrible screams that could mean only one thing. They were raping her. *Oh, my God.* Leona covered her ears and quaked. The cries continued until she wished that Andy would die and stop suffering.

An empty vodka bottle flew out from behind the building. The grinding noise rose and fell and what had to be demonic laughter rang out. Still the woman's screams continued.

The image of Bert's baby kept Leona in control, kept her a warrior. She had to save that baby. The baby would die if she didn't do her job. The empty golf cart sat there, tantalizing.

She prayed, "Please help me. Please help me." Whether it was the answer to her prayers or the effects of unaccustomed alcohol, the sounds of the inebriated monsters became slurred and sporadic. The woman's cries faded to whimpers and then silence.

One of the reptiles lurched from behind the headquarters. He glared around balefully, looking at the porta-potty shielding Leona. He took a step in her direction, but stopped and turned to a heap of bodies. He urinated on them with a snorting laugh. Smoke rose from the corpses where his urine touched their flesh. Shaking himself off, he staggered a step, and fell face down on the pile. He lay unmoving.

Leona darted from her hiding place, jumped into the cart, and made a run for the new tent.

"Roxy, Bert! Get in! Hurry!" Roxy pulled Bert out of the tent and pushed her into the cart. Leona floored it before they were seated. As they made their way toward the switchbacks and saftey, Leona drove the cart with a fury that couldn't be contained.

The area looked vacant and silent when they reached the Rim—they seemed to be the only ones still escaping. She saw a black form leaping toward them out of the corner of her eye. Leona yanked the steering wheel and manuevered out of its way. It was a very drunk demon, but still capable of killing. Other monsters clawed at them, but were too inebriated to stop the women's flight.

Leona plunged over the edge without a thought, slowing for the switchbacks, sliding into the turns, and gunning it as they pulled round each curve; she drove automatically, cart leaning into the bends as though she was riding a galloping horse.

Bud, Elizabeth, and Will sat in their cart at the foot of the cliff when the screaming started. Bud tried to hear what was being said, but the thunder in the distance obscured it. Something terrible was happening up there. Their headlights lit the path: they saw it all.

Dozens of golf carts flew over the Rim as though demons were behind them. Nyough! Nyough! Nyough! The carts flew over the edge like kids' toys, bouncing and heading down the switchbacks. Bud didn't even know they had that many golf carts—or that they could go that fast. Grandfather was in the lead—he saw them and shouted at them as he zoomed by.

"Run! Run for your lives! Run!"

Bud had never seen Grandfather run from anything. He wouldn't leave until he knew that Bert was safe. Other carts passed them, their occupants yelling, "Run! Run! They'll get you! Run to the Ballroom!"

Elizabeth stopped crying, the spectacle was so bizarre. The golf carts passed and hordes of people came running after them, looking over their shoulders with terror on their faces. "Run!" they shrieked. "They'll kill you!"

Bud wouldn't move; he couldn't.

Probably half of the people in the Meeting passed before them. Bud was ready to drive up the path alone, when he saw one of the Numenon motor homes career over the Rim.

He held his breath, expecting to see it somersault down. An RV *couldn't* go down that path. But someone very smart was driving. He didn't try to turn on the switchbacks, just moved as far out into the curve as he could, then backed down to the next one, backing as far as he could before driving forward until the subsequent turn.

Miraculously, the gigantic vehicle lurched to the bottom. When it sped past, they saw Jon Walker driving, with terrified faces massed behind him. He waved at them, frantically signaling that they should follow the crowd.

Then it was over; the screaming exodus dwindled to a few people, and then none.

"You two stay here. I'll go see if I can find Bert."

"We won't leave you," Will said.

Bud headed toward the path, into the mayhem above. They could hear screams of anguish and rage. Murder. People may have stopped fleeing the disaster, but it hadn't stopped.

None of it mattered, he had to find Bert. They'd almost hit the switchbacks. Then the final cart rattled down. Tears ran down his cheeks when he saw Bert huddled between Roxy and Leona Brand. She was safe. He waved at her and shouted, "Are you all right?"

Bert didn't answer. She looked at him, so worn down that she was lucky to be conscious. But she was there, and she was alive.

Leona nodded, looking anything but all right. "Have you seen Tyler?"

91

CARL PILOTED THE cart into the hidden canyon leading to the Ballroom. Like most of the ancestral caverns, the massive Ballroom was impossible to find without knowing exactly where it was.

"Go to the middle." Grandfather pointed toward the center of the grotto. Their cart carried eight injured and exhausted people that they'd picked up along the way. They'd started out speeding along, but their velocity slowed with each new passenger. The cart was so overloaded by the time they reached the Ballroom that it barely putted along.

"The lake is back there," the old man pointed into the blackness deeper inside the cave. "People will come through there," he said, indicating the entrance behind them. Then he pointed at their feet. "We'll put the hurt ones here."

Carl stopped. The only illumination was from the golf cart's head-lights; they lit a small arc in front of them. He couldn't see the cave's walls.

Carl stepped out of the cart and began waving his arms, jumping and shouting. Grandfather began to chant, and then turned to their pas-sengers. "Come, everyone. Chant. You're not too tired for that."

The people they'd brought along looked at the cave's ceiling in amazement. It glowed—stones and gems sparkled like jewels, and patterns of light undulated over the ceiling's surface, moving like the swell of the sea. It was exquisite. Soon the Ballroom was brightly illuminated.

"It's part of the mystery of the Bowl," Grandfather explained. Carl already knew this; he'd been to the Ballroom many times with the warriors. It was a huge cave easily capable of holding the entire Meeting. It had been used for ceremonies and group weddings for thousands of years. Now Grandfather's people used it as a training site when the desert heat was too much even for the warriors.

"The stone responds to the presence of people, and to our feelings." As the ceiling and walls lit up, the group could see beautiful rock paintings that covered every surface within reach. Three wide tunnels spread away from the main cave like fingers, heading back into the bedrock.

"The People have used this cave from the beginning of time. Tiny caves open off those corridors. Families lived in them in the old days. There is also drinking water in the lake up there. Lots of flush holes. Everything we need." Grandfather's eyes twinkled. "Aho, Carl! This is the Mogollon Hilton!"

Carl wasn't so optimistic. The cave was lit, but it wasn't comfortable. They had nothing but rock floors, walls, and twinkling lights. They had no beds, no medicine or bandages, nothing to take care of the survivors who had begun to flood in. Carl helped the people on their cart to get down. He had to lay them on the bare rock.

"Carl, me an' the boys are here to help." Carl looked up and saw a man in a khaki uniform. He had his hands on his hips and the biggest gut anywhere.

"Thank you, Elmo." Carl helped another old lady get down.

"When we heard Grandfather say y'all was goin' to the Ballroom, me an' the boys ran out to the parking lot and got a couple of AWDs. We got a shit load of hurt people outside the cave.

"We've been tryin' to uphold law and order all night. Didn't work, though." Elmo ran his hands through the greasy strands of his hair. He'd lost his hat. "Sure has been an evening."

"We appreciate your help."

"You got it. I'm under orders to lay low, but this …"

Carl looked up. He and Elmo got to work with no more conversation. It seemed like an avalanche of wounded souls entered the Ballroom. More people than Carl could count dragged themselves into the cold rock cave. A deluge of those who had been following them on foot entered. Hundreds poured in, with more arriving every instant.

Many were scantily clad; some were naked. They tried to cover themselves. Whatever insanity had overtaken them in the Bowl had disappeared. The memory of what they'd been doing hadn't. They sat down where they were, mouths gaping, tears flowing.

Grandfather took charge. "Carl, put the injured in rows so that the healers and doctors can reach them." The old man shouted, "Healers! Comfort those in need." He started chanting again, touching the traumatized people around him, and lessening their pain.

Nothing seemed to help: as soon as their shock was released, their embarrassment at what they'd done popped up.

Grandfather raised his arms again. "Chant! Let the chant carry everything away!"

Two golf carts, one carrying Elizabeth, Bud, and Will, and the other filled with Leona, Roxy, and Bert, entered during a lull. Bud gasped when he saw Bert.

They drove the carts toward Grandfather. Swarms of people milled around. Bud couldn't guess how many people were crying out for help. Some suffered silently or were unconscious. Those who hadn't been hurt were the loudest, sobbing and wailing from pure shock.

The scene reminded Bud of the Pit during the Meeting, except no one was happy.

Bud stepped down and turned to the other cart. Bert sat clutching her belly, tear tracks down her cheeks. "Bert, are you okay, honey?"

"It's been awful," Roxy said. Bert seemed unable to speak. "Bert started having contractions early in the afternoon. I don't know if she's in labor or not. It was so scary up there, Bud." Roxy shook like a tambourine. "People were killed and there were monsters. We had to hide. Oh, Bud, if Leona hadn't been there, we'd be dead." Roxy started to cry for the first time all day. Bert joined her.

"Oh, Bert. I should have been with you." He wrapped his arms around his wife. Bert's face showed every bit of her day's suffering. Bud looked to Elizabeth. "Is she going to have the baby here?"

"I have to examine her, Bud, and find out where we stand. Don't worry; I've delivered babies before."

Bud gawked at the crowd. So many of the people were missing clothes. What had happened back at the camp? No time for that. His eyes settled on Grandfather. Elizabeth had gone to him. They were in intense conversation. He could hear them talking.

"Where can I examine Bert?" she said. "Do we have any supplies? Where are the other doctors?"

"The three big tunnels have many smaller caves opening off of them," Grandfather said. "They're like this one. Make some noise, move around, and the lights go on. Go down there, you'll find a place." He pointed at the closest tunnel.

"The doctors are there." He indicated Larry Wolf, the senior internist who was supposed to be taking Elizabeth's place at the Meeting. Wolf and his pack of interns stood around a small pile of medical supplies on the floor as though they were guarding it. Elizabeth spoke with them, rummaged through the heap and came back with some lubricant and exam gloves.

"At least we have these," she said. "Come on, honey. Let's see what we've got. Roxy, you come too. I may need you." Elizabeth, Bert, and

Roxy took one of the carts and headed slowly up the corridor. Bud sat on the rumble seat in the back, facing the main chamber of the Ballroom.

If he had been standing up, Bud thought his knees might give in. He was happy to see Roxy and Leona, but he felt like he might fall apart. He didn't feel that way out in the desert, but he did now, with Bert safely in front of him.

He saw Leona Brand out of the corner of his eye. She had climbed out of her cart and pitched in helping the injured without a pause. He needed to thank her for taking care of Bert. Bud wiped his eyes with the back of his hand. That was *his* job and he didn't do it.

Bud looked up and saw that Will Duane moved into the empty cart. He sat there by himself. The white cast around his leg stood out. Duane's mouth opened and closed. He looked around like a fish in hell.

92

CARL SAW HOW bad Will Duane looked. He was headed toward him, but Leona Brand called, diverting him to helping the wounded people.

"Carl, I'll need your help." She turned to the doctors and said, "We don't have any bandages. Do you have sterile water or containers?"

"No. We got all that stuff," an intern pointed at a pile of supplies. Lubricant, gloves, and a bunch of stuff one might take to an orgy. "We didn't have time," said one of the interns.

"What did you bring to help these people?" she said to Larry Wolf, the head internist.

Larry stammered, "I jammed all the medical supplies I could into my back pack and a couple of cases."

Carl noticed his backpack and the cases the interns were carrying.

"I took all the morphine and anything people could get high on."

"How about antibiotics?" Leona barked. "Bandages? Sutures? We need those. No one wants to get high around here."

Larry shook his head. "Everything was crazy …"

"We'll figure it out," Carl said.

Carl arranged the wounded in rows and comforted them as well as he could. He was a healer, but these wounds were too severe for him to handle. Most of the time, he used his healing touch to put them to sleep. Sleeping through the coming days was probably the best thing to do.

When Carl looked over at where Mr. Duane had been, he and the golf cart were gone.

93

WILL CAREFULLY BACKED the golf cart away from the storm's epicenter. He retreated all the way to the cave's side wall and sat there, clutching the steering wheel. The cavern's entrance was to his left. Refugees stumbled through it. To his right was the corridor that Elizabeth and the others had disappeared into. He wiped his mouth with his hand. He didn't notice his rasping breathing or the way his hands clutched the wheel beneath them.

The survivors spread out before him, a moving quilt of disaster. Smells of blood and open flesh, shit and urine, booze and odors he didn't recognize permeated his nostrils. His eyes were assaulted by bright red flesh and protruding bones. Organs whose functions he didn't know poked through torn skin. Howling filled his ears.

He had to get out of there. Could he drive out the entrance and escape somewhere? Was it safe out in the desert? Was anywhere safe?

A sobbing woman staggered into the cave and threw herself into his arms. "Help me!"

Will recoiled. "I can't help you. Go over there." He pushed her toward the doctors. "Grandfather's over there, he can help you." Will had to pry her fingers from his shoulders. He couldn't help her, why did she keep asking?

A warrior approached and said, "Grandfather told me to get this." He nodded at the cart. "We need it."

Will gave the cart to him. He swayed as he stood, unsteady because of the cast on his leg.

Where was the highly paid staff he'd brought along so that he would never be stranded in a situation like this? He huddled against the rock wall, searching the crowd. The Numenon crew seemed to have vanished.

The multitudes continued to flow into the cave, most of them heading straight for the hospital area in the middle. People either stayed there, joining the moaning masses, or milled away like a river diverted by a large rock.

How could he help these people? Why should he help them? The *People* were so foreign that he would have never, ever ventured into this idiotic expedition if he had a clue that this might happen. He came to mine their sacred lands and to get Grandfather to make Marina take him back, that's all.

Will's rigid body shook as though it carried an electric current. His lips were drawn tight. His hands quivered as he passed them through his hair. He wasn't aware of how close he was to hysteria. He felt only rising energy, power to fight the chaos.

"Numenon people! Staff meeting *now!*" Will's voice rang out. His voice was loud but in control the first time he attempted to gather his flock. No one responded.

Will's voice rang out, louder, reverberating off the rock. *"Numenon staff meeting here! Now!!"*

He stood away from the wall, waving his arms. The volume and pitch of his voice increased until he was screaming. The People turned and looked at him, ducking their heads and wincing. None of them had seen Will Duane out of control.

Will paced up and down as well as he could with his leg enclosed in plaster. Where was his highly paid, professional staff? What were they doing? They were supposed to be supporting *him*.

"Numenon people! Staff meeting right now! Get over here or I'll fire you!" Will's cast made a hollow thud as he stumped along the rock floor. *"GET OVER HERE!"*

Will couldn't see any of his staff until Jon walked through the cave opening. He jumped a foot when he heard Will's voice, which echoed throughout the cave. Will stood by the wall, screaming for them to come.

Jon ran up to him. "Mr. Duane, they'll be right in. They're in the motor home, helping hurt people and unloading stuff."

Will barely registered his words.

"Mr. Duane, you have to stop. People are staring," Jon pressed harder, looking more terrified of confronting his boss than the bedlam around him. "They'll hate us worse than ever. Pretend I'm Betty—you always calm down for her. She's gone; you have to do it yourself now."

Will barely heard him. "Get over here, now! All of you!" Eyes popping, spit flying, Will stood against the wall, head wagging back and forth like one of those plastic dogs people put their cars' rear windows.

"Mr. Duane, this is not the time for a screamer!" Jon looked like he might start screaming. Will didn't notice that, either.

The Numenon staff began to stagger into the cave. They had their arms wrapped around injured people, helping them walk. Will's rage was so spectacular that his employees scarcely noticed the jeweled cave walls with their undulating lights. They crept inside, trying to get past their boss without him seeing them. It didn't work.

"GET OVER HERE!" Will shrieked at Jeff Block, the second member of his staff to enter the cave. Jeff approached cautiously. "WHERE ARE THE REST OF YOU?"

Jon intervened, "We were helping ..."

Delroy entered the cave, blinking at the twinkling ceiling. Mark was right behind him. Followed by Gil.

"*Where have you been?* Look at this!" Will didn't seem to notice what his people were doing. And then he did.

"You've been helping people. Oh. That's okay. That's a good thing to do. Put them over there and come back." He pointed to the hospital area and waited until they returned.

"Are we all here?" Will's tone softened. They gathered around him: Gil, Mark, Jeff, Delroy, and Rich. Melissa wasn't there; she was with Wesley. "Where's Doug?"

"He's with Janice. She's a woman he met this week. He and those ladies who were guarding her in the RV are with her," Jon said.

"Where's Hector?"

Jon put his hand to his mouth and gasped. "I saw him with some Indian women in the Pit."

"Did he make it out with you?"

"Not with us."

"We'll get this place tied down, then set up a search party for Hector. We'll leave as soon as possible. I'll get helicopters."

Noise from outside the cave announced the arrival of the first of Tyler Brand's assortment of trucks and RVs. Four warriors entered the cave holding the corners of a blanket. Someone was inside. His or her rump hung down, forming a V. A stream of blood dripped from the blanket's lowest point, forming a trail on the rock floor.

At the sight of the trickling blood, Will's eyes opened. He gasped and leaped forward, tripping on his cast and landing flat on his face on the stone floor. A few people—not Numenon people—giggled semi-hysterically.

Will sprang to his feet. "Who laughed! Which one of you sons of bitches laughed?" He spun around accusing anyone who'd make eye contact, snarling like a pit bull. He couldn't fix anything or even take a step. He turned on his cast like it was the enemy. "Get me out of this thing! Where are the doctors? Get me out of this!"

Will charged toward the sick bay, pushing, shoving, trampling everyone before him. "Get out of my way. Move!"

People toppled in the crowded cave, others turned and stared. Will rammed his way over whomever and whatever was in front of him.

94

"GET OUT OF my way!" Will shoved people who could barely stand.

"Get this thing off me!" he shouted when he reached the senior doctor, pointing at his cast. Will turned from side to side, eyes searching for Elizabeth. Why had she healed his leg, but left the damned cast on?

"I can't get your cast off," said the beleaguered internist. "I don't have tools."

"Why don't you have tools?" Will whispered, but his whisper was more intimidating than his screaming. "Get me out of this or I'll—"

"Maybe we've got something back at the motor home," Mark Kenna said. "Jon brought everything you can think of."

Carl said, "Send someone back there and bring anything you think could cut off a cast. Fast!"

Mark ran with Jon in pursuit. "Wait. I know where everything is."

They returned with a gigantic tool kit. Jon pulled out some huge shears. "I brought these for cutting up wild game. I thought we might shoot a buffalo or something."

"Let me see those," Carl said, reaching for the giant scissors. "If they fit between his leg and the cast, I can probably ..." And so he did. Carl cut through the plaster in an impressive display of strength.

"Thank you," Will said, rubbing his calf and looking chastened. He gave Carl his hand and the massive warrior pulled him to his feet. The only problem was he just had one shoe. "I can't walk like this."

"Take 'em both off," Carl said. "An' come over here with me."

He led the billionaire back to the place on the wall where he'd been standing earlier. Carl had a feeling he could fix something.

"Okay. Look at me," he said, resting his hands lightly on Will's shoulders and letting his energy flow. The crazy man he'd been watching for the last half hour wasn't the Will he knew. That Will was the guy who had treated Andy fairly even though she came there to spy. He'd given Carl a good job and acted like he was an equal. He told Carl that he needed him. Will was a decent person.

They made eye contact. Will slumped almost immediately, bending forward so that his head touched Carl's chest. The older man began to shudder, but not in the wired way he'd been before. Will's shoulders shook harder and tipped forward more. He was weeping.

"Talk to me," Carl said.

Will pushed away and looked up into Carl's eyes. Moisture rolled down his face. "Did you see those people? They were hacked to pieces. They were so hurt, and I couldn't do a thing. They came up to me and asked for help. I couldn't do *anything*." He waved his hand at the place his cast had been.

"I was useless." Will rubbed his forehead. "Worse than useless. Jesus. I've never seen anything like that. Like someone took a machete to them. They're going to die, aren't they?"

"Some of them."

"If I wasn't here, none of this would have happened. Enzo wants *me*, not them. I should have warned people when I found out what Sandy

Sydney was. I should have made everyone listen to Grandfather. I should have made them leave. I knew what Enzo was. He destroyed my family.

"But I *didn't* know what he was. I didn't know he could do *this*. Oh, God, this is because of me. This and that poor girl Sandy Sydney attacked. I shouldn't have come."

"You think all of this is your fault? But you didn't—"

"Yes. He did this to get me." Will covered his eyes. "All those people. Some of them had nothing on. Did you see them? That is so embarassing. And it could happen to anyone. It happened to *me*. I was in a hotel with some woman. We woke up and smoke was everywhere. The drapes were on fire. We ran out … The press was all over.

"Jesus. Those poor people. So embarassing." Will rocked from side to side. "I've got to handle this. I can't let him get away with it."

Will twisted and bolted, heading out the cave's entrance. He was so fast Carl couldn't catch him. He put his fingers to his mouth, making a piercing whistle. Warriors' heads went up and turned toward him. He ran for the cave's mouth and motioned for them to follow him.

The entrance to the cave was a fairly long canyon with a bend in it. In three places, it narrowed to just wide enough for the RV to get through. The motor home was parked just outside of the cave's mouth. Carl barreled down the gulley as fast as he could. He was in good shape, but Will Duane was a lifelong runner. A couple of days in a cast didn't slow him down. Carl didn't see him until he stood at the place where the canyon opened into the desert, watching Will run into the open plain. Running barefoot hadn't bothered him one bit.

Will kept going until he was clear of the Badlands and completely visible to anyone in the desert.

"You want *me*," he yelled at the sky. "Come and get me, you son of a bitch." He kept shouting that, facing in different directions. When he had turned around completely, he saw Carl and a bunch of warriors standing in the ravine's opening.

"Stay there. Don't come out. I know what I'm doing," he yelled.

"We can't move. We're stuck. He's around here somewhere," Carl shouted. "Don't do this. We can help the hurt people. You don't have to do this."

"It's my fault. I have to fix it." Will turned away and ran farther into the desert. "Come and get me, asshole," he screamed into the sky, turning as before.

Sandy Sydney appeared in front of him. It was as though she materialized out of nothing.

"Hello, Will. Did you come to play?" Sandy postured and preened, undulating like the whore she was. She had the same little girl voice that had driven him nuts in Numenon. She wore the tight pale blue jeans she'd had on when he saw her last, just before she escaped from the *Cass*. The same pink checked shirt, too. They were torn and dirty. One sleeve was gone. Her tits were as big as ever.

"I'm sorry I couldn't dress for our date, sweetie. But once we get going, you won't care. I hope you last longer than that Indian bitch. She couldn't take much of anything," Sandy moved closer and he could see her face in the moonlight. It looked like a puzzle that had been put together with little regard as to how the pieces fit. Her hair was matted. It might have been a wig from a thrift store.

"I don't look the way I used to, I know." She pouted. "I had to put my whole head together without a mirror, thanks to your little friend. I'll fix her when I'm done with you. Where is she? Sweet Melissa?"

"None of your business. Where is he?"

"Who?"

"Enzo?"

"Nowhere around here. He's back in Spain."

"Where did the demons come from?"

"Demons?" Sandy seemed genuinely perplexed. "Is that why all of you were running?" Fear replaced perplexity. "*Enzo's* demons? *Here?*" She backed away from Will.

Will realized that she couldn't see into the Bowl. She didn't know what had happened. "Enzo's goons tore up the whole place. There are people in the cave who will never be the same—if they live. Enzo could show up here any time."

Her face grew pale and she put her hand to her mouth.

A brilliant light appeared in the heavens, illuminating half the sky. Their eyes were drawn to it. "What's that?" Sandy pointed to a shimmering area that looked like a movie set.

A sumptuous bed with sapphire satin sheets was occupied by a naked woman. She stretched out, one hand behind her head, the other draped to the side. Her breasts were flattened as she lay on her back, but their voluptuousness was apparent. The camera—or whatever it was—lingered on her fine flesh, illuminating it slowly. It panned down her long leg and slender ankle. Slowly traveled over her foot, which protruded from the edge of the bed. The others slowly materialized. A man kneeled between her legs, bending over her.

"No," Will cried. "Don't do that! Stop!" He ran toward the image, waving his hands over his head. "Don't! Don't show that. Leave her alone!" Will was far out in the desert, far beyond the protection of the Bowl.

Two men were behind her. One grasped her wrist and held it above her head. The woman was beautiful, porcelain-skinned and elegant. Her black hair spread over the pillow. The man between her legs bent over and took her nipple in his mouth. Her chest arched and her face turned toward the camera.

"Stop it! Stop. Leave her alone! Don't show that!"

Kathryn Duane's beautiful face turned so that the lens displayed it perfectly. Hollywood didn't have a prettier one. Her eyes were half-closed and rolled back. Just enough of her pupil showed to display the flawless blue of her eyes. Kathryn was drugged.

"Stop it! Turn that off!" Will was going crazy, punching at the sky. "She's never done anything to you! Leave her alone. It's me you want! Take me!"

"All right," Enzo Donatore's face covered the sky, replacing Kathryn's image. "I've wanted to take you for a long time. I suggest a merger. We can do it in my dungeon. Or right here." Enzo bent closer, his close-cropped silvery blond hair glittering; his bright blue eyes fixed on Will. "Do you remember the fun we had in the canyon?" A huge finger materialized above Will. "Ring a bell?"

Will didn't remember what Enzo had done to him and Doug. It was lost in a sea of trauma and unconsciousness. "Shut up and get on with it." Will wasn't afraid, and he wasn't aware of the warriors massed in the opening of the ravine. "But if you take me, you can't hurt the people inside. Or up on top," he added.

"Oh? I've already hurt them. Or my children did. My wife's babes should be arriving shortly. Snakes. Do you like snakes? I love them. My wife is a serpent." Enzo chuckled. "I never could resist Najx. We made thousands of babies. Millions." Enzo looked pensive, then turned on Will.

A gigantic hand shot from the sky and backhanded Will, knocking him from his feet. He lay on the desert floor and then slowly rolled up on his hands and knees. He got up unsteadily, placing one hand on the side of his mouth.

"This is what the rest of your life will be, Will. Pain." He slapped him again, and Will went sprawling. "But you won't die, entirely. You'll live to be one of mine. More than alive, and still dead. Like Sandy Sydney, but better. You'll be smarter. No one at Numenon will be able to see that you're changed. You'll be more yourself than ever. Ruthless. Vicious. Merciless." He flicked Will's prostrate body with a finger. Ribs cracked as he rolled along the ground.

"It will be better, Will. No remorse, no sadness. All the women you want. You'll be able to keep Numenon. They're trying to take if from you. You know that, don't you? Frank Sauvage and the rest. You wouldn't keep it for six months if you went back the way you are. Soft and weak. With me, you'll keep it forever. Lifetimes will roll by, and you'll still be on top."

Enzo's skin darkened, as though something black was trying to emerge through it. He shook his head, and the human flesh grew thicker, covering his reptilian form.

"But first you have to be mine. And then you have to die and be reborn." Thunderheads mushroomed around Enzo, covering the sky. "What shall I do to you? What would hurt most?" His brows furrowed as he thought.

"Oh, I know. You can have sex with my dear Sandy Sydney. Your friends can watch." He laughed, nodding at the silent crowd in the canyon's mouth. "You'll end up with your dick burned off, but I can fix that.

"Sandy, my dear, where are you? Come out of hiding. I know you're here." Enzo raised his head and howled, a screeching sound like boulders rubbing and big cats screaming. "She ran away, that stinking puta." He cursed in Spanish and Italian. "Fucking bitch." He swore in English just as well as the other languages.

"I'll have to do it myself." A stream of saliva escaped his mouth. He caught it on his finger and moved it toward Will. The thread splattered on the ground, causing the rock to smoke. It etched into the stone. He draped the strand across Will's back. He thrashed and screamed.

"Oh, you baby. That doesn't hurt that much. But all right, I'll do something else."

Will was lying on his belly. His ankles began to spread as though invisible hands were pulling them apart. The spread widened, and widened impossibly. Will screamed again.

"You humans. So weak. But dismemberment never has been easy, Will. I'll go slowly, just for you." Enzo's floating visage gloated. Another pull, another scream. "You were too good, Will. All those computers and innovations. Your incredible market share. The growth of your product lines. I never would have noticed you if you hadn't stood out so much.

"But you did stand out. You were brilliant. I had to hate you. And want to destroy you and do this." Will's leg shot upward. A crack rang out from deep within it.

"Stop," someone said. Enzo looked up.

A tiny old man stood a few feet from Will. "That is enough."

95

"AH!" ENZO'S EYEBROWS rose. "You must be Grandfather. Or Joseph Biship as they called you in the Indian school. Or schools. You were in quite a number. Such a bright boy. And then All-Saints Seminary. Why you almost earned a PhD, but you ran off to live in poverty with that old charlatan. Was that a good example for your people? Dropping out? Not earning a living?

"But perhaps you came to join me?"

"I came to destroy you." Grandfather snorted.

"Oh, *you're* going to destroy me? And you're so big and powerful, you can do it." Enzo laughed. "You can't weigh one hundred pounds. Look at me, and all of my family." As Enzo spoke, the desert behind him began to move, undulating and twining over itself as far as anyone could see. Heads emerged, black serpents' heads. Some were squared off and triangular like vipers; others were fine and slick, but no less deadly. Water mocassins, copperheads, mambas, cobras, a symphony of venomous herpetology played in the desert. Hissing filled the air.

Above his head, the leather wings of his flying lizards flapped and fluttered, beating the air and directing the stench of the snakes toward Grandfather and Will and the warriors in the canyon. Close behind Enzo, black-scaled monsters appeared and massed. The demons' red eyes glowed, growls turning over in their chests.

"I have many children. These are just a few; the ones who didn't get to play earlier." Enzo nodded toward the Bowl. "They're hungry, and they're bored. You'll make such a little meal, but a meal. When they shit you out, I'll make you whole again. And one of my people."

The darkness that had been floating to the surface of Enzo's skin broke through. His snout emerged, he grew into his essential form. Tyrannosaurus rex was no less frightening. Throwing his head back, Enzo roared. His roar was answered by the hisses and screams of his children. They began to swarm toward the shaman and Will.

"Stop!" Grandfather ordered.

The horde stopped. They continued to howl, but in a bewildered way. All but Enzo faded from sight.

"You showed me your children. Let me show you my family," the shaman said. He raised his hand and all could see them. From horizon to horizon, moving warriors, bonneted heros. Raging horses. Champions from beyond history. Their outlines stood out like the presence of angels, radiant and eternal. Around them were the sacred animals. The white buffalo. Totems. Thunder clouds pressed against the ancient spirits. The thunder beings stood within them, raising their arms in unison, beating cosmic drums. Enzo put his hands over his ears.

"You do not exist. Leave while you can," the old man said. Enzo didn't move. Grandfather pointed to the west. "She's coming for you through the gate between the worlds. She comes from the edge of life and death."

A high tone, like a single harp string being struck, sounded. The brilliant shape swooped in so fast that no one saw its approach. The creature's razor-fronted edge was a dazzling blue; streamers of blue light flew out behind. Her eyes were barely visible in the brilliance. The eagle's feet extended, and all that was left of Enzo was his scream.

Grandfather chuckled. Then laughed. Bliss almost overtook him, but Will groaned. "Let me heal you, my son." He placed his hands on Will as he lay on the ground, popping his dislocated hips into place and healing his broken bones as well as the sores from Enzo's acid venom.

"Get up my son, it is time to rejoice. Evil has been beaten this night." He sunk into bliss and danced a few steps, then abruptly whirled and faced the warriors in the opening of the canyon.

The warriors stood, mouths hanging open. Feet spread. Speechless.

"Why are you surprised? Haven't you listened to me all these years?" Grandfather was a bit indignant at their surprise. "Tell me! What happened?"

"The big eagle, the crystal eagle, your totem, came and carried him away," one said.

"Very good. You have eyes. What *really* happened? What have I taught you?"

"Where was the *battle*? I thought there'd be a fight," the speaker was querulous. The group pulled together, nodding their heads and murmuring agreement. They thought this would be the final show-down that decided the fate of the world.

"Aho! You expected a battle to the death! Enzo and his legions of snakes and reptiles and Dark Powers against me and the Ancestors. And our Supernaturals: the thunderbeings and all those from the unseen world.

"A huge battle would take place over the desert, with lightning and explosions and armies advancing and retreating. And blood! Lots of blood, and severed limbs. Death.

"*You expected the great battle between good and evil, where the winner would be determined, once and for all.*" Grandfather paced in front of his warriors. He was furious. Hadn't they learned anything from him?

"You read too much science fiction.

"THERE ISN'T ANY BATTLE!

"Don't you understand? The Great One created *everything*, including Enzo Donatore and his spawn and castle and all those like him in the past. The Great One is the most powerful thing in the universe. *Nothing* can oppose it."

"You're saying that the Great One *made* Enzo Donatore?" Will choked out. "How can that be? Everything you've said, everything you've taught all week. It's all been about goodness and living righteously. How can you say that the One, God, created a monster like Enzo Donatore?"

"Enzo and all those like him exist at the pleasure of the Great One."

"The One *allows* him to exist?"

"Yes, of course. The One brings him and all evil into existence with just a thought. And if the One ceases to think that thought, poof! No evil."

"Why doesn't the One do that?"

"I don't know." He shrugged. "Maybe the One likes the show. The drama of Enzo and his plotting. Maybe the One likes wars. Something to think of besides bliss."

Will stood blinking his eyes. "The Great One *likes the show?*"

"Yes. We are in a play, Will Duane. A vast play that takes in everything from the world of ants and insects and germs to angels and beings we can't see. A play that extends past this planet and solar system to galaxies we do not know. The play of the One *is* the entire universe. Whatever happens in it happens at the will of the Great One. The movement of every leaf and eyelid. The One allows all of it."

Will couldn't think about that. "Is Enzo dead?"

The old man scoffed. "He is not dead, just backed off for a while. He will hide in his lair and ponder revenge. He will hate me as much as he does you, Will Duane, and try to hurt me and my teachings. You and my warriors are his targets now.

"But we don't need to fear Enzo Donatore or his spawn at this Meeting. What we need to fear is ourselves." The warriors looked perplexed.

"But we're the good guys," someone said.

"We are the good guys when we are good. But each of us is subjected to great temptation. The higher you grow, the greater the lure of evil. The traps are everywhere. *We* are what we have to fear."

They began to clamor with questions.

"No, that is not important now. Don't you wonder what happened? Why did Enzo disappear? Why did he have no power over me? This is worth talking about."

Grandfather smiled and seemed to float. "The Great One can do anything. How is not ours to know. We must go back to our friends in the Ballroom.

"But first, we must praise the Ancestors and the One."

The shaman's voice rose and fell as he sang the song. The warriors joined him, marveling. Reality was so different than the story-tellers' tales. It was much, much more miraculous and fine.

They sang a song from the Lakota mystic, Black Elk:

Peace ... comes within the souls of people
when they realize
their relationship,
their oneness,
with the universe and all its powers,
and when they realize that

at the center of the Universe
dwells Wakan-tanka,
and that this center is everywhere,
it is within each of us.
This is the real peace ...

"Now let us see what the Great One has wrought," Grandfather said, walking toward the Ballroom's opening.

WHAT COULD POSSIBLY
HAPPEN NEXT?

Find out in *Phenomenon: A Tale of Mysticism & Miracles,* Bloodsong 3

They went to hell and back in *Numenon: A Tale of Mysticism & Money* and *Mogollon: A Tale of Mysticism & Mayhem.* Looks like most of them made it. But the week isn't over.

Grandfather's Meeting runs from Sunday to Saturday, a full seven days. It's Wednesday night when *Mogollon,* the second Bloodsong book, ends. Grandfather has three more days to realize his dream of creating a world where love is king.

Will we have a planet where people cooperate and work together with mutual respect? Or will violence and corruption rule the day? Will the flawed humans who messed up creation do their own thing? Or will the Great One take the reins?

It's all in *Phenomenon: A Tale of Mysticism & Miracles.* The suspense, terror, romance, and miracles you've come to expect from Sandy Nathan ❦ reach a crescendo as the Meeting comes to a close.

Expect Phenomenon: A Tale of Mysticism & Miracles in late 2014.

ABOUT THE BLOODSONG SERIES

WHAT'S COMING NEXT? THE BLOODSONG SERIES EXPLAINED

The Bloodsong Series I envision is *big* and *long*. It's barely begun to see the light of day. The first three books are set in New Mexico at a spiritual retreat in the fabled Mogollon Bowl, a supernatural place invested with spirit and magic. After those volumes give up their secrets, the story moves to new realms.

The coming books in the series occur in a number of places. They're set in Silicon Valley, South-eastern Oregon, Montana, a magical kingdom on top of the Coastal Range in Woodside, California. In Spain, Italy, and Iceland, in addition to the good old USA.

The cast of characters changes and expands. In addition to our familiar billionaires and Native Americans, future works include socialites with secrets, a physicist who is also a witch, and musicians who rock the world. One tome stars an assassin for the Dark Lord, who hangs out with a porn queen, infamous abortionist, and a bunch of Mafiosi, and the devil. That one is a love story.

I've loosened up a lot.

All of this came from a transcendental experience—a miraculous Zap!—that came to me after a meditation retreat in 1995. The experience lasted an instant, but left behind ideas for a dozen books—and counting. The words kept pouring out, seemingly endless, until I began the rewrite of *Mogollon*.

I hit writer's block so massive and impenetrable that it is a miracle that you're even looking at this book. For years, I'd pick up the manuscript and my brain would turn to month-old oatmeal.

Finally, I pulled all the words together and emailed them to my editor, saying, "Fix it! Fix it now!" She did, cutting *Mogollon* in half by pulling out entire stories and plot lines. Seeing the manuscript with them gone was rather like noticing that my leg had been chopped off and arteries were hanging out. Painful, but the removed portions gave me a huge pool of material for short stories. Those are addition to the stuff noted above.

I've got some rewriting to do, but the writer's block seems to have gone. I know some of you felt irritated, impatient, annoyed, and even enraged about the length time between *Numenon's* release and that of *Mogollon*. Darn tootin'! Five years is a long time to wait.

I apologize for that. Writers aren't like conveyer belts, chucking out a book three times a year. (Well, some writers are like machines, but I'm not.) My books are custom made and full of spirit and excitement. The take time to write, even if it's "just" rewriting a draft. I can't guarantee that what I've described will be out soon, but I'll try my best.

Meanwhile, while you're waiting for the third installment of the Bloodsong Series, *Phenomenon: A Tale of Mysticism & Miracles*, I have more for you to read. You don't have to wait for additional work.

Yes! While I was wrestling with the rewrite of *Mogollon,* I had another transcendental experience, which turned into a whole other series of books.

The Earth's End Trilogy is sci-fi adventure set in a future world, right before we blow it up. The first book, *The Angel & the Brown-Eyed Boy* came directly from the trancendental experience (which is described in the Authors' Notes of the three books of the series.) *The Angel* shows the worst possible outcome of our current political logjam: a police state followed by the nuclear destruction of the planet. It's about a young man trying to make sense of a senseless world. And a beautiful alien trying to save her planet. I'ts a love story.

The second book of Earth's End, *Lady Grace & the War for a New World*, features the survivors of the Armageddon in the first book. They crawl out from their hiding places and find themselves in prehistoric conditions. Also, the neighbors aren't very nice. They've mutated and are downright hostile. Deadly, in fact.

Finally, *The Headman & the Assassin* is a love story throughout. It's the lifelong romance of Sam Baahuud and Emily, the federal agent he finds just before the bombs go off. It takes place in a huge bomb shelter and features a new cast of characters, plus a few from the first book, *The Angel & the Brown-Eyed Boy*.

So, if I'm hit by a truck or trapped by writer's block again and you have to wait for *Phenomenon*, I've got another series for you to read. Here's another secret, the Bloodsong Series will eventually merge with Earth's End creating a wild adventure across time and space.

It's a spectacular journey that may take a lifetime. I invite you to make it with me.

ABOUT THE AUTHOR ...

SANDY NATHAN

Sandy Nathan writes to amaze and delight, uplift and inspire, as well as thrill and occasionally terrify. She is known for creating unforgettable characters and putting them in do-or-die situations. She writes in genres ranging from visionary fiction to juvenile nonfiction to memoir and science fiction.

"I write for people who like challenging, original work. My reader isn't satisfied by a worn-out story or predictable plot. I do my best to give my readers what they want.

"My work has a visionary core. It depicts human beings on a spiritual journey. A moral premise drives each book: right and wrong underlie the action; goodness fights to be expressed. But just because my writing is about growth and transcendent consciousness doesn't mean the trip will be easy or successful. I don't guarantee happy endings.

Mrs. Nathan's books have won twenty-four national awards, including multiple awards from oldest, largest, and most prestigious contests for independent publishers. Her books have earned rave critical reviews and customer reviews of close to five-star averages on Amazon.

Sandy was born in San Francisco. Sandy grew up in the hard driving, achievement-orientated corporate culture of Silicon Valley. Holding Master's Degrees in Economics and Marriage, Family, and Child Counseling, she was a doctoral student at Stanford's Graduate School of Business. Sandy has been an economic analyst, businesswoman, and negotiation coach, as well as author.

Mrs. Nathan lives with her husband on their California ranch. They bred Peruvian Paso horses for almost twenty years. She has three grown children and two grandchildren.

www.sandynathan.com

Join Sandy'a Newletter Mailing List
http://www.sandynathan.com/contact.html

Reviews are very important in establishing a book's ranking.
If you enjoyed *Mogollon: A Tale of Mysticism & Mayhem,* consider
leaving a review on Mogollon's Amazon page and your favorite on-line
book sellers.

Made in the USA
Charleston, SC
10 February 2014